REBECCA TOPE lives on a smallholding in Herefordshire, with a full complement of livestock, but manages to travel the world and enjoy civilisation from time to time as well. Most of her varied experiences and activities find their way into her books, sooner or later. She is also the author of the Cotswold Mysteries series featuring Thea Osborne.

www.rebeccatope.com

If you enjoyed *Death of a Friend*, read on to find out about more books by Rebecca Tope . . .

To discover more great fiction and to
place an order visit our website at
www.allisonandbusby.com
or call us on
020 7580 1080

OTHER BOOKS IN THE
WEST COUNTRY MYSTERIES

A Dirty
Death

Rebecca Tope

Dark
Undertakings

Rebecca Tope

A Death
to Record

Rebecca Tope

'One of the most intelligent and thought
provoking of today's crime writers'
Mystery Women

Death of a Friend

REBECCA TOPE

Allison & Busby Limited
13 Charlotte Mews
London W1T 4EJ
www.allisonandbusby.com

First published in Great Britain in 2000.
This paperback edition published by Allison & Busby in 2012.

A CIP catalogue record for this book is available from
the British Library.

10 9 8 7 6 5 4 3 2 1

ISBN 978-0-7490-4028-4

Typeset in 10.5/14.2 pt Sabon by
Allison & Busby Ltd.

The paper used for this Allison & Busby publication
has been produced from trees that have been legally sourced
from well-managed and credibly certified forests.

Printed and bound by
CPI Group (UK) Ltd, Croydon, CR0 4YY

For Hilton and Jenny Hughes
beloved friends

CHARACTER LIST

Cattermole Family

MARTHA
RICHMOND – her husband
ALEXIS – her sister
NINA NESBITT (deceased) – sister to Martha and Alexis
CLEMENT and HUGH – Nina's sons
NEV – Nina's husband
LADY HERMIONE NESBITT – Nev's mother

The Quakers

HANNAH GRATTON
BILL – her brother
CHARLIE (deceased) – her nephew
SILAS DAGGS – her cousin
CLIVE and MANDY ASPEN – the Wardens
DOROTHY MANSFIELD
VALERIE TAYLOR
POLLY SPENCE
MIRIAM SNOW

Others

FRANK GRATTON – estranged from his family
DETECTIVE CONSTABLE DEN COOPER
LILAH BEARDON – his fiancée
MIRANDA BEARDON – Lilah's mother
RODDY – Lilah's brother

PROLOGUE

Charlie saw the horse coming towards him from the other end of the field. He recognised its rider with some surprise and raised his hand to wave. The bridle path ran along beside the hedge and its accompanying ditch, and the horse trotted easily along the well-defined route.

The rider did not wave back. Instead the horse was urged to greater speed, heading directly for him, until Charlie wondered how it was going to avoid him. But he wasn't afraid. There was no room in him for fear, not with everything that had happened in recent days still raw in his mind. Nina was dead and the shocking horror of that fact pushed everything else out of awareness.

Even so, the thundering horse was definitely going to knock him down if it kept on its course. He looked into the face of the rider and was jolted to attention by its expression. Hatred sat there like a grotesque mask, twisting the features almost out of recognition. Charlie's heart stopped. 'No!' he shouted. 'What are you doing?'

And then he turned to run. He ran into the corner of the field and turned sharply right, to follow another hedge. There was a gateway only thirty yards distant with the gate closed across it. He could vault over and save himself.

He knew all along he couldn't outrun the horse. It cut the corner, coming at him from the side and rearing up as it got within a yard of the hedge. He saw its muscles working the powerful forelegs and felt his own puny powerlessness. High above his head, the face of the rider flickered, leaning forward, urging the horse to do its worst.

A hoof caught him on the temple and he fell to the ground, dizzy but still conscious. 'No!' he tried to scream again, but the word emerged breathy and low. He looked up, knowing he should be protecting himself – but needing to see the rider's face again, to comprehend this madness. Both front hoofs, their metal shoes brown and heavy with mud, the elegant equine legs above them forming a graceful arc against the sky, came down onto his head.

He tried, even to the last, to believe it was all the horse's doing. All some crazy accident and not the rider's deliberate act.

CHAPTER ONE

The task of compiling Nina's death notice fell to Alexis. 'Make it something meaningful,' said Martha. 'Not just *dearly loved sister* and all that guff.'

'Trust me,' said Alexis. 'I'm good with words.'

The *Daily Telegraph* woman made no comment when the copy was telephoned through, except to say that it would cost rather more than three hundred pounds. 'It'll be worth it,' said Alexis. 'Would you read it back, please?'

NESBITT, Nina (aka Nina Cattermole) on Thursday 25 March, from her own sheer carelessness, at the wasteful age of 35. Her younger sisters, Martha and Alexis, will share their diminished lives with her sons, Hugh and Clement, and other family members. Nina was an untamed spirit who believed herself to be invulnerable. We all believed it too. The funeral is on Wednesday 31 March at High Copse Farmhouse, at 12 noon, followed by burial under the great oak tree. Phone Alexis on 01837 565654 for directions. Bring flowers.

The mountain created from nearly a hundred floral sheaves, cushions, wreaths and posies made an impressive display, taking up a large part of the garden. 'Princess Diana has a lot to answer for,' grumbled Richmond. 'What the hell are we going to do with all these afterwards?'

'That doesn't matter,' Martha reproached him, softening the words with an affectionate rub just above his elbow. 'For now, they're wonderful.'

The lower of the two fields had had to be commandeered for car parking and the hired marquee was not quite roomy enough for everyone to squeeze into. The chipboard coffin, unadorned with false handles or brassy screw-tops, had been painted by Alexis and Clement with abstract red and purple swirls, and rested on trestles at one end of the tent. Outside it was coldly drizzling and a slow steam was rising from the warmly-dressed people as they crammed together, generating a welter of heat and emotion. Glasses of wine were being issued by two village women from a table beside the entrance, but no food was on offer. 'They'll just have to go home for a late lunch,' Alexis said. 'We can't possibly feed everyone – especially as we've no idea how many might come.'

'Where's Charlie?' fussed Alexis now, stroking a finger downwards between her eyes. 'He can't abandon us at this stage. Clem—' she bent towards her younger nephew '—surely you've seen Charlie?'

The boy shook his head, then winced as if the movement hurt him.

'I always wanted to arrange a funeral like this,' sighed Martha. 'I thought it would be romantic. It just shows you should be careful what you wish for; it can be so terrible when you get it. And I've got no idea what we're supposed to do next. I can see the sense in an established ritual after all.' She was standing close to the coffin, where the family had instinctively assembled.

'Nobody's going to know if we get it wrong,' Alexis reassured her. 'Just look confident.'

Richmond was in charge of the marquee and had filled a small corner with equipment for music. He anxiously fiddled with wires and muttered about being given the worst of all the jobs. His large bald head was blotchy, and his round, reproachful eyes darted incessantly from one face to another. Hugh was beside him, looking much more familiar with the gadgetry.

Martha climbed onto the platform they'd erected, almost tripping over her long skirt. It was dark blue, a colour that seemed right for a funeral, but the length was obviously wrong. All the other women had hemlines just below the knee. She stood still and gazed at the crowd. People she had only ever seen in old jeans and anoraks were dressed up in smart clothes which made them barely recognisable. She wished they'd thought to say *casual dress* in the newspaper.

Hugh switched on the sound system and inserted a CD, just as his aunt opened her mouth to speak. A ripple of surprise swept across the faces as the people realised what they were hearing. It was a young boy singing the hymn 'Dear Lord and Father of Mankind' in a slow, pure voice that filled the air with sadness. As soon as it was finished, Hugh played it again, glancing at the crowd defiantly. There was complete attention as the words began to make sense.

> *Breathe through the heats of our desire*
> *Thy coolness and thy balm;*
> *Let sense be dumb, let flesh retire;*
> *Speak through the earthquake, wind and fire,*
> *O still, small voice of calm!*

The tent itself seemed to exhale in silent reaction to the hymn.

'What are you going to say?' Alexis whispered to Martha, as the last line died away. Martha looked at her uncomprehendingly and made no reply. 'Come on – now you're up there, you'd better make some sort of speech. Why did you go up there, otherwise?'

Martha shook her head in confusion. 'Not yet,' she said. 'I'm not ready yet.' And she jumped down again.

Alexis went over to Hugh. 'Why did you play that? Nina wasn't one for hymns.' He turned to look at her, his face stiff with gritted jaws and tired eye muscles. He had discovered that if you kept blinking and squeezing, you could stop tears from flowing.

'It's written by a Quaker,' he told her. 'You should know that. Charlie said we should play it.'

'But *she* wasn't a Quaker.'

The boy just looked at her. 'She said that's what she would have been, if she'd been anything,' he said carefully. 'And she liked that hymn. She used to sing it. You must remember.'

Alexis pulled a face. 'She was such an awful singer, I probably wouldn't have recognised it. Is Charlie here, then? Have you seen him?'

Hugh turned his face away as if the question

didn't concern him. 'Nope,' he said. 'Why don't you ask Clem?'

'I have. Where on earth can he be?'

The older boy glanced over at his brother, but Clem made no response. 'He'll be somewhere around,' Hugh told Alexis. 'He's your boyfriend – you should know what he's doing.'

'I've been busy,' she frowned, with yet another futile glance around the marquee. She sucked in her top lip anxiously for a moment and then returned to more immediate concerns. 'So what do we do next? The masses are growing restless.' It was true: the crowd was unitedly facing the platform, glancing at each other and mouthing questions. 'A lot of animal rights people. They won't get difficult, will they?'

'They've come because Mum was their leader, that's all. They're just ordinary without her.'

Alexis looked at him with admiration. 'You're right,' she said. 'I hope they don't abandon the cause because she's—'

Hugh's expression was blank as he turned back to the sound system. His movements were slow and clumsy as if he'd reached the end of a long, weary journey. 'Don't worry,' he said ambiguously and slotted another disc into the machine. Seconds later an Alice Cooper song crashed out, the husky tones bringing a very different set of expressions to the gathered faces.

Martha gestured urgently at the boy to turn the volume down. He ignored her. She stormed over to him. 'Turn it *down*,' she hissed.

'She liked this one,' he said stubbornly. 'This is my last chance to play it for her.'

'It's loud enough to wake the dead,' she bellowed at him.

Hugh looked at her, white and bitter. 'No,' he shook his head. 'No, it's not.' And he pushed the volume lever even higher.

Angrily she yanked at him and squeezed his arm hard. Rage at Nina crackled between them. Then Martha reached for the volume slider and pushed it down as far as it would go. The throbbing beat died, leaving an auditory nakedness that chilled the crowd. They waited, edging back against the sides of the tent, as far as possible from the coffin. Many had come from curiosity, as much as grief or sympathy, and their confused motives created a sheeplike atmosphere, everyone watching everyone else for a lead.

Alexis took charge, standing tall on the platform and clapping her hands in the waiting hush. 'Friends,' she announced, 'we have no set order or ceremony for this ritual. We want you to make it special by remembering Nina as she really was and helping us to face her death. We ask you to tell us stories about her, what you knew of her, what you liked and disliked. We need to feel that

16

her life was not wasted in spite of her early death. Will you help us?'

A murmur went round. Many people tried to shuffle behind others, afraid of having to speak. 'Well, I'll start off, then,' said Martha, moving forward like someone wading through a lake of blood, and climbing once more onto the stage. 'Nina was my older sister, so I've known her all my life. She lived here at High Copse, even when she was married to Nevil, and had both her children here. For her to die whilst protesting against the fox hunt is something we're still coming to terms with. It was a stupid accident and we feel no sense of blame towards anyone.' Here she paused and looked at Clement, then at Hugh and Alexis. One by one they nodded agreement. 'Nina was an original. We often argued with her, sometimes disapproved of her. But we have no idea how we'll manage without her . . .' She stopped, brushing the back of her hand against her dripping nose, and retreated from the platform.

A man's voice came from the middle of the crowd. 'Could I say something?' he called in ringing tones. Everyone craned their necks to look at him, mostly in vain. Many of them recognised his voice.

'Good God,' Alexis muttered to Clement, who had pushed under her arm and was nuzzling his face against her ribs. 'It's bloody Gerald.'

The speaker proceeded: 'I must admit I find this funeral highly unusual,' he began, with a minimal flare of his nostrils, 'and I might be speaking out of turn, but it does seem to behove me to express my gratitude for what Mrs Taverner has just said. I imagine you are all aware that it was my horse, Shamrock, which dealt Mrs Nesbitt the fatal blow, and some of you may be wondering what happened to him afterwards. Well, I consulted the authorities and the clear advice was that no blame of any sort can be attached to the horse. I will not be riding him to hounds next season, as a mark of respect, but he will remain in my possession and we will do all we can to ensure that nothing so tragic ever happens again. Thank you.'

Glances of approval, cynicism and scorn passed around the marquee, spiced with some subdued hissing from one corner, where three or four young men were gathered. Richmond murmured in Martha's ear, 'Brave of him, wouldn't you say, Mrs Taverner?' Martha never used her husband's surname and grinned briefly at his gentle jibe. 'Sounds as if some of the activists can't stomach what he said. Or do they want the horse shot?'

She widened her eyes at him in mock apprehension. 'Don't let the boys hear you. They've been worrying about that.' He put a finger over his lips. Briefly she pressed close to him, gripping him tight around his broad chest.

'Now, now, you two,' came a cool voice behind them. 'There's a time and a place for everything.'

Martha met the eyes of an olive-skinned woman. 'Hello, Polly. We were just hoping that your crowd would let Gerald leave with his dignity intact. Does he realise how many people here would like to inflict long and agonising torture on him?'

The woman smiled, her full mouth twisting lopsidedly. 'He's safe enough. We're too upset about Nina for any trouble-making. It's so *awful*, I still can't believe it. I wanted to ask – have you thought of some kind of memorial for her? Something that'll carry forward her name and what she believed in?'

Martha grimaced. 'Like what?'

'Maybe a trust fund for animal rights, or a bursary into research into the suffering caused by hunting – that sort of thing. Everybody here would contribute. You'd have thousands before you know it. Come on, Martha,' she said urgently, 'don't waste the opportunity.'

'I can't just invent something out of the blue and ask people to give money. I'll think about it.'

'Well, Val or I will remind you when you've had a few days to recover.' And she moved away in the direction of the hissing youths.

'*A few days!*' Martha repeated incredulously.

She turned to Richmond. 'Did you hear that?'

'You haven't heard the last of it,' Richmond predicted. 'Intriguing girl.'

'Hey!' Martha protested.

'Don't worry, definitely not my type. But she's a puzzle, you must admit. I never understood why she deferred to Nina all the time, when she's at least as strong a character. I often get the feeling she's playing some sort of game.'

'Talking about me?' Alexis demanded, overhearing his last words.

Martha laughed. 'If the cap fits. No, not you, Polly Spence, if you must know.'

'Yes I must,' Alexis shot back. 'I've been keeping an eye on her lately. I think she's nursing some naughty ideas about Charlie. They've been spending a lot of time together.'

Richmond sighed melodramatically. 'You women!' he said. 'You don't know the meaning of the word "trust", do you?'

The sisters exchanged cynical glances and said nothing. A swell of conversation began, as moments passed with no further speakers. Alexis pulled at Martha's cotton sleeve. 'We can't let it go at that. Somebody else should say something.'

'I don't think you can force them. We haven't prepared this very well, have we? Even Nina wouldn't know where to go from here.'

Hugh looked up at them from his place at

Alexis's side. 'Can I say something?' he said, gesturing towards the crowd.

'Oh, darling – yes, if you're sure.' Martha was careful to resist the urge to stroke his cheek. 'Of course you can. Shall I shut them up for you?'

He nodded and she clapped her hands, as Alexis had done not long before. This time the sound was swallowed up and went unnoticed. 'Wait,' she said and went to the sound system. Within seconds a sudden blare of Alice Cooper effectively silenced the throng. Martha turned it off again and nodded towards Hugh without a word. The boy began to speak, his gaze fixed on the far end of the tent.

'My mother was a very annoying person,' he said. 'She talked to my friends as if she was the same age as them. She borrowed my shirts and never changed my sheets. She was a useless housewife. She let my father leave us for months at a time, because she neglected him. Now she has let herself die. But she was a great friend and being dead is even worse than all the other things. Being dead is completely terrible. This funeral is the only way we could think of to be honest about her. Please try to say what you feel.' His breath all used up, he stopped abruptly and smacked his hand on the coffin next to him. Then he made a fist and pounded it down again and again. Alexis caught him before the next blow and held him to her. The silence was full of thumping hearts and gathering tears.

Two or three others in the crowd contributed anecdotes about Nina, but nothing came close to Hugh's despairing outburst. Inexorably, attention was dissipated. Yet again Alexis scanned the crowd for sight of Charlie, with no luck. Instead, her eye was caught by a young woman with a very short haircut, who waved at her hesitantly.

'Isn't that your friend Lilah?' she asked Martha. 'What *has* she done to her hair?'

Martha took a while to follow the precise direction of her sister's nod. Lilah was standing between two older women; an air of self-possession formed an invisible bubble around her. 'I'd better go and speak to her,' she said.

'Remember when we were last at a funeral?' said Lilah, as Martha came within speaking distance.

'Your dad,' nodded Martha. 'Let's hope there won't be any more for a long time.'

'Poor Nina. It's so hard to believe. Den told me about it, of course, as soon as it happened.'

Martha's eyebrows asked the question; Lilah went pink. 'We're engaged now, actually. He's just got into the CID. He was at the hunt on Thursday – he saw the whole thing. It's true, you couldn't blame the horse. It only nudged her.'

'Head-butted, the way I heard it.'

'She was standing so close to it. Silly, really.'

'Very silly,' Martha agreed. Tall and thin, orange hair tied back from her face, the eccentric long skirt hanging crookedly from narrow hips, she looked like a prettier version of Virginia Woolf. 'But it shouldn't have killed her, all the same.'

'Some people's skulls are thin. What did the Coroner's Officer tell you?'

Martha shrugged. 'Nothing much. A freak accident. The knock drove her nose upwards and inwards and caused a massive haemorrhage at the front of the brain which cut off all her vital processes. She lost consciousness within a few seconds.'

'Well you're giving her a lovely send-off. All this . . .' she swung her head in an arc to take in the marquee. 'Amazing.'

Martha leant forward and whispered, 'We have no idea what we're doing, to be honest. We let the boys decide most of it, but we all knew we couldn't use the village church and the impossible Father Edmund. Nor some ghastly cremation. It was a process of elimination, really.'

'I thought Charlie Grattan must have been behind it. That's what people are saying. Except he doesn't seem to be here?'

'No. Alexis is a bit bothered about that. We're beginning to wonder if he's all right. He was so devastated by what happened, he probably can't face going through all this.'

Lilah nodded doubtfully and Martha caught the implication. She pulled a rueful face. 'It sounds awfully feeble, doesn't it? But you don't know him. He's hopelessly thin-skinned. I bet he'll turn up as soon as we've got the burial over with.'

'Alexis seems to want you,' Lilah observed. Martha turned to see her sister beckoning and obediently returned to the waiting coffin. A subtle change in the atmosphere told her that there was no deferring the final stage of the proceedings. After a short exchange with her sister, Martha came forward and held up her hands, appealing for silence once more.

'Thank you, everybody,' she called. 'You've been wonderful and we're sorry if all this seems rather disorganised. Now I think we must move on. Nina died as she lived, impetuous and impossible to ignore. And I know none of us can quite forget the element of farce attached to her death. Although her cause might have been noble, the way she died was almost ludicrous. There must be a thousand perfectly ordinary ways to die – trust Nina to find a new one. Now, when you're ready, we'll carry her out to the grave and . . .' *Bury her*, she wanted to say. But the words were too stark and she let them hang unspoken.

* * *

Afterwards the sisters and their nephews and Richmond gathered in the kitchen. Alexis tried to phone Charlie, but was told by his aunt that she hadn't seen him for two or three days. 'I thought he was with you,' she said, with a touch of alarm.

'We haven't seen him since Sunday,' said Alexis. 'Don't worry, he's sure to turn up soon.' She put the phone down and frowned at Martha. 'Where the hell *is* he?' she said.

'He'll turn up,' said Richmond, echoing Alexis's own words. 'You must be used to him doing this sort of thing by now.'

'Well, I'm not,' she retorted. 'If he couldn't be here for me, then he should have thought of the boys.'

'We're not *his* boys,' said Hugh. Everyone understood the unspoken thought. Hugh and Clement were the sons of Nevil, not Charlie, close friends though the two men might be. And Nevil had missed the funeral, too.

Alexis looked at each face in turn. Richmond flinched under her gaze and heaved himself to his feet. 'Can't sit around here,' he said. 'Things to do. I ought to see how much damage all those cars have done to the lower field.'

After his departure the conversation returned to Charlie. 'I thought . . . well, maybe he can't cope with what we're doing,' Martha suggested. 'I was talking to Lilah and that seemed a possible explanation. Or could be he disapproved?'

'He'd have said something,' Alexis asserted. 'And he's a Quaker, not a Jehovah's Witness. Quakers approve of more or less anything, apart from violence.' She put a hand to her middle, wincing and rubbing slightly. 'I'm beginning to be really worried about him. My stomach's gone fluttery. He might have gone off by himself somewhere, all upset. He might be feeling guilty. He was ever so fond of Nina, after all. Just because they argued most of the time doesn't mean he didn't like her.'

'For heaven's sake!' Martha slapped the table and repeated the reassurance she'd convinced herself was true. 'There's nothing to worry about. Charlie's the least of our problems.'

Alexis took a deep breath and worked her head in a circle, easing the tension in her neck. 'It's so weird,' she said. 'Who's going to massage my neck now Nina isn't here to do it?' Both the boys swallowed visibly. The family had made a pact to speak about their mother as naturally as they could, but it was proving much more difficult than they'd expected. Every time her name was mentioned, they all experienced a flash of renewed knowledge of her death, along with the pain and loss, anger and embarrassment that still accompanied it.

'Lilah's engaged to that detective, did you

know?' Martha continued, desperate to change the subject. 'The one who tried to revive Nina.'

'What'll happen when she marries him?' asked Alexis, doing her best to play along. 'Will he turn farmer, or will she leave Redstone for her mother to run?'

'God knows.' Martha was sunk into apathetic exhaustion. When the phone rang, she reached a slow arm to where it lay behind her on the draining board. As soon as she realised who was speaking, she came back to life.'

'Nev!' she shouted. 'Where the hell *are* you? . . . Trust you . . . No, it never is, is it? . . . What? . . . When? . . . No, we won't meet you, get yourself down here on a train and then take the bus. Your sons need you here . . . Oh, okay.' She waggled the receiver under Hugh's nose. 'Talk to your father. He's stuck in Singapore until tomorrow.'

Hugh took the phone cautiously. 'Nev?' he said. 'What's happening?' He listened for a while, unsmiling. 'We're all right,' he said at last. 'Clem's here as well.'

Clem moved to take the phone, but Hugh held onto it. After a few seconds he said, 'Bye then,' and pressed the Off button before handing it back to Martha. 'His money ran out,' he said to his brother with a shrug.

'It wasn't his fault,' said Martha, trying to be

placatory. 'There was a volcano in New Zealand and the flights are all in chaos.'

'Small volcano, nobody hurt,' said Alexis. 'So small it wasn't on the news. That's his story and he's sticking to it.'

'*I* wanted to talk to him,' Clem said reproachfully. 'He never talks to me.'

Before anyone could speak, the back door crashed open and Richmond stood framed against the late afternoon sky, his eyes bulging grotesquely, chest heaving with exertion.

'It's Charlie!' he gasped. 'I've found Charlie.'

CHAPTER TWO

Detective Constable Den Cooper was waiting for Lilah at the police station. She was meeting him after work, having gone home from the funeral to change and see that everything was running smoothly on the farm, before driving into town. As soon as he saw her, Den stood up and drew her to him in a warm embrace, resting his chin on the top of her head.

'How was it?' he asked.

'Peculiar. The grave was so shallow! I don't know how Martha and Alexis can go on living there, with their sister rotting at the end of the garden. I'd have nightmares if it was me.'

'They are peculiar people,' he mumbled. 'And what a way to die!'

'I didn't think it was as bizarre as people are making out. A horse is a big thing. If you try to headbutt one, you can expect to get hurt.'

'I wonder whether it had a headache afterwards? I suppose it's lucky to be alive. Some people would have shot it there and then.'

'Gerald made sure everyone knew there was no chance of that happening. He loves that horse.'

Den sighed. 'Just like you love your cows?'

She cuffed him. 'Don't start that again. Although, I prefer them to horses. Give me a cow any day. But we're not talking about me. Nobody blames that horse. It would be terrible to blame it for something it couldn't help. You know that as well as anybody. You saw the whole thing.'

'I did.' He was drawn into yet another retelling of the story. Each time, he recalled another detail, reliving the extraordinary events of the hunt protest. 'She was waving her *Ban the Hunt* placard, trying to stop the riders going through the gateway. She stood right in front of Gerald, yelling and shouting. He was clearly annoyed, but he never raised his crop or anything. The horse just lowered its head, probably to get a better look at her, and she did the same. It was very funny. Two or three people laughed at her. Then the animal jerked its head up again and the bony edge of its nose caught her full in the face, with a hard knock. The worst you'd expect was a nosebleed, but she dropped to the ground instantly, out cold. I was the first to reach her. It was obvious she wouldn't make it, even though I tried some mouth-to-mouth.'

'She must have had a very fragile skull.'

'Stupid way to die. It was practically the last hunt of the season as well. The whole protest was a waste of time. I blame that Charlie fellow as much as anyone. Rushing round like a lunatic, he was, getting everybody worked up.'

'That's what people were saying at the funeral. Charlie wasn't there, by the way, which we all thought rather odd. Not only was he Nina's co-protester, he's going out with her sister.'

'Funny beggar,' Den commented. 'Those poor kids, too. What'll they do now?'

Lilah shrugged. 'They're quite able to fend for themselves. I used to babysit them when they were little, you know. I was only about fourteen and we played hide and seek all over that enormous house. It was wonderful.'

'Well, come on, then. I'm cooking. You don't have to get anything, do you?'

She shook her head. 'It all seems to be under control. Amos is really good with the cows. Better than Daddy or Sam ever were. They seem to read his mind. I can't help feeling we're exploiting him, but he won't have it.'

'You saved him from a miserable old age. He

can't believe his luck, having your mum at such close quarters and plenty to do all day.'

'Well it's working like magic.' Amos and Isaac Grimsdale had lived on the land adjacent to the Beardons' farm, but the sudden death of his brother had been the final blow to Amos's independence. Moving in with Lilah and her family had been the obvious solution to a number of connected problems.

Den clambered into the passenger seat of Lilah's car, folding his long legs into the small space. But before she could start the engine, a young uniformed policeman came running after them.

'Den!' he called. 'Hang on. There's just been a call. Someone's found a body in a ditch. The Chief thinks you ought to go with the others.'

'What the hell for? I've done my shift for today.' Den frowned up at the man; Lilah sighed and let go of the ignition key.

'It's Charlie Grattan, they think. The hunt protester. He's had his head bashed in; been there a day or two. Your patch, mate. You'd better be in at the start.'

Lilah leant across Den, her expression bemused. 'Found in a ditch with his head bashed in? Where, exactly?'

'High Copse Farm. Belongs to the same family as that woman who died trying to stop the hunt.'

Lilah stared at him, disbelieving. 'But I've only just come from there.' She looked at Den, wide-eyed. 'They've been looking for him all day.'

Den began to move, unclipping his seatbelt. 'Don't wait for me,' he said. 'I might be some time.'

Den had been transferred to plain clothes a few months earlier, after the CID training course, which he had enjoyed enormously, much to his own surprise. He had not expected involvement in violent death to be a major element of his work when he first applied to join the police force, but he had quickly discovered that the public perception of Devon as a sleepy rural idyll was an illusion. When a person died on a farm or in a remote hamlet, they often did it messily, long before an ambulance could navigate itself down the maze of narrow lanes. And by no means all of those deaths could be attributed to natural causes. It soon became obvious to Den that the apparently peaceful routines of agricultural life were beset with lethal equipment, convenient murder weapons and ominously tangled relationships.

Charlie Grattan's body was found curled tight as a hedgehog, hands covering the head as if to ward off the savage blows that killed him. His knuckles were split; blood from them and the dreadful head wounds had combined to form a repellently crusty cap and mask.

'I couldn't even recognise him at first,' said Richmond faintly. 'He was just a mass of blood, with grass and flies and stuff sticking to him. Never seen anything like it.'

Martha and Alexis sat on either side of him, slight beside his bulk. The two boys had been sent to bed with difficulty. The news of Charlie's death had produced the same numb effect in them as it had in the adults.

Richmond had told the police how he had been walking across the lower field after Nina's funeral, when he noticed a smell familiar from his younger days on a sheep farm. 'That ditch is fairly deep,' he explained, 'so I thought an animal of some kind had got itself stuck and died there. Been there since Sunday, do you think? That's when we last saw him.'

Den was non-committal. There had been a team working along the ditch and across the field it bordered, in the hour or two of daylight remaining, and now they were packing up, preparing to take away their findings for analysis. A WPC had been despatched to break the news to Charlie's immediate family. Eventually his body would be delivered to the mortuary for post-mortem examination. Richmond provided an identification of Charlie Grattan not just from his clothes, but the colour of his hair and those few features still discernible. According to the preliminary findings of the police doctor, he had indeed been dead for over twenty-four hours.

Den had returned to High Copse Farmhouse in the early evening, under instructions to make a start on an inquiry into a death which showed every sign of being unlawful. Slowly the threads of the incident would be teased out like the unravelling of a tangled piece of Fair-Isle knitting. Too new at the job to distinguish any kind of pattern at this early stage, he was nonetheless acquiring a degree of confidence in his questioning.

'Could you tell me a bit about Charlie?' he asked. 'What his connection with your family was; where he worked; anything you think would be useful.' A computer search had already revealed certain facts about the deceased: a man already well known as an animal rights activist, with prosecutions for disturbance and trespass as well as a reputation for unruly behaviour. Den had personal experience of this, having witnessed Charlie's antics at the protest which had led to the death of Nina Nesbitt.

Martha spoke tonelessly. 'He wasn't in work. He was giving all his time to the protests. The hunt season finishes in another week or two and Charlie was going to get a summer job before the new campaign next winter. He spent a lot of time here . . .' She glanced at Alexis and raised her eyebrows, but Alexis made no response apart from an almost invisible shrug. Martha heaved a weary sigh, which made Den wonder how she would find the strength to carry on. He wondered also how anyone could be cruel enough to kill Charlie in the week the Cattermoles were burying their sister.

'Charlie was Alexis's boyfriend,' Martha said. 'They'd been together for about six months.'

'Longer than that,' said Richmond, who'd said almost nothing thus far. 'Must go back to July last year.'

'He was a Quaker,' said Alexis. 'You should know that. It was important to him.'

Den noted the ready use of the past tense, while searching his memory for any information about Quakers. It came up blank.

'Was he a member of the local Quaker . . . group? Church? What do they call it?'

'Meeting,' supplied Alexis. 'They use a lot of archaic terms. There's a Meeting in Chillhampton. It's very small. Eight or nine people. Very close-knit, like a family, really.'

'Do Quakers approve of animal rights activism?' Den asked.

Alexis smiled sourly. 'Some do. Some followed Charlie as if he was a new Messiah. Others thought he was bringing the Meeting into disrepute. It might give you an idea of how it was if I say that Charlie tried to understand everybody and ended up offending them all. He told Nina she was simplistic and naïve. He called Gerald Fairfield a monster to his face. You'll soon hear from them all, I'm sure.'

I'm sure I will, thought Den without enthusiasm. A murdered Quaker was beginning to sound like a very complicated crime to investigate. The Detective Inspector was going to want full explanations that he felt seriously inadequate to deliver. 'I won't keep you much longer,' he said. 'Just the basics. You last saw Mr Grattan on Sunday, is that right?'

'Yes,' confirmed Martha. 'He was here at the weekend. We had to prepare Nina's coffin and just . . . get through the days, I suppose. Trying to keep the boys going and get hold of their father. Charlie seemed to wander off at some point. We can't remember exactly when.'

'But he lived at Chillhampton? That's what – four miles from here?'

'A bit less across the fields. He could walk it in forty minutes – and frequently did. He gave up his car last year.'

'Oh? Was that ideology or necessity?'

'A bit of each. He didn't have any money coming in and there's usually a vehicle here to use in an emergency. But he didn't like cars much anyway.'

'He lived with his parents?'

'Officially, yes. But they're not his parents, you know. I mean, Bill is his father, but Hannah is his aunt. Everybody makes the same mistake.'

Den made no move to record this information. He wasn't likely to forget it, and the G5 had already been completed, with the salient points surrounding the death itself all filled in neatly. Until the post-mortem was performed, there was little more to be done.

'Somebody will come back and take statements,' he told them. 'After they've done the post-mortem. Meanwhile . . .' He looked at Alexis. 'I'm sorry you've had so much trouble.'

His words sounded hopelessly inadequate, but Alexis nodded vaguely and attempted a smile. She had run her hands distractedly through her hair so many times it stuck out in tangled chunks, making her distress a tangible thing. She gave Martha a desolate look. 'I'll have to go and see Hannah and Bill,' she said.

The room felt cold; the stark fluorescent light exaggerated their pale faces and shadowed eyes. Den wanted to leave on a positive note. 'Lilah said to give you her condolences,' he offered, deliberately invoking his fiancée's name, hoping to build a closer tie, to remind them he was just a local lad who already knew where the family fitted into the scheme of things.

'Lilah was at the funeral,' Martha remembered. 'That was nice of her. Did she think we were very odd, burying Nina in the garden?'

Den shook his head. 'She thinks it's your business. Losing your sister like that was . . .'

'It's all right,' Alexis interrupted. 'You can say it was tragic. This is beginning to feel like something out of *Hamlet* or *Macbeth*, anyway.' She shook her head and closed her eyes. 'Nobody ever tells you how much it *hurts*,' she moaned.

Den shifted in the chair, his bony knees sticking out awkwardly, as they always did. A mark like a smear of dirt on the side of his long face was the slowly fading legacy of a violent blow sustained in the course of his duty nearly a year before. He put his fingers to it gently, thinking for a moment about Nina Nesbitt and the casual knock her head had received. By rights, he should be dead and Nina none the worse for her experience.

Martha stroked her sister's arm and made hushing noises. She took up the idea. 'For once, tragedy is probably the right word to use. After all, she did bring it on herself. It was even quite a noble cause in a small way.'

Den began to grasp the essential connections at the centre of the inquiry. Trained not to jump to conclusions, he had gone too far in the other direction. *Gather as many facts as you can*, was the first rule, and he believed he was doing quite well there. Facts alone, however, were not going to produce a conclusion.

He pushed back the chair and stood up. 'We want to know exactly who's been here since you last saw Charlie. Every single visitor.'

Alexis gave a mocking laugh. 'Including the hundred-odd who were here today at the funeral?'

Den did not react to the provocation; he knew it was not meant personally. 'Fortunately no,' he said. 'It's already clear that Mr Grattan died before the funeral took place. But it does include relatives and close friends.'

'We can tell you that now,' said Martha. 'Since we last saw Charlie, the only people to visit have been Nina's mother-in-law, Hermione Nesbitt, and a couple of reps for Richmond. They all came on Monday. Hermione wanted to see Nina, but she didn't come to the funeral. She hurt her arm on Monday doing something with a horse, and says she's in a lot of pain.'

Den made a note this time. 'Mother-in-law?' he repeated. 'How old is she? Where does she live?'

'She's in her late sixties, a widow. She lives at Bradstone, just above the Tamar.'

The penny dropped. 'Oh,' he said. 'She must be the lady who took the boys away, after the accident at the hunt . . . their grandmother.'

'That's her,' said Martha.

Den flipped his notebook closed and crammed it into his pocket. He crossed the room, then hesitated in the doorway, realising that nobody was going to see him out. Either they were in no hurry to get rid of him, or they were so sunk in misery and shock that they'd forgotten the social niceties. But he couldn't just disappear like that.

Martha was the first to notice his discomfort. 'Oh, sorry,' she said. 'I'll come to the door with you, if you think you might get lost.'

They stepped out into the dark corridor. The house felt huge, with doors opening on both sides into large, gloomy rooms. The only light came from the kitchen and the landing at the top of a long staircase. Martha went ahead and switched on a light in the small porch beyond the front door.

'This is almost more than we can take,' she said quietly. 'None of us can think straight this evening. We'll try to be more helpful tomorrow.' Suddenly she jerked her head as if someone had called her name. 'Dear God!' she exclaimed. 'You're looking for the person who killed him, aren't you? I'm being terribly stupid. I didn't hear everything you said when you arrived. Charlie was murdered, is that right?'

Den cleared his throat. 'He had very severe injuries, the worst ones to his head. It seems beyond reasonable doubt that there was foul play. But we won't know anything for sure until the post-mortem tomorrow.'

'Well,' she said, 'if I was being uncharitable I'd suggest you start with our friend Gerald. Although to be honest I can't see even him going that far. Poor Charlie! What can he possibly have done to deserve such a death?'

Den made no attempt to answer that. He took two or three steps towards his car before turning back for a moment. 'One last thing,' he remembered. 'Do you keep any horses on this property?'

'No,' she said, wide-eyed. 'Why? What are you thinking?'

'I'm not thinking anything,' he assured her. 'I'll see you tomorrow.'

He thought about the High Copse family as he drove away. As far as he could tell, everyone he'd seen was genuinely shocked and grief-stricken by the death of Charlie Grattan. The coming days were going to be gruelling. It was his first murder since joining the CID, and the fact that he knew the people involved, if only casually, gave him a central role in the investigation. He imagined he would have the task of interviewing a number of them, as well as visiting members of the Quaker group . . . Meeting . . . whatever they called it. It would mean delving into the activities of the animal rights people. With a sigh, he remembered that Lilah was waiting for him to spend what remained of the evening with her. Murder was a real pain, he concluded. And recalling his last brush with it, he once again fingered the mark on the side of his face.

CHAPTER THREE

WPC Jane Nugent had taken the news of Charlie's death to the people she too had initially assumed to be his parents. 'Mrs Grattan?' she had asked on the doorstep, when a woman in her sixties answered the door.

'*Miss* Grattan, actually,' came the reply, somewhat to Jane's confusion. It took a few moments to ascertain that this was indeed the woman who had brought Charlie up, along with his father, Mr Bill Grattan. They were brother and sister.

'I'm extremely sorry to tell you that his body was found this afternoon at High Copse Farm.' Jane didn't mind being the bearer of bad news; it made her feel essential, at the heart of things,

doing a job that could not be left undone. She
had a useful knack of being both warm and
businesslike; sympathetic but unsentimental.
People generally demanded facts and Jane Nugent
was adept at providing them.

'He's been taken to the Royal Devon and
Exeter for a post-mortem,' she explained. 'And
I'm afraid there will be a police investigation
into who was responsible for his death. Is there
anybody I can telephone for you? Anybody you'd
like to have with you?'

She watched the old man, Bill, with some
curiosity. Ten years or so older than his sister, he
sat in a deep armchair, head bowed in silence. He
had a large head, with bushy iron-grey eyebrows
and thick hair of a similar colour. His eyes were
framed in pleated flesh which hung loosely under
his lower lids, showing a rim of red. The overall
impression was of a desperate vulnerability, an
almost unbearable misery. With his chin in one
hand, the little finger caught between his teeth,
he presented a picture of such complex layers of
pain that Jane had to avert her inquisitive gaze.

The sister, however, seemed very much less
disconcerted. 'Thank you for coming, my dear,
but I don't think we need any further help,' she
said. 'Is there anything more you want from us
this evening? Will we be required to identify the
body?' Her face was pale, her hands clasped

tightly together at her waist, but her voice was steady.

'No, I don't think so,' said Jane. 'I believe someone from High Copse has already done that.'

'Ah yes. Probably Mr Taverner. He's a good man, although I can't say I really know him.' Her expression suddenly changed, as if something cold had brushed against her face. She frowned and gave a little shake. 'Poor Charlie,' she breathed. 'He must have been terrified.' Her frown deepened and she looked into Jane's eyes. 'Has this got anything to do with the accident last week?'

Jane blinked. 'You mean what happened to Mrs Nesbitt at the hunt protest,' she said, after a moment's incomprehension. 'Well, it's too soon to say, and anyway . . .'

'You wouldn't be permitted to tell us, I expect.' Hannah glanced at her brother. 'And I can see that I should not have asked.' A sharpness in this last remark caught Jane by surprise.

'It isn't that. The fact is, we really don't know ourselves at the moment. Until the post-mortem . . .'

'That's all right,' Hannah stopped her. 'Now I'm sure you've got things to do. We appreciate your coming, dear, but we'll manage. We've got each other. And we have friends. We'll be well supported by the people from the Meeting.'

'Er . . . ?'

'Friends' Meeting. Quakers is what you probably know us as. The Society of Friends is our official title. We're very small, so I'm not surprised you don't know of us. I happen to be the Clerk. Bill and I have been Quakers all our lives. Charlie too, of course.'

'I'm sorry to be so ignorant,' said Jane sincerely.

'Don't be. We're not very visible these days. In fact, we're very much a dying breed, I fear. There's not much of the original passion left any more.' She sighed. 'Three hundred years ago, the Quakers were very much a force to be reckoned with.'

'Well, I hope you'll get all the support you need from it.'

'Oh, yes,' Hannah nodded slowly. 'Oh yes. We will.'

Jane allowed herself to be ushered out, pausing only to tell the Grattans that they could expect to be interviewed about Charlie's movements and other relevant matters. His bedroom would be examined, and other aspects of his life explored.

'It all sounds rather intrusive,' Hannah demurred, with another worried glance at her brother.

'We try to avoid it feeling like that, but of

course, if we're to understand exactly what happened, it can't really be avoided.'

'No,' said Hannah cheerlessly. 'I don't suppose it can.'

WPC Nugent took her leave in a thoughtful mood. The only thing she could remember about Quakers was that they made a fuss about nuclear bombs and wars. She'd had no idea there were some of them living right here, on her patch.

Silas Dagg hated the telephone. His cousins had insisted he have one installed after he twisted his back and lay for two days on the floor before anybody found him, but he never used it. Very few people were given his number, so when it rang at seven-thirty that evening, the shock was considerable. Angrily he snatched up the receiver, having dumped his elderly corgi roughly on the floor from her snug place on his lap.

'Who might that be?' he demanded.

'Silas, it's Hannah,' came the gentle reply. The voice was slow and musical, as always, but he could hear grief and trouble coming out of the grubby plastic gadget in his hand, like something tangible. Like rain in the midst of the hay harvest or a scouring disease running through the calves.

'What?' he said, his shoulders braced squarely for whatever she might have to tell him.

'They found Charlie.'

'Was he lost? First I've heard of it.'

'We hadn't seen him since Sunday, but we thought he was with the Cattermoles. He's been staying there a lot lately. The police were here a little while ago, to tell us they found him at half past four today, in a ditch.'

'Dead?' The question was unnecessary; he'd already heard the answer in her voice.

'They think he was murdered. Silas – who in the world would want to murder Charlie? When did he ever hurt anybody?'

Silas shuddered as the fact behind the words struck him. Hannah and Bill were his cousins. Together they formed the core of the Quaker Meeting – Birthright Friends, whose great-grandparents had worshipped at the little Meeting House at the end of the village street. Farmers, builders, traders: their straight dealing often leading to an affluence they found burdensome. The meeting waxed and waned, attracting occasional newcomers, but rarely numbering more than twenty or thirty members. The loss of Charlie was a great blow; the fact that his death had been brought about with deliberate malice was far worse.

'Shall I come?' he asked.

'I think we should hold a special meeting.'

'What – now? Surely that's too quick?' And

yet the thought appealed to him: to have his fellow Friends around him was always a comfort, even in recent times, with so much turmoil and disagreement causing divisions and unkind words. Silas always looked forward to the silent hour each Sunday morning.

'Not *now*,' she said, on a single breath of impatience at the suggestion. 'On Friday. At eleven. I'm sure everyone will be able to come.'

'Are you? *Everyone*?' He put a world of meaning into the word; there were people who might be deeply embarrassed to be asked to remember Charlie Grattan with fondness. *Who could possibly want to hurt Charlie?* Hannah had asked. Silas could have answered with a string of names. Charlie had been a fool in more ways than one and caused many a wounded soul to curse him in their hearts for his intemperate ways. Hunting was about much more than chasing a fox across wintry fields. It went far deeper than that, as Silas well understood. To condemn it as barbaric was to ignore tradition and age-old practice. It encompassed something visceral, unspoken, to do with man's place on the land. As a Quaker, Silas had never personally indulged in hunting, but he respected and understood those who did, and he had flinched at Charlie Grattan's behaviour towards them.

* * *

Thursday morning was busy for Den. The pathologist had performed a post-mortem on Charlie and preliminary results indicated that he had died of a fractured skull; fractured, in fact, in no fewer than four places. The object responsible had been a horseshoe, or possibly two horseshoes. The curved shape had been distinctive and there were matching marks on his face and shoulders. The blows had been delivered with some considerable force. The time of death could get no closer than between seventy-two and forty-eight hours before he was found. And that meant he had been killed on Sunday or Monday. These basic facts were circulated to CID by eleven that morning.

'Either someone bashed him with a horseshoe, over and over, or he was trampled to death by a very determined horse,' summarised the Inspector, briefing Den and two others. 'And at the moment it looks a lot like the latter, given that a horseshoe on its own is not a very credible weapon. Even if you snatched one up on the spur of the moment, it would be almost impossible to hold it at such an angle as to inflict these wounds or to wield it with sufficient force. There was substantial weight behind the shoe when it connected with his head.'

'How bizarre,' breathed Den. 'Especially after Nina Nesbitt.' The others eyed him expectantly.

'You know – the woman protesting at the hunt. Killed by a horse. Coincidence or what?'

The Inspector remained impassive. 'Plainly not,' he said. 'Same farm, as well as both involving a horse. But no suggestion of two murders. There's not a whiff of foul play about the way the woman died. Am I right, Cooper?'

Den nodded. 'It was definitely an accident, no question. So maybe somebody wanted to deliberately echo that death in the way he killed Charlie? As a way of making a connection. That would make sense, wouldn't it? Somebody trying to get some sort of point across.'

'Right. Good thinking. Now I want interviews, lots of them. All the family background you can find, plus close scrutiny of the animal rights crowd and the people who live at the place where he died. Close liaison with forensics, obviously, and take on board anything they can tell you about the churned-up ground by that ditch, hairs from horses and humans – everything. Plus – and this should come first, now I think about it – get people out to all the local riding stables and check horses' feet for blood, or new shoes being fitted urgently, that sort of thing. It's a faint hope you'll find anything, all these days later, but it has to be done. We need to know who knew Grattan best. Who loved him, who hated him. Cooper, I gather your girlfriend knows the High Copse people?

That might be useful, but don't let her cloud your judgement.' He noticed Den's wary reaction. 'I don't mean anything heavy. We're not taking her on as a temporary WPC or anything. Just don't waste her, if you see what I mean.'

Den nodded and relaxed. 'All right, sir,' he said.

After further deliberation, DI Smith decided he had enough grounds to bring Master of Foxhounds Gerald Fairfield in for questioning. DC Phil Bennett and DS Danny Hemsley were dispatched to collect him, before proceeding to an examination of local horses. Danny groaned. 'Growth industry, horses. There are scores of the things within ten miles of here.'

The Inspector ignored him. 'Cooper, you can help interview Fairfield. If we get anywhere with him, you might be able to forget half those people we've just been talking about.'

'Yes, sir.' The Inspector was, on the whole, an easy man to work with. His reasoning was generally sound and his demands rarely beyond the achievable. Den just wished he could like him. An occasional smile would help; a glimpse of someone with ordinary human emotions beneath the calm, wooden face that he presented to the world would work wonders. Smith's career had not been unduly strewn with obstacles. He had never been shot or held hostage; had never uncovered a ring of satanic paedophiles or a drug-based gang holding the town in a reign of terror. Badger baiting could be nasty, admittedly, and old ladies tended to make a tremendous fuss when they were burgled, but by and large, as far as Den could tell, the task of enforcing the law in the heart of Devon need not automatically turn you into an icy-hearted cynic.

People boxed themselves into corners: that was how Den saw it. They never meant to become criminals, never intentionally turned themselves into outlaws or reprobates. Something just got twisted inside them. Some inner failure took hold of them and they simply never found their way back up the greasy pole to conformity and social compliance. That didn't necessarily make them likeable or easy to understand, but it kept Den himself from disillusion with the world at large. 'The trouble with you is, you always want to be nice,' said Lilah. 'You want to hold on to the moral high ground and not let any of this muck stick to you.'

She was right, and he saw no reason to change.

Gerald Fairfield came willingly when invited by the police officers, who were careful not to mention Charlie Grattan. He strolled into the police station behind them, head held high, and looked from face to face with curiosity. Even at a glance, Den sensed that this was not a guilty man. Stripped of his hunting pink, his commanding horse, his entourage of beaters and whippers and terrier men, he was still an imposing presence.

Detective Inspector Smith fought hard not to be intimidated. 'If you would just come this way, sir, we have a few questions for you. It won't take more than a few minutes.'

'Delighted to be of help,' Gerald smiled. The interview was to be taped and Den sat at a distance from the main action. Smith and Fairfield faced each other across the table, two men approaching fifty who had spent much of their lives in the area but never met before. Fairfield had gone to boarding school and then done a spell in the army, waiting to inherit his father's estate. Smith had attended the local comprehensive, followed by police college; he lived in a three-bedroomed house in a row of others just like it. The abiding assumptions of the British class system, personified as they were in these individuals, quickly put both men at their ease. They knew what to expect from each other.

Nonetheless DI Smith's opening words came as a surprise to Gerald. 'We're investigating the death of Mr Charles Grattan,' he began. 'His body was found yesterday. He appears to have been dead for some time.'

Fairfield reared back, chin tucked into his neck.

'Good God!' he said. 'I had no idea. I thought you wanted to go over the Nesbitt woman again.' He paused and inhaled deeply. 'Grattan dead, eh? You astonish me.'

Den more than half believed him. The flicker of glee, the triumphant twitch at the corners of his lips, seemed too genuine for this to be old news. On the other hand, Fairfield was as undemonstrative as anyone of his background, and the clues as to his mood were so fleeting they might have been mere imagination.

'It looks very much like murder,' Smith continued. 'He was attacked by a horse, which as you know, is unlikely to occur without the involvement of a human being.'

'Wait, wait.' The Hunt Master put up his hands. 'You're telling me that both these antis have been killed by horses within a few days of each other? That's incredible. Somebody's playing a game.'

Smith manifested puzzlement. 'What do you mean by that?' he asked.

'Nothing in particular, just that Grattan always sailed closer to the wind than was good for him. If he's been bumped off now, it strikes me that's too much of a coincidence. Wouldn't you say? I'd call it a game,' he repeated.

'A game with very high stakes,' Smith remarked coldly. 'Now, sir, if you could tell me where you last saw Mr Grattan and fill in your own movements as fully as you can for Sunday and Monday, perhaps we can eliminate you from our enquiries.'

'You think *I* did it? You think I'd ride out, chasing after Grattan and somehow get poor old Shamrock to repeat his performance of last week? Ludicrous, Inspector, if I may say so. Surely the poor creature's in enough trouble as it is. I've had to keep him in, with a lock on the stable door, in case any of those hooligans take it into their heads to avenge the Nesbitt girl.'

'Would you just answer the question, sir?' repeated Smith flatly.

'I last saw Charlie Grattan a week ago. Thursday, at eleven in the morning, when my horse had just killed his fellow protester. He was shouting and wailing in a highly uncontrolled fashion, which I admit to finding most unpleasant. On Sunday I drove down to Penzance and back, to visit my sister. On Monday I was mostly in my estate office, although I did call in on Bruce Wragg in the afternoon. He's the Field Master and we wanted to discuss the Hunt programme. We also discussed whether either of us would attend the funeral at High Copse. You may know that I did eventually go along and made a short address. I felt I owed it to the family. And of course Hermione's a personal friend.'

Smith made a few notes, before raising his gaze interrogatively. 'Hermione?'

'Nesbitt. Mother-in-law of the deceased. Keen huntswoman in her own right. Highly embarrassed by the girl's antics, I can tell you. Dotes on the grandsons, of course.' He turned to Den for the first time. 'I seem to recall you were there last week,' he said. 'You saw how she was with them.'

Den nodded minimally and Smith intervened. 'We're here to investigate the death of Charlie Grattan,' he said. 'Not Nina Nesbitt.'

'Seems to me you can't separate the two,' argued Gerald. 'I've always thought that's a failing with you police people. You don't see the wider picture.'

'And it seems to *me*,' Smith snapped back, 'that you're avoiding the subject of Grattan's death.'

'Not at all,' Fairfield disagreed. 'It's just that I have nothing whatsoever to say about it. It's too bizarre. Besides, I hardly knew the fellow. What makes you think it was a deliberate killing, anyway? Couldn't he have fallen somehow, or got himself kicked accidentally? Horses don't attack people, not around here at least. They're all far too well bred for that.'

Den could not restrain a slight hiss of disagreement. Both the older men looked at him.

'Sorry, sir,' he said. 'But I wouldn't go along with that. Remember that little girl, eighteen months ago, who had her back broken when her pony knocked her down and rolled on her?'

Smith nodded briefly and repressively, and Den understood that arguing with the interviewee was not part of his role. Fairfield sat passive and patient, ready for the next question.

After a short silence, Smith said, 'I take it the news of his death is not entirely unwelcome to you?'

'Steady on! Young man, presumably with a family, life ahead of him. I wouldn't wish death on anyone. Whatever you might think, I'm still trying to get over last week. That was a terrible thing. He'll tell you—' He nodded at Den. 'That crack, bone on bone . . . ghastly thing to happen. Sorry, sorry.' He raised his eyes to the ceiling. 'Doing it again, aren't I. But you see, Grattan's a pinprick compared to that. I can't pretend I liked him. Thought he was a complete nutcase, if I'm honest. But I didn't kill him. I can see the way your mind's working, and I admit there's a kind of logic to viewing me as a suspect. But you'll have to think again, Inspector. I promise you that nobody who works with horses would deliberately use one to kill a man. The psychology of that is way off the mark.'

'Perhaps, while you're here, we could ask

one or two technical questions?' The Inspector adopted a subtly submissive demeanour as he said this.

'Fire away,' the landowner invited, placated.

'Firstly, what would be a reasonable distance for a rider and horse to travel, say in two or three hours? At the sort of pace designed not to attract attention.'

Fairfield answered unhesitatingly. 'Fifteen, twenty miles, maximum. Further than that, and they'd be cantering. Though I'm not sure anybody would take notice of a rider cantering along some of the quieter bridleways. Thirty-five miles wouldn't be impossible for a good animal. Opens up a pretty wide range of possibilities for your enquiries, eh, Inspector? Glad I'm not in your shoes.'

DI Smith made some notes, thanked his witness and suggested that Den drive him home again. They parted with high civility, each acknowledging that jobs must be done and roles must be played. But as he walked out to the car, Den knew that Gerald Fairfield still had to feature significantly on the short list of those who had means, motive and opportunity to kill Charlie Grattan. Indeed, Den concluded with a wry smile that Gerald was on a very, very short list of such individuals.

In the car they talked inevitably of Nina. Den

was aware of a mutual need to replay the scene of her death with someone who had been there. 'I've been dreaming about it,' Gerald admitted. 'In the dream, the horse is covered in blood. Nobody ever asked about his welfare, you know. Whether the poor lad had a bruised nose. All that shouting and screaming upset him; he's been off his fodder ever since. I'm not complaining, obviously. I'm probably lucky nobody's demanded he be put down.'

'They *are* animal rights activists,' Den pointed out. 'That presumably extends to horses.'

'Hah!' Gerald laughed sarcastically. 'You're joking! You, of all people, must know what they get up to, what they do to police dogs and horses. They're nothing but hypocrites and fools. Surely you're with me on that?'

'I think that's a bit sweeping,' Den ventured. 'I haven't much personal experience, but from what I'm hearing about Charlie, he was no fool. He had a lot of respect from a lot of people. He was a Quaker, too. I don't think they're generally regarded as hypocrites.'

'A Quaker, eh? Like old Barty White, my terrier supplier. He's no hypocrite, either, though I bet his Quaker pals think he is. He'll know your Charlie, I suppose.' He gave a slight chuckle. 'I don't envy you sorting this one out. That Cattermole family defies comprehension, for a start. You won't have known the old woman, I imagine? Died four or five years ago now.'

'Old woman?'

'Eliza. Mother of the three girls. Amazing character. When I was fifteen, I was insanely in love with her. Never really got over it – though that's off the record.'

'But she must have been . . .'

'Mid-thirties, at least. Hadn't had any of the girls at the time. She was working on it, though. Eliza Cattermole brought the sixties to Devon all by herself. God, it seems like another world now.'

'What happened to her husband?'

'No such person. Didn't hold with anything so conventional as marriage. You ask Martha – she'll cheerfully tell you. She's the best of the bunch by a long way. The only one with a proper job and her feet on the ground. Not that any of that's got anything to do with this business.'

Den wasn't so sure. In his limited experience, he had already learnt that motivation for murder was highly likely to extend a long way back into the past.

'So who's their father? Is he still around?'

'It wasn't just the one chap,' Gerald explained patiently. 'There were three different ones. Nobody from round here. She'd go off to London or wherever and come back pregnant. Did it deliberately. We assumed it was because she couldn't find anybody good enough for her on this side of the country.'

'How did she manage for money?'

'Hasn't anyone told you this story?' Gerald stared at Den, turning sideways in the car. Den shook his head. 'When she was eighteen, her parents sent her to London for the society season. I don't know how it happened, but she was taken up by some film agent chap and given a star part in a big American film. Paid her very generously, took her to California for a year or two – real fairytale stuff. She met Monroe, Ava Gardner, Cary Grant – the whole shooting match. But she only ever made the one film – which was a big success – and came back in about nineteen fifty-five with her pockets full of cash.'

'What was the film?'

'Can't remember now. I suspect she was cast for her looks, not her talent. But she made the money work for her and it saw her through when she needed it. Mind you, living at that place, before they sold off most of the land, can't have been easy. I remember they cut down acres of fine oak and beech, to use on the open fires that were all they had for heating.'

Den dropped his passenger outside his own impressive house, built from old, mellow stone with a creeper covering the façade. Stables, offices, a large stone-built barn and an open-fronted shed housing two gleaming new tractors formed three sides of a muck-free yard. For some people, the vagaries of contemporary agricultural politics hardly seemed to impinge at all.

He drove back to the police station thinking about the Cattermole inheritance, which may or may not still exist. High Copse had struck him as being in decline and not at all the home of people living on substantial private means. Had the daughters squandered it, or had there never been as much as local rumour believed?

One note found its way into his jotter before he went on to the next job: *Gerald Fairfield was once in love with Eliza Cattermole*. It seemed to be a small detail that was unlikely to be substantiated by any of his forthcoming interviews.

CHAPTER FOUR

Back at the station, Smith called Den in for a talk about Fairfield.

'He talked about the Cattermoles in the car,' Den reported, and summarised the handful of facts he'd gleaned.

'Interesting. Now let me try this one on you, just off the top of my head.'

Den leant back against the table behind him. It made him appear less tall, a wise move when face to face with DI Smith, who stood a full five inches shorter. 'Okay,' he invited.

'Imagine the disgruntled Gerald is out for a ride – probably on one of his hacks and not the ill-fated beast that killed Mrs Nesbitt. He heads towards High Copse, either out of curiosity or because it's as good a route as any. Meets Grattan, who starts abusing him, calling him a murderer, being thoroughly provocative. With me so far?'

Den nodded. 'Sounds like the Charlie Grattan I saw last week.'

'After a bit of this, he sees red, charges after Charlie, and the horse tramples him, maybe by accident. But nobody's going to believe that, are they? So he puts on the act we've just witnessed, and bloody good it was, too. He persuades his sister in Penzance to give him an alibi – we've phoned her by the way, and she backs his story. What d'you think?'

Den examined a worn patch in the vinyl floor covering, trying to find the right response. 'It's possible,' he said. 'Except—'

'Yes? Except what?'

'Well . . . would he have gone to High Copse, after what happened? He doesn't strike me as the sort of horseman who goes out for a casual trot along a bridle path. He's got enough land of his own. And if Charlie had yelled and screamed at him in that field, someone from the house would most likely have heard him. It's not very far away.'

'Interesting,' said Smith again. 'Thanks, Cooper. You're coming along, you know.'

Den watched in vain for a smile to accompany the words.

* * *

Given the task of going back to the scene to ask a whole tranche of new questions, Den rehearsed his enquiries as he drove south-westwards towards High Copse. He had lived in the area all his life, going to school with people from a range of outlying villages, but there were still isolated settlements that he had never visited, within the triangle formed by Okehampton, Tavistock and Launceston. There were perhaps fifty tiny communities, some of them nestling at the end of high-banked country lanes, others bordering the busier roads. High Copse was two miles from any of these; their closest neighbour was a white cob farmhouse almost half a mile away.

The outline of Brentor seemed to follow him as he drove, a landmark visible across the whole area, with its almost comical little church perched crazily on the granite outcrop. Den found his gaze drifting towards it more than usual.

Jane Nugent had spoken to him briefly about Hannah and Bill Grattan and their Quaker Meeting. 'Doesn't sound like any church I've ever come across,' she said. 'She never mentioned God or forgiveness or any of the usual religious stuff. And yet it sounded . . . *nice*, somehow.' She laughed in embarrassment, hearing herself. Perhaps her words were still in Den's mind as the church in the sky watched him drive through the narrow lanes.

The big house was a worthy partner for Brentor. Visible from a lesser, but still impressive, distance, nestled halfway up a steep hill, as many houses were in this uneven landscape, High Copse had definite presence.

From the gravelled car-parking patch at the front of the house, Den could see the red mound of earth bordered by banks of vivid funeral flowers that was Nina's grave. It was sheltered by a spreading oak tree, at least three hundred years old and not yet in leaf. The grave's distance from the house was an unsettling forty or fifty yards, but it could only be seen from one or two windows. Perhaps they would grow a thick hedge around it. They must have stronger stomachs than his, though, to live with the knowledge of her lying there, decomposing year after year.

Martha came to the door with young Clement at her side. She invited him in, and he wiped his feet before stepping into the long, dark corridor that ran through to the back of the house.

'Alexis isn't here,' Martha told him, when they were once again in the warm kitchen. 'She's gone to see Charlie's family. I don't think she'll be long. Clem . . .' she put a hand out to the boy as he stood at the table flipping through a comic, 'can you go somewhere else? I don't think the policeman needs you to be here.' She raised an eyebrow at Den, who shook his head.

Clement sighed and stayed where he was. 'What's he want, anyway?' he demanded.

'He's come about Charlie. I told you.'

Clem narrowed his eyes. 'Everybody's dying,' he muttered. 'I don't like it.'

'Me neither,' Martha agreed. 'It's a bummer. But keep smiling, eh? Nev should be here tomorrow – that's something to look forward to, isn't it. And Hugh's up there in the rumpus room, isn't he?'

The child shrugged. 'He won't let me do anything with him today. He says I'm a nuisance.' The petulance was exaggerated, but even so he cut a pitiable little figure.

'Oh, Clem.' Martha tightened her lips, turning them inwards to be caught between her teeth. She averted her face from him, blindly holding his hand in a tight squeeze. 'This won't take very long, I promise. When Alexis gets back, I'll do us some lunch. How about putting a video on in my room? You can choose anything you like.'

With a show of reluctance Clem left the kitchen. Soon Martha and Den heard him going upstairs, his pace quickening as he climbed. She smiled. 'Special treat, he's got a thing about old musicals, but Hugh laughs at him about it. He'll be all right for an hour or so now.'

'Nice little kid,' said Den. 'What's going to happen to them?'

She gave him a challenging stare. 'Nothing's going to happen to them. They live here. They were born here.'

'Unusual,' he commented with a touch of apology. 'These days, anyway – a real extended family.'

'I don't know why you say that. If this was an inner-city estate you wouldn't be at all surprised to find a set-up like ours. Your problem's with the house, not the people in it.'

He leant back in the chair, fixing his gaze on a large cobweb in the corner where two walls met the ceiling. The police were trained to deal with unexpected hostility from the newly bereaved. They'd all done the role play and watched training videos. The vital thing was not to respond to it. Besides, what Martha had said was true, at least in part.

'I have to ask you some questions,' he said firmly. 'Following on from yesterday, can you think of any connections between the two deaths?' He held up his hand as she began to speak. 'No, wait. I don't need convincing that your sister died by accident. That isn't what I mean. But can we have a list of people who knew both her and Grattan? And what was the relationship between the two of them?'

Martha clasped her hands together into a double fist and rested her chin on it. 'That could take all day. You're asking me to give a complete account of their lives.'

He nodded. 'That's generally the way of it in a murder inquiry, unfortunately.'

'I've been thinking . . . isn't it possible that Charlie also died by accident? I didn't take in much detail, but Richmond says he might have been knocked into the ditch by a horse that was just being a bit too exuberant, and then he got kicked in the head. Are you quite sure that couldn't be what happened?'

Den pursed his lips. 'Doesn't fit the facts – sorry. If someone riding a horse had just knocked him over by mistake, it stands to reason they'd do something to help him. They wouldn't just keep quiet about it and go home as if nothing had happened. Have you got a large horse liable to go wild, with access to that field?' She shook her head regretfully. 'No, I thought not. And nobody's reported seeing a loose horse. Did Charlie have a mount of his own?'

'No. He had a thing about "slave animals" as he called them. Said humans exploited them for their own ends. He had all sorts of silly plans for buying land and turning animals loose on it to live free. He was never going to have the money for anything like that. And of course it could never work, if he had.'

'I see. Well, we're still looking for a horse,

then. I can't tell you much, but I'm afraid there is no doubt at all that your sister and Charlie Grattan both died from violent contact with a horse.'

Martha worked her mouth, her flexible features making a succession of faces. Den read worry, hesitation, disbelief and resolve, one after the other. 'If it's about horses, well . . . there's Frank,' she said at last. The words emerged explosively, as if escaping against her will. She put one hand to her mouth. 'But—'

Den waited. Better if she elaborated without any prompting from him.

'Charlie's brother, he's called Frank. He lives near Ashburton, across the moor from here. Breeds horses for riding stables. He and Charlie scarcely saw each other; the family have more or less disowned him. I wonder if they've even thought to tell him the news.'

'Older brother or younger?'

'Older, by quite a bit. You need to ask Alexis, she knows more about him than I do. I think she even met him once. If we're talking about horses, you can't really ignore Frank.'

Den made a long note on his increasingly scruffy notepad, and tried to suppress his excitement. 'Did he know Nina?'

'Not really. But he did come here once, some weeks ago, and talked to her for a while. There was nobody else here, so I've no idea what was said. I just know she was rather upset afterwards, and kept talking about "the brother from hell". Charlie asked why she didn't like him, and what he'd done to annoy her, but she didn't have much of an answer.'

'And he'd never been here before?'

'Not to my knowledge. I assumed he wanted to see Charlie, and someone had told him he'd probably find him here. Frank didn't wait around, though. I don't think Charlie's seen him for months, maybe even years.'

Den nibbled his pencil, trying to think of further questions. The link between Nina and Charlie was still frustratingly tenuous. 'Nina was well known, I gather? A lot of people came to her funeral, according to Lilah. Would any of them blame Charlie for her death?'

'Hang on,' Martha protested. 'One thing at a time. Yes, she was well known. She got herself into the news often enough, and not just because of animal rights. She was against the supermarket coming to town, the bypass, the closing of rights of way, packaging, cuts in bus services . . .' She ticked them off on her fingers.

'Packaging?'

'You know – using stupid plastic trays for four apples, so you can't buy one or three or five, and wrapping everything up in three layers of

73

impenetrable polythene. Quite honestly, that was the cause I had most sympathy with. I've written one or two letters to supermarkets myself about that one.'

'So she would have upset plenty of people.'

'Very much so. Although she was charming to them all individually. I don't think many would have borne a grudge for long. And anyway . . .'

'Yes, I know. And anyway, her death was an accident. Which brings me to the next question. Charlie's involvement in what happened at the hunt.'

'You were there. You saw it for yourself. How could it be Charlie's fault?'

'If he was seen to be the ringleader, sending her into a dangerous situation . . .'

'You obviously didn't know Nina,' she said scornfully. 'Nobody could *send* her anywhere. Nina did what Nina wanted to do. It would be lunatic to think of blaming Charlie.'

The banging of the front door interrupted them. They waited, without moving, until Alexis came into the kitchen.

CHAPTER FIVE

Den gave Alexis his full attention. Her wide mouth and grey eyes were attractive, but she had too narrow a head and too short a neck for him to find her seriously pleasing to look at. Her thick black hair seemed to resent any attempts at control. Martha was preferable, despite the same narrow head; she seemed to be more in proportion and her apricot-coloured hair singled her out as a person to be noticed.

'I've been to see Hannah,' Alexis said. Den noticed her hands were shaking. She stood in the kitchen, making no move to sit down.

'How was she?' Martha patted the back of one of the wooden chairs and her sister obediently pulled it away from the table and dropped into it heavily.

'Shell-shocked. At least . . . I suppose that's how you'd describe it. On the surface, she's quite calm, her usual self, but her eyes are weird. She didn't look at me once. It was as if she was looking for Charlie, expecting to find him behind the sofa or in the fireplace. And Bill's a total wreck. He just sits in that chair like a great sack of rubbish that no one wants. Considering Charlie was his son, not Hannah's, you'd think he'd be getting the sympathy.'

'How do you know he isn't?'

'People kept coming to the door. Well, two did. Mandy from the Meeting House and another Quaker, whose name I can't remember. The drippy one. Anyway, they only talked to Hannah and more or less ignored poor old Bill.'

Den tried to remind them of his presence. 'If I could just . . .'

'Sorry,' said Alexis curtly. 'What do you want to know?'

'When exactly did you see Charlie last?'

'Ah, yes.' Her face seemed suddenly longer and greyer. 'As we've already told you, we can't be very exact about that. He was here on Sunday morning. We didn't have a proper lunch, people just got themselves a sandwich. The boys went off to their gran's in the afternoon and I thought perhaps Charlie had gone with them. But Hugh says he didn't. Richmond thought he'd gone for a lie-down. It was all so chaotic here, you see.'

'Was your sister's body here on Sunday?' The question was difficult to phrase tactfully.

Martha answered. 'No. We brought her back here from the hospital in Exeter early on Monday, once we'd painted the coffin. We put her in the dining room with candles all round her, and she stayed there until Wednesday morning.'

'So Charlie didn't see her?'

Both sisters shook their heads. 'We thought it was because he couldn't cope with it,' said Martha. 'He was soft like that.'

'But all the time he was lying dead in that ditch,' moaned Alexis. 'Why didn't we go and look for him? Why did we assume he was just being a coward? We *knew* he wasn't a cowardly person.'

'He seemed very distressed at what happened to Nina,' said Den, remembering his own experience of Charlie. 'If you saw him like that, you'd naturally expect him to find the business of the funeral difficult.'

'You don't understand,' said Alexis unhappily. 'Charlie wasn't like other people.'

'Oh?'

'He wasn't *thick*, or anything like that. He did brilliantly at school. But he had . . . gaps. He couldn't do more than one thing at a time. And he didn't know how to play the usual social games.

He told people what he thought, no matter the consequences. But there was real magic in him. Charisma.'

Den nodded, trying to form a picture of the dead man. 'And when you said about him going for a lie-down – which room would that have been in?' he asked delicately.

'Mine of course. He was sleeping with me. He was more or less at the point of moving in here. We were going to get a bigger bed.' She tailed off, the lost future a great pit in front of her. 'Charlie was part of this family,' she wept.

Martha made soothing noises; Den permitted a short silence. Then Martha took up the thread. 'It's true. We'd come to see him as a permanent fixture. He and Nina did a lot together, too. With Nev away so much, it was good to have Charlie here as another man about the place. He helped Richmond with some of the heavy work now and then.'

'Nev?'

'Nina's husband. Father of Hugh and Clem. If you're looking for nice, normal nuclear families, that's the nearest we can offer you.'

'And where is he now?'

'Probably Singapore Airport. He phoned us yesterday and said he'd try and get here sometime tonight or tomorrow. He was in Vietnam when Nina died. It took ages to contact him. In this day and age, you'd think a person could get back within a week, but there you are. Apparently there was a volcano somewhere which delayed things. And once he knew we weren't holding the funeral back for him, another day or two wasn't critical. But it isn't really fair on the boys. They can hardly wait to see him again.'

'How long has he been away?'

'Oh . . .' Martha stared at Alexis, trying to work out her reply.

'Five or six months,' the younger sister supplied. 'I think he went in September or October.'

Den closed his eyes a moment, trying to disentangle the morass of carelessly dropped loose ends. *Nev Nesbitt phoned Wednesday afternoon, check flights* he wrote on his notepad. 'The boys' gran,' he remembered. 'That's Mrs Nesbitt senior, Nev's mother, right? You mentioned her yesterday. She sees a lot of the boys, does she?' He reran the scene at Nina's death, when an elderly woman had appeared from nowhere to scoop up both boys like a protecting angel. It could only have been Hermione Nesbitt.

'She's very fond of them,' Martha nodded. 'But she doesn't like us much. She doesn't approve of us. Couldn't stand Nina. Didn't even come to the funeral, although she did show up on Monday morning and spent a few minutes with the body.

And she brought Hugh back at the same time.'

'Er . . . could you explain that?' Den asked.

'Oh, I think there was some problem with his bike, so he stayed the night with Hermione. Clem was here on his own on Sunday evening. You remember, don't you?' Martha checked with Alexis. 'We played Downfall with him.'

Den summarised. 'Let me get this right. Both boys cycled to Bradstone on Sunday. Clem came back alone and Hugh was driven home next morning. Isn't it rather a long way for a young boy on his own?'

'I don't think so,' said Martha stiffly. 'Only about four miles as the crow flies. They go across the fields. There's a path some of the way. It's very ancient actually, a bit of local heritage.' She lifted her chin and stared out of the window for a bit. 'Hoskins mentions it.'

'And who might Hoskins be?' asked Den, irritable at this sudden glimpse of Martha the schoolteacher.

'He wrote books about Devon. And other counties, I think. He lists everything of interest. I'm rather shocked you don't know that.'

'Well, I'll know another time, won't I?' he flashed back, before catching himself and smiling an apology. 'Where were we?'

The two women looked at him and said nothing. 'Just working out where everybody was,' he said. 'Hugh at his gran's, Clem here, having got home safely on his bike.' He wrote a few words. 'Lucky boys, having such freedom,' he added.

Alexis snorted and Martha cast a quick glance at the ceiling in ill-concealed exasperation.

'I'd better go and talk to Mr Taverner, then, if you'll just tell me where I can find him.'

Outside, Richmond was pretending to be busy in his office. High Copse Farmhouse no longer operated as a farm, despite retaining twenty acres of land, comprising two fields, a generous garden and a large apple orchard behind the house. The barns were mostly offices, the pigsties provided a playground for the boys and the former shippon was now a large warehouse full of animal feedstuffs. The business of supplying feed to smallholders and rural families with domestic pets was a thriving one, selling at low cost as it did. Bulk bags of dry dog food; layers' pellets for hens; powdered milk as substitute for nursing mothers, whether bovine, canine or feline; and a hundred different kinds of food and equipment for horses, ponies and donkeys, formed the main stock. There was also tinned dog food and cat food, hay, straw and corn. Combined with Martha's work as a teacher and Alexis's as a conference organiser, the family's income was adequate to sustain a reasonable lifestyle. The stream of cash-and-carry customers brought a variety and vitality to the place which everyone living there seemed to relish. Richmond was a man inclined to bonhomie, living up to his surname of Taverner, conjuring images of rotund ancestors standing beside the firkin and holding forth on the politics of the time.

Nonetheless, Richmond had resented the fact that Nina contributed scarcely a penny to the family budget. Admittedly she had the boys to take care of, but once Clement had started school, he saw no reason why she shouldn't pull her weight. Instead she spent her time flying round the countryside with placards, leaflets, megaphone and a perpetual sense of outrage. Richmond had found her both frustrating and embarrassing. When he married Martha, four years earlier, it had not been with a view to spending so much time with her sisters. 'We'll have our own rooms,' she had promised him. 'We'll hardly know there's anyone else in the house.' At first they had tried to keep it that way, but their official sitting room was dark and cold. It was the original dairy and looked out over the converted shippon in all its cement-block-and-steel-girder glory. Before long, they were in the kitchen with everyone else, any idea of genuine privacy abandoned. Being the only man amongst three women and two youngsters had brought with it a whole set of mixed blessings. Not one of them waited on him; if he wanted a cup of tea he had to make it himself. On the other hand, if a household gadget broke down, he was expected to fix it. Nobody wanted to hear his stories of late deliveries, awkward customers or sudden hikes in feed prices. Instead, they jabbered on about village gossip, Martha's efforts to instil a respect for English literature into stubborn young heads or Nina's latest exploit. For this reason, if no other, he had welcomed Charlie Grattan into the family circle with some relief.

Richmond supposed the police would want to interview him again about finding Charlie's body. He had escaped to the office to keep himself occupied before they came looking for him. There was plenty to do, if only he could apply himself to it. Normally he enjoyed his work, being in charge, making decisions. He ran the whole operation entirely on his own, employing no outside help. Since Hugh had turned thirteen, he had sometimes been roped in to do some of the tidying up or a bit of gentle stock-taking; and any one of the sisters would take a turn at serving customers if Richmond had to go out. If none of them was available, he would put a large CLOSED notice on the gate and people came back another time. The sign was up now, as it had been since

Nina died. Tomorrow, though, they'd open up again, before too many customers were lost for ever to a rival. Already some people had ignored the sign and pushed through, desperate for a bale of hay for their precious animals.

He knew he would have to think about Charlie in another few minutes, but he put it off as long as he could. He had trembled on Martha's bosom in bed the night before, unable to forget the awful mess their friend's head had been in. He had tried not to look at it, once he'd recognised the jacket and old trainers belonging to Charlie. But the pitiful posture, Charlie's useless attempt to shield himself with his hands, had been impossible to forget. He didn't think he would ever recover from the shock of stumbling on the body on his own land. Richmond was scared and sad and confused, as he waited for his interview with Den Cooper.

The return of the forensics team to the ditch was disconcerting, too. Were they going to collect every blade of grass, every tiny fragment of hair, every speck of dried blood? He could see them crawling all over the area from his office window, despite it being the length of a field away. What a job, he thought. What kind of people spent their working lives poring over the unsavoury detritus of a murder?

* * *

High Copse lived up to its name, Den noticed, as he and the boy Hugh crossed the gravelled area and walked towards Richmond's new barn. Behind the house, a steep hill was crowned with a copse of old English trees: beech, oak, ash. It had been reduced in size by the Cattermoles' need for firewood, but not by very much. When the sisters were still small, Eliza, their mother, had sold the higher stretches of the land to an affluent incomer, who preserved it with almost religious fervour. Between the copse and the house an apple orchard straggled up the slope, the trees old and misshapen, a large hencoop positioned between them and a row of beehives along one hedge. On two sides there were more hills, and beyond the one to the east the rising outline of Dartmoor was visible. Below the house stretched a nostalgic scene of small fields and high hedges, a world seemingly untouched for centuries. No new fences or roads; no modern primary-coloured EC-subsidised crops such as linseed or rape – at least not this early in the season.

'It looks the same as it must have done for hundreds of years,' Den remarked to his young guide.

Hugh looked doubtful. 'Wait till you see Richmond's warehouse,' he said, and gestured towards the building, set on a level below the house. Very little of the original shippon remained, beyond the basic shape and size. New wooden door and window frames still looked raw and unfinished. The silvery metal cladding made an unnatural splash amongst the trees and grass.

'I see what you mean,' said Den ruefully.

Hugh took him into the office and then slouched on a stool near the door while the two men shook hands and Den sat down on a chair that looked as if it had been rejected from the High Copse farmhouse. One leg felt wobbly and he leant as heavily as he could on the table between himself and Richmond.

'Lunch is in half an hour,' Hugh said. Richmond nodded, keeping his eyes on the detective.

'Tell me,' said Den, to the boy, 'when did you last see Charlie?'

Hugh wriggled his shoulders and frowned. 'Must have been Sunday,' he said. 'When Clem and Alexis were painting the coffin. Friday and Saturday were crazy days. The phone kept ringing and Martha was shouting at everybody. Charlie didn't come again after Sunday. I thought he had the right idea. But he was dead, wasn't he? He died days ago. I heard Richmond saying he did.' His voice rose higher and his sentences became more childish as he spoke, until he seemed to Den like a much younger child. *Poor little chap*, he thought.

'We're not quite sure of the exact day,' he told Hugh, with a glance at Richmond. 'Did you like Charlie?'

Richmond stirred at this and pushed forward his hands, clasped together, making a big beefy V with his arms, flat on the table. His knuckles were only an inch away from Den's left hand. Den glanced at him, but did not withdraw the question.

Hugh nodded, a single duck and lift of his chin. 'Yeah,' he breathed. 'He was cool.'

'Do you know anyone who didn't like him?'

The boy considered. 'The hunting people and the man at the battery farm. I don't know. Lots of people got annoyed with him, but I don't think they didn't *like* him. Same as Mum – she was always fighting with him, but she was his friend, really.'

'Look,' Richmond interrupted. 'I'm not sure we can let you question Hugh like this. He has nothing useful to tell you, and he'll get upset if you carry on. Can we let him go now?'

Den was on sufficiently shaky ground not to insist. He had hoped for some sort of background information from Hugh, some detail which would bring the picture into focus, but seemed destined for disappointment.

He nodded. 'Thanks for your help,' he said.

Hugh slid off his stool and paused. 'It was a pleasure,' he said politely. 'I hope you catch the person who murdered Charlie. So does Clem. Goodbye.' And he left, closing the door behind him.

'Nice boy,' Den said.

Richmond smiled. 'Say what you like about Nina, she was a good mother in her way. But you have to remember who they are. Breeding shows in people, even now. Take their grandfathers – younger son of a baronet on one side, and the owner of a hefty tract of farmland on the other. Bet Martha never told you that.'

Den shook his head in puzzlement. 'My information is that Nina's father is unknown.'

'Ah, yes. Sorry, I meant the boys' *great*-grandfather on that side. Eliza's dad, Nina's grandad. Owned a fair part of the land you see from our front garden at one time. Sold it, though, when Eliza was a girl. Then she did the same thing, with most of what was left. It was always assumed that it was the lack of a male heir that motivated them, in both cases. If you ask me, Eliza was just desperate for some ready cash.'

'Did you know her?' He was sketching a family tree on his notepad.

'I did indeed,' Richmond assured him. 'A legend in her own time. I didn't stand a chance with Martha until the old girl was dead. As it was, I had to jump through any number of hoops. If they hadn't needed someone to sort them out financially and find some way to survive apart from farming, I doubt if I'd ever have been taken on. She wouldn't change her name to mine and she says she's never going to give up her job. It doesn't look as if I'm ever to be blessed with a son and heir, either.'

'You make it sound like a marriage of convenience.'

'A convenient marriage, certainly,' Richmond agreed. 'But make no mistake, I love that woman. And she loves me. I would die for her, without a moment's hesitation.'

'And would you kill for her?' Den asked, surprising himself.

'That remains to be seen,' smiled Richmond with no sign of agitation.

CHAPTER SIX

As he drove away down the winding lane from High Copse, Den felt he had been there for days. His head was filled with snatches and snippets of information, very few of which seemed to connect to the murder. The main item of interest so far was the brother Frank and his horse-breeding; that was surely of real relevance. If Phil was available, he assumed the two of them would be despatched to Ashburton later that day to have a word with Mr Frank Grattan. Plus, he supposed, Mr Nev Nesbitt, when he finally showed up. Something felt iffy about that particular individual – not only the arm's-length marriage to Nina, but the leisurely return home to his bereft sons. Checking passenger lists was a job for Jane Nugent, in the scheme of things.

He felt he'd been immersed in an atmosphere like nothing he could recall experiencing before. The ramshackle, unkempt house, containing people who might have come from another age, or another planet. The strangeness of the relationships, Nina with her absent husband; Charlie, apparently close to both Nina and Alexis; Martha's patient and surprisingly ordinary husband. And the orphan boys with their bizarrely aristocratic bloodlines and their enviable freedom, living lives that Den could not begin to comprehend. Hugh, so obviously mourning for his mother to the exclusion of everything else; his pale little brother moving from one sheltering aunt to another, more ready, perhaps, to accept a substitute for Nina. And both craving the return of Nevil, their father, if Martha could be believed.

It was time for lunch. He would stop at the village shop in Chillhampton and get himself a pork pie. Then he had to go and talk to the Grattans, who lived at the northern end of the village. From them he hoped to draw forth a more complete picture of Charlie. Why, for example, was a man of thirty-three still living with the people who'd reared him, and why did he not have a proper job? And what, if anything, did being a Quaker really mean in this day and age?

* * *

The interview was painful. Hannah Grattan gave unadorned facts in a soft, patient voice which betrayed none of her feelings. Charlie's mother, Bill's wife, had died when the boy was two years old. Hannah had come back from working in Nigeria, in the aftermath of the Biafran War, and had devoted the rest of her life to caring for the two men. Yes, there was another Grattan son, Frank, who had been seventeen when his mother had died. He had left home a week after Hannah arrived, and she had seen very little of him since.

Den asked to be shown Charlie's bedroom and Hannah led him up the twisting cottage stairway and onto a landing. Four doors opened from it and she indicated the first one. 'In there,' she said. 'We haven't touched anything.'

The room was square, with a low ceiling, the view over open fields. A single bed with a wooden slatted headboard was covered with a handmade patchwork quilt. A large desk was covered with magazines, including *Horse and Hound, The Friend, The Vegan* and *Resurgence,* as well as a chaotic litter of papers. A computer sat in one corner, with an expensive-looking laser printer on a second table alongside. Clothes were obviously kept to a minimum, in a neat three-drawered chest under the window. The wall above the desk was covered with newspaper articles, hand-written addresses, phone numbers, reminders, all attached with Blu-tack.

The impression was in complete harmony with Alexis's assessment of Charlie: a man with a one-track mind, a total obsession with animal rights. Den picked up a copy of *The Friend*, realising it to be the weekly magazine for Quakers, and found a red felt-tipped slash in the margin against a letter from someone insisting that Quakers had a moral duty to defend all creatures from exploitation. On the front cover of one of the copies of *Resurgence*, the words NATURE, SCIENCE and SOCIETY shouted at him.

Beside the bed was another small table holding an alarm clock and a framed photograph. It showed a woman in her mid-thirties with a young child in her arms and a teenage boy at her side. The boy had a large head with shaggy dark hair and a long chin. Den could see a clear likeness to Bill Grattan, the wrecked man downstairs. The child was under a year old, sitting on his mother's arm, looking straight at the camera, his face serious. Pale, with colourless hair, he resembled his mother in the round face and small mouth. Den assumed Charlie kept this picture as a memorial of the dead mother he surely couldn't remember – and perhaps of Frank, the estranged older brother. If Hannah's story was true, Charlie had lost two of his closest relatives when he was only two years old.

Something about the room took Den back to his own boyhood. Despite the magazines and adult clothes, Charlie seemed to have lived more like a teenager than a man in his thirties. There was a certain purposefulness, an absence of the mess and self-indulgence of a single man which was intriguing. Den recalled his own piles of comics and schoolbooks, the forgotten coffee mugs and mismatched socks which had typified his room when he was sixteen. Charlie's room was tidier than Den's had been, but in some ways it was almost the same.

It was mid-afternoon when he made his report on progress so far. The Inspector had an air of urgency, muttering about the first forty-eight hours being the most crucial, insisting that every detail, every impression, be noted. 'We don't know these people,' he reminded Den. 'Our job is to get under their skin, understand how they operate. Write it all down, Cooper. That pad's nowhere near as full as it ought to be.'

Hastily Den opened his notepad and added *Hannah Grattan – Charlie's aunt, not mother* to the few lines of notes he'd made so far. He was longing to make a joke about 'Charlie's aunt' but could see the Inspector was not in the mood. For good measure, he also wrote, *Bedroom very boyish, CG somehow not fully grown up. Hints from AC suggest the same sort of thing or cd be plain Quaker lifestyle?*

'What next then?' the DI pursued. 'List the priorities for me.'

'The brother, sir. Frank Grattan. Breeds horses, lives near Ashburton. Several years older than Charlie – some trouble in the family. Martha Cattermole told me about him. Seems to think he should be questioned.'

Smith nodded. 'Fair enough,' he agreed. 'Get hold of Phil and the two of you can get over there soon as you like. Got the address, have you?'

'Not yet, sir. Give me a couple of minutes.' Den reached for a telephone directory from a high shelf level with his head and opened it at very nearly the right page. *F.* Grattan was conveniently listed, with enough of an address to make finding the stables an easy matter. 'Got it, sir,' he said.

'What else?' Smith pursued. 'There should be a pageful of names by now.'

Den took a deep breath. 'I've spoken to . . . seven people this morning,' he said calmly, having done a hasty mental count. 'If you count the younger boy, Clem. As soon as the boys' father gets home, I think I should have a word with him. Plus the people who go to the Quaker meeting.'

'Ah, yes!' The DI seized on this. 'When do they meet, do you know?'

'They're having a special meeting tomorrow morning, sir, in memory of Charlie. Eleven o'clock, I think. Miss Grattan mentioned it.'

'Be there,' instructed Smith.

Den gulped. 'Right, sir.'

Detective Constable Phil Bennett turned up from a series of visits to local equestrian establishments smelling slightly of manure and shaking his head glumly. 'Too many of the bloody things,' he said. 'They're taking over the world. It's a needle in a haystack job if ever there was one.'

Den explained with some diffidence that Phil had yet another similar call to make that day. 'But this one's much more promising,' he said encouragingly. 'And it'll be a nice drive.'

'All in a day's work,' said Phil, with unnerving good cheer. 'And you might be right. I shouldn't wonder if Brother Frank's got plenty to tell us.'

There were certainly horses in plenty in the fields to either side of Frank Gratton's entrance drive. The low-lying land, poorly maintained and apparently boggy in places, conveyed a depressing atmosphere. The horses, however, looked bursting with health. Two mares had young foals alongside them, and leggy colts nudged and shouldered each other in a group close to the drive. 'Everyone's gone horse mad, seems like,' said Den. 'Useless creatures, Lilah calls them.'

'Little girls love 'em, though. My Sophie's as bad as any,' Phil admitted. 'She can't wait for Saturday when she goes for her lessons. Not that I get involved with it. But even I can see that these'd be way out of her class. These beauties are strictly for the grown-ups, if I'm any judge.'

Den assessed the depths of his own ignorance concerning horses, and deemed them profound. He had never once been on the back of one, never attended a race meeting, never thought to distinguish between hacks and hunters, Arabs and Shetlands. He had a vague idea, gleaned from the film *Gandhi*, that a horse wouldn't willingly trample on a human being. On the other hand, there sometimes wasn't much option available to the creature. If you got yourself under the hoofs of a large galloping horse, you couldn't blame it if your head got broken.

Frank Gratton himself was standing in the muddy yard, halfway between the modest bungalow and extensive stables, watching their arrival with only the vaguest hint of concern. He looked at least fifty, with narrow shoulders, a sparse scattering of long grey hair and ruddy cheeks. Den could see a likeness to Bill now only in the deepset eyes. He narrowed these eyes until they almost disappeared, waiting for the police detectives to leave their vehicle.

'Good afternoon, sir,' said Phil easily. 'Mr Gratton?'

'Come about our Charlie, I reckon,' he replied bleakly. 'Wondered if you'd be bothered to come and see me. Wasn't sure you'd even be told I existed.' He ducked his head, so they couldn't see his face. Then he braced himself, hefting two buckets by his sides. 'Just let me take these . . .' he nodded at the buckets and then at the stables. The message was clear and the visitors were left in the yard.

'D'you want to come in the house?' Grattan asked, on his reappearance. Without waiting for a reply, he led the way to a plain green-painted door, which scraped on stone flags as he pushed it open. Two thin black cats came rushing to greet him and he shoved them away with his boot. A breath of cold air hit the two policemen as they stepped cautiously inside. On a mild April day, it was noticeably warmer outside than in.

The trio moved into a dark, untidy room with a huge table pushed under the window at one end and a sofa covered in newspapers at the other. When Gratton hesitated, Den and Phil sat down firmly on upright chairs at the table. 'We're sorry about what happened to your brother,' Phil said, without embellishment.

Gratton nodded. 'Sounds like someone did it

on purpose,' he said with a frown. 'Must have had too much of his animal rights antics.' His accent was intriguing, Den noted: educated middle-class overlaid with a deliberate uncouthness, as if he possessed no respect for his origins. Everything about him suggested a purposeful movement down the social scale, away from wherever he'd started.

'When did you last see him?' Phil proceeded, producing a notepad and ballpoint.

'Weeks ago,' came the ready response. 'Months, even. We had little to do with each other.'

'Could you be more precise?'

'Let's see.' With exaggerated care, Gratton scanned his memory. 'It was in that cold spell. Early February, must have been. First week of the month, near enough.'

'And you were on good terms with him, were you?'

'Not so sure about that. Every time he saw me he'd get on to the subject of the horses, how I was condemning them to a life of misery, with a stream of novices trying to ride them and no chance for them to be their real selves. Sheer bloody nonsense, every word of it. I'll never understand where he got it all from.'

'How did you react to that sort of thing?' Phil asked.

Gratton shrugged. 'With a laugh, usually. It made no odds to me, when it came down to it. My horses are the best you can get. I told him he should be glad of people like me. Without us, horses would probably go extinct. They'd suffer, at any rate. They're nothing more than a hobby for idle rich people these days, I know that. But they pay well and the beasts are well looked after. It was the stupidity of it I couldn't get used to. Some causes you can see the point of, but not this one. Nobody but our Charlie could have made a campaign for the liberation of gee-gees.' He laughed sourly, but Den noticed that the frown had returned to his face and a twist of pain lurked around his nose and mouth.

'Are you familiar with the Cattermole family and the farm where your brother was found?'

Again a shrug, half-suppressed. 'In a way,' he answered. 'Been there once or twice. I knew Charlie was seeing one of the sisters. Heard about the woman being killed in the hunt protest.'

Den gave him a close look and said, 'You mean Nina. You paid her a visit not long ago, I understand.'

Frank rubbed a grimy hand down one cheek; stubble made a rasping noise against the rough skin. 'That's true,' he said.

'For what purpose?'

Frank was silent for a long minute. 'I was passing and called in on the off-chance of a cup of tea.'

Den gave him a sceptical look before asking, 'So what was your reaction to her death? Especially as it was inflicted by a horse. It must have struck you—'

'It struck me as damned carelessness,' Frank said heavily. 'A senseless waste of a life. It also struck me . . .' he turned his head away, but darted brief glances at Den as he spoke, 'that people would probably think Charlie was to blame.'

'And you?' Phil interrupted eagerly. 'Did *you* think that?'

Frank's head sank further into his shoulders, like a turtle withdrawing from the world. 'It crossed my mind,' he said.

Den couldn't stop himself. 'Nina's death was an accident,' he said. 'I saw it happen myself, and—'

'Okay, Den,' said Phil repressively, reminding his younger colleague that personal observations were inappropriate. 'Now Mr Gratton, can I ask you whether you know of anyone who might have wanted your brother dead? Anyone who had a grudge against him?'

Gratton's mouth worked a little as if tasting something bitter. 'Nobody I know would want Charlie dead.' He tapped a forefinger on the table. 'Charlie was . . . well, people wanted to protect him,' he finished weakly. 'It didn't matter what he said or how much of a nuisance he made of himself. There's nobody would wilfully kill him.' His eyes grew shiny and he swiped a hand across his nose.

'And can you account for your own movements earlier this week?' Phil proceeded, having made a brief note on his pad. 'Sunday and Monday in particular.'

'I've been here all week. In and out, of course. Monday I did a bit of shopping in Newton Abbot. Sunday I never went anywhere, so far as I can recall. You'd need to be more precise.'

'Who told you about your brother's death?' Phil asked suddenly.

'Aunt Hannah. She phoned me first thing this morning. I offered to go to her, but she told me not to. I don't go there any more. Haven't been there for years.'

'Why not?' asked Phil baldly.

Frank's expression changed. His cheeks darkened and he turned his face away. 'Just a silly family thing,' he muttered stiltedly. 'Too late to mend it now. I speak to Hannah now and then, but the old man won't have me in the house.'

Den stirred, feeling somewhat left out of the interview. 'Could you elaborate on that?' he said. 'We'd like to know exactly why you're not welcome in your own family's home.'

'Look at me,' Frank invited. 'You've seen them, I suppose?' Den nodded. 'Everything clean and neat and ladylike, if I remember rightly. I don't fit in. It goes back a long way.' His head sank even further into his shoulders and both detectives waited in silence for more. Frank attempted a rueful smile; it was a horrible failure. 'These things happen,' he said unconvincingly. 'I think we've all forgotten what it was about by now.' His flush deepened further, but his lips clamped tight against any further explanation.

'But you saw Charlie from time to time?' Phil said.

'He came over here every few months. In spite of his lunatic ideas, I liked to keep up with him.' To Den's watching eyes, Frank suddenly became a near replica of his father, racked by an identical sadness. He took a deep shuddering breath before whispering, 'I'm really going to miss him.'

Phil became brisk. 'You're not married, are you, Mr Gratton?'

The man smiled bitterly and shook his head. He cast a long look around the room. 'No,' he conceded. 'I'm not married.'

Phil nodded as if satisfied and wrote quickly in the notebook. Then he raised his head. 'One last thing. I take it you're a good horseman?'

'Me?' Frank responded with a slight nod of his head. 'I can ride anything. There isn't a horse alive that's not putty in my hands. I love them, you see. Wife, family and friends, my horses are. Anyone'll tell you.'

CHAPTER SEVEN

The Quaker Meeting House was an unimpressive Victorian building, with a more modern two-storey extension that provided accommodation for the Wardens. Inside the front door, leading off a small hallway, were a kitchen to the left and a dusty book-lined room to the right. Directly ahead was the Meeting Room itself. This was fitted with wooden benches on all four sides, arranged in gently-rising tiers. An old oak table stood in the middle of the room, covered with a lace cloth, a vase of flowers placed dead centre. Heat was provided by ugly storage heaters crammed into any available space, with a further set of convector heaters high up on the walls. These had been switched on a few minutes earlier and were crackling and spitting as they expanded.

On Friday morning, at the special meeting for Charlie Gratton, Den Cooper entered by the front door and stood conspicuously in the hallway, utterly at a loss. He was a few minutes late. Ahead he could see the large Meeting Room already dotted with people. Nobody seemed to be on any sort of door duty, so he edged slowly forwards, wondering how many iron Quaker rules he could unwittingly contravene in the next hour.

He recognised three faces as he entered the room: Hannah and Bill Gratton, he on the corner of one of the lower benches and she at the back of the tier facing him; and Alexis Cattermole on the second row facing the door. Six others were also present, scattered around the room.

Hannah and Alexis both looked at him, Hannah with a gaze of unsurprised acceptance; Alexis with narrowed eyes and obvious resentment. He sat close to the door, crossing his legs and trying to shrink in size. The silence in the room was like a mountain mist, cool and tangible. As he looked across at Bill Gratton and the other people on the same bench, he observed that their eyes were closed. They sat upright, but with relaxed shoulders, chins tilted slightly upwards. They were like people waiting for something.

Hannah was to his left; when he gradually turned his head to catch sight of her, she too had closed her eyes. *What are they all thinking?* he wondered. *How do they manage to keep so still and quiet?*

A mucousy sniffing came suddenly from Alexis, abnormally loud, and he watched her wipe a fingertip impatiently under first one eye then the other. At least she was thinking about Charlie, Den presumed.

He tried to focus on his own reason for being there. He was above all an observer, seeking to learn more about the Quaker group to which Grattan had belonged, and to watch for any significant reactions amongst those who knew him. The meeting was open to anyone to attend, although it didn't feel like that: the sense of alienation was acute. He had no idea how to behave, what to expect, or, indeed, what might be unusual behaviour for a Quaker. He inwardly cursed DI Smith for sending him. It was one of the hardest assignments he'd been given so far.

Mercifully, within ten minutes of Den's arrival, a man stood up. Very dark, in his late thirties or early forties, with a ringing voice and a gimlet stare, he began to speak with no preliminary clearing of throat or other warning. Den was aware of Hannah's startled twitch at the first words.

'Friends, this is a dreadfully sad time for us all. Our beloved friend Charlie Gratton has been killed in a terrible, shocking manner, and we can only come together and grieve for him and for those who loved him. We remember Charlie as a man of strong principle and outspoken opinions. He was a person who could never be ignored. He was a person who will never be forgotten. Perhaps I could give special sympathy to his family, Bill and Hannah, in what must be a time of great pain, and also to his friend Alexis, who has lost not only Charlie, but also her sister in recent days. It seems to be a cruel fact of life that troubles do indeed come in battalions and we pray that Alexis will find all the support that she needs at this time.'

Den watched Alexis and saw her give a weak smile of acknowledgement. One or two heads nodded in agreement with the words. But one or two mouths tightened, as if suppressing irritation. Bill Grattan made no response, but continued to sit like a statue on his bench.

There were two other elderly men besides Bill. At first glance they seemed very alike: small, neatly dressed and still. But one had a round head, with thick, faded brown hair, and the other had a long, lined face, large ears and only a scattering of white hair across his narrow head. Something about the expression of the latter, and the set of his shoulders, made Den think that perhaps he was a relative of Bill and Hannah. He rehearsed in his mind how he would approach each person at the end of the meeting, in order to find out who they were and why they were here.

The man who had got up to speak was flanked by a woman of a similar age: probably his wife, Den decided. She was colourlessly pretty, her hands folded passively in her lap. She had shown no sign of interest or agreement when the man had been speaking, but had continued to stare at the floor, as she had done all along.

The last two people were both women, one elderly and one in her thirties. Den could not see the former at all; she was sitting directly behind him, in complete silence. The younger one was plump, with wavy hair styled in a rather old-fashioned bob. He scrutinised her boldly as she sat with closed eyes not far from Alexis. She had rich, creamy skin; her neck was a warm hue somewhere between beige and magnolia. She looked solidly rooted, heavy, almost languorous, on the bench.

The meeting settled back into silence. With a furtive glance at his watch, Den discovered that only twenty-three minutes had so far elapsed. His buttocks felt sore already from the hard bench. He tried to concentrate on the inquiry into Charlie's death, to assess the chance that the person who killed him was there in the room. Any of the men, apart from poor old Bill, would probably qualify. The Junoesque woman could doubtless handle a sturdy horse, and even the subdued little wife might be stronger than she looked. He wondered whether the people gathered around him represented everyone who had genuinely loved Charlie. Were they actually grieving in their silent absorption, without shedding a tear or stifling a sniff? Apart, that is, from Alexis, who was by her own account no Quaker.

Just when he thought he couldn't possibly bear a further thirty-five minutes, another person stood up. It was the long-faced man. 'Charlie was an angry chap,' he began, his voice louder than his elderly frame suggested, 'and he upset a lot of people with his carryings-on about animal rights and that. But he was young and he was one of us and his manner of dying was an abomination. An *abomination*,' he repeated, making much of the word. 'As Quakers, the one thing we refuse to bear is violence. Our Peace Testimony is more important than anything. It is hard for us, knowing that one of our Meeting has been killed by a savage act of violence.' He began to sit down again, but straightened once more. 'And we must give our love to all his friends – yes, we must.' And he fixed Alexis with a gaze both fierce and affectionate.

Den had assumed the meeting would last for an hour, but two minutes after the second speaker sat down there was a general rustling and opening of eyes, and all the people stretched this way and that to shake hands with whoever was closest to them. Den found a hand appearing over his shoulder, and turned to face the elderly woman he had hardly glimpsed so far.

'Welcome,' she said. 'I'm Dorothy Mansfield.' He took her hand, finding it cool and supple. Meeting her eye, he realised he already knew her. With difficulty he restrained himself from exclaiming; time enough for that when he'd gathered all available information from the assembled Quakers. The need to avoid distractions seemed even greater than usual, in this place.

Alexis came directly to him, followed closely by Hannah. 'What on earth are you doing here?' Alexis demanded. Before he could answer, Hannah laid a reproachful hand on the younger woman's arm, with awesome effect. Alexis dropped back, wiping her finger under one eye again, and let herself be accosted by the dark man who had first spoken.

Den addressed himself to Hannah. 'I need to know who all these people are,' he said apologetically. 'I hope you'll understand why.'

'Let me introduce you,' she said. 'Everyone

here wants to give you all the help they can.'

She began with the long-faced man who had spoken last. 'This is Silas Daggs, my cousin,' she said, inadvertently boosting Den's confidence in his detective abilities. 'He lives out on the Launceston road. Like us, he's been a Quaker all his life.' Den took out his pad and noted the name and relationship.

Then there was a general silence, which Den realised was probably an expectation that he would try to interview everyone on the spot. He forced a genial smile. 'Don't worry,' he said to the room at large. 'My colleagues and I will want to speak to you in due course, but for now I'd just like names and addresses. I hope you don't feel this is an intrusion . . .' He tailed off, silenced by their obvious patience and understanding. How would he have felt if a policeman had invaded such a peculiarly emotional and spiritual occasion as this had been? For the fact that they all knew he was a policeman, in spite of his plain clothes, was beyond doubt. He presumed he was better known in the area than he'd appreciated in the past. His height; his presence at times of crisis; even his relationship with Lilah Beardon – it all made him visible. It did at least avoid the need for awkward explanations.

Hannah led him round the rough circle that had formed. 'Clive and Mandy Aspen,' she said.

'They're the Wardens here, so you won't need to ask for their address.' The weak joke was received without humour by Clive Aspen, the dark man who'd spoken first. He made a stiff little bow to Den and laid a hand on his wife's back, between the shoulder blades. She nodded and then tried to turn away, perhaps to escape her husband's proprietary touch. Den noted down their names, with *Wardens* after them. If he could have been sure that nobody could read his jottings, he'd have added *Not a happy couple*.

'That leaves Val Taylor,' Hannah continued, gesturing at the creamy-skinned Juno, 'then Dorothy Mansfield and Barty White,' indicating the other elderly man. 'They can give you their addresses themselves. I ought to go and see to Bill.' Together they looked at her brother, who had not moved since the meeting ended. 'He's really not dealing very well with all this.' Worry tinged her voice and Den felt a surge of pity for the man and his shattered life.

Addresses duly noted and a few vague indications given as to when each person might expect to be interviewed, Den prepared to make his exit. The sense of being an intruder had not lessened, in spite of the easy welcome. Alexis followed him to the door. 'Sorry,' she muttered. 'I wasn't thinking straight. Even so . . .' She screwed up her face, looking very like Martha.

'I'd hoped to get away from it here. From the . . . nastier elements of what's happened.'

He made an understanding grimace. 'Not possible, I'm afraid,' he said. 'But I hope I didn't wreck it for you completely.' He looked around the room. 'They seem to be very nice people.'

'They are,' she said. 'But I assume you think one of them could have killed Charlie.'

He'd seen the question coming. 'We're not ruling anything out,' he said.

When he'd gone, Mandy appeared with a trayful of teacups. Hannah was the first to take two from her and carry them over to Bill. 'Why can't she ever make it hot?' she said to him, after her first sip. 'Lukewarm tea's disgusting.' Bill drained his own in a few seconds and wiped his mouth with his hand.

'Disgusting,' he agreed thickly, though he clearly didn't really care.

Hannah sat beside him, watching the others in the room, trying to see them as the young police detective must have done. Clive was escorting Mandy, taking cups from her tray and handing them out, proffering a plate of plain biscuits. The Aspens had come to Quakerism slowly, making it the rock – or safety net – of their marriage. The story they had told on their arrival was a sorry one. Clive had been a product of the eighties, working fourteen hours a day and earning a six-figure salary in something to do with oil, a rising star. Then their first – and only, as it turned out – child had died, and Clive had broken down spectacularly, spending two years looking out of the window and letting his life disintegrate. Finding a Quaker Meeting marked the first stage of his recovery, and six years on he glowed with zealous gratitude.

Hannah transferred her attention to Alexis, whom she herself had asked to come to this special meeting. The younger woman had been to two Quaker meetings with Charlie during the past months and confessed to finding them very uncomfortable. Sitting still for an hour on a hard wooden bench was physically demanding and on the first occasion she had panicked and almost left. Hannah had watched her with interest, guessing at her feelings. She knew there could be something awful about being forced to sit there in silence, in a virtually solitary intimacy that was everything and nothing. Some people closed their eyes, but others did not. Alexis had tried it both ways, but in either case had to fight to quell the thoughts crowding her mind. On that first visit, nobody had spoken throughout the entire hour; Hannah was in no doubt that it felt to Alexis like a complete waste of time.

On the second occasion, Charlie himself had

risen to 'give a ministry' as he himself called it. He had spoken about anger, in his usual direct fashion. Hannah had been proud of him and had seen how impressed Alexis had been.

Today her quiet crying had not gone unnoticed. They were all feeling for her and the space to weep freely seemed like a great gift.

Dorothy, tall with a great mane of long silver hair and disconcertingly acute brown eyes, approached Alexis now and patted her on the shoulder. 'There's nothing anyone can say to make it better. We just have to keep going, one day at a time.' Dorothy could always be relied on, Hannah thought. Intelligent, good-humoured and possessed of a transparently clear conscience, there were moments when Dorothy was almost frightening.

The other member, Bartholomew White, kept his distance from Alexis; she had never spoken to him, as far as Hannah knew. He'd farmed all his life on an isolated property to the north of High Copse. He'd been a Quaker for decades, but rarely involved himself in anything more than the Sunday meetings. He'd been 'convinced' as the archaic language put it, in his twenties, and been staunchly loyal ever since.

Preparing to get Bill to his feet and make the short journey home, Hannah was once again drawn to look at Clive Aspen, hearing his voice rising above the general murmur. Clive always seemed more self-consciously Quaker than any of the others, on whom faith sat lightly and unobtrusively. Clive talked about 'God's work' and 'spiritual paths' more like an Anglican vicar than a Friend. He complained constantly of the small size of the Meeting, and urged everyone to find ways to bring in new people. Hannah had eventually spoken to him about it. 'We prefer to leave people to find their own way here,' she had said. 'We do no good by forcing them.'

His manner, then and now, conveyed reproach, a sense that nobody quite came up to his expectations. Here was this most wonderful of all religious groups, ready for the taking, and the perverse human race failed to avail themselves of it. For Clive, this was inexplicable. He couldn't help but evangelise.

Now he was saying to Dorothy, 'I hope this meeting has been helpful,' with a self-conscious glance at Hannah. When he met her eye his normally pale skin seemed to flush. She could see his jaw clenching, his body taking on a momentary rigidity. Clive Aspen was a trial to her, in her capacity as Clerk to the Meeting. All around him conflict was generated; arguments, misunderstandings, a sort of deception. Clive lived by a set of precepts that disturbed Hannah. Not least, there was his treatment of Mandy, who seemed to melt away, diminished, when in his company.

Nagging at the back of Hannah's mind was the memory of a scene between Clive and Charlie on the day before Nina Nesbitt died. Charlie had found out that Clive intended riding to hounds in the hunt meeting, and was upbraiding him ferociously. The exchange had taken place in the Meeting House kitchen, while Hannah had been in the small back room, trying to find a particular volume. It all seemed a long time ago now, but Clive's words were etched on her memory.

'I'll do what I like, Charlie Gratton. There's nothing wrong with following the hunt. It isn't for you to dictate how people behave. *If you try to stop me, you'll be very, very sorry. I'm warning you – don't try to interfere with me.*'

The words themselves were bad enough, but the tone had made Hannah shudder. She had never before heard such hatred in a man's voice.

CHAPTER EIGHT

Back at High Copse Alexis told Martha all about the Quaker gathering and what they had said about Charlie, going on to describe a strange encounter with Val Taylor just as she was leaving.

She had been intercepted at the door by Val's plump arm encased in an expensive silk blouse. Val had begun slowly, apologising for not having been at Nina's funeral because of a vital case conference, commiserating on the appalling impact of the two deaths so close together. 'We all loved Charlie,' she had continued in a low, strangled voice. 'He was the life and soul of the Meeting. We might be small in numbers, but we have a force, something good and vital. Charlie did that. Without him, it's going to fall apart.'

Alexis had looked nervously over her shoulder at the other Quakers, still chatting over their tea, but they didn't seem to have heard.

Val went on, 'Some people think everything can go on the same, but it can't. Some people even think that without Charlie it might be *better* than before. He caused trouble, yes, but it was *good* trouble. It challenged all the bad things. Look – I can't talk to you now. Can I come and see you at High Copse? Tomorrow afternoon? Four o'clock? I know Polly already said something to Martha and you probably think it's a bit soon, but I think we should start a collection right away.'

Alexis had been bemused, but there'd been no reason to refuse the woman's request. 'All right,' she said, 'but I don't really understand . . .'

'You will,' said Val.

'So she's coming here,' Alexis told Martha. 'To talk to us about some sort of memorial to Nina. I have no idea what she has in mind. To be honest, I've never taken much notice of her before.'

'Polly Spence was on at me about the same idea, at the funeral. Nina groupies, both of them. They probably want to build a statue to her outside the village hall.'

'If they do it for her, they should do it for Charlie as well,' said Alexis vehemently.

Martha spread her hands. 'Don't ask me. I

would have said hero-worship isn't very Quakerly anyway.'

Alexis snorted. 'If you want my opinion, the Quakers themselves wouldn't know what's Quakerly and what isn't. One minute they're making banners and handing out leaflets about animal cruelty; the next they're complaining that Charlie gives them a bad image.'

'That's what comes of not having a proper doctrine, I suppose,' murmured Martha. She returned her attention to a button she was sewing on to Hugh's trousers.

'How do *you* know they haven't got a . . . doctrine? Whatever that is?'

'Charlie told me. You must have known that.'

'What makes you so bloody well-informed all of a sudden? What's *doctrine* got to do with anything?'

Martha bit her lip and said nothing. It was the strategy she had always used when dealing with her younger sister's anger.

Den made a start on his interviews early that afternoon, beginning with Clive and Mandy Aspen. The Wardens of the Meeting House lived in a spacious first-floor flat attached to the premises. As Den raised his hand to ring the bell, he was surprised by the door silently opening and Clive Aspen appearing. He was dressed in a long black coat, which combined with his black hair and deep dark eyes to give him the appearance of the villain in a Victorian melodrama. The two men stared at each other speechlessly for some seconds, before Clive said, 'You're not wasting much time, are you?'

'I'm sorry to be a nuisance, but I would appreciate a few minutes of your time.' He noticed how difficult it was to speak calmly in the face of Clive's hostility. He felt as if he were interrogating a known felon with the requisite anti-police grudge, rather than a respectable Quaker.

'I'm just going out,' said Clive superfluously. 'Can't it wait? Or maybe Mandy would do? She's upstairs.'

'I'm sorry, sir, but I think it would be better if I could speak to the two of you. It won't take very long.'

Clive was tall, but still three inches below Den, and the disadvantage clearly discomforted him. His face flushed, and he glanced over his shoulder. 'Oh, all right then,' he capitulated. 'You'd better come in.'

The door led directly into a hall and up a steep flight of stairs. The Meeting House on the ground floor had its own entrance. Clive led the way, calling for his wife as he reached the top of the stairs. There was no response. 'Mandy!'

he tried again, a harsh note in his voice snagging Den's attention. A door opened, and the woman stood in the doorway, her head turned towards the stairs.

'Yes?' she said, the word carrying a wealth of resentment and misery. As Den approached her, he could see the marks of tears on her face.

'That policeman's here, wanting to talk to us about Charlie.'

'Well bring him up,' she said wearily. 'We knew he'd come.'

Clive preceded Den up the stairs in silence and then into the living room. The couple took up positions of distinct unease, Mandy leaning awkwardly against a table and Clive standing in the middle of the room, as if guarding his territory.

'Come in. Sorry about the mess,' he said curtly.

The flat was not messy in the least. Two or three books lay on the table, and a piece of knitting was just visible under a cushion on the sofa. Otherwise, it was almost inhumanly tidy and clean. The contrast with the shambolic but life-filled High Copse Farmhouse was almost ludicrous.

Den sat down on the sofa, encouraged by a wordless wave of Mandy's hand, and took out his notebook. 'I'm going to need to run through a few points with you.'

Clive went to an old-fashioned Ladderex storage system and opened the flap of a desk. He took out a slim booklet and brought it to Den. 'This is the Monthly Meeting Membership List,' he said. 'Our Preparatory meeting is here, look. All Members and Attenders are listed. I think you'll find twelve names in all. We're an extremely small Meeting.'

'Thank you,' smiled Den. 'May I keep it for a day or two? Or should I copy the names out now?'

Clive shrugged. 'Keep it. I know them all by heart anyway.'

'Thank you,' repeated Den, wishing they would both sit down and relax a bit.

'Would you tell me anything you knew about Charlie Gratton that you think might be useful?' he began, having learnt the value of non-specific questions of this type. If you stuck with stark facts, when you knew almost nothing about the set-up, you were virtually certain to overlook something vital. Encourage people to waffle, and important information sometimes emerged.

Not with these two, though. 'I really don't think we can usefully contribute to your investigations,' said Clive stiffly. 'You'll already be aware that Charlie lived with his father and aunt, that he was heavily committed to animal rights activism, and that Alexis Cattermole was his girlfriend.'

Den looked casually at his own feet, and asked, 'Did you like him?'

Clive's breath hissed as he drew it in sharply. Mandy suppressed a small moan. *No* and *Yes* respectively, Den guessed. 'He was all right,' Clive managed. 'Made a lot of trouble for everybody, and had some intensely stupid ideas, but he was sincere. The Quaker way is to find something to value in everybody.'

'But it's easier with some people than with others,' Den supplied recklessly. 'Bound to be.' He looked across at Mandy, as if for support.

'He's a great loss,' she said in a voice overlaid with a strong Birmingham accent. Accustomed to the musical rhythms of the Devon dialect, Den found the strained, nasal flatness of the woman's speech jarring.

He wanted to ask: *To you or to the Meeting?* but didn't dare with her husband present. To judge from the tear stains and her hesitancy, there was no need, anyway. If he'd read the signs correctly, Mandy Aspen was missing Charlie Gratton very much indeed.

'Were either of you involved in the animal rights activities?' he continued. 'I assume from what you've just said, Mr Aspen, that you're not in much sympathy with it?' Again he glanced at Mandy, trying to invite her to make her own contribution.

Clive drew himself up tall; his nostrils flickered. 'No,' was all he said. Den heard a wealth of suppressed contempt behind the word.

'And yet a number of other Quakers seem to have agreed with Charlie,' Den remarked. 'As I understand it.'

'One or two,' Clive acknowledged. 'There's an element of Quakerism which attaches a lot of importance to the welfare of animals.'

'Which you don't endorse?'

'That's right.'

'I see. Now, I just need to check a few dates and so forth, and I'll be out of your way. How long have you lived here at the Meeting House?'

'Three years.'

Den made a careful note, mindful of his Inspector's censure. 'And do you work anywhere else – or is this your sole occupation? Being Warden, I mean?'

'I freelance in a small way as a software consultant – working from here – and both Mandy and I assist the community by giving our time to local schools. You probably know how eager the Government is to ensure computer literacy in the next generation. Unfortunately, the teachers aren't always up to the challenge. So I go into the local primary school and Mandy performs a similar role at the comprehensive in Tavistock. She couldn't find paid employment here. She's a trained librarian, as it happens.'

'So you both work mostly without payment?' Den queried. The couple nodded in unison.

'We didn't come here in order to get rich,' said Clive stiffly. 'Besides, we have a small private income – inherited from my parents – which gives us a certain amount of freedom.'

'And the Wardenship?' Den pursued. 'What exactly does that entail? I gather it's not in any sense like being a vicar or priest.' He spoke cautiously, uncertain of his ground.

'The Society of Friends does not favour any sort of priesthood,' said Clive pompously. 'We have a Clerk, who conducts our business meetings, and two Elders. Our job here is to keep the place clean, to welcome visitors and show them around if necessary, and to take responsibility for lettings of the Meeting House. At the moment it's only used on one afternoon a week, by a small discussion group, and one evening a fortnight, by what was Charlie Gratton's Animal Rights Campaign. We provide tea and biscuits for the Sunday meetings, and ensure that the heating, water, electricity, rubbish collection and telephone are all maintained and regularised.' Den could almost hear the quotation marks from the Wardenship job description.

'Thank you,' he said. 'That's all very clear.' Though just where it left him in regard to his murder inquiry, he had very little idea. Clive's manner was offputting and mildly intimidating, but there were no detectable signs of guilt. He decided to wind up his interview with the usual unsettling request.

'Could you both tell me where you were on Sunday and Monday of this week?' he said flatly.

Clive answered for them both. 'We were both here on Sunday morning, of course, for the meeting. Mandy was at the school all day on Monday, but Monday is one of my free days . . .'

'So is Friday, by the look of it,' Den remarked.

'We're here today because of this morning's special memorial meeting for Charlie,' said Clive acidly. 'We were needed here. I had hoped to make up the time this afternoon instead—' His sigh was loud and exaggerated.

'I don't work Fridays,' Mandy offered. 'Not usually, anyway.'

'I'm sorry,' Den retreated. 'If you could just—'

Clive took up his thread. 'I was here on Monday morning, and went out in the afternoon to see a friend. It is rather difficult, Constable, to account for every moment of two whole days, as I'm sure you'll appreciate.'

'May I ask exactly who this friend was that you visited?'

Clive frowned almost imperceptibly. 'It was Miriam Snow, one of our members. You'll find her in the booklet, including her phone number, if you want her to corroborate what I've told you. She lives alone, and tends to get agitated about small difficulties. She wanted to complete her tax return, and asked me if I would help her. I was happy to be of that small service.'

'How long did it take?' Den queried.

'The whole afternoon,' he said shortly.

Den made another few lines of jottings, and then looked up. 'Just one last question,' he smiled. 'Do either of you ride?'

He could see that Clive was under no illusions as to the import of the question, but Mandy seemed to be enlivened by it. 'Oh yes!' she beamed, finally pushing herself away from the table. 'We both do. It's one of our greatest pleasures. We hire horses from the riding stables, every chance we get.' Suddenly aware of Clive's silence, she cut herself short. 'Don't we?' she asked anxiously, pressing him for agreement.

'We do,' he said. 'We find it very . . . therapeutic.'

'And did you go riding on Sunday or Monday this week?'

'No,' said Clive emphatically. 'Definitely not.' Mandy blinked, but said nothing. Den made another superfluous note.

'Well, I'm sorry to have disturbed you,' he said, putting his notebook away. 'Especially as you were just going out.'

'That's all right,' said Mandy quickly. 'We're all very upset about Charlie, you know. He was one of our most energetic members.'

Just about the youngest, too, thought Den, trying to imagine what a thirty-three-year-old animal rights activist could get out of membership of such a peculiar outfit as this small group of Quakers seemed to be.

CHAPTER NINE

The investigation was showing every sign of stalling when Den reported back to the station. DI Smith had drawn one of his elaborate diagrams on the whiteboard, listing names of all the people involved, and a cluster of headings *Mo, Me* and *Op*, with strange jottings beneath them. Den deciphered them with relative ease: *Motive, Means* and *Opportunity* – the basic catechism used in murder investigations, but which barely embraced the whole story. The means with which Charlie had been killed was straightforward, if unusual. *Lrg hrs* was written underneath *Me.* Motives had burgeoned over the day, too. *Aml rghts, Money? Rvnge? Poltcs, Jlsy? Women?* were all scribbled under *Mo. Op* still headed a blank column – which

Den thought he could now fill all on his own. He stepped forward and uncapped the blue marker pen on the ledge below the board. Carefully, he wrote *Clive Aspen, Quaker Warden*. Stepping back, the incongruity struck him. Violence was anathema to Quakers. But perhaps this had been precisely the kind of attack a Quaker might be able to live with – if he could convince himself that the horse had been the killer. A barely-controlled stallion, given to rearing and kicking out with its forelegs, could be blamed for the incident with the rider virtually exonerated. The idea, perhaps, sown by the manner of Nina Nesbitt's dying. The only flaw there, thought Den dourly, was the failure to report the incident. Whatever the precise truth of the matter, by not calling for help that horse rider had effectively committed murder. And somehow Den could all too clearly envisage Friend Clive doing exactly that.

He stepped forward again and added *Frank Gratton* to the *Op* column. Frank, the estranged brother, who had a whole yardful of horses at his disposal, and who had been named by Martha Cattermole as a likely suspect. The obstinate demeanour of the man had piqued Den's curiosity. And why – *why* – had his virtuous Quaker relatives seen fit to ostracise him so comprehensively?

* * *

Having left some notes for DI Smith, and looked in vain for any evidence of progress made by Danny and Phil since he last saw them, Den took a quick solitary tea break in the canteen before returning to his interviews. The drive to and from Chillhampton was becoming familiar already; he was in no doubt that before the case was closed, he'd be thoroughly sick of it. Originally he had hoped to offload some of the Quaker interviews onto Phil, but since the meeting that morning he felt much more inclined to follow everything through himself. He would be a familiar face to the remaining four he'd met and the others who had not attended the meeting would no doubt have heard of him by the time he reached them.

He chose Dorothy Mansfield for his next interview. Her address was simple enough: 1 Hawthorn Way, Chillhampton. The unimaginative and unexciting little development of new homes lay behind the village hall, two hundred yards from the Meeting House and all too easy to locate.

Mrs Mansfield opened the door ten seconds after Den had rung the bell, and greeted him with an encouraging smile. Before embarking on his formal questions, he permitted himself a personal touch. 'You used to be Mrs Maples,' he said with a smile. 'I came to you for piano lessons.'

She laughed. 'I wouldn't be at all surprised,'

she agreed. 'But I'm definitely not Mrs Maples any more, and I didn't even bring the piano with me when I moved. You must have been terribly young – I don't remember you at all.'

'I was six and it was twenty-one years ago. I didn't stick it for very long.'

'Well, come in. This must be my turn to be grilled about Charlie?'

'I'm afraid so,' he admitted. 'There's still a lot I need to know.'

'I expect there is,' she said. Den followed her into the house.

It was very small and betrayed no sign of any Mr Mansfield. The ground floor evidently consisted of nothing more than a long, narrow room, arranged to provide comfortable seating at one end and a dining table at the other, with a small kitchen adjacent to the eating area. Stairs and a narrow hall completed the rectangular layout. It was altogether familiar and curiously depressing in its predictability.

Mrs Mansfield, however, was not predictable at all. 'Horrible, isn't it,' she said cheerfully. 'There's almost nothing you can do with a house like this. Not downstairs, anyway. It gets more interesting on the upper floor – but I don't intend to show you, unless you decide I'm a prime suspect, in which case you'll want to do a thorough search. You can if you want, of course.'

He forced a cautious laugh, wondering whether he was going to need to ask questions at all, or whether the whole story – if there was a story – would be presented to him rehearsed and unprompted.

'Coffee?' she asked him. 'I've got some good stuff. You should taste the disgusting muck Mandy gives us after meeting. It's a little-known fact about Quakers, that they serve the most unspeakable hot drinks in the civilised world.'

'Thanks,' Den accepted, and he followed her through to the little square kitchen.

'So . . . Charlie,' she continued, turning to face him, meeting his eye with a direct gaze that he found disconcerting. An echo from the piano lessons rang in his head. *Denholm Cooper, you're absolutely hopeless! Why on earth did your mother send you here? You'd be much better off wielding a cricket bat.* He wanted to tell her now that she'd been right, that he had never wanted to play the piano, never for a moment enjoyed the silly little tunes he'd been required to learn. Fortunately for all concerned, his mother had been quickly persuaded to let the whole thing drop after a couple of terms.

Mrs Mansfield's eyes were a light brown, like a wild animal's. Her hair was a softly glistening silver, and she had it tied back in a long ponytail. She was narrow across the hips and shoulders, making her seem taller than she really was, and she was unnervingly schoolmistressy. He supposed she must be in her seventies, although her face had few wrinkles and her hands looked strong and unmarked. He had learnt to add a good ten years to most women's ages, from the evidence of their appearance. Most of them had been ignoring all the old rules about hair and clothes for a long time now.

'Yes, Charlie,' he confirmed. 'I'm sure you're aware that he was almost certainly murdered. We can't be sure of the exact day it happened, but it looks like late Sunday or early Monday.'

'So I understand. Some time between the death of Nina and her funeral. Two deaths within a few days – it has naturally shaken us all up rather badly. What must it be like for poor Alexis? I keep thinking I should go and see her, but I'm not sure I would be welcome.'

Den tried to visualise the scene and failed. Where strong women gathered together, it was hard to predict what might happen. 'We're still trying to understand the precise connection between Charlie and the animal rights protests, and the Quaker Meeting. Would you be able to throw any light on that for me?'

She busied herself with the coffee for a minute and then handed him a mug. 'You take this and I'll bring the biscuits,' she said. 'Sugar?'

'No thanks.'

She settled herself and Den on two armchairs beneath the front window and took a hearty gulp of the coffee before answering. 'Charlie was the philosophical ringleader, so to speak. As opposed to Nina Nesbitt, who was the organiser, the pragmatist. Charlie believed in it all quite desperately. I felt sorry for him, to be honest, banging his head on such a solid brick wall. He was never going to get hunting stopped, not to mention virtually all modern farming practices, which is what he wanted. Anything at all that involved what he called "slave animals" was evil in his mind. Quite frankly, I found the whole business rather irritating. Especially when it came to Val and Miriam – and Polly Spence, of course.'

'They all agreed with him?'

'Miriam will agree with anybody. The woman's weak-minded. I don't mean that unkindly – she can't help it. We're all immensely patient with her, I promise you. But she's a great one for causes and Charlie found her a lot of simple jobs to do. Val's a political animal. She thinks the future lies with animal rights and she's furthering her own agenda, or whatever it is they say nowadays. I can just see her as Chair of the District Council in years to come – assuming she learns to be a bit more conciliatory first. At the moment, she's intent on alienating some very influential people, which isn't too sensible.'

Den made rapid notes. 'And Polly Spence?'

'Val's poodle,' came the prompt reply, followed by a half-serious hand to her mouth, eyes wide with self-reproach. 'Oh, no, that's putting it too strongly. Polly has time on her hands and a good heart. She needs a banner to march behind, and Charlie supplied it. I like Polly the best of them all, taken all round. She's also an artist of sorts, which endears her to me. Not that she's got much to show for it.'

'What does she do for a living?'

'I think she works as a receptionist at the Dartmoor Hotel. But she fancies herself as a potter, and has a stand at craft fairs from time to time. Some of her things are rather interesting.'

Den sat back in the expensive easy chair and assembled his thoughts. Garrulous as the woman was being, he had no sense of getting close to the kernel of truth that would pin down the killer of Charlie Gratton. It all felt like background, an intriguing picture of an interesting collection of people; but nothing about them pointed towards a vicious murder. 'Charlie,' he prompted. 'How did these people feel about Charlie?'

'They worshipped him,' came the ready response. 'That's not a very Quakerly way of putting it, I suppose. They took their lead from him, they believed in him. He was very charismatic, you know.'

Den sucked the end of his pencil and looked at her thoughtfully. 'Charismatic,' he repeated, remembering that Alexis had said the same thing. But he also remembered the protester he'd seen on the day Nina died. Thin, with pale skin and gingery colouring, something very earnest in his demeanour; Den had gained an impression of a young man with a mission, a persona probably adopted as an unconscious strategy to mask an immaturity or lack of confidence that went very deep. *Charismatic* didn't ring true, somehow.

But Dorothy stuck to her point. 'Definitely,' she insisted.

Den let it go and moved on. 'So you wouldn't say that any of the Quakers disliked him?'

'That's not what I said,' she rebuked him. 'You only asked me about Miriam, Val and Polly. There's a lot more to the Meeting than those three.'

'Of course.' He shook his head, impatient with himself. 'I was forgetting Bartholomew White.'

'You were forgetting the Aspens,' she said severely. 'And that's something you must not do.'

'Ah!' Den emitted a short syllable of surprise. 'But I've already interviewed them.'

'And you think they were both as fond of Charlie as everyone else, do you? You must be a very poor judge of character if that's the case.'

Den lifted his chin, hanging on to his dignity as best he could. The careful words came slowly. 'I merely meant that I have no need to ask *you* about them, because I've seen for myself. But if you think there's anything I should know, I'd appreciate hearing it.'

'Clive loathed Charlie,' she said simply. 'He made no secret of it, either. He thought Charlie was giving Quakerism a bad name. And he didn't – doesn't – like Alexis very much, either.'

'How well does he know her?'

'Enough to disapprove of her. I haven't quite worked out what he has against her. It might be straightforward jealousy.'

He cocked his head to one side invitingly. 'Jealousy?'

'Of her easy life. There's a blitheness about the Cattermoles that annoys Clive. He has known hard times. He thinks that's done his soul good, taught him that life is meant to be a struggle. When he sees people who are congenitally happy, with money and health and lots of friends, he gets very agitated. He can't work it out, and looks for something below the surface – evidence that all happiness has been bought at a price.'

'You make him sound almost . . . well, *disturbed*.'

'He didn't tell you about his breakdown, then?'

Den reluctantly shook his head. 'I don't suppose he thought it was relevant.'

'It probably isn't,' she agreed. 'But it's left him with an exaggerated respect for the psychiatric profession. Therapists, counsellors, shrinks – he believes they can do no wrong. And he fancies himself as an amateur practitioner. He reads a lot of books on the subject. Research papers.'

'What is it they say about a little knowledge being a dangerous thing?' Den said thoughtfully.

'Exactly.' She sat back in her chair and smiled. 'I must say I never thought you'd come to anything. You were a truly terrible piano pupil, you know.'

'I thought you couldn't remember me.'

'Well now I do. Little Denholm Cooper. Your legs were unnaturally long, even then. I don't think there's anything more I can tell you now. I'm not sure I've been of much help.'

'Did *you* like Charlie, Mrs Mansfield?'

The hesitation spoke volumes. 'I found him very *entertaining*,' she said at last. 'And probably quite a useful irritant to the more pompous of our citizens. But I suppose I have to be honest. No, I didn't really like him. There was something volatile about him, something unsettling. I could never really believe he had the same blood as Hannah and Bill. But he had a rocky childhood, what with his mother dying and his brother running off. I did my best to give him the benefit of the doubt. It's the Quaker way, you know.'

'Yes, I know. You always look for the best in people. Clive told me.'

'And if anyone knows the finer points of Quaker faith and practice, it's definitely Clive,' she said, with a wry sigh.

CHAPTER TEN

Den spent Friday evening in his flat only a couple of streets away from the police station, curled up on his comfortable settee with Lilah. She had delegated the afternoon milking to her brother Roddy, who was at sixth form college, and tended to regard farmwork as beneath his dignity. The compromise Lilah had reached with him was that he would take over for two or three afternoons a month, 'just to keep his hand in'. He had a friend, Jeremy, who was romantic about farming and very much enjoyed taking part once in a while, as well.

The herd had changed considerably in the year since Lilah had taken over. Smaller in size, it concentrated on the speciality market for creamy Jersey milk. While the nation's dairy farms seemed obsessed with the high-quantity-low-fat Friesian stuff, the Beardons stuck with the old-fashioned bad-for-your-heart product. 'The tide will turn again, you see,' Lilah insisted. 'I haven't noticed the rate of heart attacks coming down since people changed to milk without any cream on it.'

But twice-daily milking was a straitjacket from which there was no escape. It was Lilah's first thought when she woke up, and the first consideration when she tried to arrange any sort of social life. Even though she had Amos and Roddy as back-up, the real onus of responsibility fell squarely onto her shoulders.

'How well do you know the Cattermoles, really?' Den had just asked her. She was considering her reply.

'Not terribly well now,' she concluded. 'Martha was a brilliant teacher, and she and I would meet after school sometimes to talk about books. When I was doing A-level, she gave me a bit of extra tuition at her house, in return for babysitting the boys now and then. But that was ages ago, and I've only seen her three or four times a year since then.'

'They're not *her* boys,' Den objected, needing to keep the convoluted facts of the High Copse family straight in his mind. He pulled her head onto his shoulder, and wrapped a long arm round her. The ruby ring on her left hand gleamed at him.

'No,' Lilah agreed. 'But Nina used to go off and leave them. Alexis wasn't there very much in those days – she was doing some sort of public relations course in Liverpool, I think, which lasted a couple of years. It was just after the old mother died. Martha wasn't married then, and she was off courting with Richmond. It's a fabulous house. I loved going there.' She twisted her face to look at him, and grinned. 'It was always an adventure.'

'I only saw the kitchen and that hideous new shed. What's so great about it?'

'There's a secret passage, for one thing. It goes from Martha's room up to the attic, up a tiny little staircase with a hidden door. I think it's Elizabethan. The boys are lucky to have such a place to live. They've had a much freer life than most kids get these days.' They both fell silent for a moment, thinking about country children and their relative freedom. Their favourite topic of conversation in recent weeks had been where they would live when they married, and how many children they'd have.

'They don't seem to take much care of it,' Den commented lazily. 'It was full of cobwebs and dust.'

'It always was like that, although they used to have a cleaning woman. Remember Hetty Taplow, from our village?'

Den wrinkled his brow, but could not honestly say he did. Lilah carried on. 'She works in the pub. Has done for years. She also used to do a bit of housework at High Copse. I don't think she does any more.'

'Evidently not, I'd say.'

'Funny she wasn't at Nina's funeral, come to think of it. Hetty always loves a funeral. Perhaps she didn't approve of the way they were doing it.'

Den had little interest in Hetty; it was the Cattermoles who intrigued him. 'Did you know Nina?' he asked.

'Not really. To be honest I was a bit in awe of her. Very forceful. I sometimes suspected that Alexis didn't really like her, even though they were always joking around when they were together. People keep saying now how close those two were – but it never felt like that to me.'

'Did you know,' he began hesitantly, unwilling to gossip, 'that Nina, Martha and Alexis have three different fathers?'

'Oh yes,' she said readily. 'Everybody knows that. Thanks to Hetty, probably. My mum was very impressed. Well, you know what she's like. She always wanted to be friends with the old woman – Eliza Cattermole – but she never got

146

the chance. You don't think *that's* got anything to do with what happened to Charlie, do you? It couldn't possibly have.'

He shook his head slowly. 'Hard to imagine how it could,' he agreed. 'Unless one of the fathers turned up and took a dislike to Charlie. Say it was Alexis's father. Conservative with a capital C. When he realised she was having it off with a Quaker animal rights activist, he saw red and ran him down with his horse.'

'No,' Lilah judged. 'I don't see it, somehow. Implausible, Constable.' She adopted the tight-lipped wooden look that Den often used when imitating his Inspector.

'You're right,' he admitted, and shifted slightly, so as to reach her mouth for a long kiss.

With a small sigh, he tried to relinquish his duties as a criminal investigator. They were definitely at odds with his desire to spend a lazy, sensual evening with his beloved. He half-wished he hadn't broached the subject of the Cattermoles in the first place. He half-wished he was in some other line of work entirely. When pursuing a murder inquiry, you had to notice every detail. You had to try and make connections and understand what motivated people. You had to be suspicious and persistent and rude and intrusive. But he had first come together with Lilah during the investigation into her father's murder, and the habit of discussing a case with her had been formed from the start. Ten minutes later, his questions resumed.

'What about Charlie Gratton, then? Had you ever come across him?'

'Hardly at all,' she responded willingly. 'Too far away. Us varming volk don't get out much, remember. High Copse is the furthest afield I ventured for a long time. The Grattons are another three or four miles from there. I knew they were Quakers, and that Charlie was anti-hunt – and that's only because I'd seen him in the paper. My dad would have said Charlie was fouling his own nest, making such a commotion so close to home. I'd think he must have made quite a lot of enemies.'

'Which is where I come in. Trying to identify these enemies isn't going to be easy.' He sighed, and added, 'Nasty way to die. You should have seen the look on his face, what was visible of it. Terrified.'

'Poor chap. Someone definitely rode a horse over him, then?'

'It still isn't certain how deliberate it was. Forensics are arguing over it. But even if it wasn't premeditated murder, we've got someone failing to report a fatal accident, which is serious enough to warrant a few days of our time. We're hoping they'll have settled the main facts by tomorrow, anyway.'

'So we won't think about it any more now. Okay?' She glanced out of the window. 'Looks like rain again.'

'Course it does. It's Easter next weekend. It always rains at Easter – especially Good Friday. It's getting in some practice.'

'Maybe we should emigrate? That would settle the argument about where we're going to live, once and for all. We could run an ostrich farm in Swaziland.'

'I think I'd rather teach wind surfing in Barbados. Once I've learnt how to do it myself, of course.'

'No, no. There have to be some animals involved. I know – we'll breed llamas in Peru.'

'Scuba diving off Casablanca.'

She won the fight by tickling him in the one place that always got results.

In their modest cottage at the very end of the village street, Hannah and Bill Gratton were struggling to maintain a semblance of normality. Bill sat where he always sat, in a big old high-backed chair beside the fireplace. He had a table close by, on which were assembled three or four books, a plastic bottle of pills, a fifty-year-old Parker fountain pen and a notepad. He had suffered a slight stroke the previous year, affecting the right side of his body, and was determined to relearn the copperplate script for which he had always been well known.

Hannah was polishing the dining table with beeswax, having already vacuumed and dusted the room thoroughly. Three cards of condolence stood on the mantelpiece, delivered by hand at the first news of Charlie's death. Bill glanced at them repeatedly. He had not wanted his sister to display them, but she had insisted, saying that the people who sent them would look for them when they came to visit – which they inevitably would through the coming days.

They would have spoken very little to each other, even without Bill's stroke. After living together for most of their lives, there didn't seem to be much to say, even in the face of such a calamity. *Or perhaps*, thought Hannah, *we just haven't the courage to say what we're thinking.*

She was battling hard to repress the growing feeling of resentment against Bill and his son. It wasn't fair of her – nobody could blame Bill for Charlie's death. But the fact remained that, along with Charlie, very nearly everything that Hannah lived for had disappeared. It was difficult not to take it as a personal affront – a deliberate snatching away of the ground beneath her feet. She knew, of course, what people thought of her. They believed that she had clung to her nephew tighter than many a mother would have done.

Still living there in his thirties, with no proper job and everything done for him – many people made no effort to conceal their disapproval. 'That lad should have left home years ago,' they muttered. 'Tied to Hannah's apron strings, even if she isn't his real mother.' Only Hannah and Bill knew that it wasn't like that at all. Only they understood that they had no choice but to keep him with them as they did. Hannah and Bill had known that it would not be a good thing for Charlie to move in with Alexis and form a permanent relationship with her. *At least*, their eyes had said, as they'd looked at each other that evening when the girl from the police had brought the news – *at least now we don't have to worry about that.*

CHAPTER ELEVEN

Saturday afternoon at High Copse Farmhouse did not go according to plan.

'We'll light a fire and put a video on,' said Martha to the boys. 'Just chill out and do nothing for a bit. If anyone comes for the shop, Richmond can deal with them. Most people probably assume we'll still be closed.'

'It's all right for you,' grumbled Alexis. 'I've got this woman coming.'

Martha looked at her. 'What woman?'

'I told you yesterday. Val, from Quakers. Remember?'

Martha shook her head. 'Sorry. My head's not working properly at the moment.'

Alexis spoke with an exaggerated patience.

'She was one of Nina's animal rights cronies, and she's known Charlie for ages. She and Polly Spence – the one who spoke to you at the funeral. I suppose she might turn up as well. They want to make some sort of memorial for Nina. I told you.'

'It all sounds a bit unnecessary. And yes, I do remember Polly saying something. I thought I told her to leave it for a few months.'

'Well, they won't do that. It's not at all unnecessary to them. They've lost both their leaders in one week.'

Martha sighed. It was true her head wasn't working that day. She had barely managed to drag herself out of bed, feeling the loss of Nina more keenly than at any point so far, having dreamt that her sister was miraculously alive and still waving banners in front of horses' faces. 'What do they want *us* to do about it?' she asked tiredly.

'I'll tell you after I've seen her.' Alexis was wandering restlessly round the big living room at the front of the house, where Martha was half-heartedly trying to get a log fire going. The room was dusty and rather dark. A big holly tree grew outside the main window, and had not been cut back for years. The furniture was heavy and solid, made from oak and mahogany: a large sideboard containing the best china and cutlery; a bureau with a bookcase on top of it. Seating was provided by an oak settle, dating back to the late eighteenth century and upholstered in a brown velvet which had been snagged by cats' claws and children's sandals over the decades, and two mismatched armchairs. A big television sat in one corner. It had been Richmond's when he married Martha, and he had brought it with him, hoping it would make the living room more appealing to some family members. The wholesale crowding into the kitchen was a constant annoyance to him.

Clement and Hugh lay on the floor in front of the TV, with big cushions under their heads. The once-expensive Persian carpet was warm to lie on, but gritty and far from sweet-smelling. Dogs and cats used the room in summer evenings when the kitchen became too hot for them.

'I hope you won't want to bring her in here,' said Martha. 'You'll have to vacuum it and tidy up a bit, if so.'

Alexis shook her head. 'The kitchen will do. Everywhere else is in too much of a mess. We've missed the spring cleaning season again, I suppose.'

'You can clean at any time,' Richmond said mildly. He was perched on a narrow window seat at the end of the room, with sections of the Saturday *Guardian* scattered all around him.

'Most people do it more often than once a year, or so I understand.'

'Poor fools,' said Martha. 'Nothing better to do. I'm just grateful that none of us was born under the sign of Virgo. We'd really be in trouble then.'

'Hugh's a Taurus, and that's nearly as bad,' said Alexis. 'Though it might be useful to have someone who liked cleaning. The windows are so filthy, you can hardly see out.'

'There!' Martha crowed. 'Success!' The fire had finally taken hold of the pieces of bark and small twigs she had laid on top of several twists of newspaper, and she delicately placed larger logs on top. 'That should be all right now.' Something about the sturdy little flames made her feel better. She looked round at the others. 'There's nothing like a fire,' she said idiotically.

'We live like people in the Stone Age,' said Hugh. 'It's embarrassing.'

'At your age, old son, everything's embarrassing,' Richmond told him. 'It gets better with time. You can leave home and get a nice modern house on an estate in – oh, four or five years from now. Meanwhile, you're stuck with us.'

Hugh cocked his head to look at his brother, and the boys exchanged a long glance. Martha, watching them, wondered what had passed between them. As a teacher, she had some experience of the way children exchanged wordless messages, and she had learnt not to ignore them. 'Hey!' she said. 'Let's not talk about people moving out. We're a *family*, and this is our home. It's true the place is a mess, and with all these visitors, we're noticing it more than usual. But it's a great house. It loves us. We understand each other.'

'Don't start that stuff,' Alexis said violently. Everyone stared at her. 'It's just a house. I hate sloppy talk like that – pretending it can have feelings. It makes me feel as if I've got no choice but to live here until I'm ninety. If Charlie hadn't died, I might have got away. We could have lived somewhere else, like normal people. As it is – well—' she threw a trapped look from one corner of the room to another. 'I don't know whether I can *bear* to go on living here, especially with that bloody grave in the garden.'

Martha breathed out, a long, steadying bid for time. Then she closed her eyes for a moment. 'Alexis, what are you saying? I asked you, only a few weeks ago, what you and Charlie were planning, and you said you couldn't imagine ever leaving High Copse. What's changed?'

Alexis laughed harshly. There was no mirth in the sound. 'I should think that was obvious,' she said, in a choked voice. 'As far as I can see, just about everything has changed. Hugh's right. We're huddled here like neolithic cavemen, letting the house fall apart, too selfishly caught up in our own stupid projects to see what's happening, ignoring everything that doesn't suit our warped view of the world. And it was all because of Nina. Big Sister who controlled us with her iron will and her impatience with any arguments. What did we say in the newspaper – *diminished lives*. Well, so they might be, but I'm not going to let it stop there. When I woke up this morning, my first thought was, *No more Nina*. And I was *glad*.'

'Shut up,' Martha shouted. 'Stop it. You don't know what you're saying. In front of the boys, too. You should be ashamed of yourself.'

'Well I'm not. It needed saying.' Alexis gave one more sweeping look around the room, pausing a moment to focus on the two boys, before striding out. The door was pulled shut behind her, but it wouldn't slam. A drift of rucked-up carpet had prevented it from fully closing for several months past.

Five minutes later Martha and Richmond heard the car driving up their track before the dogs began to bark. They kept two collies outside, as if they were a real farm; the dogs were under-stimulated and something of a liability at certain seasons of the year. These included lambing time on neighbouring farms, which lasted from January to April, and the summer separation of lambs from their mothers, which made the collies restless and wistful, wanting to join in with the commotion. Their best friend was Clem, who took them into the larger of their two fields and taught them tricks.

Now they belatedly set up a frenzied barking which brought the boys out of their trancelike attention to the television. 'Nev!' they said in unison. 'That's Nev!' In a scramble of limbs, they were up and out of the house before the adults could move.

'How do they know?' puzzled Richmond.

'The dogs know the engine, and the boys know the dogs,' Martha explained. 'He must have collected his car from his mother's already.' She made no move to get up from the settle, but pressed a hand to her temple as if struck by a sudden headache.

'Come on,' Richmond urged her. 'You have to face him sometime. Best get it over with.'

They paused in the doorway, watching the scene. The dogs and children were all trying to win the newcomer's regard, jumping and pulling at him, as he stood with his back to the vehicle. He was suntanned and lean, with long brown hair tied back from his face. He looked like an advertisement for lager or Levi's. Except that there were tears on his cheeks, and he stared at one of the upper windows of the house, as if waiting to see a familiar face.

He laid a hand loosely on each boy's shoulder, and forced a smile at Martha. 'Sorry I'm late,' he said. His accent was cultured, betraying his origins and the years spent at Winchester School. Nev Nesbitt had been a great catch when Nina Cattermole married him, despite his extreme youth. Only the High Copse matriarch had been dubious. 'Apart from having a name like a hamster, he's awfully inbred,' Eliza had said.

'Nonsense, Ma,' Nina had breezed. 'You can't get finer breeding than his. We'll make wonderful sons for England, you see if we don't.' And the family agreed that she had been perfectly right.

'Come in,' said Martha impatiently. 'You must be exhausted. What time did the flight finally get in?'

He shrugged. 'No idea,' he said. 'I'm not even sure what day it is.'

'Nev,' said Clem, into a moment of silence, 'are you going to stay with us now? We buried Mum over there, look.' His thin arm, in a grubby sweatshirt, pointed waveringly across at the oak tree. 'You have to stay here now. Don't you?'

The boys' father slowly turned to follow the pointing finger, and then he removed his hands from the children and took a step away from them. The dogs watched hopefully, but made no further noise. 'I'll go now,' he said. 'Get it over with. Give me a few minutes, will you?' He looked down at Clem. 'Back soon – okay?'

'I'll come with you,' said Hugh, importantly, putting out a hand to prevent his brother from interrupting.

'No,' said Nevil sharply. Then in a more gentle voice, 'No – I need to go and talk to her on my own. When I get back, I'm going to be gasping for a cup of tea, and we'll talk and talk.'

Minus Nevil everyone wandered back into the house. Only then did Martha notice that Alexis hadn't come out to greet her returned brother-in-law. *Typical*, she thought crossly. *Trust Alexis to keep herself detached.*

But she regretted her unkind interpretation when they all went into the kitchen and found Alexis drooping over the sink, washing mugs and saucepans, with tears dripping into the bowl of grey water. 'Oh, Lexi,' she said. 'What set this off?'

With a big sniff, and a swipe of a damp wrist across her eyes, Alexis tried to smile. 'This,' she said, half laughing, half sobbing, and held up a bright red mug with black and gold lettering all around it. A flower was shedding its petals, and attached to each one was a phrase – *She Loves Me* or *She Loves Me Not*. 'Charlie and I bought it a fortnight ago at Tavistock market. They say it's the little things, don't they.'

'Nev's here,' said Hugh, a hint of warning in his voice. 'He's gone to look at the grave.'

'Oh,' gulped Alexis. 'I'd better pull myself together, then, hadn't I.' She reached for a grubby tea-towel and wiped her eyes with it. 'Can't let him see me like this.'

'Why not?' Martha wondered. 'He's upset too.'

'Oh, I can't *cope* with this,' Alexis wailed, and she dashed the new mug violently onto the lino-covered floor. It shattered loudly. 'It's like the end of the world. I want Charlie back. I've got so much I want to say to him.'

Everyone watched her, wary of what she might do next. As the youngest, Alexis had always been given to tantrums and demonstrations of strong emotion. The usual strategy was to ignore her until she settled down. This time, that didn't seem to be an option. She said again, with intensity, but recovered from the former hysteria, 'I want Charlie. I can't go on without him.'

A voice from the corridor brought distraction. 'Charlie? Why – what's happened to Charlie?'

Martha put a weary hand to her head, and reached for Hugh as the nearest source of support. The boy squared his shoulders, and looked directly at his father.

'Your mother didn't say anything, then?' Richmond said.

Nev shook his head, his expression confused. 'I only stayed a few minutes. She was busy feeding a litter of puppies. Tell me.' His tone was urgent.

'Somebody murdered him,' Hugh said, slightly too loud. 'Richmond found him in a ditch.'

Nev's eyes seemed to grow a filmy skin, like a sick cat's. He blinked, and moved his head in a jerky fashion, as if recoiling from an expected blow, only to stop himself midway. It was terrible to see. 'What?' he whispered. 'What did you say?'

'Sit down,' Richmond ordered him. They slowly arranged themselves into a rough circle, with Nev as its focus. Richmond leant against the Aga; Alexis remained at the sink. Nev, seated at the table, seemed barely conscious.

Alexis spoke first, not looking at anybody. 'It happened on Sunday or Monday. We found him on Wednesday, a few hours after Nina's funeral. He'd been lying there for two or three days. We missed him, but nobody went to look for him. We were too busy.'

'Busy,' Nev echoed, disbelief resonating in his voice.

'*You* should have been here,' said Hugh harshly. 'We needed *you*. You had the whole week to get here.'

'Hardly,' Nev shook his head in disagreement. 'It was late Friday where I was when you phoned me, and that was two hundred miles from an airline office. I had to pack up, tie up one or two loose ends, especially as I didn't have any idea when I'd be back again. They got me on the first available flight, but it was delayed. I told you. There was no way I could be here any quicker. It's a long way from Vietnam to here, you know.'

'You shouldn't have gone in the first place,' the boy persisted. Reproach was pouring out of him, an uncontrollable spate of feeling. His blue eyes stared accusingly at his father and he spoke hoarsely, as if the words were hurting his throat.

'Don't give me that.' Anger flashed into Nevil's eyes, and he put up a hand like a traffic policeman. 'We've been over all that before.'

'Well, you can't go away again,' the boy stated flatly.

'No, you can't,' chimed in Clement, like a little echo. 'We won't let you. There isn't anybody to be our dad now Charlie's gone.'

'You've got Richmond,' Martha interrupted.

The boys' eyes met, and Hugh gave a small frown. 'We really want Nev,' said Clem, with a polite smile at his aunt. 'He's our proper father.'

Nev clasped both hands around his head, and squeezed. A groan came from somewhere deep inside him. 'What a fucking mess,' he mumbled. 'I can't deal with this, I just can't.'

'Tough,' spat Alexis. 'That's really tough, kiddo. Because as I see it, you don't get any choice. As Hugh so rightly says, you are their father.'

Nev raised his head, and stared hard at her. 'Since when have fathers been so bloody important around here?' he demanded.

A renewed barking outside effectively halted the conversation. 'Somebody's here,' said Clem. A minute later, there was a knock on the front door.

Alexis was forced after all to lead Val and Polly into the living room, because the kitchen was so crowded. The fire was smouldering uncertainly and she added two more logs. She directed the visitors towards the settle, and took a window seat for herself. The weak light from outside was enough to throw her face into shadow, so that neither visitor could fully make out her expression. She, on the other hand, could see them only too well, and was struck by the vivid contrast in their appearance.

'I hope you don't mind Polly coming as well?' Val said carelessly.

Alexis shrugged. 'It's all the same to me,' she said. She wasn't in the mood for bland courtesies after the events of the day so far.

Polly Spence had her thick black hair pulled away from her face and tied at the back of her neck. Her movements were economical, graceful, betraying her Indian grandmother as much as her skin colour did. A persistent tension between her obvious strong feelings and her cool manner made her a fascinating figure.

'We've come about Nina and Charlie,' said Val, at the outset. 'I'm not sure I made that clear yesterday? After all, they were both part of the protest movement.'

'Even though they hardly agreed on anything,' said Alexis dryly. 'Funny, that.'

'Funny that you should think it true,' observed Polly. 'It bears little relation to the way I saw it.'

'Anyway,' Val ploughed on. 'We've had a phone-round, and everybody agrees that there should be a proper memorial to them, Nina especially. She was our leader, and we're going to be lost without her. She was such a special person, too. The favourite idea is a charitable fund of some sort. We'd set it up properly, and get a committee to run it. It could be quite a big thing – a national appeal. Honestly, Alexis, you probably don't even realise what a significant name Nina was.'

'You weren't at the funeral, were you?' Alexis shocked the woman into silence with her question. Polly sat back, awaiting her moment. Val's mouth fell open.

'What? Oh – I wrote to tell you – didn't you see my letter? I had a case conference, which I absolutely couldn't miss. What difference does that make?'

'Sorry. None, I suppose,' Alexis shook her head. 'Except that Polly already mentioned all this to Martha, and we're frankly not very impressed by the idea. Nina was a rebel by nature. And a good organiser, I admit. But her claim to fame was as a sort of gang-leader, if we're honest. I'm not sure that her reputation bears much scrutiny. Now, Charlie was different. He had it all sorted: the ethics, the psychology, the tactics – everything. I'd be more interested in memorialising him, quite frankly.'

Val hastily nodded concurrence. 'Yes of course. As we said . . .' She looked to Polly for help. 'At least, we thought Nina's name should be on the appeal. But there'll be plenty of opportunity to talk about Charlie. Although – um – he was in fact *murdered*, wasn't he? I'm not sure—'

'You think that tarnishes his image?' said Alexis. 'Perhaps you're right. It isn't very glamorous being bashed to death, is it? I do see.'

Polly stirred uncomfortably. 'We are *terribly* sorry about Charlie,' she said earnestly, her large brown eyes widening with sincerity. 'And it's all so recent – you can't possibly have got used to it yet. We should have waited before coming to see you – but it is rather urgent. The hunt season ends in a few weeks, and then everything goes quiet for the summer. We did want to get the appeal launched right away, you see. If you could just give it your consent, we can get out of your way.'

'Why do you need my consent? What have I got to do with it?'

Polly looked shamefaced. 'We need to know that you won't try to prevent it. We're very keen to avoid any embarrassment.'

'I see.' Alexis smiled at a passing thought. 'After all, we Cattermoles are a highly embarrassing family.' She waited a moment, aware of the undiminished tension in the room. 'Well, I'm sorry, but I can't give you what you want. I think the idea stinks, quite honestly. My sister was no saint, and not a suitable figurehead for any appeal. If you'd listened to Charlie, you'd know that fox hunting is doomed anyway. I know he put a lot of energy into the protests – but he believed he was just hammering a few more nails into its coffin. It doesn't matter how much money you raise or what rallies you organise. It's over, already. Stop wasting your time and go back to doing something useful. That's my reply. Sorry.' She regarded the stunned faces with some pleasure, and something lifted slightly inside her. She thought she could hear Charlie faintly applauding her for the stand she had taken.

Polly Spence stood up. 'All right,' she said, inclining her perfect oval head on the swanlike neck. 'Come on, Val. We did our best.'

'You can't mean it,' Val blustered. 'It isn't just hunting. What about live exports, battery farms, genetic engineering?'

'And pollution, packaging, population and prison reform?' added Alexis with sarcasm in her tone. 'Charlie cared about it all, and a lot more. But it needs real live people out there, getting publicity and taking risks – not people salving their consciences by giving money to charity. No appeal fund in the world can make a real difference.' Her voice became quieter, serious. 'As I see it, the world's doing pretty well, in spite of all these problems. I think you protesters are misguided, in a way. Charlie knew how I felt about it. It's entirely a matter of perception. But I don't want to argue with you. Go, please. Leave us in peace with our grief.'

The women left, Polly with dignity intact, Val bristling with outrage and disappointment. Just before Alexis closed the door on them, Val turned, and said, 'You haven't heard the last of it, you know.'

CHAPTER TWELVE

Eight Friends gathered at the usual meeting for worship on Sunday, at eleven a.m. Three Elders – Hannah, Bill and Silas; two members – Dorothy Mansfield and Miriam Snow, and one attender, Polly Spence; plus the wardens. Nobody spoke throughout the Meeting, but Hannah Gratton found herself fighting back tears as the silence deepened. Her emotions began to swirl uncontrollably, laced with memories and increasingly uncomfortable thoughts. The police had been restrained in their account of how Charlie had died, but enough of a picture had been given for Hannah to feel a sense of horror at the brutality of it.

She knew Silas would waste no time in going

over all Charlie's misdemeanours yet again, as soon as Meeting was over. Her cousin had always been a trial to her, and there seemed to be no respite to be expected in the old man's lifetime. She winced at the idea – it came close to wishing him dead, and that was an unwholesome thought to be having at any time, let alone during Meeting for Worship. Families could be a curse, she knew only too well. They could bring more acute suffering than anything else, as well as the most love. Yet she had come back to the family when she could have made a life for herself in Africa or Eastern Europe. Hannah had given ten years of her early life to a village school and other work in Madagascar before coming back to Devonshire and her brother with his motherless sons.

At the time, she had confided in Sarah Beamish, the wise Elder, who had lived far into her nineties, and been forced to agree when Sarah said, 'My dear, caring for those boys is Quaker work, just as much as bringing education to little African children.' So Hannah had made the best of it, and become a mother to Charlie, in her prime, when she could have done anything, gone anywhere. She might even have married Benjamin.

Unbidden, the image of her lover formed behind her closed eyelids. So tall and strong he'd been, with skin like nothing she had ever known before, and a mouth that could consume her in flames. He only had to smile and show the tip of his crimson tongue for her to lose all sense of who and where she was. That was over thirty years ago now, and the power of her feeling for him was as great as ever. She had been thirty-five and her African lover only twenty-two – but the age difference had no meaning to them. Leaving him behind had been the hardest thing she had ever done.

Because it had been impossible for them to make a life together in Britain. He could never have settled in this alien land, with its rain and its unwelcoming people. Benjamin was born to live in the sun, to walk ten miles a day and work his magic on his own people. And Hannah was called home to give stability and love to Charlie and Frank. *Surely, Lord*, she thought to herself now, *I might have been given a little more reward for my sacrifice? What have I now, but one dead nephew, and one who feels himself lost to us because of what he did?* A bitter taste filled her mouth. She recognised it as self-pity and resentment. And anger. Not against Frank or Silas or even the wreckage that was now Bill. No, the person Hannah was enraged with was Charlie, dead in a ditch with the marks of horseshoes all over his head.

Bill came to her side, as soon as hands had been shaken, and the announcements given out by Hannah herself, in her capacity as Clerk to the Meeting. His shoulders were hunched, his skin an unhealthy grey. Bill was a naturally silent man, poor company by any standards; the loss of his younger son had only driven him further into his own lonely world. *What must we look like?* Hannah wondered, thinking of Charlie's girl Alexis, who had come to the special meeting a few days ago. *What a strange lot we are.* She looked round at the small group, waiting for the undrinkable tea which Mandy had scurried off to make. It seemed to Hannah that they all had some peculiarity which set them apart from the modern world. Silas was an old curmudgeon, living in the past, afraid of his telephone and ridiculously doting on his smelly dog. Clive was walking wounded, though he would never admit it. His zeal for Quakerism made the others uncomfortable – people who needed to would find their way to the Meeting without being rounded up by the Warden. Over the centuries, there had been a diminishing enthusiasm for evangelism amongst Quakers, until now it was quite frowned upon. Clive stood slightly aside now, his dark features set in a fixed expression which betrayed nothing of what he was thinking. 'Probably the oddest one of all,' thought Hannah, taking care not to meet his eye.

Dorothy and Miriam were chatting with

some animation, and Hannah moved over to join them. 'Oh, Hannah,' said Miriam, laying a soft, well-manicured hand on Hannah's arm, 'I did want to come on Friday, but it was just impossible. You know how *terribly* sorry I am to hear about Charlie. It's just too horrible for words.'

'Thank you, dear,' said Hannah. 'That's kind of you.' She did her best to like Miriam, but the white hair and the pink face conveyed a vacuity which Hannah found it difficult to embrace. It was unusual for such persistent lack of intelligence to find satisfaction in Quaker activities. The silence of the Meeting, and the assumption of honest integrity, threw people onto their own resources, drawing out whatever nascent qualities lay within. Miriam was something of a failure in this respect. She drifted with whatever media-induced breeze might blow, rising to give ministry about fleeting headline trivia, which she became deeply concerned with for a brief period, before something new caught her attention. Miriam had taken Charlie and his animal rights very seriously for a while, particularly when he made the front page of the local paper for three weeks in succession.

'Bartholemew was here,' said Dorothy. 'Pity you missed him.'

Hannah inwardly smiled at this small piece of

mischief. It was no secret that Miriam harboured an unsuitable affection for Barty which was sternly and consistently rebuffed.

Regret flitted over Miriam's face, and she said nothing.

'Have you and Bill made any plans for the funeral?' asked Clive from behind Hannah's shoulder. She jumped violently, and swung round with a frown on her face. 'Sorry,' he said carelessly. 'I didn't mean to alarm you.'

'Well, don't creep about like that,' she said tartly. The shock on his face was almost comical. 'Especially when everyone's nerves are so jangled. My nephew has been *murdered*, you know.'

'I'm aware of that,' he told her gravely. 'An awful thing to happen, especially amongst Friends.'

'We're not immune to violence,' she said quietly. 'Just unlikely to be the practitioners of it. At least, we like to think so.'

'We do indeed,' he nodded. 'I can't think of a single Quaker murderer, throughout history.'

'I can't either,' she said. 'But I dare say there have been one or two.'

'The funeral?' he prompted.

'We have to wait for the police to deliberate. If there's a prosecution, their defence is entitled to call for another post-mortem. That means we can't have a cremation. If the inquiry is prolonged, then I understand they would give permission for a burial after a certain time. We just have to be patient and do what we can to assist the police in their investigations.'

'Of course,' said Clive. 'I didn't realise what was involved. What a business this is! If only Charlie could have been a bit more—'

'A bit more *what*?' demanded Hannah. 'Prayerful? Ready for an early death? What do you wish he had been, Clive?' Irritation was overflowing, and she could do nothing to stem it.

Clive looked at his feet and pursed his lips in exaggerated compassion. 'No, no. Just . . . well, he was rather confrontational, wasn't he. Showed the Quakers in a poor light, in that respect.' He glanced up and noticed her expression. 'I'm sorry. I ought not to criticise him now he's not here to defend himself. I did say it to his face. He knew how I felt.'

As if that makes any difference, thought Hannah sourly.

Polly's was the next orbit to coincide with Hannah's. The tea was now being distributed, as always so slowly that it was cold before it touched one's lips. In such a small group, this was hard to understand, but it was always so. People hung back, the cups were wide-brimmed and cooled quickly, and Hannah suspected that Mandy never waited for the kettle to reach boiling point before making the tea. She always took a cup, and always found it revolting.

'No Val today?' she asked Polly, who shrugged.

'I don't consult her before Meeting, you know,' she said impatiently. 'We don't come in the same car. We live six miles away from each other. It's strange the way people think we're inseparable or something.'

'You're quite right,' Hannah placated her. 'I can see it must be annoying.'

'Oh, I'm sorry,' the woman exhaled, with a long, mournful breath. 'I'm in a foul mood.'

Me too, thought Hannah, grimly. But she was an Elder, she had duties. 'Anything you'd like to tell me about?' she said gently. 'It's a pity to feel like that after Meeting. We always hope it will improve people's state of mind.'

'No, no. I'm really sorry to dump it on you, when you've got so much to cope with. Unforgivable of me. But everything seems to be falling apart just now. Do you know, they're shipping another load of calves from Plymouth tomorrow? They're older than before, but it's just as cruel. After everything we've tried to stop them! There's just so much cruelty going on. I sat there in Meeting, going through it all, and getting myself more and more upset about it. And wishing Charlie was here to give us some guidance. It's going to be very hard to carry on without him. Him and Nina, of course.'

Hannah made a great effort. 'Nina?' she queried, before recollecting herself. 'Oh, yes. Alexis's sister. Poor girl. You'll miss her?'

'Of course. She was amazing. A wonderful person. We want to start a special fund in her memory, although her family aren't entirely co-operative.' She gave herself a little shake. 'Well – we probably approached them too soon. It was an absolute *tragedy* when Nina died. Such a silly accident, too. And here I *can* speak for Val. She feels just the same as I do about it.'

Hannah could do no more than shake her head. She felt suddenly weak, giddy and faint, and put out a hand to catch the edge of the table. She leant heavily, causing the tray of empty teacups to rattle.

'Oh dear,' wailed Polly. 'You poor thing. Sit down, for goodness' sake. It's shock, I expect. After everything you've been through.'

Mandy, Miriam and Dorothy all gathered round Hannah to express their concern. Bill stumped over, and gruffly announced that he would take her home, and they needn't worry. 'Hasn't been eating much,' he said, by way of explanation. 'Difficult time.'

Silas tagged along behind them, muttering grumpily. They usually took him back to their cottage and gave him a good Sunday lunch. Hannah turned to speak to him.

'Silas, can I ask you not to say anything about Charlie on the way home? I know what you thought of him, but I really can't bear any more just now. Is that all right?'

Silas stared at her, mouth half-open, and gave a confused nod. Hannah smiled slightly. For once she had managed to silence her cousin. It was a small source of satisfaction.

Left to themselves, with the little Meeting kitchen to clean up, Mandy and Clive were preoccupied at first. 'They never realise how much work they make after a meeting,' Mandy said after a few minutes, as she mopped up wet patches left on the worktop and folded the tea towel neatly before placing it on its rail. Clive had stacked the cups in precise ranks and disposed of the teabags and biscuit wrappers.

'All part of the job,' he said. 'Nothing to grumble about.'

'It doesn't occur to them, either, how late our lunch always is on a Sunday. I can't peel potatoes and get them roasting as well as being in here till half past twelve. I'm not complaining, Clive, but I think a bit of acknowledgement now and then would be nice.'

'It wouldn't occur to them that we eat a roast

lunch, just the two of us. They'd think it was old fashioned.'

She looked at him anxiously. 'But you still want it, don't you? You said—'

'Of course,' he said shortly.

Although they'd finished all the work, Mandy continued to fiddle with teaspoons. The roast needed all her attention upstairs in the flat, and the vegetables had to be prepared; they'd be lucky if it was on the table by two o'clock. But she had something to ask her husband and the necessary courage was slow in building.

'Clive . . .' she managed at last. 'Why did you lie to that policeman on Friday? About us going riding on Monday, I mean. I could have told him you didn't go anywhere near High Copse. It wouldn't have done any harm to tell the truth. After all—'

'I know what I'm doing,' he said through tight lips. 'It's a matter of committing a small sin to prevent a larger one. It seemed to me that it would save a great deal of police time if we were simply eliminated from the enquiries from the start. Do you understand?'

Not in the least, she wanted to say. *What you just said is madness.* But she merely smiled and nodded.

'It's so sad for them, isn't it,' she changed the subject, as they finally went back up to the flat.

'That poor family! Two deaths in less than a week. However will they cope?'

Clive sighed impatiently. 'I expect they'll cope quite well. People can deal with these things. You managed it; I managed it. If we can, I'm sure those transgressors at High Copse can get through.'

'Transgressors?' she echoed, a flash of defiance breaking through the meekness. 'What a word to use! They're just ordinary people, Clive, and you know it.'

He took a step towards her, towering over her, seeming much larger than he actually was. His black eyes glared piercingly down. With difficulty she stood her ground; she had learnt over the years that it was the only way to handle him. He seemed to hover for a moment, predatory, dangerous, before stepping back and thumping down onto the sofa behind him. 'Better get on with that dinner,' he said. 'Tell me if you need any help.'

She left him with relief, quietly preparing the traditional meal, as if for a real family.

CHAPTER THIRTEEN

On Monday morning, the police team met for a summary of progress so far. Den sat between Phil and Danny, new notebook on his lap, the first few pages covered in jotted notes. He had distilled them from his High Copse interviews, and gazed at them now with a sense of inadequacy. Nothing seemed to shed much light on the death of Charlie Gratton.

The Inspector sat informally on the edge of the desk at the front of the room, and invited each man in turn to discuss his findings. Danny spoke first. 'Forensics have made a thorough search of the scene, and concluded that the victim was trampled at a short distance from the ditch where he was found. There are several hoof prints, as well as traces of blood on the grass. Unfortunately, it rained on Tuesday and Wednesday, which hasn't made it easy. From his position in the ditch, it would appear that his injuries were inflicted in the open field, as he lay with his hands over his head, curled as small as possible, in an effort to protect himself. Then he either rolled or was pushed into the ditch. The only visible footprints are the victim's, which suggests that the horse rider never dismounted. Assuming, of course, that the horse wasn't acting on its own,' he added conscientiously.

The Inspector gave a slow, satirical nod. 'That is indeed the assumption,' he said. 'Otherwise, we wouldn't be wasting our time investigating a murder, would we? They don't send horses to trial these days.'

Den Cooper coughed and everyone looked at him. 'Shouldn't we have some evidence for that?' he ventured.

'Such as?'

'Er . . . such as, there was no loose horse reported with blood on its feet. Somebody obviously took it home and cleaned it up.'

'Point taken,' said the Inspector, with an implausible air of patience. 'Carry on,' he nodded to Danny.

'Right sir. So it seems there are several possibilities. Perhaps Charlie staggered to his feet and was kicked into the ditch by the rider, still on the horse. Or he might have dived into the ditch in the hope of escaping further attack. Or the horse itself knocked him into it. On balance the pathologist and forensics all favour the last one. There's a rough area of grass and weeds about a foot wide at the edge of the ditch. The most obvious marks on the ground are within another foot of this area, which doesn't give the horse much room before virtually landing in the ditch itself. It could even be that Charlie was half into it before the blows were ever struck. It's nearly three feet deep. He could stand in it and be vulnerable to the hooves of a rearing horse. There was another small amount of blood underneath the body, suggesting that he actually died in the ditch, but within a very few minutes of getting there.' He glanced up, to assess the reaction.

The Inspector smiled grimly. 'Good,' he said. 'Anything else?'

'From the depth of the wounds and the horseshoe marks, it must have been a fair-sized animal. Certainly not a pony. The marks all point the same way. The edges of the shoes did the worst damage, as if the hooves kicked forward.' Danny made prancing motions with his hands, then stamped down on an imaginary skull. 'The hands are badly damaged, too, where they tried to protect his face. And they think there might have been one or two more blows after he'd fallen, although that would be hard to explain if he was lying in the ditch by then.'

'Too much to hope that the animal hurt itself in the process, I suppose? Any vicious brambles in the hedge at that point?'

'Afraid not, sir. Even if it had ended up with one of its forelegs in the ditch, standing on the victim's head, it could probably have backed out quite easily.'

'How exactly was he lying when they found him?' asked the Inspector. 'Face up or down?'

'More or less down, sir. One of the worst injuries is on the back of his head, quite low down. That might even have been the fatal blow. The brain is badly damaged at that point. One hand is much more affected than the other, too.'

'Which hand?'

Danny consulted his notes. 'The right, sir. Which suggests that he could have rolled on to his left side during the attack. His right cheek and temple are also more badly hurt than the left. A horse's hoof is a big thing, sir. One direct impact, with the weight of the animal behind it, can do a great deal of damage.'

'I can imagine,' agreed the Inspector.

Den heard an echo from earlier in the week. Talking about Nina Nesbitt's death, Lilah had said, *A horse's head is a big thing. If you try to headbutt one, you can expect to get hurt.*

He shivered at the similarities. There surely *had* to be a connection somewhere . . .

'Bennett?' continued the Inspector. 'What joy with the background stuff? What've you turned up about Gratton's past?'

Phil sat forward. 'Quite a file on him, sir. Unruly behaviour at the protests, public nuisance – all connected to animal rights. He was only charged twice, though. No hint of violence. He went to a Quaker school as a boarder until he was eighteen, then worked for Greenpeace for a few years. Office stuff, mainly, it seems. Can't see anything that might lead to a murder motive. Nothing linked to a specific individual, anyway.'

'Right,' was Smith's only response. After a moment he pursued a new tack. 'I gather you went back yesterday to update the Grattons on the forensic findings?'

This was news to Den, and he had to suppress a stab of annoyance that the suffering Grattons had been subjected to yet another police intrusion. It must look like inefficiency when different officers kept turning up on their doorstep, no doubt asking the same questions as the one before. He waited tensely for Phil's report, fearing that his colleague's impressions and findings would be at variance to his own. He even wondered whether Phil had been sent deliberately, because DI Smith

186

didn't trust Den to gather the important facts.

Detective Constable Phil Bennett had a thin neck and a very small chin. His head widened at the temple, and domed on the brow, giving him a look of top-heavy intelligence. His habit of speaking slowly, consideringly, added to this impression, but Den had sometimes felt it belied the truth.

'Something strange there,' he began. 'Bill Gratton – the father – was all over the place. Could hardly get a sentence out. Said he didn't know anything about anything. Hadn't seen Charlie for over a week. Seemed to think the lad might have married the Cattermole girl and moved into High Copse with her, given time. Quite honestly, I got the feeling he never much liked Charlie. Couldn't get him to show any grief, anyway.'

Den coughed again, attracting another beam of attention from the room. 'That wasn't my impression, sir,' he said carefully. 'I think the old chap's very upset indeed.' He wanted to state it even more strongly, the image of the wreckage that had been Bill Gratton still vivid in his mind.

'Hmm,' said Smith, and turned back to Phil. 'Did you ask him about the other son – Frank?'

'That was even worse. Clammed up completely. I asked who'd told Frank about Charlie, and Hannah – Miss Gratton – said she'd phoned him. That ties in with what Frank told us. Miss Gratton said he was "estranged from the family". They haven't seen him for years.'

'So, this brother and sister have lived together for how long?' the Inspector asked. 'Is there anything we ought to be noticing in the set-up?'

'Over thirty years, sir. She's the boss. He looks to her for everything, seems like. He isn't in very good health – I presume he's had a slight stroke or something. She came back from Africa or somewhere, when Charlie was two, because his mother had died. Frank's fifteen years older, and was off their hands soon after his auntie arrived. They just told me dates, facts, no feelings, no little stories or contradictions. It was obvious that something's locked away tight in the cupboard.'

'Right.' The Inspector almost rubbed his hands together. 'Very promising, Phil. I know you've got a lot more for us, but let's just hear Den out, with his thoughts on the High Copse family, and then we can really put our heads together. Okay?' He turned to Den invitingly.

'It's not a lot, sir,' he admitted. 'Hard to grasp any direct link between Nina's accident and Charlie's death. Going in cold, like that, not knowing anything about the way it all worked – it was difficult. They're a very weird family. Three sisters, all with different fathers. Gerald Fairfield told me that last week. I gather it's common knowledge, and they've got no hang-ups about it.

'Martha, the middle one, has a husband, who was brought in to set them on a better business footing. Swears they love each other, though. Even said he'd die for her. The two boys are Nina's. Thirteen and nine. Sounds as if everyone took turns at minding them. Alexis, the youngest sister, has a temper. Restless, furious at the whole thing. She struck me as a bit unstable. Charlie was her boyfriend for eight months or so. She'd been to a couple of Quaker meetings with him, met his family, apart from the brother. There's also Nina's husband, Nevil. I haven't seen him yet, but I've asked Jane Nugent to check the airlines, make sure he was where he claims he was.'

'Good,' Smith nodded. 'Give me a bit more about the atmosphere at High Copse.'

'They all seemed genuinely stunned. Not surprising, finding a body on the day of your sister's funeral. That's another thing – Nina's grave out there, under that great tree. Morbid. Spooky, too. I don't think it's right, not with the youngsters living there.'

'Summarise, Den, there's a good lad. Off the top of your head – did any of the Cattermoles kill Charlie?'

Den shook his head hesitantly. 'No motive I could find, nor much opportunity. Means – well, they don't keep horses, but I doubt if they'd find it hard to get hold of one. The whole area is lousy with them. They live on a bridle path. Richmond sells horse feed, and there are notices in his shop for all kinds of horsy stuff. Means wouldn't have been a problem. But, no, sir. I'd say I've drawn a blank at High Copse.'

'Disappointing, Cooper,' sighed the Inspector. He sank his chin on his chest for a long moment. Then he looked up. 'How's this for a summary? Our villain knew Charlie had a habit of walking about the fields, so he hung about on horseback on the bridle path, looking like any Sunday rider out for a stroll – if a horse can be said to stroll. As soon as the man in question comes into sight, man and horse charge across the field, pinning Charlie against the hedge and forcing the horse to rear up and bash him to death. The field can't be seen from the house, although loud noises would carry to anybody in the yard or adjacent fields. He'd have to take that risk. There's little danger of anybody noticing the disturbed ground. The body's neatly hidden in the ditch. All he has to do is ride away again without ever setting foot on the ground. When he gets home he cleans any blood off the horse and maybe gets it reshod.' He raised his eyebrows invitingly. 'Any comments?'

Den spoke cautiously. 'First, sir, we don't know that Charlie was in the habit of walking in that particular field. No one seems to think he was. Secondly, anybody hanging about on a big horse on that path for more than a few minutes might attract notice. Thirdly, how could he be sure it would work? That the horse would oblige?'

'So you're saying it was opportunistic?'

'Yes, sir,' said Den firmly. 'I think it must have been. You couldn't plan something like that. Our killer happened across Charlie – maybe knowing there was a chance he'd do so – and gave it his best try. Maybe he never really meant to kill him, but just give him a fright.'

The Inspector nodded. 'You're right, Cooper. This is the worst kind of investigation you can get, just about. We have to either produce cast-iron evidence, match the horseshoe marks to a real live horse, or else hope someone incriminates himself. There isn't even a watertight case for calling it a murder at all, as you so rightly pointed out. What if a runaway horse got itself tangled up with him and he rolled into the ditch to get away from it? I can just hear a defence team pushing all the way for that.'

Den pursed his lips. 'Horses don't often run away in these parts. They're too well fenced in. Too precious. But I suppose accidents can happen.'

'And horses do sometimes bolt or escape

from their fields. If they're startled by something they can do a fair bit of damage. Now I'm not saying we give up. But we're not going to get any special favours resource-wise on this one. No extra personnel, very little overtime.' He sighed and turned over a sheet of notes in front of him. 'Now, the Quakers. Any progress there?'

Den cleared his throat and mustered his thoughts. 'I went to see the couple who live over the Meeting House. Clive and Mandy Aspen. Early forties, probably. No sign of any kids. They both do a bit of voluntary work in local schools, and seem to survive on a pittance paid them by the Quakers plus a bit of freelance computer work on his part. I guess they've got some sort of private income as well. He obviously didn't like Charlie one bit. She gave me the impression she was a lot more upset than she dared show. She'd been crying when I got there.'

'What do they do all day?'

'Among other things, they're both keen horse riders,' said Den with a flourish. The reaction was every bit as gratifying as he could have hoped.

'Bear them in mind,' instructed the DI. 'And speak to all the other members of this – church? Sect?'

'Meeting,' Den told him, with authority. 'It's called a Meeting. I've already made a start, sir. I've interviewed Dorothy Mansfield, who's a member, and she gave me a lot of useful background. I've got five others on the membership list to see yet.' He looked at his notepad for the names. 'Silas Daggs, Miriam Snow, Bartholomew White, Val Taylor and Polly Spence.' He already felt tired at the prospect.

'Then get to it, lad. We've a way to go and I want reports on all of them by this time tomorrow. Phil – you'd better make sure Jane's followed up the airlines. Then a bit of rummaging in the background of these Aspen people. Anything else you can suggest?'

Phil cocked his head. 'There's more to Frank Gratton than we're being told,' he said. 'The separation from his family, I mean. He called it "a silly family thing" when Den and I went to see him. It's niggling at me.'

Smith looked at Den. 'Keep coming back to that in your interviews,' he advised. 'Somebody somewhere must know the secret.'

'Right, sir. So I'm doing all the interviews, am I?'

'Is that a problem?'

'Well . . .'

'Phil's needed at the computer for a while, before getting back to the local horsy types, and Danny – as you've probably forgotten – is due to start a three-day training course in Bristol this afternoon. We're going to have to manage without him for a while.'

Oh well, thought Den. *It's my own fault. I shouldn't have been so keen.* And armed with the list of Quakers, and his almost-blank notepad, he hurried off for his next interview.

CHAPTER FOURTEEN

'How's it going?' Lilah asked Den that evening.

He shook his head wearily. 'I've been surrounded by Quakers all day. They're all very nice people, really friendly and open – and I don't feel as if they've got me anywhere at all. I've seen Dorothy Mansfield – that was yesterday . . .' he began ticking them off on his fingers. 'And Silas Daggs—'

'What a wonderful name!' Lilah exclaimed. 'I've never heard of him before.'

'He's not very sociable. Lives with a smelly old corgi and a lot of valuable-looking antiques. He's Bill and Hannah Gratton's bachelor cousin, and their grandad left all the family heirlooms to him, for some reason. The others got hardly anything, as far as I can see. He didn't approve of Charlie, in a general sort of way. Been a pig farmer for much of his life, but thanks his stars he's out of it now. Thinks the world has gone to rack and ruin.'

'Carry on,' she prompted.

'Right. Dorothy, Silas, Miriam Snow, Barty White and the two younger ones – Polly Spence and Valerie Taylor. I haven't seen the last two yet. They weren't in when I tried.'

'I have heard of Barty White,' Lilah nodded. 'He used to have a big herd of Friesians. Actually, thinking about it, I remember my dad and I went there once to have a look at his set-up. He was milking ten at a time, when we were only doing three. He had an ACR system, which we thought was amazing.'

'Do I know what ACR stands for?'

'I can never remember exactly. Something like Automatic Cluster Removal. Basically, the unit comes off when the cow's finished milking, of its own accord. Saves a lot of time.' She grinned. 'We decided not to bother with it. Dad said it was bound to lead to mastitis, you see—'

'I don't want to know,' Den decided. 'Anyway, Barty told me a bit about his life. He sold nearly all the land three years ago, when he hit sixty, and let his son keep the house. He lives in a bungalow across the road now and dreams of past glories.

He also breeds Jack Russells – for the hunt.'

'Which can't have endeared him to Charlie Gratton.'

'I tried to ask him what the Quakers thought about it. He said it wasn't their business, that hunting was a time-honoured country practice and that if he didn't sell dogs to augment his pathetic pension, he'd probably starve. I was fairly well convinced.'

'So who is Miriam Snow?'

'She lives in that tiny village west of Chillhampton – bet you've never been there. Kilworthy. Wonderful scenery, like going back a thousand years. She cycles through the lanes to Meeting. Doesn't even have a car. She seemed lonely and a bit helpless. Mrs Mansfield said some quite rude things about her.'

'So she isn't one of your suspects?'

Den shook his head. 'I can't bring myself to imagine it. I asked her if she rode a horse and she went pale at the very idea. Partly because horses frighten her and partly because Charlie told her it was exploitative, I think.'

'Or because she felt guilty?'

'I don't think so. But you're right – I should have kept an open mind to the possibility. I'm a hopeless policeman – it's so difficult to think the worst of people all the time.'

'You don't have to do that. Just allow for the

possibility that they're lying to you. They might be doing it to protect someone else. Or because they're being threatened. And watch their body language.'

'Yes, miss,' he said meekly. 'I'll do better next time. Anyway, Miriam Snow was one of Charlie's most ardent followers – she swallowed all that stuff about slave animals and human beings not having the right to use other species. Except she didn't seem to have any real grasp of what it meant. She's got a cat and two budgies and her garden obviously makes full use of a host of pesticides. I saw a box of slug pellets on her windowsill.'

'Does Barty White ride?'

Den sighed. 'Unfortunately, he does. Not only that, but he's got a seventeen-hand stallion in his paddock. Said it belongs to his son and doesn't often get ridden. But he lends it out from time to time to anyone who fancies a gallop and can handle it. Looked rather a nasty brute to my ignorant eye.'

'Seventeen hands is enormous. Did you ask him where he got it from?'

'Apparently it was a reject from somewhere, because its temper's not too good. His son said he would give it a home.'

Lilah looked at him in excitement. 'But it might be the very one you're looking for! Has anyone examined its hooves for bloodstains?'

He nodded. 'A team went over this afternoon. I called them right away. They didn't find anything. It's hopeless, quite honestly, over a week after the event. Just walking about on wet grass for all that time would be enough to clean everything off. It hadn't been given new shoes, so there's the very faintest possibility they'll match against Charlie's wounds, but I'm not holding my breath. I can't see Barty doing the deed, and his son was away in London over the crucial period.' He sighed. 'I'm not really getting anywhere at all.'

Before Lilah could adequately sympathise, Den's doorbell rang. 'Expecting anyone?' she asked. He shook his head and slowly stood up. 'I'll go,' she offered. But perhaps because they'd been talking about murder, or perhaps because he was a policeman and therefore a natural protector, he went to the door.

His visitor was so out of context that he merely gaped at her for a few seconds. 'Sorry to intrude,' she smiled. 'I'll go away again if you're busy. But I gather Lilah's here and I was hoping for a little chat.'

Lilah appeared behind Den. 'Martha!' she yelped. 'How did you know I was here?'

'I phoned your ma and she told me. Is this a bad time? Are you in the middle of something?'

'Well—' Lilah hesitated and looked to Den for a contribution.

'Of course we're not,' he said heartily, suddenly enlivened by the unexpectedness of the visit. 'It'll be great to talk to you. You won't be surprised to know we were discussing Charlie. Come in.'

Martha stepped confidently into the house and began to unwind a scarf. 'It's got cold again,' she said.

They settled her down with a mug of coffee and waited to hear the reason for her visitation. Den forced himself to do some quick thinking. He had a duty to be cautious, even suspicious, with this woman who could herself have murdered Charlie Gratton. She certainly had the opportunity. By paying this call she might even be increasing his suspicions. The obvious conclusion was that she wanted to discover how the inquiry was going and where police attention was most sharply directed. Under the guise of a somewhat moribund friendship with Lilah she might very well be trying to ferret out information that it would be unwise to share.

But at the same time, he was aware of a strong feeling of sympathy for Martha, fortified by knowing that she was – or had once been – Lilah's friend. He himself had been a pupil at the same school where Martha had taught English to Lilah and befriended her as a sixth former, but he had left before Martha arrived, and knew her only by reputation. The connection worked both ways, of course. If Martha turned out to have killed Charlie, then Den for one was going to be both amazed and distressed. The mere possibility was supposed to be enough to keep him at a professional distance, and he did his best to maintain it.

Martha began to speak almost immediately. 'I suppose you know about me and Nina and Alexis all having different fathers.' She sounded relieved to say it, as if she'd been holding the words in for too long already.

Den and Lilah both nodded with a hint of sheepishness.

'Okay. So I assume you also know the essential facts: the three daughters of Eliza Cattermole,' born within seven years of each other. Nina, then me, then Alexis. We don't know who any of the fathers were – *are*. It was a village scandal, thirty-five years ago. If you asked, even now, there are plenty of people who'd tell you all about our wicked mother. She was actually a lovely person. She was all give, no take. Our mother was the daughter of gentry. High Copse was the Big House, with a capital B, capital H. The manor house, at one time. It's been changed a lot, of course—' She paused, staring vaguely out of the small window onto the street below, apparently seeing High Copse as it once was, and not a side street in Okehampton.

Martha took a deep breath, and Den understood that she was making an effort to speak steadily. 'Ma had brothers, too. Uncle Luke and Uncle Paul. They gave her shares in the house. Luke was a somewhat unorthodox civil servant with the Foreign Office and Paul was a psychiatrist, firmly in the R.D. Laing mould. In fact, I think he came to the same conclusions ten years before Laing did. Never occurred to him to write books about it, though.' She laughed. 'Is this getting boring? I am getting to the point, honestly. About my mother. She was even more in the middle of things than her brothers. She met W.H. Auden and Stanley Spencer – definitely the bohemian end of the spectrum – and she brought us up at High Copse in as liberal an atmosphere as you can get.' She stopped abruptly.

'And she's dead now?' asked Den, well aware of the answer already.

Martha nodded. 'She died five years ago, at the age of seventy-six. She came to motherhood quite late, you see. Very late, by the standards of the time. She was forty-six when she had Alexis. Uncle Luke's in a nursing home in Kent and Uncle Paul went a bit strange. The last we heard he was in New Zealand, building himself an ocean-going boat. He'd be nearly eighty now.'

'And you really don't know who your fathers were? Not any of them?'

Martha shook her head. 'We never really asked. She convinced us that it didn't matter. They weren't chosen with any real care, as I understand it. These days, they'd have been anonymous sperm donors from a private agency. They weren't local. She always insisted on that. It was about the only thing she ever told us. It isn't so very unusual, you know. I could show you five or six women with children by three different men. Three seems to be the favourite number. Maybe there's an evolutionary significance to it. Her only deviation was in not marrying any of them.'

'The *point*, Martha,' Lilah prompted.

Martha said nothing for an uncomfortably long time. 'I could give a variety of answers to that. First of all, I'd like to set the record straight, so you don't rush off looking for Nina's outraged father seeking vengeance on Charlie for her death. Nina's father almost certainly doesn't know she ever existed.'

Den considered his next words carefully, swallowing back those which first came to mind. *We never seriously thought of looking for Nina's father.* In the complex game that every murder inquiry turned into, sooner or later, he wondered just what part it was that Martha was trying to play.

'What else?' he asked.

She smiled. 'I want to make sure you know exactly how peculiar we are. And how, by associating with us, Charlie also became peculiar. A lot of locals resent us.'

'I'm not really sure—' Den began.

'Neither am I,' Lilah chipped in. 'You're obviously trying to tell us something, but I've no idea what it is.'

Martha flushed, her clear skin deepening into a shade resembling a recent tan. Den felt the same warmth in his own cheeks, watching her. She certainly rewarded close observation. Initially striking because of her hair and height, it took time to realise just how lovely she was. The clear gaze and confident tilt of her head gave the impression of dignity and authority. Den hoped again that the outcome of his inquiry was not going to bring any further grief onto Martha's shoulders.

'I've been thinking about something one of the other teachers said to me at school today. Term finishes this week and we've been having parents' evenings. I overheard one chap saying he wondered what the parents would think about meeting me. *After all, there's probably a murderer in the family* – that was what he said. It never really occurred to me until then that people were thinking that. The papers have concentrated on us, because Charlie was found on our land –

and because of Nina, I suppose. But they seem to be assuming that one of us actually killed him. So I wanted to make sure that you don't think that. Because it would be an awful waste of your time if you did. It would distract you from finding the real killer.' She met Den's eyes, unblinking, for the last part of her speech. 'Did you go to see Frank?' she asked after a brief pause.

He nodded but offered no further information. Martha leant forward urgently. 'It must have been someone good with horses, and someone with a precise knowledge of where they could find Charlie. You might think that rules Frank out, but I know he would have been able to find Charlie if he wanted to.'

'How would he?' Den asked, before he could stop himself. He hadn't wanted to get drawn into this conversation.

She leant back again and folded her arms. 'He . . . knows people locally.'

'But who? How do you know? Does he know you and Alexis?'

'No,' she said with resignation. 'I've hardly ever met him. I think Nina ran into him once or twice. But he does know Nev. You see, Frank Gratton is Nevil Nesbitt's godfather.'

'I think I'll go back to High Copse,' Den told Phil, after lunch on Tuesday. 'I had a rather unexpected visit from Martha Cattermole last night and it's had the opposite effect from what she intended.'

'Oh yeah?' Phil said inattentively.

'She seemed to be trying to divert us away from her family onto Charlie's brother Frank. So I'm wondering what it is we've missed up there.'

Phil fingered his narrow chin for a moment, obviously thinking hard. Den had no illusions that the thoughts he was focused on concerned him or anything he had said.

'Any inspiration?' he asked hopefully.

'Hang on a minute.' Phil put up one finger. 'Right. Got it. Sorry. You're talking about the Gratton thing, right?'

'What else would I be talking about?'

Phil rubbed his chin again more vigorously. 'Plenty,' he grinned. 'But it's good to see you concentrating on the job in hand. So you're going back to the big house. Who's going to be there? The sisters both work, and the kids'll be at school, won't they? That just leaves the chap who runs the feedstuffs business.'

'And the kids' father. He must have got back by now.'

'Oh – did you hear what Jane unearthed? About the airline? We were going to make sure you got it.'

'No. What?'

'He was on a flight – Qantas, I think – days earlier than he claims. He landed at Heathrow in the early hours of Monday morning. They'd given him a special seat – one of those reserved for people rushing home for funerals and suchlike. Paid two thousand quid for it.'

Den's mouth dropped open. '*Monday!*' he echoed. 'Then he could have . . .'

'Exactly.'

'So where was he? They had a phone call from him on Wednesday, saying he was still in Singapore.'

'Why should they doubt him? He could have been anywhere.' Phil's expression contained a patient reproach, thick with implication that Den was being very slow. 'They phoned him midday on Friday, our time – nearly midnight where he was. He set off right away – let's say – and was in Singapore by sometime on Sunday, easy. Onto the Qantas flight and bingo! We didn't follow his steps from Vietnam to Singapore, though we might yet have to.'

'Two thousand quid,' Den muttered.

'And the rest. That's just the return ticket from Singapore.'

'Return?'

'Open dated. Any time in the next six months.'

'Bloody hell. What does the DI say about it?'

'He says it would be useful if you could go and talk to him, without letting on what we know of his movements. He was going to see you himself, in about ten minutes' time, but I doubt he'll have to now. He thinks you're well up to the task. Watch the bloke's face, when you ask him about times and dates and addresses and so forth.'

Den's mind was reeling. Was this not clear evidence that Nev Nesbitt killed Charlie? Should there not be a carful of officers preparing to go and arrest him? 'Why so softly softly?' he asked.

'It's not adding up to the DI's satisfaction, seems like. All those Quakers and horses and animal rights, muddying the water. Nobody liked the Gratton chap very much, but nobody *hated* him, as far as we can see. The Quakers look too meek and mild to be true—'

'Not Clive Aspen,' Den interrupted. 'Nor Bartholomew White. And they both ride big, strong horses. Smith's right – we can't give up on the Quakers just yet.'

'Very wise. But all the same, the Nesbitt chap looks the favourite now. Strikes me it went like this – he hears the news about his missus, sees red, breaks all records getting home, blaming Charlie for the whole thing. Grabs himself a horse from somewhere – didn't you say his mother's a keen hunt follower? – and then rides the poor chap down. Then off again for a few days, pretending he's waiting for a flight in the Far East. Fits like a dream.'

'Wouldn't he know we'd check the flights?'

Phil shook his head. 'I bet you he's never given it a thought.'

On his drive to the farmhouse, Den passed three horse riders, each strolling in solitary splendour along the roadside. Acutely sensitised to them by the murder inquiry, he made every effort to observe their faces. All three were women, astride large, well-muscled horses, and clearly in absolute control of their mounts. Any one of them looked as if she could ride down a pedestrian with no trouble at all. Two of them looked to Den as if they'd rather enjoy the novelty of so doing. Both these were in late middle age, wearing hard hats and regulation jodhpurs, apparently going nowhere, simply 'out for a ride'. The futility of it struck Den for the first time. Of all life's more pointless activities, this must rank right up there with golf and collecting postmarks.

The third rider was less forbidding. In her twenties, dressed in jeans and sweatshirt, she didn't even sport a hard hat. Briefly Den wondered if there was a law against going bareheaded on the open highway whilst in charge of an equine mode of transport. He thought there very probably was. But at least he could get a good look at her face, and be assured that it was nobody he recognised.

CHAPTER FIFTEEN

A stranger met him at the front door of High Copse Farmhouse. A lean, long-haired individual, who appeared to be in his mid-thirties. As Den drew closer, he discerned the sweet smell of cannabis, with very little surprise.

'Hi,' said the man, easily. 'Nobody's here but me. What can I do for you?'

'I'm Detective Constable Cooper,' said Den. 'I'm investigating the death of Charlie Gratton.' Involuntarily, Den glanced to his left, where the field and ditch were located. Between the house and the field lay Nina's grave, its flowers still bright under the sheltering oak tree.

'Aha!' the man responded. 'I should have known.'

'And you are—?' He knew, of course, what the answer would be. He was busily trying to establish a sensible sequence of questions for the man who suddenly looked like the prime suspect.

'Nev,' came the anticipated answer. 'Nevil Nesbitt, if we're being official. Husband of Nina, father of Clem and Hugh. I got back on Saturday. They didn't wait the funeral for me.'

'So I understand.' Den cleared his throat. 'I was there when she died. It was a terrible accident. I've never seen anything like it before.'

'Yeah.' Instead of inviting Den in, Nevil came out, closing the door behind him. 'It's a nice day,' he said. 'We can chat out here. The kids'll be back soon. It's weird being here on my own, rattling around in this great big place. The house is usually full of people. I still expect the old lady to show up – when I first lived here, she was still very much in charge.' He sighed and looked up at the house behind him. The upstairs windows seemed to look back at him sadly.

'Do I understand that you and Nina were separated?' Den wasn't sure whether he was making small talk or pursuing his investigation. Nev had a dreamy manner, manifesting little sign of grief or anxiety over the events of the last week, not at all the standard police interviewee.

Den was halfway to deciding he didn't really like the man.

'Separated?' Nev repeated. 'No way – except by distance. I travel, see. It's what I do. She came with me a few times. No, no, not *separated*. I was always going to come back.'

'This travelling – is it part of your work? How long had you been away?'

'It's what I do,' Nev repeated, to Den's irritation. 'I'd gone out last year – September, October – I don't remember. Vietnam. Ever been there?' Den shook his head. 'You should, man. It's magic. Upcountry, away from the cities, it's another world. Amazing people. You know – after that obscene war, and the chemicals and napalm and stuff – they just laugh about it now. Get on with their lives, go with the flow. Time passes, the rice grows, the babies get fat. They work – don't get me wrong – but they're into some amazing rhythm. I can't get my head round all this hassle here. People battling over fox hunting and sentimental bullshit like that. Totally futile.'

'Sentimental?'

'Absolutely. Marshmallow for backbones. And that includes Nina, up to a point. She knew how I felt about it, what my take on her protesting was. Never thought it'd kill her though.' He shook his head. 'There'll never be another one like Nina. Christ knows what'll happen now.'

They had strolled across the stretch of gravel in front of the house, and were now leaning on the rail fence which divided the car parking area from the rather neglected lawn and garden, which sloped downwards to the two fields still attached to High Copse. To their left the approach drive also sloped away, down to the road at the foot of the hill, where Den assumed the school bus would deposit the sons of the house in due course.

'We'll be needing a bit more detail on the timings of your flight,' Den said as firmly as he could. 'Just to check you got back into the country when you say you did.' Watching Nev's face, he felt momentarily ashamed of the deception. Fear was unmistakable in the grey eyes. 'And an address in Vietnam, just in case,' he added desperately.

'Shit,' said Nev. Den waited. The tension slowly deepened until Nev broke it with a boyish smile. 'Well, I'd better confess then, hadn't I,' he said, holding his arms away from his sides, as if waiting to be frisked. 'Is there any hope you'll keep it to yourself and not tell Martha or Alexis?'

'For now,' Den nodded. 'But if it comes to court . . .'

'I got into London about six on Monday morning,' Nev told him. 'Stayed with a friend there until Saturday. I know it looks bad, but Christ, I couldn't face all this—' He indicated the direction of Nina's grave. 'I didn't want to be here when they buried her. I phoned them, and they were nagging at me to hurry up. Just like it used to be – ordering me about. So I took my time. That's all.'

'Could you give me the address in London?'

Nev rolled his eyes up to the sky. 'I'll never live this down,' he groaned. 'It's a girl, if you must know.' He breathed deeply, then grinned sheepishly. 'Look – surely you can see that if I'd killed Charlie, I'd have gone to more trouble to cover my tracks? And I can't see where you think there's a motive. He was my mate. Our mothers were friends for years.'

'I'm just collecting the facts for now,' Den said stiffly. 'If you could let me have the address and your flight times, that'll be it for the time being. Except I'll need to speak to your mother, too.'

'She's going to love that,' Nev remarked. 'She can really go to town, telling you what a disappointment I am. She might even go along with the idea that I killed Charlie. It wouldn't surprise me. I could have borrowed that bloody horse of hers – which I expect you've heard all about?'

Den tried to think and drew a blank. 'There are

a lot of horses around here,' he replied carefully.

'You said it, mate,' Nev sighed. 'Come on, then, and I'll fill you in on the details before the boys get home. You won't be arresting me just yet, will you?'

'I'll need an undertaking that you won't leave the area without informing us. There's a good chance you'll be invited in for questioning when I've reported what you've told me today, and when we've checked all the facts.'

'I like *invited*,' said Nev, and added, 'The boys would probably be rather pleased if I was thrown into jail for a few years. They'd know where I was then. Always moaning about the way I go off, they are. You should have heard Hugh on Saturday, telling me off for not getting here sooner.'

'One more thing,' Den remembered. 'Charlie's brother is your godfather – have I got that right?'

Nevil blinked and put a hand flat to his own chest as if in pain. 'Frank . . .' he said quietly. 'I suppose he is, yes. Although I should think he's forgotten all about it by now. He was never much good at it. He sent me birthday cards and one or two nifty presents when I was little, but that's about as far as it went.'

'And Charlie started a relationship with Alexis last year. Did you know about that?'

Nev nodded. 'I was here when it happened.

It was weird. It seemed almost like incest. At least—' He paused and rubbed a finger between his eyes. 'That's not really right. More like two brothers marrying two sisters. It used to happen a lot you know, in country areas like this.'

Den cut him short. 'The addresses?' he said. Nev dictated the three he needed – a small Vietnam village, a flat in Bayswater and his mother's house a few miles away, alongside the river Tamar.

'Go carefully with her,' he advised. 'She's really upset about what's been happening. Whatever she might think of me, she's crazy about the boys.'

Den remembered Richmond's comments about the boys' ancestry; something about aristocracy on both sides. Nev added further comment, as an afterthought. 'She loathed Nina, of course. And it was mutual.'

'Really?'

'Oh yeah. Because of the hunting. My mum's a demon for the hunt. I gather she fell off a few days ago – the day before they buried Nina – she wrenched her shoulder. Used it as an excuse to miss the funeral. But she's a devoted grandma – has the boys for most of the summer holidays. They get up to all sorts of adventures.'

Den cast a sweeping glance across the unpeopled hills and fields before him and raised an eyebrow. 'Can't they get up to adventures here?'

Nev laughed. 'Course they can. The little buggers are spoilt rotten.'

Den waited just long enough to witness the two boys returning home, and greeting their father with an enthusiasm that contained an air of desperate relief, as if they'd half expected him to have disappeared again before they reached home. Den felt for them. He could imagine the insecurity of never knowing when their sole remaining parent might wander off to some godforsaken corner of the world and simply forget all about them. He sat in his car for a minute, making notes on his pad, trying to control the excitement he felt at having extracted such an easy admission from Nev that he had lied.

At the foot of the drive, he met Richmond, in his four-wheel-drive vehicle. They had to manoeuvre carefully past each other, and Den gave a polite wave, to indicate that he had no wish to speak to the man again just now. He saw Richmond shrug and shake his head slightly, before driving quickly up to his house, in low gear. *Like a bull at a gate,* thought Den. *Or a horse ridden deliberately at someone it was going to kill.*

Den found an excuse to pass close by Redstone Farm that afternoon and decided to call in. Lilah would probably be out in the fields, planting some crop or clearing out a ditch, but he might still manage to snatch a few words with her. She was running the farm these days with very little help, and with extreme financial constraints, thanks to a succession of government moves – or failures to move. Her mother had taken on an outside job which brought in just enough to keep destitution at bay. For a girl in her early twenties, Lilah was performing miracles, but Den wondered how she could possibly hope to keep it up.

He liked to imagine himself living here with her, helping with the animals on his days off, and enjoying the country life. He liked the friendly little Jersey cows and the ancient rhythms of the seasonal work. He even fancied the idea of driving a tractor, throwing bales around, attending the births of lambs and calves. He wanted to see Lilah in context. But she seemed reluctant for him to come to the farm, as if she felt it an invasion of her personal territory. She preferred to visit his flat in the evening – often staying the night as well. All he could do was to make unscheduled visits and hope she'd be available and glad to see him.

But he knew, as always, it wasn't going to be easy to find her. He drove down the familiar lane, with its ruts and sharp bends, into the muddy farmyard, relieved at least to see Lilah's car standing in its usual place beside the small front garden. She had rebuffed Miranda's suggestion that they share a car when they sold the unsuitably large vehicle that had belonged to Lilah's father. Miranda had got herself a cheap hatchback and the consequent independence now seemed to both of them an absolute necessity.

As he stood quietly listening for the sound of a tractor or anything to indicate where his fiancée might be, he found himself pondering his murder investigation once again. This farm was nothing like High Copse where Charlie had died, but it was enough to remind him of how it must have been to die in a ditch, your head smashed in by a heavy iron horseshoe. He tried to visualise exactly how it might have happened – the horse first rearing up to knock the man to the ground and then trample him. Would the animal have been blindly obedient? Or was it more likely that it had been afraid, nervous, resisting this terrible act it was being asked to commit? Had it first been made to chase Charlie across the field, so they clashed unavoidably when they reached the hedge? The forensic people had traced the horse's progress part of the way, surmising that it had been travelling at some speed shortly before the encounter with Charlie. It was a heavy animal – a hunter or a hack – the sort of horse a full grown man would ride, not a riding school pony or a delicately-bred Arab.

He smiled to himself, remembering Lilah's words. *Give me a cow any day.* But even cows would attack, given the right circumstances. He recalled a recent story of a woman killed by a herd of highly protective cows with calves, which had taken exception to the presence of her dogs.

There was no sound coming from the outbuildings, or the closer fields, and he had just decided to give up when a voice accosted him from the direction of the milking parlour. 'Den? What are you doing here?'

It was Roddy, Lilah's younger brother. He wore rubber boots and ragged jeans, and Den noticed how much he had grown in recent months. He was never going to be as tall as the police detective, but he had overtaken Lilah by two or three inches.

'I could ask you the same thing. Shouldn't you be at school?'

'It's the Easter holidays. We've got an inset day. Most people finish tomorrow.'

'And then you've got your A levels, right?'

'No, that's next year. I'm taking an AS this year and a couple of extra GCSEs. It's all a bit complicated. You looking for Lilah?'

Den nodded. 'I was passing and thought I might catch her.'

'She's discing, in the far field, that way. It would take you ages to get there. Aren't you working today?'

'Meant to be, yeah.' He pushed an indecisive hand through his hair. 'I'd better get on with it. By the way, did you know Charlie Gratton?'

Roddy shook his head. 'Not at all.'

'But you know Martha? What about Nina?'

'Steady on,' Roddy protested. 'Don't come the detective with me. I've had enough people die around me. This one isn't my problem. Lilah started talking about it this morning and I shut her up. From now on, I'm sticking with the living.'

'Sorry. And of course you know Martha – she's still teaching English, isn't she?'

'Yeah, but I've never been in her group. Lilah's her pet, not me. I tell you, Den, you can leave me right out of this one. I'm not even going to play guessing games with you.'

'So you're not thinking of a career in the police force?'

'Not bloody likely!' The boy's eyes widened in disgust at the idea. 'There's no shortage of jobs to suit me. Computers, accountancy, retail, even teaching . . .' He ticked them off on his fingers. 'The careers office is throwing out new suggestions every day at the moment.'

Den looked at him sympathetically. 'And it doesn't sound to me as if any of them has really taken your fancy,' he said gently.

Roddy frowned, his dark brows coming together. 'There's no hurry,' he said defensively and swung the stick he was carrying.

'Well, must get on. Will you tell Lilah I dropped in? I'll see her this evening, anyway.'

'Okay.'

The interlude had unsettled him and distracted him from his pursuit of Charlie Gratton's killer – but it had also given him a perspective on the case. Most people in this village, and others in the area, cared little for the death of a man eight miles away, even if he had been killed deliberately. They had their own troubles. Even now, in the age of technology and worldwide communications, their insular lives encompassed the same small area they always had. Some of them might have access to email and Internet, carry mobile phones and have offspring on the other side of the world, but the focus of their daily lives was on the land that they could see and feel and cover in an hour's walk. Lilah was discing – breaking up the clods of ploughed earth ready for seeding – giving the job her undivided attention. Den liked the picture this conjured; the timelessness of farming reassured him. The machinery they used might change, but the tasks remained the same. If only she could be persuaded to let him join in, then everything would be perfect.

'Did you ever meet Nevil – Nina's husband?' Den asked Lilah, soon after she arrived at his flat that evening. She frowned thoughtfully, then nodded.

'Once or twice. He didn't make much of an impression. I remember Hugh missed him, though, when he was on his travels. Talked about him all the time, when he was little.'

'Nevil's mother's minor aristocracy, apparently. Takes the boys over in the summer holidays, to give them a change of scene. Compared to most, they're horribly privileged.'

'For all that, they go to the local schools and muck in with everybody else. Martha's got her feet on the ground – she wouldn't let them get above themselves.' She delved into a plastic carrier bag which she'd dumped on the floor on arrival, and produced two large mackerel. 'Look what I got at that fish van. Aren't they gorgeous! I hope you know how to cook them.'

Den narrowed his eyes. 'What are they?' he demanded. 'I'm not very good with fish.'

'Mackerel, you fool. I think you cut the heads off, open them flat and grill them. I saw it on the telly – but I thought you'd know.' He could see her disappointment, and did what he could to summon enthusiasm. His memories of mackerel included a lot of bones, a pungent flavour and acute indigestion afterwards. He doggedly returned to the former conversation, the death of Charlie Gratton very much a priority.

'The boys – what must the other kids make of them, coming from such a weird family?'

Lilah shrugged. 'Families ain't what they used to be,' she said, with a rueful grin. 'No one's normal these days. Who else have you seen today?'

'I caught up with Polly Spence this morning and made her late for work. The only thing worth noting was that she seemed passionately fond of Nina and hardly less so of Charlie.'

'Maybe she's one of those people who gushes over everyone indiscriminately. I saw her at Nina's funeral, talking to Martha. She's very attractive, isn't she?'

'The sort who turns heads,' he agreed. 'But she struck me as a bit shallow. Never been married, no sign of a boyfriend. Must be something wrong.'

Lilah hissed disapprovingly. 'Careful,' she warned. 'Maybe she prefers women.'

He considered for a moment. 'Maybe she does,' he nodded. 'If so, it could be Val Taylor she's paired up with. People do seem to talk about them as an item, now I come to think about it. I haven't seen Ms Taylor yet.'

'Well it sounds as if you're well stuck in,' Lilah encouraged.

He shrugged. 'At least the DI seems pleased with me, Christ knows why. We haven't got any hard evidence to point us at anybody. It's just a lot of guesses and hints and nothing concrete. The sort of case every policeman dreads, I suppose.'

'Clive Aspen sounds the most sinister one to me,' she interrupted as she sawed through the mackerels' spinal columns to remove their heads. 'If all Quakers are like him, I'm going to stay well clear of them.'

'They're not,' he defended hotly. 'Not at all. Hannah, Dorothy, Barty White – they're all, I don't know, *centred* might be a good word for it. They don't play games like most people. It sounds naïve, I know, particularly in the present circumstances, but I'm sure they're saying what they mean and giving me the truth as they see it. Clive Aspen is a recent convert and he's got a history of disturbance and trouble. They're not all like him, definitely not. Even Miriam Snow and Silas Daggs and Bill Gratton – they might not be perfect human beings, but there's a *simplicity* about them. It's very refreshing.' He stopped and eyed her anxiously; she'd suspended her attack on the fish and was looking at him with raised brows.

'Okay,' she said. 'They're not all like Clive.'

'He's going to have to be watched,' Den admitted, slightly embarrassed after his emotional outburst. 'Particularly as he and Mandy both ride horses. And he wasn't too keen to volunteer that information – she butted in before he could stop her.'

'Everybody in this case rides horses,' she said. 'My dad always said horses were useless parasites. He'd drive right up close behind them, if he came across them on the roads. Their muck's not much good, either. Makes the ground sour.'

'Your dad—' Den began, and then shook his head. Lilah's father was still a tangible presence nearly a year after his untimely death. She talked freely about him, constantly quoting him, copying many of his ways of doing things. Den could never decide whether the man had been a monster or simply too clever and too energetic for the sleepy Devon countryside he'd found himself in.

'Phil went to see the riding school where the Aspens hired their mounts,' he said. 'They weren't particularly helpful, apparently. Gave cast-iron promises that their beasts wouldn't hurt a fly. Obviously they'd be unlikely to admit it, even if someone brought a horse back with blood on its hooves and murder in its eye. The trouble is, there are just too many of the damned things to even begin to inspect them all. I met three on the road only today. Phil's interviewed some more hunt people, and he's still got a list a mile long. That's the obvious place to look. Some of those animals are *huge*.' He shuddered, remembering yet again the strong, shapely head of the horse that had killed Nina Nesbitt, its height and weight such that a mere nudge from the sharp nose bone had been fatal.

The mackerel were surprisingly good, and the evening passed pleasantly. Lilah stayed the night, but set the alarm for six. 'My turn to do the milking – again,' she sighed, carefully adjusting the buttons on the clock. 'We're going to have to make some changes at this rate. I don't like having to be in two places at once.'

'There is an obvious solution,' he mumbled sleepily. 'But now isn't the time to bring it up.'

She poked him painfully in the chest. 'Say it,' she ordered.

'I could come and live at Redstone.'

She was quiet for too long. He raised his head from the pillow to look at her. She was sitting up, hands crossed over her chest defensively. 'What?' he asked.

'It wouldn't work,' she said softly. 'With Mum there all the time, and Roddy in and out. Sorry, but we'll just have to stick with things as they are. Which means I'd better get to sleep this minute.'

Which she did, leaving Den to lie wakefully beside her thinking darkly about her remarks.

As it happened, Den was quite happy with the six o'clock alarm call; he had dropped off to sleep eventually, only to dream about a killer horse which was besieging his flat. Waking to a cold, drizzling April morning after about four hours' sleep was a decided relief.

They parted warily, conscious of the minefield between them. 'I'll see you tonight,' she promised. 'Same time as usual?'

'I'll be here,' he nodded. 'Unless something develops on the Gratton case. I'll phone you if that happens.'

Wednesday morning's briefing was repetitive and conducted under a cloud of depression. As far as Den could see, they hadn't uncovered a single new fact since the previous morning, and the trail of the killer got colder by the hour. Den once more summarised his enquiries to date, by making three verbal headings. 'One, the Quakers and the animal rights stuff. Let's lump all that together since there are people who fall into both groups.'

'Seems reasonable,' nodded the DI. 'Go on.'

'Group Two is the Cattermole family. Nina's husband was Charlie's friend – or so he says. His mother rides to the hunt and has a fair bit of contact with the two boys. She hasn't been interviewed yet. She lives near one of the bridges over the Tamar, if I've read the map correctly. Looks nice.'

'Nice, Cooper? Are we working for the Devon Tourist Board now? Make sure there's an interview report on her by the end of today.'

'Yes, sir. I was going to, sir. I've been wondering what she thought of Charlie. It can't have been anything complimentary, to say the least.

'Thirdly,' Den continued, with a flourish, 'comes the Gratton family itself. We've got four people – the chief mourners, if you like. His father, Bill; aunt Hannah – who was in effect his mother – cousin Silas, and brother Frank. They've all been interviewed, but I think we should see them again. That's it.' He sat back with a sigh, but then jerked forward again. 'Oh, yes, I nearly forgot. Martha Cattermole tells me that Frank Gratton is Nevil Nesbitt's godfather. He was only fourteen or so when the kid was born, but their mothers were apparently best friends. I can't see that it's remotely significant, apart from proving that the link between the two families goes back a long way.'

DI Smith narrowed his eyes and stared at the floor for a long minute. 'Hmm,' he said. 'That does surprise me. Can't say quite why, except I understood that the Nesbitts were aristocracy, near enough, and the Grattons are . . . well, something else.'

'They're not exactly ordinary, though,' Den said. 'Silas Daggs owns some pretty good stuff – grandfather clock, antique table and chairs. Frank must have had a bit of cash to get those stables going. And women make unlikely friends when they've got little kids.'

Inspector Smith shook his head. 'It still feels odd,' he said heavily. 'And those headings of yours have left one big staring gap.' He looked at Phil, like a schoolteacher waiting for the right answer.

'Horses?' Phil said, as if the answer were blindingly obvious. 'Isn't this whole thing to do with horses?'

Den began to reply. 'Yes, of course, but—'

'But you haven't actually got them listed, have you?' Smith observed. 'Fair do's, it's Phil's side of the business, but you two need to pool findings. Half-complete lists are no good to anyone. Right?'

'Right, sir,' chorused the two detectives in unison.

'That means we go on looking for connections

between Charlie Gratton and the hunt, anyone with a powerful horse, stables, and so forth,' their superior spelt out.

Between them they shared out the day's interviews. 'Makes a change from house-to-house,' Phil commented, as they scrutinised the map. 'I'll be spending half the day nice and warm in the car by the look of it.' His schedule included as many prominent members of the hunt as he could locate. Den was to see the Grattons again, as well as Hermione Nesbitt and Val Taylor; he also had to follow up the addresses given him by Nev.

'Oh, yes – and have a think about money,' Smith added as they were leaving the room. 'Sounds to me as if there's quite a bit of it about. Keep rummaging around for any links – okay? That goes for both of you. I want *links*. The way it feels to me, at this stage, is we're missing something. I'm not getting any feeling for Charlie Gratton as the object of anyone's hatred. You don't ride a horse over someone and chuck him dying in a ditch if you don't loathe him pretty fiercely. Off you go, then, boys. Same time tomorrow, unless you've got something that won't wait. You know where you can find me.'

Den retained the impression that the investigation was running out of steam. They were already repeating themselves, chasing up dead-end leads which had all the promise of an over-chewed stick of gum. *Maybe*, he thought grimly, *nobody killed the bloke at all. Maybe it was just another freak accident.* And how foolish they'd look, wasting all this time pursuing a murderer that never even existed.

Waiting for a mug of coffee to cool, Den sat down at the computer and began to do a search on names. He started with *Gratton*, ignoring the well-studied file on Charlie and finding no further entries under that name. He then tried *Cattermole*, entirely fruitlessly. Almost idly, he entered *Nesbitt*, knowing there would be a recent report on Nina's sudden death and forthcoming inquest. He was surprised, however, to find a second entry under the same surname, with the same address.

Nesbitt, Clement. Born 8.8.1991.
Address: High Copse Farmhouse,
Brimaton, Devon.
Subject of investigation into possible abuse (sexual?). Anonymous informant. September 1998. Referred to Social Services. No prosecutions brought. No further action.

Den sat back in his chair with enough of a thump to bring the front legs off the floor. *Anonymous informant?* He went back over his first visit to High Copse, thinking of the moment when the younger boy came hesitantly into the room and had been treated with such gentleness by Martha. The boy was pale, small for his age, quiet. But then, his mother had just died – Den had naturally assumed that he was suffering from shock and sadness and bewilderment. If, however, this was how he *always* looked, then it wasn't difficult to understand how someone – a teacher, or the parents of another child – might worry that something was wrong. Especially these days, when abuse was suspected if a kid had a grazed knee.

But no action had been taken. It had apparently been a false alarm – a groundless accusation. It surely wasn't anything to do with the death of Charlie Gratton. Or was it?

Den's training had only just been completed. His head was still full of dictums: *Pay particular attention to apparent coincidences* and *Watch out for the same names appearing in different contexts.* He tried to imagine how it had been for the family, under the scrutiny of Social Services. Had they taken Clem away for medical examination? Had they questioned Richmond and Nev – and Charlie? Had the adults closed ranks and defended each other – or had there been a scapegoat?

The experience could not fail to have left a

mark on Clem, if not on the whole family. And perhaps it had left resentment, too. And who was the *anonymous informant*? Who would be so malicious – or so sensitive to the possibility – as to make such a charge?

CHAPTER SIXTEEN

'You are going to stay with us, aren't you, Nev?' Hugh said, for the tenth time in three days, as they walked together from the barn to the house early on Wednesday morning. 'Just for the summer. We can go to Granny's if you don't like it here. Or maybe we could come with you to somewhere foreign. We've only got one more term, and then it's the long holiday. Will you stay till then? We've got the school trip in July and they want someone's dad to come. Would you do that? You're good at travel things. You'd like that, wouldn't you?'

Nev put a slim hand on the boy's shoulder. 'I ain't got no plans to go no place,' he drawled. 'Might think about that there camping trip.'

Hugh smiled politely at the attempt at humour and suppressed the urge to show excitement at the semi-promise. His experience of Nev from the very beginning had taught him to place little credence on anything his father said. Everyone, himself included, wished he would stop laying himself open to disappointment, but the wellspring of hope was yet to run dry.

'I heard that,' came Martha's voice from an open window. 'Sounds a great idea to me.'

'What does?' Nev asked, peering into the room. 'These windows are filthy, d'you know that?'

'Camping,' she said, firmly ignoring the comment. 'Hugh's in Year Nine now, and they always have a week on Exmoor every summer. It's very popular and everybody loves it.'

'So why is there a vacancy for "someone's dad"?'

'Because most of the dads are otherwise engaged.' The *obviously* was clearly implied.

Hugh drifted away, unsure whether or not to be grateful for Martha's intervention. Nev was just as likely to be deterred by what he interpreted as nagging as convinced by a commercial for the Year Nine Trip. All the old ambivalences attached to his feelings for Nev were coming back, just as they always did. It was as if the most fantastic meal imaginable, made with all your favourite ingredients, had been dished up sprinkled with some sort of bitter herb. You had to scrape it off, work around it, try to ignore it – but the fun was spoilt, just the same.

The Easter holiday was just about to start: two and a half weeks in which to make sure he'd get what he wanted. So long as he could keep Nev in sight, it would probably be okay. It was going to school that had always been such agony. Every day he imagined his father stealing away with no warning, off on yet another of his mysterious and apparently pointless trips. The other kids did their best to understand. They liked Hugh, despite his reluctance to join in; perhaps they found him intriguing. Several of them had absent fathers, so the habit of inventing reasons for their non-appearance was deep-rooted and entirely accepted. The shared anxiety this gave rise to was a bond, particularly amongst the boys.

But Hugh was unusual in his insistence that *his* father was not absent – not really. His parents weren't divorced. Nev came back at intervals and behaved like a proper father. It was his *job* to be away, like a soldier or a geologist. 'So what is his job then?' came the obvious query. And Hugh could never find a satisfactory answer to that.

Martha was a complicating factor in his school life which he often felt he could do without. It wasn't as bad as having a *parent* for a teacher, like poor Richard Rivers, whose mother taught geography and was one of the least popular teachers in the school. But an English teacher aunt with frizzy orange hair and clothes like someone out of the Addams Family was nonetheless an embarrassment. Fortunately, everyone liked her and nobody ever suggested she was anything but a brilliant teacher. And on Wednesdays and Fridays she drove him to school instead of leaving him to get the bus. On those days she had to get there early enough for Hugh to catch registration; otherwise, she timed it to arrive two minutes before First Lesson, which wasn't soon enough for Hugh. 'Besides,' she said, 'it's good for you to be with the others on the bus.' He was still trying to work that one out.

Today was Wednesday, the last day of term, and they were due to leave in five minutes' time. Nev, for once, had got up before nine and had gone out to the barn with Richmond, saying he'd like to see the changes he'd made. Hugh had taken the opportunity of going with them.

'Don't go wandering off!' Martha had called after him through the window. 'And where's your schoolbag?'

'In the car,' he called back. They only stayed a few minutes in the barn before coming back to the house – Hugh didn't believe Nev knew or cared anything about Richmond's business.

It had been a silly whim. Nev hadn't asked any questions and Richmond hadn't bothered making any explanations. Nobody imagined Nev would ever offer to take a share in the work.

Now, two minutes before he and Martha were due to leave, Hugh fixed Nev with a long, hungry stare.

'Don't worry, mate,' Nev laughed uncomfortably at him. 'I'll still be here when you get back.' The fact that Nev knew what he was afraid of did nothing at all to quell his anxiety.

Martha chatted steadily in the car, as she always did. But this morning she had a disconcerting new plan. 'I was talking to Richmond last night,' she said, 'and we thought it would be good if you boys had some sort of proper holiday, at half term at the end of May. Richmond thought he might take you somewhere abroad, Italy maybe. What do you think? It could be a late birthday present for you.'

Hugh frowned. 'Why Richmond? Why not Nev?'

'Good question,' she nodded. 'Why not indeed? But you know Nev. He'd never be pinned down to a precise date, and he's not one for the sort of thing we had in mind. Another time, maybe – when Clem's a bit older – he can take you to some remote rainforest. But for now, we thought something a bit more normal. A nice package holiday with a swimming pool and a beach nearby.'

'But . . .' Hugh's stomach clenched with all the things he wanted to say. 'But we're *Nev's* sons, not Richmond's.' He wriggled uneasily as he heard the way that sounded.

'I know you are. We're not trying to *steal* you. But we owe something to Nina. Besides, I think you need to get away for a break after all that's happened. Clem as much as you. More, probably. He's been so quiet and pale, poor little chap.'

'Okay,' he muttered, more to shut her up than in agreement with the proposal. Italy with Richmond may or may not be a good idea. Just at that moment it simply didn't feel relevant.

A mile or two before reaching the school they overtook a rusted and smoking Mini. Hugh looked back over his shoulder. 'That was Mrs Aspen,' he said. 'Her car doesn't look good.'

'The woman who helps in the IT department?' Martha queried vaguely.

'That's right. She knows Alexis and Charlie. She . . . she cried about Charlie yesterday.' His voice tailed away and he looked back again, seeming anxious, although the Mini was no longer visible.

Martha screwed up her face in puzzlement. 'When? I mean . . . explain.'

'She was helping me with the computer and

suddenly seemed to recognise me. I think it was because I'd put my address on the screen – we were writing letters. And she said wasn't that where Charlie Gratton had died, and I said yeah and she started crying. Just quietly. Nobody else saw.'

'Did you try to comfort her?'

'Sort of. I said I didn't think he suffered much. That's what people usually say, isn't it?' He glanced at her and caught her eye as she gave him a swift look before returning her attention to the road.

'Yes, that's what people usually say,' she agreed. 'Whether it's true or not.'

At High Copse Farmhouse that morning, Alexis, Richmond and Nev all found separate ways of keeping busy. Richmond dealt with a succession of customers for animal feed, trying to ignore their curious glances at the new grave under the oak tree and the field where they assumed Charlie's body to have been found. Only one person openly referred to the dramatic events, and that in a manner irritatingly oblique.

'Be expecting a third, if the old stories are to be believed,' said Bartholomew White, as he hefted a sizeable sack of Pascoe's Complete Dog Food onto one shoulder. Richmond held the door open for him and made no reply.

'Us'll miss Charlie at Meeting,' Barty went on. 'Doubt the youngsters'll keep on coming, without 'e.'

Richmond sighed. 'I certainly doubt you'll be seeing Alexis there again,' he agreed. 'Though you never can tell. Your dogs doing all right on that stuff, are they?'

'Right enough. Don't know it's worth the price, though. If it were down to me, they'd have offal and tripes, same as always, but that Fairfield's a fussy chap. Got to be just right for'n. Dogs eat better than people these days.'

Richmond shrugged. He hadn't warmed to Bartholomew from what he knew of him. A self-contained man, seeming older than his years, he kept a pack of Jack Russell terriers on behalf of the local hunt, their yapping resounding famously across the neighbourhood. Richmond's acquaintance with Charlie had led him to assume that Quakers found hunting anathema; one day, he promised himself, he'd ask Barty how he reconciled the two.

'You been interviewed pretty thorough, I dare say?' Barty asked, as he got into his battered pickup truck. 'Had a young chap call on me a day or so ago, asking about Charlie. Didn't seem to have much idea about anything. Can't see it being a proper murder, anyhow. Seems to me that someone's horse got out of hand and Charlie was in the way. Be typical, that would. Even if it were done on purpose, the trail'll be cold before they got themselves together.'

'You've got a horse yourself, haven't you?' Richmond asked.

'My son's. I never ride him. Too big for me now. Never did feel too easy on anything bigger than fifteen hands. He didn't go unnoticed, though, if that's what you're axing me.'

Richmond merely nodded vaguely and stood back, hoping the man would drive away. Barty turned on the engine, but threw one final remark at Richmond before moving off.

'You be careful, friend,' he said. 'It never stops at two.'

Alexis was planning a conference to be held in Plymouth next October. She specialised in small-scale events, where she had sole control of the arrangements; payment was modest, but satisfaction high and the majority of the work could be done from home. She never quite understood why it was that people hired her at all, when the whole thing was usually so simple that anybody with a telephone and a filing system could do it all for themselves. She assumed it was because they liked to have someone to blame when things went wrong.

Fortunately, things very rarely did go wrong.

She handled the advertising, booking, payments, meals and hospitality for the speakers with care and full attention to detail. She produced programmes, organised stalls in the foyer, and ensured that delegates were well plied with tea and coffee in the intervals. She was bossy where necessary and always insistent on deadlines. Her workload varied between two and four events per month, which gave her a great deal of free time. She believed she had the perfect job, and most people agreed with her. At least, she *had* believed that, twelve days ago, when she had two sisters and a boyfriend. It felt different now. The phrase she'd used in the press announcement of Nina's death returned relentlessly, echoing in her mind. *Diminished lives,* she'd said and it seemed to get more true with every day that passed.

Without Charlie the evenings were long and achingly dull. Without Nina the days were flat and two-dimensional. There was nobody left for Alexis to talk to: Martha was out all day and distracted in the evenings; Richmond and Alexis had little to say to each other; and Nev was beneath contempt. A week after burying Nina and finding Charlie's body, there seemed to be little reason to go on. Almost overnight, her life had lost all its colour, its direction. Alexis was frightened, although she tried not to admit it. The only future she could see for herself now was a desert of tedious, repetitive work and a slow, crumbling monotony of daily life at High Copse.

And yet she hadn't been aware of any great expectations built around Charlie. She had known, somewhere inside her, that it wasn't going to last for ever. She and Charlie had been good together, but not paired-up-for-life good; he was both too similar to her, and too different. Being Nev's friend had made him almost part of the family; being a Quaker had made him an alien. The animal rights obsession had made him downright dangerous. It was true they'd talked about setting up home together, and she supposed she might have done it, but High Copse was a hard place to abandon and Alexis wasn't convinced she could have made the necessary effort.

As she scanned through her files for the conference, she was aware of Nev roaming restlessly through the house, in and out of Nina's room, up and down the stairs. She tried to ignore him. Her own room was large and light, at the front of the house on the first floor. Of the five bedrooms, it was the second best and she had turned it into more of an office than a place to sleep. The bed, which had been rather narrow for her and Charlie to share comfortably, had been pushed into a corner. Since Charlie died, she had slept very badly, vividly recalling the nights he had spent with her there.

She supposed that Nina's room would quickly become Nev's own space, if he stayed. Although he had very few possessions with which to fill it. The house was accustomed to changes, people coming and going, boundaries shifting. It was full of the ghosts of previous inhabitants, the air thick at times with their dust and detritus. Charlie would leave a lesser trace than the others: his distinctive way of running up and down the stairs, a heavy thud alternating with a lighter step; his tuneless whistle as he shaved; the newsletters and notices that he left everywhere, advertising another protest rally or setting out reasons why fox hunting was morally untenable. He had been more like one of the children than a new adult around the place, which might explain why Hugh and Clem had been so cool towards him. However hard he'd tried to win their affection, they had maintained a certain distance.

'They're slow to trust men,' Martha had explained. 'With a father like Nev, it isn't surprising.'

'But they like Richmond,' Alexis had argued.

'They do *now*,' Martha agreed. 'I seem to remember it took them about two years before they'd even raise a smile at his jokes.'

Charlie hadn't seemed bothered about the

boys' behaviour. He never made any special efforts to win their approval and Alexis had been frustrated by this, compensating for it as much as she could by suggesting he take Hugh and Clem with him when he went to look for fox earths or badger setts. Nobody had been very enthused by her suggestions, although once or twice she'd successfully insisted they all three go off together.

Part of her unhappiness now was due to the knowledge that she had been less than honest with Charlie and with herself, in the final weeks of his life. She had let him believe she was fully committed to their relationship, that she might even consider marrying him at some future date. He had begun talking about their future to other people, with a silly grin of complacency that had made her cringe. She'd even heard him say to the boys one day that he, Charlie, would 'fill in' for the absent Nev, once he was living there full-time. Nina had also heard him. 'Steady on, Charlie,' she'd called out crossly. 'They don't need any of that while they've got me. Nobody's "filling in" for anybody, okay?'

Alexis hadn't wanted to get involved. It was one thing to try and ensure that Hugh and Clem liked Charlie, and quite another for him to offer his services as a substitute father. If she did go through with it and marry the man, she supposed she'd have to go the whole hog and produce two or three babies in due course, for him to father for real. Not that she'd ever encouraged him to broach that particular subject with her. She had been miles away from that sort of decision – and now she'd never have to make it at all.

A noise outside drew her to the window: a clash of metal on metal, followed by some shouting. Easily alarmed now, she found she was shaking before she even focused on what had happened.

A pickup truck had come to a halt part way down their drive, alongside a large Range Rover. The drive was not wide enough for two such big vehicles – a fact both drivers appeared to have ignored. The two vehicles were in uncomfortably close contact. The man who'd been driving the pickup was standing in front of the Range Rover and Richmond was trotting down to join him. Alexis knew only too well the identity of the woman sitting in dignified immobility in the vehicle, in complete certainty that none of this was her fault.

Alexis sighed and clasped her hands together. The last thing she wanted to face was a visit from her sister's mother-in-law. But what Alexis might or might not want was, as always, of total unconcern to Hermione Nesbitt.

CHAPTER SEVENTEEN

Den's discovery of the file on Clem Nesbitt had brought an urgent need to return to High Copse. 'You'd better both go,' DI Smith decreed, when Den had managed to locate him and explain his findings. Neither Den nor Phil had even considered arguing with him.

In the car they discussed strategy. 'The father first,' said Phil. 'Then Uncle Richmond. That takes care of the men, though I guess the most likely scenario is that it was Charlie.'

'If you ask me, the most likely scenario is that nothing happened at all. It was a storm in a teacup, a false alarm. Social Services couldn't find anything.'

'Couldn't *prove* anything,' Phil corrected him. 'It's not the same thing.'

'Same outcome. If they couldn't when it was first reported, what chance have we got now?'

'You might be surprised,' said Phil.

'So are we thinking that the family somehow got together, six months later, and killed Charlie collectively?' Den leant his head on the rest behind him and stared at the roof of the car. 'The timing stinks, if so. They'd have been far too preoccupied by what had just happened to Nina, wouldn't they? And Alexis was his *girlfriend*.'

Phil snorted. 'Grow up, Den. Picture this – Alexis catches him fingering the little lad one day. Or worse. Wouldn't you say she'd be the *most* likely to want to tear his head off – or something rather nastier? Because she'd been deceived? And if she enlisted Martha and Richmond – and maybe the old grandma too, for good measure – they'd be very nearly as outraged as she was. It's a theory, anyhow.'

'It could fit,' Den agreed slowly. 'Especially if it was planned in advance. I've been worrying about who would know Charlie was going to be in the field at that particular time. Even so, I still think someone might have come across him by accident and decided to seize the opportunity to wipe out a nuisance.'

'You *prefer* to think that because you've got friendly with the family,' Phil accused. 'Have to be objective, mate. It's the only way.'

'I know. But I can't see it. This whole abuse stuff's too much of a cliché. Too obvious. And which one of them would you put down as the horse rider? As the one who actually finished him off? They *knew* him. He was part of the family. As a means of execution, it's ludicrous. They'd have had much better opportunities. A massive dose of sleeping pills in his tea, for example. And why wait six months?'

'Well, just hang on to the possibility for now,' Phil insisted. 'We can put it to them and see how they react.'

Den pulled a face. 'Ludicrous,' he muttered.

'We're there, look. Brace yourself.'

Den felt even more uneasy as he stood on the doorstep of the farmhouse waiting for someone to answer their knock. This was his fifth visit in a week and they were hardly any closer to a resolution. Every time the murder ran through his head, all theories seemed fatally flawed. Even if one of the Cattermoles had got hold of a horse and mown Charlie down with it, he assumed they'd have their story word-perfect by this time. The theory that Charlie had been killed for abusing young Clement made no sense to him, given what he knew of the family. They were unusual, even eccentric, but he didn't think they could be guilty of anything as malign and underhand as that.

Nevil, Richmond and Alexis were all at home. Martha would get back from school at about four that afternoon and the boys would come on the school bus soon after that. Phil and Den decided to start with Nev.

Den could see the man was unnerved by a second police interview in two days, despite the earlier warning that there were still details to be pursued. They asked him for the precise date he had left for Vietnam the previous year; he answered with some difficulty. Fetching a battered rucksack from his room, he upended it and finally unearthed a boarding pass for a flight to Hanoi on 20th September. The anonymous call about Clem had been made two days later. When told about it, Nev was impressively shocked.

'Abuse?' he gasped. 'Do you mean *sexual* abuse?'

'There was a suspicion of that, yes,' said Phil firmly.

'Rubbish,' affirmed Nev. 'Total and absolute rubbish.'

'How can you be so sure? You haven't had very much continuous contact with your sons, have you? Do you think you'd notice if something like that had been troubling them?' Phil was finding his feet rapidly. As Den took notes he watched the interviewee's face closely; Nev had gone pale and his hands were rigid claws on the table in front of him. The accusation of abuse certainly seemed to have taken him by surprise.

'Wait a minute,' Nev objected. 'Who exactly are you accusing of this . . . this—'

'Outrage?' Phil suggested blandly. 'We're making no accusations, sir. We're just putting you in the picture. In the light of Charlie Gratton's death, you wouldn't be surprised to hear—'

'Oh, I get it.' Nev shook his head in relieved amusement. 'You think it was Charlie, and when they found out, the family closed ranks and bumped him off.'

'They?' shot Den, remembering his previous interview with Nevil. 'Why do you think we wouldn't be including you?'

'Ah. Well, I grant you I could just conceivably have made it down here in time to do the deed, but how do you suggest I took part in the conspiracy with the others? Long-distance phone calls? Emails?'

'Neither is impossible,' said Phil. 'Far from it.'

'But it didn't happen. All I can do is ask you to believe that. And—' he looked suddenly alert, 'what about poor old Clem? What's going to happen to him with all this innuendo flying about?'

'Why should anything happen?'

Nev glowered. 'As I understand it, kids get

taken into care if there's even a suspicion of anything like this going on at home.'

'I don't think we need worry about that,' Den said, feeling a pang of sympathetic alarm. 'Not at the moment, anyway. Social Services are no longer pursuing the matter.'

Phil sighed and said there were no more questions. Den quickly contradicted him. 'Just one,' he said. Phil and Nev both raised their eyebrows expectantly.

'When exactly do you plan to return to Vietnam?'

'Oh . . . no plans at all for that,' Nev replied easily, relief clear in his voice.

'Then why buy a return ticket?' Den pounced.

Nev blinked at the swiftness of the question, but soon recovered his composure. 'Because,' he said patiently, 'I had no idea what I would find here, for one thing. Plus it costs pretty much the same as a one-way. Plus . . . well, I'm the sort of guy who likes to keep his escape routes open. The ticket might be handy to have.' He turned his head from one to the other, relaxed and boyish now the session was almost over.

Richmond was even more thunderstruck at the detectives' revelation. 'Why didn't anybody tell us at the time?' he demanded. 'Were we being investigated without ever knowing it? Where did such a filthy idea come from – that's what I want to know.'

When Phil suggested a family execution of Charlie might have taken place, Richmond's disbelieving laughter seemed genuine. He reminded them that he had found the body himself. 'And don't think something like that could have been carried out without my knowing about it,' he said flatly. 'The idea's absolute nonsense. A waste of time even talking about it. Besides, if Social Services had taken it seriously, they'd have informed us. We know nothing whatsoever about this allegation. That proves it was completely groundless.'

Alexis was far more furious. Once she'd grasped the full import of what was being mooted, her mouth dropped open. '*Charlie?*' she repeated incredulously, her colour deepening. 'You must be mad. Christ Almighty, the idea's *insane*. Clem's never been abused, sexually or in any other way. We *love* him. He's surrounded by people who want more than anything for him to be happy and secure. If you want my opinion, you should be looking for the dirty-minded nutcase who made the accusation in the first place. I don't suppose you'll tell me who it was.'

Den and Phil exchanged glances and Phil gave a small nod. 'It was anonymous,' said Den softly.

'There you are, then!' she triumphed. 'Someone with a grudge against us. When did you say this was?'

'Last September,' Den told her.

'Well, nobody ever came to see us about it,' she said firmly. 'They must have known it was crazy from the start.'

'Possibly,' said Phil. 'There might have been some sort of investigation through the school. Perhaps his mother was contacted. We're still checking that.'

Alexis shook her head fiercely. 'No way. She'd have told us.'

Literally drawing a line in his notes under that particular subject, Den looked her full in the face. 'Can we backtrack a bit?' he asked. 'Just a few loose ends from my interview last week.'

'Go on,' she invited sulkily.

'Who would you say was closest to Charlie, after yourself? Who was he most fond of?'

'You're asking his girlfriend that? Well, to the best of my knowledge, I'd say Nina, his aunt Hannah and Nev. He worked very closely with Nina on the protests – they supported each other. He was very upset when she died.'

'He was devastated,' said Den quietly. 'I saw him.'

'Who wouldn't be? Nobody should die like that.'

'And perhaps he blamed himself,' Phil ventured.

Alexis shook her head, the mass of thick hair a dense cloud around her narrow face. 'I don't think so. No way was it his fault.'

'So how would you describe him in the days after Nina died?'

'Oh, I don't know.' She scowled impatiently. 'I didn't see much of him, and we were all so busy the whole time. He was around on Sunday morning, and then – as we've all told you a dozen times – none of us can remember seeing him after that.'

'And would you disagree with the word "devastated" as a description of how he took her death?' Phil nodded towards Den as the eyewitness.

Again she shook her head. 'He might have been. He took things to heart. That was the main thing about Charlie – he was very thin-skinned.'

The police detectives withdrew after that. 'What do you think?' Den asked his colleague, once they were again in the car and out of earshot.

'They weren't happy, were they?'

'They were horrified.'

'But then, people generally are,' Phil added. 'They don't like the idea of something like that affecting their own family.'

'So where to now?' asked Den.

'The nearest pub,' Phil told him. 'We can talk about it then.'

They found a pub advertising BAR SNACKS and sat in a deserted saloon to assess their progress. 'We're going to have to see Hermione Nesbitt,' Den said urgently. 'She ought to have been interviewed days ago. Her name comes up too often.'

Phil shrugged. 'Yeah, but what's she going to tell you? She loves her grandsons, enjoys the hunt and probably thinks her son's a wastrel. Which he is,' he added forcefully. 'Typical spoilt little rich boy.'

'She missed Nina's funeral,' said Den. 'Accidentally on purpose. And she was a close friend of Charlie's mother. She knows – or knew – Frank Gratton. I don't know about you, but I've got plenty to ask her.'

'Not a Quaker as well, is she? Just to neaten everything off.'

Den shook his head. 'But she keeps and rides horses. On that fact alone, she should be seen.'

'*Okay*, Den. I get the point. You go off and see her now, if you want to. She sounds pretty intimidating to me. I just hope she doesn't eat you.'

'I can't,' Den pointed out. 'We've only got one car and we need to report back on this morning.' He concentrated on his drink for a minute, then started a new tack. 'You ever been on a hunt, Phil?'

Phil shook his head with a grin. 'Takes guts, though. Remember that chap last year, broke his back jumping a hedge? And those dogs are quite something, working in a pack. It'd be a shame if it was all banned, don't you think?'

Den pushed out his lips. 'Can't say I'd care one way or the other.'

'Well, it could still turn out that the Nesbitt woman's accident does the trick. They haven't confirmed a date for another Meet, you know. Probably scared of aggressive antis.'

'That's a funny thing,' said Den absently. 'Meet and Meeting.'

'What?'

'The words they use. For hunting it's a Meet – for Quakers it's a Meeting. Capital M both times. Maybe they're not as different as they think they are.'

That afternoon DI Smith set them to combing through all the notes and tapes they'd made to date, watching for timings, checking and double-checking where each person claimed to have been for as much as possible of Sunday and Monday. Having listened to the feedback from that morning, he shook his head knowingly. 'I didn't think there'd be much mileage in it,' he said, much to Den's annoyance. 'Had to check it out though,' he added kindly.

'Shouldn't someone go and see Mrs Nesbitt?' Den persisted. 'It's a week since Charlie was found, and we still haven't interviewed her. It's been on my to-do list for days now.'

'If there's time,' Smith agreed. 'Otherwise it'll wait until tomorrow. I doubt she's going anywhere. You've got something about her in the notes, anyway, if I remember rightly. Didn't she drop in on the family, on Monday last week?'

Den was impressed. The fact of a brief visit by Hermione on the Monday morning before Nina's funeral had been a short two-line note buried amongst a scatter of scribbles. 'She did,' he confirmed. 'Hugh had stayed the night with her and she was bringing him back.'

'You need to see those boys again,' Smith said, much to Den's surprise. 'Kids notice things. They pick up on atmospheres. And it wouldn't hurt to try to have another look at the young one after this abuse accusation.'

'I ought to have a WPC with me, then.'

'I'm aware of that,' Smith snapped. 'Jane Nugent can go with you. She's good at that sort of thing.' He looked at his watch. 'My, my, how the day flies! If you go at about three-thirty, the boys'll just be getting home from school. Last day of term, if I'm not mistaken. They'll be excited

– Easter eggs and all that. Keep it low-key. The family aren't going to be too co-operative, seeing you back again so soon, but it would be good if you could get the kids on their own. Just for an informal chat. They might know the rules that say that's not allowed – so try and get their Auntie Martha, if you have to have somebody there.'

Den was impressed afresh. To his knowledge, DI Smith had never met the Cattermoles and had nothing more than Den's own reports to go on, and yet it felt as if he knew them inside out. 'Martha would be best,' he agreed.

Yet another trip to High Copse might have been tedious, but the presence of Jane Nugent beside him gave it a new angle. She chatted sporadically, talking as much about her plans for a fortnight in Egypt as the murder of Charlie Gratton. She also admitted to considerable ambition in the uniformed police. 'Don't fancy CID much,' she laughed. 'I wouldn't feel like a proper copper without the outfit.'

An atmosphere of weary depression greeted them at the house. Martha had only just got home and was in bare feet, holding a substantial sandwich. 'Last day of term,' she said, as if in explanation. 'Look, I should be there when you talk to the boys, but I'm too whacked. Leave the door open and I'll just sort of listen in. Is that okay? Don't upset them, will you? I hope I can trust you on that. They've only been home about five minutes.'

They were ushered into the gloomy living room and the door was left open. Hugh and Clem sat together on the sofa. Jane and Den took two armchairs. It was scarcely informal, but Den supposed it was the closest they were going to get.

'Would you tell us, in your own words, what happened between the day your mum died and the day of her funeral?' he asked gently. Between them, the children described the arrival of the coffin, unfolding it, applying the first coat of white paint; Charlie disappearing at some unnoticed point.

'We never said bye-bye to him,' noted Clem wistfully.

'Don't be so—' Hugh began, before checking himself. He gave his brother's arm a punch; not vicious, but not good-natured either. Den scrutinised each boy in turn, remembering fleetingly that parallel universe you inhabit as a kid, where adults totally fail to see what's going on. Even those who made an effort to understand usually got it completely wrong. He remembered when his own mother married for a second time, importing young Gary as a step-brother and worrying about all the wrong things. She'd made promises about fairness, about nothing in Den's life changing, when what he'd really wanted was to take the little chap about with him and teach him the rules of Warhammer and Masters of the Universe. The adults had been so worried about jealousy that they had effectively confined the boys to separate cages and wasted what could have been a very affectionate relationship. Seven years his junior, Gary could almost have been a practise son. But Den hadn't given up – they saw each other regularly now.

None of which was much use in working out what was going on between Hugh and Clem. 'So who's in charge here now?' he asked. 'Or does the place run itself? I remember it was Clem who fetched the eggs last time I was here. You're lucky there aren't any cows to milk, or fields to plough. My girlfriend lives on a farm where there's never any let-up. Jobs to be done, the whole time.'

Hugh frowned and circled a forefinger on the worn arm of the sofa. His head was held at an awkward angle against the cushion behind him, making an uncomfortable picture. 'It's not so different from before,' he muttered. 'Richmond does most of the work, and Martha's out every day at school, same as us. We like it like this.' He looked up defiantly. 'Don't we?' he appealed fiercely to his brother. Clem just nodded half-heartedly.

Den remembered the accusation of abuse and gave the younger boy a closer inspection. He was certainly alarmingly pale; his skin looked thin, almost transparent, and there were blue shadows under his eyes. He gave every sign of being completely dominated by his older brother. Den wondered whether there might be some value in getting Clem on his own for a chat: a simple conversation might at least settle one or two doubts. He glanced at Jane and wondered if she would co-operate in such a dubious strategy.

'Well, I don't think there's anything more to ask you,' he said. 'It seems to me you're going to be okay, when all the fuss dies down a bit. Life goes on, eh?'

Hugh's frown reappeared. 'Not for my mum, it doesn't,' he said. 'She's out there in that grave. Dead!' He slammed a fist on the sofa, and repeated the word. *'Dead!'* Clem gave a supportive murmur. Den noticed tears hovering on his lower eyelids.

He stood up slowly. 'Well, I think we'd better get going. Although it's so nice up here, it'd be good to stay. Especially with the sun shining like it is. Those primroses of yours are really something. And did I see beehives up in the orchard?'

'Those are Martha's,' said Clem. 'She's good with bees.'

Den looked at Jane again, meaningfully. 'Would you show me?' Den asked Clem. 'Just for a minute?'

'Yeah – go on,' said Jane carelessly. 'I'll keep Hugh company.'

The man and boy walked up to the orchard, behind the house, following a steep path. 'You must keep fit, coming up here every day,' Den remarked. 'Seems as if you've got your share of the jobs, even though you are the youngest.'

The child shrugged and said nothing.

'Did Charlie do anything around the place? He was more or less living here, wasn't he?'

'Charlie was useless,' said Clem, matter-of-factly. 'Richmond said he wasn't all there in the head. Couldn't even tie his own shoelaces.' Den could hear the quotation marks – the line evidently originating directly from Richmond.

'But you liked him, didn't you? Hugh said he was cool.'

Clement sighed impatiently. 'We wanted Nev, not Charlie,' he said simply. 'Look, these are the hives. That one's new. It's a bait hive – waiting for a swarm in the summer. Martha's always lucky getting new swarms, even though there aren't any other beekeepers for miles. Last year we had nearly five hundred pounds of honey. Richmond sells it for us.' He waved at the row of hives, under a hedge. Den counted six, each painted with bold colours and swirling patterns. He was reminded suddenly of Nina's coffin, as he'd heard it described.

'Nev and Charlie were best friends, is that right?' he went on. 'Nev must be really upset now.'

'He's got us. And he's got Granny. He'll be all right. He'll have to stay here now, you see.' Suddenly the child's face was earnest, even enthusiastic. 'Hugh says so. Nev'll have to stay and be our guardian. Nev's *really* cool.'

The word *guardian* echoed for a moment, oddly old-fashioned.

'Is he a guardian because he guards you from something?' he ventured, trying to make it sound jokey.

'Oh, no. We don't need guarding. Not now, anyway. Everything's okay now. Except we're sad, of course. About Mum. I like the grave being there, you know,' he confided. 'I can go and talk to her any time I want. I can tell her things – Martha says she might be able to hear me. Nobody knows for sure, do they? And it's sort of good, really, about Charlie.' He looked suddenly anxious. 'I don't mean *good* – but, well, we didn't need him hanging around, making trouble. Richmond said he was a pest.'

Den marvelled at how ineffective his lengthy interviews had been. How wrong his assumptions were turning out to be . . .

'So you think you'll be okay now, do you? No need to send the social workers in?' The risk was calculated, and his heart pounded briskly at the implications. With justification, as it turned out. Clem's lower lip was instantly seized between sharp little teeth and his hands turned to fists. He shook his head violently, and said nothing. Den had all the answer he needed.

'Okay, forget I said that. The hives are great. Shall I help you with the eggs?' Stiffly, Clem moved to the hen coop and lifted a large flap at the back. A clutch of five eggs waited for him. Den carefully slipped two into each jacket pocket, and let Clem carry the fifth.

CHAPTER EIGHTEEN

Alone in his flat for an hour before paying an evening visit to Val Taylor, Den made himself a sandwich and arranged himself on the sofa, legs stretched out so his feet hung over one arm. A sofa big enough to accommodate Den's length would have taken up too much space, but he'd long ago developed a technique for getting comfortable. He reached out to put a CD in the player, and tried in vain to think of nothing. It was no good, there were too many things he ought to be getting on with; too many things that might be happening without him. *When this is all over*, he promised himself, *I'm going to have a week just doing nothing at all.*

* * *

The first task was to keep his fiancée sweet. Miranda answered the phone at Redstone and he asked her to tell Lilah he was expecting to be out later than usual. This being so, she might not feel it worthwhile coming over to the flat that evening. 'She can get an early night and I'll try and see her tomorrow.'

'*Try?*' Miranda repeated.

'It's this murder,' Den said slowly. Miranda had that effect on him. 'Charlie Gratton. A lot of people are only at home in the evenings and we're getting behind with the interviews.'

'Can't you insist on seeing them at work?'

'They're not suspects. It's not always a good idea to embarrass people unless you have to. You lose their goodwill that way.'

'Yes, I suppose you do,' she said drily. 'I'll tell Lilah when she comes in. She'll probably welcome the early night, as you say. She's looking tired today.'

Den felt a stab of alarm. If Miranda had noticed, then Lilah must be looking *really* rough.

It was almost six. He'd give Val another hour and then call in on her. Outside the light was fading, the sky an appealing display of pink-tinged clouds. Suddenly his flat felt too constricted, his head too crowded with jumbled theories and unfinished investigations. It hadn't been helped by the few minutes' conversation he'd had with DI Smith on his return from the session with Hugh and Clement Nesbitt.

'Sir!' he'd called, catching up with an impatient superior. 'I've seen the High Copse kids – can we have another think about this alleged abuse? The kid is obviously allergic to social workers and he seems rather glad that Charlie's permanently out of the way. Shouldn't we order up the full report from Social Services?'

'Already done,' said the Inspector. 'But it doesn't get us very far. No names named and the whole thing dismissed as a piece of mischief. Not before they'd investigated, of course, and had a quiet word with the mother. She just laughed and the social proceeded to comprehensively traumatise the poor little bugger.'

'Christ!' spat Den. 'Why can't they be more sensitive?'

'Not really their fault,' Smith chided mildly. 'Blame the person who gave the tip-off in the first place. You know as well as I do the social workers had no choice after that.'

'What if the informant was deliberately pointing the finger at Charlie? Then the same person flipped last week and mowed him down with a horse.'

'Charlie hadn't been going out with Alexis more than a couple of months when the accusation was made. He'd been nowhere near

High Copse before then, as far as we know. I really don't think the abuse thing has anything to do with him.'

'He was Nev's friend for years, so he probably had been there,' Den argued, feeling an odd pang of disappointment at this mistake on the DI's part. 'And . . . what if Charlie himself was the informant? He might have noticed something going on and done it from the best of motives. There's probably some moral requirement to blow the whistle if you're a Quaker.'

Smith shook his head. 'Only if you're a hundred per cent sure of your facts. Otherwise it's malevolence.'

Den felt defeated. 'I'm interviewing Valerie Taylor now,' he said. 'She's only at home in the evening, which is rather a nuisance.'

'I'm sure it is, Cooper, but this is a murder investigation. We don't stick to nine to five at a time like this. I thought you understood that. You keep going until you've got a full report on every one of those Quakers who knew Charlie. By rights, it would have been finished days ago. Understood?'

'Yes, sir.'

He wasn't sure whether to regard it as lucky or unfortunate when he discovered that Polly

Spence was at the home of Val Taylor when he arrived for the interview. It was very likely that neither woman would be as frank and open with an audience as she would have been on her own. And in the event that either or both of them had been directly concerned with Charlie's death, they could flash unspoken signals to each other as he posed his questions and he'd have little chance of intercepting or interpreting them.

Never mind, he decided – it was something to have caught up with Val and thus to complete, for DI Smith's gratification, his report on the entire membership of the Chillhampton Preparative Meeting, as the local Quakers called themselves.

The two women made a fine couple. Val's house was furnished with great care and some expense. Nothing on the shelves except books and one or two framed pictures. No untidy piles of newspapers or unpaid bills. A modern oak desk stood beneath the generous bay window and on it was a stack of leaflets and envelopes. This apparently was the reason for Polly's presence. She sat silently, folding the leaflets and putting them into envelopes, as the interview proceeded.

'To start with,' said Den, 'would you be kind enough to tell me where you were on Sunday and Monday of last week?'

'Sunday morning I went to Meeting, then came

back here for the rest of the day. On Monday I was at work,' she said promptly.

'Did anybody see you on Sunday afternoon?'

'Half a dozen people, actually. I had a bit of a party, which started at six and went on until about nine. It was by way of a small celebration. My younger brother just announced his engagement and I invited a few people here to get to know his fiancée.'

'Could I have the names of the guests?'

She blinked at him. 'All of them?'

'Please.'

'Right. Well, Paul Taylor – that's my brother. Jenny Samuels is his fiancée. Then there was Andrew Pickering, who works with me and knows Paul, with his girlfriend Annie. And there was another woman, a friend of mine. She's called Helena Fairfield.'

Den reacted quickly. 'Fairfield? Is she any relation to Gerald, the Master of Foxhounds?'

Val turned pink and looked worriedly at Polly. 'Well, yes. She's his daughter. But I hope you won't give her away to her father. He doesn't know she's friendly with me.'

'How old is she?'

'Twenty-two, I think. She doesn't live at home any more. In fact, she's in her probationary year as a social worker. And she's deeply involved in animal rights work. That's why her father—'

'I understand,' Den interrupted. 'Her secret's safe with me.' He hoped this was true. He could think of a few scenarios whereby Gerald would have to hear about his daughter's activities via the police. 'What time on Monday did you arrive at work?'

'Eight forty-five, as always. If you're thinking of me as a possible suspect for the murder of Charlie Gratton, I'd say I've got a fairly good alibi. People don't go riding around after dark and I'd have had difficulty in getting hold of a horse at any time.'

'Sunday afternoon?' Den suggested. 'It looks as if there are a few hours unaccounted for then.'

Val laughed. 'That's true, I suppose. I was cooking and cleaning, but I can't prove it. I might add that I'm a hopeless rider, and I liked Charlie far too much to kill him.'

Den smiled absently. Something had just struck him: *People don't usually ride around after dark*. It was far too dangerous on the roads, but might they not trust to the animal's senses in the fields? Or could they make the assumption that Charlie had died during the hours of daylight?

'Anyway, it's against our principles,' put in Polly, from the table. 'Riding, that is.'

'Slave animals?' Den said, growing tired of this particular emotive but meaningless phrase. Both women nodded vigorously.

'So you endorse Charlie Gratton's protest activities?' he asked, eyeing Polly's leaflets.

'Absolutely. And Nina's,' Val confirmed. 'It seems a great pity that poor Nina is being forgotten in all this. We're going to carry it on for both of them, although it will be extremely difficult on our own.'

Den closed his eyes for an unwary moment, and once again the details of Nina's death replayed themselves. 'She isn't forgotten,' he said softly.

'Oh, you were there, weren't you,' Val remembered. 'You were the tall plain-clothes officer who tried to revive her. I phoned the ambulance,' she added proudly. 'Fortunately I had a mobile in my bag.'

'Yes,' Den confirmed uncomfortably.

Bare facts elicited, he did his best to assemble his thoughts. *Watch out for inconsistencies. Get a feel for the atmosphere. What* aren't *they telling you?* He let a small silence develop while he tried to focus.

'Are you aware of anybody who might have wanted Charlie dead?' he asked, hoping to catch them unawares.

Val laughed harshly. 'Only about twenty people, and that's just the locals. He was a hunt saboteur. He understood how to get the best publicity for himself and his beliefs. He wasn't going to stop.'

'So somebody stopped him,' Polly put in, softly. 'We think it must have been someone from the Hunt.'

'Anybody in particular?'

'I hope it wasn't Gerald Fairfield,' said Val. Polly sniffed derisively and Val's head snapped round to glare at her. 'What does that noise mean?' she demanded.

'You hope it wasn't Gerald because you're so *very* fond of his simpering daughter.' Sensing unsheathed claws and barely concealed passions, Den misguidedly tried to head off the fight.

'Can we stick to the subject?' he said. 'Are there any other hunt people you think might have been involved?'

Val ignored him. 'Don't make yourself look stupid, pet,' she said with withering contempt. 'There's nothing whatsoever between Helena and me.'

'Oh no, and birds don't fly, I suppose.'

Den had heard that lesbian quarrels could be every bit as vicious as the heterosexual equivalent, but he had never experienced one. He had no difficulty in recognising it for what it was, however, and he knew he couldn't disregard it. If these two were really a couple, the police would be foolish to ignore the fact.

'I take it you two are . . . partners?' he said boldly.

It stopped the fight, at least. 'Partners?' repeated Val icily. 'As in *lovers*, do you mean?' She turned away from Polly as she spoke and Den watched the latter's expression betray pain and then rage.

'That's the impression I'm getting,' he said. 'Forgive me if I'm wrong.'

'You're totally wrong and I find it hard to forgive you. That sort of assumption – *innuendo* – leads to nothing but spiteful gossip. A tarnished reputation. Have you any idea what it would do to my career, if it was believed that I was a lesbian?'

'Well, these days . . .' began Den.

'These days, nothing! Whatever the politically correct attitude might be, the reality is very different. My sexuality is entirely irrelevant to all this. It has nothing whatsoever to do with Charlie Gratton. He was in love with Alexis Cattermole. We all knew that.'

'Okay,' Den conceded. 'And what about Nina? From what I personally witnessed, he was profoundly upset by her accident.'

'Of course he was,' said Val scornfully. 'We all were.'

The scraping of Polly's chair interrupted them. With a hand to her face, fingers clasped over her mouth, she was making for the door. 'Oh, Poll,' cried Val, impatience, capitulation and concern all in her voice. 'Come back.'

Polly looked back, her eyes wet, and shook her head. Den knew betrayal when he saw it. 'I'll see you tomorrow,' said Polly thickly, and left the room.

'That was *your* fault,' Val accused, a moment later. 'Are you always so tactless?'

'And are you always so heartless? That poor girl!'

'She's not a *girl*. She's thirty-eight and she's been in love with practically every woman this side of Exeter in her time. Polly *is* a lesbian – you got that part right. But she isn't my lover, much as she'd like to be. I meant what I said about my job. If I slept with Polly, it'd be common knowledge in two shakes. Besides, I don't dislike men – only the ones who chase wild animals for the fun of it.'

'Women do that too,' he reminded her.

'Not the way men do. You should see how excited they get when they scent a fox. It's obscene.'

Den didn't argue; the fox hunting battle would run its course without any contribution from him. Apart from a vague distaste for the kind of enthusiasm Val had just referred to, he found it hard to understand how the sport could engender such passions.

But he had to pursue the relevant angle.

'With Charlie gone, would you say your protest activities have been severely weakened?'

Val pursed her lips and sighed. 'In the short term, they might be. We can't do everything ourselves. With the loss of Charlie and Nina, some of the energy has gone out of it. But there'll be new people coming along. It's growing every day. We're an irresistible force.'

'But what if someone realised that you'd be badly thrown by their loss? When Nina died they did some quick thinking and went after Charlie as well?' Even as he spoke, he knew the idea was implausible.

'Sorry, I can't see it. The battle's lost for the hunt lobby anyway. All such an act would do would be to delay the inevitable.'

'Can I ask you about the Quakers? I understand you attend regularly. I've seen Mr and Mrs Aspen and all the others. I understand that not all of them approved of Charlie's activism?'

'Clive certainly didn't,' she agreed. 'He made no bones about it. Said it was casting a slur on the law-abiding reputation of the Meeting. Which is ridiculous, given our history of protest and rebellion. Clive's not very representative.' She grimaced, as if this was a serious understatement. 'He actually sneaks off to follow the hunt sometimes, which I think is despicable. I have a feeling that Mandy secretly sympathises with our protests, but she would never say anything against Clive.'

'I'm still a bit hazy about Quaker values,' he said apologetically, 'but Mr Aspen did strike me as rather . . . *old-fashioned*.'

'He's crazy,' she said with sudden emphasis.

'Oh?'

'I know I shouldn't say it. He can't help it. It's because of his illness. He's been to hell and back since his breakdown – you can see that just by looking at him.'

'Breakdown?'

'Their baby died, and other stuff was going on, too. He had two years of total dysfunction. Mandy had to carry him.'

She seemed to think she had said too much, and shrugged. 'He's harmless enough, just a bit obsessive. Finding this position as Warden was the best thing that could happen to him. It's secure and undemanding and he can get his life back on track. It was all going so well when he first came, but then he lost his job and that set him right back again.'

'What job was that?'

She laughed rather nervously. 'He was running the after-school club in Okehampton. Silly to jump into something as stressful as that. Some of the children are only six or seven and they get tired and whingy. Apparently it was a disaster from the start. I don't know what fool took him on in the first place, but he was never liked by the children.'

'Is he well liked by anybody?'

'We're Quakers,' she reminded him. 'We do our best.'

'I don't think there's much more to ask.' He stared at the scanty jottings on the current page of his pad. 'Just this – how well do you know the family at High Copse?'

'We knew Nina, of course,' said Val readily. 'We would have done anything for her. And we knew Alexis slightly because she was Charlie's girlfriend.'

'Have you ever been to the house?'

'Polly and I were there on Saturday to talk to Alexis about a memorial for Nina. We probably should have waited a while. She wasn't really ready to talk about it. Frankly, she was very rude.'

'You're a social worker, I understand? What's your speciality?'

'Child protection,' she said shortly. Den made a note and closed his notepad.

'Well, that's been very helpful,' he said blandly. 'I'll be on my way now. If I could just have your phone number in case I think of anything else?' She supplied the number and he took his leave.

Three items seemed to him to be significant. In the car, he wrote them down.

Clive Aspen helps at Clem's school, having lost a job working with young children.
No mention of Frank.
Social workers. Clem Nesbitt and Val Taylor linked?

CHAPTER NINETEEN

At the Grattons' home that evening, the telephone rang, as it had done many times over the past week. 'Hannah? Is that you?' The tone was gruff, the delivery impatient; Hannah knew exactly who was speaking.

'Hello, Frank,' she replied. 'How are you?'

'Well enough. Now, this business with Charlie. Have you got the funeral sorted out yet? I didn't expect you to consult me, but I'd like to come along, all the same. I take it there'll be no objections?'

'I've just had a call from the police, as it happens. They say we can't go ahead for a little while yet, but they'll get clearance as soon as they can. It's easier if it's a burial – in case of complications – so we're going to bury him in the Friends Cemetery, behind the Meeting House. I think he'd have wanted that, anyway. Of course we'd be glad to see you, Frank, when the time comes. Why shouldn't we?'

He snorted softly, and said, 'I'll come then. You'll let me know what day, won't you?'

'I promise we will. In a way, it's just as well there's a delay. It's so soon after poor Nina Nesbitt. I think it's good if people get over that first.'

'All the same to me,' he said carelessly. 'Don't expect me to take an interest in that side of it. It's another world, after all this time.'

'And yet you still want to come to his funeral.'

The silence on the other end of the line was broken by a harsh breath which Hannah had no difficulty in interpreting. 'He's a loss to us all, Frank,' she said gently. 'Including your father. He won't make any difficulties about you coming to share in our grief. You know that, don't you? He's never had any hard feelings towards you.'

The bitter laugh was more painful to listen to than the stifled weeping had been. 'Easy to say,' he grated. 'Easy enough to say, Aunt Hannah. And what are the chances of the truth coming out, now the boy's dead? They say it's impossible to take a secret to the grave, don't they?'

Hannah closed her eyes. 'It wasn't Charlie's secret though, was it Frank?'

'I'll see you at the funeral,' he said and the line went dead.

Hermione Nesbitt also paid a second visit to High Copse that day. She reappeared in the evening, having been invited to dinner with the whole family. She sat on the long antique settle in the front room waiting for the summons to the dining room, with her son and two grandsons dancing attendance on her. Alexis had pulled out all the stops with a huge beef stew and three kinds of veg, but her normally unreliable culinary skills were further undermined by an inability to concentrate. One by one, members of the family popped into the kitchen offering helpful suggestions, or sometimes whispered comments about the effect Hermione was having on the household.

'She's trying to play draughts with Clem,' Martha reported in exasperation, 'but she keeps forgetting about her sling. She's knocked everything over twice. No wonder she drove into that pickup this morning. She's not fit to be out.'

The seven people assembled around the large mahogany table in the seldom-used dining room shivered and chewed valiantly, six of them wondering how Hermione could cause such turmoil by her mere presence. The matriarch herself behaved with precarious dignity. Not only was one arm in a sling, making eating very awkward, she was also nursing a slight bump on her temple, consequent on the impact with Barty White's vehicle. Nev, Hugh and Clem had all shown concern for her injuries, but the others were sparing in their sympathy.

During her visit that morning, Hermione had spent twenty minutes at Nina's graveside, kneeling unselfconsciously on the grass and speaking in a low voice. Nev had approached her warily, and together they stood quietly for another five minutes. Alexis had watched with so many conflicting emotions she felt sick. Richmond had hovered worriedly. 'She ought to get that bump seen to,' he muttered. 'Should I drive her to the doctor?'

'Yes – do that, and then take her home. Make her rest. Then you can bring her back later on and she can drive herself home when it gets dark. She always says the roads are safer at night and I think she's got a point. At least the headlights will let her know when there's anything coming.'

So it had been arranged, with both visits from the police fortuitously occurring in the interlude when Hermione was recovering at home.

It wasn't as if she really disliked the woman, Alexis had to admit to herself, as she chopped carrots and onions. In many ways she was utterly admirable. Her own mother, Eliza, had found plenty to admire in her son-in-law's mother, although she had never sought her company. 'A bit horsy,' she said by way of explanation. 'Otherwise, for somebody with so much money, she's remarkably human.'

There had, however, been a very strange encounter between Alexis and Hermione at Christmas, when they'd found themselves side by side at a big village party. Charlie had been there, as well as all the Cattermoles and most of the hunting fraternity. Nina had gritted her teeth and ignored Gerald Fairfield and his cronies, but Charlie was less restrained. Alexis had taken him to task with some ferocity.

'You and Charlie are going out together, are you?' Hermione had enquired. There had been a deep frown between her eyes and her lips seemed pale, as if with suppressed tension.

'That's right,' Alexis had confirmed carelessly. 'Since the end of July.'

'I honestly don't think he's right for you, dear. I know there's nothing I can say to change your mind, but go carefully. That's all.' The older woman shook her head, and Alexis thought she caught the sparkle of a tear.

'But—' she had started to protest in bewilderment.

'His mother and I were best friends,' Hermione said. 'You might not have known that.'

'Yes I did,' Alexis contradicted. 'Nev's said so many a time. But I don't see why—'

'There's nothing to see,' Hermione said. 'Nothing alarming or sinister. But I know you both quite well, and I wish I could convince you—' She turned away with a sigh that Alexis saw rather than heard. 'Never mind. We just have to trust to fate, I suppose.' And she returned to her hunting friends without another word.

Now that Charlie was dead there didn't seem any sense in even remembering the mysterious conversation. Fate had indeed intervened and Hermione no longer needed to worry about an inappropriate connection – whatever that might mean.

Around the dining table now, the conversation drifted by inches to the matter of Charlie's death, yet nobody wanted to be the first to utter his name. Clem sat between Nev and Martha on one side of the table; Hugh was flanked by Alexis and Hermione on the other. Richmond took the large carver chair at the head of the table, more because it contained his girth more comfortably than from any sense of patriarchy. It was past seven and the light was fading. The room had two large windows on two walls. From one, the big oak tree and Nina's grave were visible; Clem,

Nev and Martha could all see it if they tried, but they made sure this didn't happen. Instead, they focused with determination on their food, or the faces of those across the table.

Alexis was the first to raise the topic of the police interviews. 'At least they've done us all now,' she said. 'Between us we must fill quite a dossier. Heaven knows what they make of us.'

'They haven't seen me,' put in Hermione. 'Ought I to feel left out?'

'Oh, we've all taken your name in vain,' Nev told her. 'They got your address out of me this morning.' His attempt at Richmond-style joviality was not a great success; they all heard the strain in his voice. 'You'll probably find them on your doorstep first thing tomorrow – unless they're there now, searching the stables for you.'

'Good luck to them,' said his mother shortly.

Martha finished her food, and put down her fork. 'There's something I've been meaning to ask you,' she said to Hermione, fiddling with a button on the cuff of her shirt. 'Why is Frank Gratton Nev's godfather? I mean – apart from anything else, Frank must have been a Quaker, and they don't go in for godparents, do they?'

A snort of surprise came from Nev. Hermione looked at him dispassionately. 'It's rather a long story,' she said, 'and it might not make much sense after all these years. I'm surprised you even know about it. Who told you?'

'I did,' Nev said. 'We were talking about it with Nina, ages ago. Clem had been doing comparative religion at school and he wanted to know about baptism. It came up then.'

'Who's Frank?' Clem asked, looking at Martha. 'I don't remember.'

'I don't think you've ever met him. He's Charlie's older brother, and Nev's godfather. None of us know him really.'

'His mother was my best friend,' Hermione interposed. 'I'm sure you knew that.'

Various heads nodded and Alexis spoke. 'Which must make Charlie's death a special sort of loss for you,' she ventured.

Hermione smiled, with a kink of self-mockery at the corner of her mouth. 'I can't pretend I saw very much of him, once he grew up. He couldn't really remember Eloise, and Hannah has been much more of a mother to him.'

'But *Frank* remembers her,' Martha said. 'Do you see much of *him*?'

The elderly woman closed her eyes and again she smiled the same perplexing smile. 'Very little,' she said softly. 'Frank's fully occupied with his horses. He has his own life well away from here.'

'But why the godfather thing?' Martha persisted.

'It just seemed right at the time. Nev was six months old, Frank was fourteen or fifteen and disenchanted with the Quakers by then. He liked babies, and was always saying he wanted a little brother. As it happened, Charlie was born about a year later, so he got his wish. Oh, I can't explain it to you.' She threw down her knife impatiently, having struggled to eat one-handed without any help, and glared at Martha. 'What's the point of discussing this? It was thirty-four years ago. When Charlie was born and Frank had a baby closer to home to play with, he never bothered much with Nev – just sent him a birthday card now and then.'

'He must have bothered enough for Nev to know about the relationship,' Alexis commented.

'Actually, he sent me birthday cards right up until I was eighteen,' Nev corrected his mother, with an air of nostalgia. 'And presents when I was younger. Good things they were, too. Clever things, that nobody else would think of. And he took me fishing once on the Moor. Then he just lost interest. Not surprising, when you think about it. I can't imagine why he ever wanted to bother with me in the first place.'

'Maybe now Charlie's dead, he'll remember you again,' said Hugh, speaking for the first time.

Martha remembered naming Frank to Den Cooper as her first choice of suspect for Charlie's murder, and shivered. 'We know nothing about him,' she said tightly.

'He's a thoroughly nice chap,' Hermione said to Hugh. 'You have my assurance on that.'

'And Granny's always right,' said Hugh to the room in general. Clem nodded vigorously.

'Thank you, boys,' she said, a new twinkle in her eye. 'I can always rely on you two, can't I?'

'They're very lucky to have you,' said Richmond, with his habitual knack of closing a topic of conversation. He smiled sweetly at Hermione. 'What's for pudding, Alexis?'

The turmoil of clearing away plates, producing a large overcooked apple crumble and resolving a recurrent argument over whether to have custard or ice cream with it prevented further conversation for several minutes. When everything settled down again, Nev asked, 'Exactly how did you hurt your shoulder, Ma? You never told me.'

'It was that bloody Boanerges,' she said with her mouth full. 'He'll have to go if he doesn't shape up soon.'

'Oh, Granny – *no!*' cried Hugh.

'Boanerges?' queried Richmond. 'First I've heard of him.'

'It's the stallion I got from a man in Taunton. Beautiful beast, just what I need to cover the mares this year. But I'm hoping his temper won't pass to his offspring.' She looked severely at Hugh. 'And no amount of pleading will save him if he doesn't start behaving himself.'

'How exactly did he damage your shoulder?' asked Richmond.

'It was silly, really. I had him on a leading rein and he suddenly jerked sideways. I hung on, but it caught me at a funny angle and wrenched the joint backwards. Half pulled it out of its socket. It'll be better in a few days.'

'You need to slow down a bit at your age,' Nev laughed.

'One thing leads to another,' she said obliquely, before filling her mouth again.

The meal concluded, a debate developed on whether Hermione was fit to drive herself home. She insisted stoutly that she was perfectly capable and the general inclination was to agree with her. Thanks to the quirks of Devon lanes, the journey was at least ten miles by car, but less than five on foot.

Hermione easily prevailed and climbed lithely into her handsome Range Rover. 'Come and see me soon,' she told Hugh and Clem. 'Cleopatra is definitely in pup – due in a couple of weeks. She'll want you to come and admire them.'

Whoops of enthusiasm followed her down the drive and Martha silently marvelled at the woman who could tame wild horses, control a large group of huntsmen with a look, and at the same time attract such adoration from her grandsons. And yet there was something lost and lonely in Hermione's eyes, when she thought nobody was watching. Some secret grief that had always been there. It wasn't the death of her husband – she had weathered that with true British aplomb. Who, Martha wondered, had died or departed from Hermione's life, long before she met the Cattermoles? Nobody sprang to mind apart from Eloise Gratton, long-dead mother of Frank and Charlie.

CHAPTER TWENTY

Den received a worrying phone call at the police station next morning. 'Are you going to be busy this evening?' Lilah asked him. 'We need to talk.'

He felt the familiar lurch of anxiety that men everywhere experienced at these words. *She's going to finish with me*, he thought, in a strange mixture of panic and resignation.

'I can't say for sure, but I think I should be free by eight at the latest. Is that okay?'

'It'll have to be. Let me know if you can make it any sooner. I'm here all day.' She sounded friendlier now, and his heartbeat slowed slightly.

'Will do.'

'I'll see you, then.'

A small black cloud remained with him

all day, thanks to the call. He knew what he'd done – he'd suggested he move into Redstone permanently – but he didn't know why he was being punished for it. He didn't see what was so terrible about the idea. But from the sound of it, he was soon going to find out.

Detective Inspector Smith's briefing that morning lasted precisely seven minutes. Phil Bennett had gone back to Gerald Fairfield's place to question the two men employed as farm and stable hands. He hadn't gleaned anything useful from either of them.

'It would have been too obvious, anyway,' muttered Den, when Phil's lack of findings was revealed.

'There's still all the other hunt people,' said Phil defensively. 'It's still the most credible motive – and they had the means. No shortage of opportunity, either, come to that.'

WPC Jane Nugent, invited to join the briefing for the first time, spoke up. 'I've got a few interesting connections on the computer, and a bit of background on the Grattons,' she offered. She went on to flesh out a few details concerning Charlie's family. 'Frank Gratton, born nineteen fifty-two. Mother Eloise, then aged twenty-two, father Bill, twenty-four. Married for fifteen months when the baby arrived. Charles born nineteen sixty-seven. Eloise died two years later.

Possible suicide. Bill's sister Hannah was called back from some sort of missionary work in Africa, moved in to replace Eloise. Frank moves out less than a year later and maintains very little contact. Silas Daggs is first cousin to Hannah and Bill. The family have been Quakers for generations. No sign of trouble, no police records, no obvious gossip. You probably knew all that, anyway,' she concluded humbly. 'I just printed off everything I could find.'

'*Possible* suicide?' DI Smith queried. 'Where did you find that?'

'Local newspaper report, sir. The woman drowned in a pond behind their house. It was never explained how she came to fall in. The inquest called it accidental death, but one person testified that she'd been in a disturbed frame of mind ever since Charlie was born.'

'Postnatal depression?'

'Very likely, sir.'

'Who was it that said that?'

'Silas Daggs, sir.'

'Cooper?' Smith fixed his searching gaze on Den. 'We have an interview report on Mr Daggs, don't we?'

'Yes, sir. I couldn't find anything of significance in what he had to tell me.'

'Go through it again,' Smith invited. 'Just in case we missed something.'

Obligingly, with the aid of his notepad, Den recalled as much detail as he could of his interview with the man he'd heard referred to as 'curmudgeonly'. Silas Daggs had a Dickensian name and lived in a suitably Dickensian fashion. 'But he's not so much a Mr Smallweed as an elderly Joe Gargery,' Den suggested, not sure how well up on Dickens his listeners might be. To his relief, all three of them chuckled at the image conjured up. 'The house was clean and tidy and the old man himself was dressed in a suit with collar and tie,' Den recounted. 'But I don't think he'd put on his Sunday best for the police. I got the impression that was how he always dressed.'

In a flash of total recall, Den was transported back to the interview. He had been invited to sit on a small, uncomfortable sofa with a carved wooden back and sagging red upholstery. Although no expert, he suspected that it might be an antique of some value. A grandfather clock stood incongruously at the bottom of the stairs – the only space with sufficient headroom to hold it. *Another valuable heirloom*, Den had noted.

Silas appeared to be about seventy and he suffered conspicuously from arthritis. His hands were warped into tight claws and walking was clearly painful. He let himself drop heavily into an upright chair and leant down briefly to pat the head of the corgi sitting patiently beside him.

Den had savoured the little tableau the man and dog presented and described it fully now for his audience, to lukewarm response.

'Sounds as if you weren't in any hurry to get started,' Smith remarked. 'Don't make a meal of it, there's a good chap.'

'I asked him what he knew of Charlie, including his early life,' Den quickly proceeded. 'He didn't have much to say. Certainly nothing to suggest the mother killed herself. Not that I pressed him,' he admitted.

He'd asked Silas about the Quakers, and had been rather moved by the simple statement of commitment to attending every Sunday Meeting. 'It's obviously very important to him,' Den said. 'Probably the most important thing in his life. But he did say it wasn't the same as it used to be, with "the new young people changing the way things are done". I assumed he meant the Aspens – they're young compared to him – but there was Charlie and Val Taylor and Polly Spence as well. All the animal rights crowd.'

'What about the famous Quaker tolerance?' put in Phil.

'I think it's still there. He didn't say anything against them – just regretted the way things are changing. Like any old person would, really.'

'So he didn't hate Charlie?' prompted Smith.

'I'm sure he didn't,' Den said firmly. 'In fact I

got the distinct impression that he dislikes Clive Aspen far more than he ever disliked Charlie.'

'Why do you say that?'

'"Clive Aspen is no Quaker. Say what you like, that's my opinion." I wrote that down. It seemed quite a strong thing to say. He went on about George Fox—'

'Who?' Smith frowned. 'Have we spoken to him?'

Den suppressed a smile. 'George Fox – the founder of the Quakers, three hundred years ago. They quote him a lot. Silas doesn't think he'd approve of Clive Aspen. Clive's rather too keen on dragging new people in, apparently, whether or not they can sit still for an hour or even understand what it's all about. They don't stay long.'

Smith was visibly losing interest. 'I think you're right. Nothing of significance in any of that.'

'Except to confirm my hunch that Clive had no affection for Charlie, and vice versa. Silas didn't spell it out for me, but I couldn't miss the basic point.'

'So Silas was on Charlie's side.'

'I'm not sure about that. He treated me to a speech about animal rights. "God gave us animals to be used" was one comment he made. Seemed to think Charlie was a bit cracked, even if he was family.'

Smith held up a hand and stopped him. 'It might be an idea to go back and ask him a bit more about this mother of Charlie's. Eloise. Keep it as casual as you can, but say you've spoken to everyone else and he's the only one who can help. Something like that. Flattery usually works.'

'Yes, sir,' said Den dispiritedly. What was the point of pursuing a death that happened over thirty years ago? 'I'll get on to it right away. But, sir, we still haven't been to interview old Mrs Nesbitt. Something always seems to get in the way. Don't you think—?'

'Quite right, Cooper. Fortunately for you, the day is yet young. Silas Daggs first, and then Mrs N. Don't let *anything* stop you.'

'*Anything*, sir?'

'Anything short of a second murder. Or a confession to this one.'

Silas did not feel particularly flattered at being singled out for more police attention. Den therefore decided to go for the frank approach. 'To be honest, Mr Daggs, we're not getting anywhere with this inquiry. Your cousin Charlie seems to have been an irritant to a lot of people, but nothing worse than that. We haven't found anything close to a motive for murder. All we can think of is to have another look at his early life and see if anything emerges from that. I remember you said when I last visited you that you remember his mother.'

Silas wouldn't meet Den's eye, but nodded briefly. 'Plenty who remember her besides me.'

'But you saw quite a lot of her? Living so close by, I suppose you must have done.'

'She came to chat with me now and then,' Silas admitted. ''Specially when she had Charlie. She liked to have another person around, after he was born, and Bill never seemed to be there when she wanted him.'

'Why? Was Charlie a difficult baby?'

Silas shrugged. 'Not 'specially. She was just a bit thrown by having him after such a long gap. Seemed to send her out of true, if you know what I mean.'

'I understand she died when he was very small?'

Silas leant down and patted the corgi at his feet, in a gesture Den was coming to recognise as habitual. Then he slowly extracted a very large white handkerchief from his trouser pocket and blew his nose. Finally he nodded. 'She did,' he said.

'And then Hannah came back from abroad to look after Bill and Charlie, and the older boy, Frank.'

The gnarled hands reached for each other, forming a tangled double fist that looked like a complex wood carving. 'She did,' he said again, almost in a whisper.

'Did you see much of the family at that time?'

'We all went to Meeting every week. All except Frank, that is. He stopped going as soon as he could. Must have been nine or ten the last time he went. Some youngsters are like that – they just never settle to it. Never see what it's all about.'

'That must be difficult. I mean, families generally want their children to follow their own faith, don't they?'

A slight shake of the head. 'Wanting and getting don't always match up.'

'And when Mrs Gratton died – had she been ill?'

The old man closed his eyes as if against a sharp pain. Tears leaked out from under the lids. Den felt the emotion in the room, his own eyes prickling slightly at the obvious distress. He'd seen this before in old people – a story from thirty, forty, fifty years ago recurring as if it was last week, along with all the feelings associated with it, as fresh as a May morning.

'She was . . . ill, aye,' came a low whisper. 'Though none of us would admit it. I was as bad as the rest of 'em, pretending nothing was going on. In the end, she just couldn't go on living. She just couldn't. It was like trying to force a bat to live in the glare of the light, or a butterfly to live under a stone. It went against nature.' He tightened the grip of one hand on the other. 'We lived with the shame of it for many a year.'

Den knew he had to proceed with extreme caution. 'What would you say was the matter with her? Some sort of postnatal depression?'

Silas rejected the modern term. 'My old mother would have called it soul sickness. That's all I can say about it. She never went to a doctor for it.'

'But she did go to Meeting.'

Silas nodded bitterly. 'She did and we failed her. Just like we failed Charlie and others in between.'

'*Failed* him?' Den asked gently. 'How did you fail him?'

Silas shook his head and was silent for a long moment. Then he spoke softly. 'We left him too much to himself, thinking Hannah would ask if she needed our help. We could see how it was – they sent him to boarding school in the end, which made it easier.' He was making little sense to Den, who concluded that Charlie must have been a troubled adolescent. It was with considerable inner violence that he asked his final question.

'Mr Daggs, I must ask you this, painful as it's bound to be. Did you ever believe that Charlie's mother, Eloise Gratton, took her own life?'

Silas exhaled, part annoyance, part relief. He met Den's eye at last, with his own red-rimmed gaze. 'It was as plain as can be,' he said. 'But you won't get a soul to say it but me. Now, that's an end to your questions, however hard you press me. There's things you don't need to know, police or not. If you must keep axing about it, you must go to Hannah for your answers. I've said all I'm going to.'

Den believed him. 'I accept that,' he said formally. 'And I'm very grateful to you for giving me so much of your time.'

Silas guffawed. 'Got plenty of that these days,' he said bitterly.

CHAPTER TWENTY-ONE

Hermione Nesbitt lived close to the immensely scenic A384, a road which scarcely earned its appellation of the letter *A*, leading insignificantly from Tavistock to Launceston; a mere thirteen miles of existence. A road which Den presumed almost nobody outside west Devon would ever have cause to notice. And yet it was as beautiful as many a more famous stretch of highway. As it approached the river Tamar, it rendered views guaranteed to suspend a person's breath.

He had intended to emerge onto the road a few hundred yards from the bridge over the Tamar, but a wrong turning sent him too far east and he found himself enjoying the full glory of the vistas to the south. For a few moments he forgot where he was going and why. Fancifully, he imagined he had wandered into a forgotten land, where nothing had changed in a thousand years.

It was a short-lived interlude. As he climbed a long gradient, his car phone began to warble and he slowed a little to answer it.

'Cooper?' The voice was crackly and indistinct, as usual; it was no longer feasible for local police stations to call their officers directly on the phone and everything was relayed through a central point near Bristol. 'Where are you?'

Den hesitated. 'On my way to an interview for DI Smith,' he said. 'Five or six miles south of Launceston. Why?'

'You're needed at a place called . . . er . . . High Copse Farm? It's between two little villages. Let's see . . . Chillhampton, I think. That's one of them . . .'

'Yes, yes,' said Den furiously. 'I know where it is. What's happened?'

'There's a child gone missing. They asked for you particularly.'

'Oh Christ. I'm on my way.'

He jammed on the brakes as he drew level with a field gateway, and slammed the car into reverse. Before he had fully turned round, he realised there must be a shortcut through the lanes, if only he could find it. Otherwise, he would waste precious minutes going via Tavistock, with all its slow-moving traffic in the town centre.

But the lanes were treacherous. Narrow, meandering, half of them not even marked on the maps. You really had to know what you were doing. Helplessly, he dithered, wasting precious time. *Clem – it must be Clem,* he thought. *Whoever murdered Charlie has snatched the little boy, afraid he'll talk. Clem knows who the killer is.* At this very moment the child might be suffering – strangled or knifed – *Oh, God!*

He jerked the car forward, heading back the way he'd come. He would risk the lanes. High Copse was north-east of where he was. Before long, the familiar outline of Brentor would appear to guide him. A Devon man, born and bred, he should be able to navigate by instinct. And so he did. Some invisible hand guided him, some sixth sense alerted him on the two occasions on which other vehicles surged towards him around blind bends. He reached High Copse almost sobbing with relief and anxiety.

There was nobody in sight as he pulled up alongside a police car on the gravel in front of the house. A quick scan of the two fields and the orchard showed nothing. Rising above the apple trees was the copse crowning the hill – doubtless another favourite haunt of the boys. The view downhill from the house was no longer an uplifting sight. Now it merely represented countless square miles in which a small boy could lose himself – or be deliberately concealed.

'Hello.' The voice came from behind him, almost too quiet to carry across the parking area. Den swung round to see Hugh standing in the doorway of Richmond's office. 'They told me to wait here, in case anybody phoned, or . . .'

'Or Clem came home?' Den suggested. The boy was very pale, his eyes glittering. He nodded.

'Everyone's still looking for him, then? How long has he been missing?'

Hugh didn't move, but seemed to be thinking. 'Since about two o'clock. Not long really.'

'And haven't you any idea where he is?'

Hugh shook his head. 'Sorry,' he mumbled. He looked wretched.

'You know, people almost always turn up again quite safe and sound, and as you say, he hasn't been gone very long. He knows his way around these parts well enough.' Den paused. 'Has he ever done this sort of thing before?'

'What sort of thing?' The boy frowned.

'Going missing. Does he go off on his own when he's upset? Has he got a special secret place?'

Hugh wriggled his shoulders impatiently. 'They already asked me all that. I don't know where he is, okay?'

So what am I supposed to do now? Den wondered. *Search the house, orchard, warehouse . . . ?*

Another car came racing up the drive, rattling alarmingly. 'It's Mrs Aspen!' said Hugh, clearly astonished. Den peered through the windscreen as the Mini skidded to a stop, and recognised the driver.

'So it is,' he said, loping to the car with his long strides.

Mandy tumbled out, her face pink with excitement and concern. 'Clem,' she gasped, as if she'd run up from the road, rather than driven. 'Are you looking for him?'

Den's mind clicked and whirred into action. A picture of Clive Aspen performing depraved and cruel acts on the lost boy came into his mind, with the helpless Mandy taking the only action she could think of. But almost immediately he realised this notion made no sense. 'Yes we are,' he said. 'Clem's missing. Why?'

'I saw him, half a mile away. He was walking along the road. I stopped and called his name, but he must have ducked into a hedge or through a gateway, because he disappeared. Anyway, he looked ever so upset, so I decided to come up here and tell somebody.'

'How did you know where we lived?' Hugh asked her coldly.

'Oh, *Hugh!* Everyone knows High Copse. I gave Charlie a lift here once, just to the bottom of the drive. I think you ought to hurry,' she said to Den. 'He could be quite difficult to find if we leave it too long.'

'Come with me,' he told her, waving towards his car. 'Hugh, can you stick to your post here? Tell anybody you see what's going on. Can you do that?'

'Of course.'

Mandy hopped quickly into Den's passenger seat and he turned the car round with some difficulty in the cluttered forecourt. She directed him to turn left as they reached the road and then tried to identify the exact place where she'd seen the child. It was barely half a mile from the house. Den parked on a grass verge, leaving scant space for other vehicles to pass, and got out of the car. 'You can stay here if you like,' he told Mandy. 'Hoot the horn if you see him.'

'No need,' she said triumphantly. 'There he is, look.' She pointed into the nearby field, which contained a jumble of large round silage bales wrapped in black polythene and left out since the previous autumn. Clem was sitting on the ground with his back against one of them. He seemed to be rubbing his face with one hand.

Den ran to him, a distance of roughly two hundred yards. Clem looked up and twisted away for a moment, like a hunted animal, before slumping back against the bale. Unhesitatingly, Den picked him up and turned back to the car. Clem struggled. 'I can *walk*,' he protested. 'I'm not hurt.'

'Okay,' Den panted. 'Keep still a minute and we'll have a proper look at you.' He deposited the wriggling burden safely onto the back seat of his car and knelt beside the open door. 'What were you doing?' he asked. 'Everybody's out searching for you. They're terribly worried.'

'Wasn't doing anything,' Clem muttered. 'Just wanted to get away.'

'Your face is scratched,' Den observed. 'And you're very muddy.'

'I climbed through the hedge when *she* saw me.' He ducked his chin defiantly at Mandy, who was twisted round in her seat to look at him. 'How did you know who I was?' he demanded. 'I don't know you.'

To Den's surprise, Mandy flushed a deep red and gave no answer. 'Doesn't she work at your school?' he asked, his mind still fuzzy at the speed of events. The child shook his head. Den raised his eyebrows at Mandy, but she maintained her silence. 'Never mind,' said Den. 'First things first.' He shut the car door and went round to the driving seat, reaching in for the radio phone. 'Let's send out a message that you're okay, shall we? I know a lot of people who'll be very glad about that.'

Clem made an inarticulate sound, which Den interpreted as disagreement. He glanced back at the boy. With bowed head and gently shaking shoulders, the child was crying.

CHAPTER TWENTY-TWO

Den had been at home for only half an hour when Lilah arrived. She came in through the unlocked front door and threw her jacket on the sofa, just as she always did. Then she kissed him and routinely asked him if he'd had a good day. He laid a hand on either side of her face to prolong the kiss. Her cropped hair felt softly energetic under his fingers, its thick waviness one of her most attractive features. It was nothing like her mother's poker-straight pageboy style, beginning to go grey around the ears. Lilah, he felt sure, was never going to look anything like her mother.

He tried to look into her eyes as she pulled away from him, but couldn't quite find the courage. His insides were spasming with anxiety.

He couldn't bear to lose her now, not when she had become a central part of his future. If she dropped out of his life, there'd be no light, no laughter; he'd have to revise so many of his plans. And when she asked, 'And how's the murder inquiry coming along?' he felt every element in his life meshing together, making perfect sense. Because Den Cooper was a police detective with his sights set on a promotion ladder that led to the dizziest of heights, as well as Lilah Beardon's future husband. *Perhaps*, he thought, with a stab of insight, *I'd feel just as anxious if faced with the loss of that plan as well.*

'Untidily,' he replied to her question. 'Bits and pieces all over the place and nothing to link them together. To cap it all, young Clem Nesbitt went missing this afternoon. We all thought he'd been abducted.'

'My God! Did you find him?'

He nodded. 'He wasn't gone for long, as it turned out. Just wanted to go off on his own for a bit. He's upset about something. Wouldn't say what.'

'Of course he's upset! His mother just died.'

Den shook his head. 'No, it's more recent than that. Something happened today. He went running off with no coat, no idea where he was going. He'd got half a mile along the road, that's all. But it wasn't planned. You know how little kids often think about running away and hoard apples and pocket money and stuff?'

She smiled. 'Not really. But I'll take your word for it.'

'Anyway, it doesn't look to have been that sort of running away. I think he was scared. He didn't seem to want to go home although he settled down when Martha took over. Christ, was she glad to see him! She'd walked halfway to Cornwall, looking for him in the wrong direction.'

'Exciting,' Lilah commented.

That wasn't how Den would have described it. 'All part of a day's work,' he replied ruefully.

'And what about the rest of the investigation?'

He tried to concentrate, pushing out his lips and rubbing his chin with a long hand. 'I'm still looking for evidence of how people felt about Charlie before he – or Nina – died. And there's just no sign of anything strong enough to warrant murdering him. I can't uncover any real passion or genuine anger towards him.'

She tossed her head impatiently. 'Then somebody must be a very good actor. It's a bit optimistic to expect your murderer to start gnashing his teeth and spitting at the mention of Charlie's name.'

He sighed helplessly; she clearly wasn't in a very understanding mood. His stomach, now full of marshmallow or cotton wool, was making breathing difficult, and he seized his courage. 'You said we should have a talk,' he managed. 'Hadn't we better get on with it?'

Her whole manner changed as he watched her. She drooped and went pale; her bouncy hair seemed to go limp. She bit her lower lip. 'I did say that, didn't I? Have you been thinking about it all day?'

'Just a bit.' He made the irony unmistakable.

'It was when you suggested moving into Redstone.'

'I worked that much out. So what's the problem?'

'It's hard to explain rationally. It wasn't really about you . . .'

'Why do people always say that?' he interrupted. 'I *want* it to be about me. And I don't care how irrational it is. I just want to understand.'

'*Just* probably isn't the right word. When you said what you did, I had this picture of a great iron gate, like a portcullis, coming down between me and the world. I felt I'd never escape from the farm, if you were there as well. I only go out now to see you. We'd be like prisoners in an open prison, never going more than a couple of miles from home. I've lived at Redstone nearly all my life. I'm stuck with it, and I do love it most of the time. But I panic when I think it's the only place I'm ever going to see. All my friends have gone to uni, and then to America or Israel or into high-flying London jobs. Most of them have graduated by now and here I am, doing the same as I've always done. Left behind. You're my ticket at least as far as Okehampton. It isn't much, but it's a start.' She came towards him and he held out his arms. Her head fitted comfortably under his chin and she rubbed her face on his shirt. She didn't seem to be crying, but tears were obviously not far off.

'I do see what you mean,' he mumbled into the top of her head. 'And I can't tell you how relieved I am. I was scared you were going to dump me.'

She tilted her face up at him. '*What?*'

'You seemed so cross with me.' He pulled a little-boy face, pushing out his lower lip in an endearing pout.

'You are *so* insecure!' she said. 'I can't think why. You seemed pretty well in control at school. What went wrong?'

'Is this a cue for me to talk about my unhappy childhood? Because there's quite a long story to be told, if so. We ought to have something to drink if we're getting into all that.'

'Go on, then. Find a bottle of wine and let me know the worst.'

Three minutes later, they were cuddled together

on the sofa and Den was trying to recapture the salient points of his early years. The experience with Clem Nesbitt made it easier, because somehow Den had identified with the lost and confused little boy.

'I really should have told you all this before now, but I hardly ever think about it. I never did, because I can't actually remember it. The fact is, I spent nearly a year in a foster home when I was very small. My mother had a big operation on her back when I was a year old, and it went wrong somehow. I was packed off until she recovered. And naturally enough I was a real handful when she got me back again. I probably had no idea who she was by then. I used to cry all night, apparently, and my dad got sick of the whole thing and buggered off when I was five. It was a pretty rough time for all of us.'

'But I've met your dad. Did he come back?'

'He's my stepdad.'

'How could you not tell me before now?' She seemed genuinely horrified at what must look like a deception.

'It sounds daft, but it never occurred to me. He's been around for so long, I just forgot to start with. And then it all seemed a bit complicated to explain.'

She pulled away from him. '*Complicated*? But we're supposed to be getting *married*. Is there anything else you haven't got round to telling me? For God's sake, Den.' Implications flew at her. 'Will your real dad want to come to the wedding? Where is he? Have you got brothers and sisters I don't know about?'

'He died three years ago. No known siblings. He didn't marry again.' He picked at the palm of one hand, waiting for her to subside.

'Oh dear. I'm not being very grown up about this, am I? And I can't pretend my own family is altogether normal.' She relaxed against his chest again. 'Sorry. I'm glad you've told me. Considering all that, you've turned out pretty well, on the whole.'

He tightened an arm around her and she snuggled closer. 'So it's all right, is it?'

She took a swig of wine, reaching awkwardly for the glass. 'Apart from my silly restlessness, yes. We haven't resolved that problem, though, have we? I'm too young to be a farmer, that's the trouble. I love Redstone, but I live for the hours when I can get away from it. My mother drives me mad and Roddy's so unconcerned with the farm that he seems more like a ghost than a brother. The *real* ghosts are bad enough . . .'

'Are you telling me you've been seeing ghosts?'

She laughed. 'They're not the visible sort, but they're there, just the same. Daddy and Sam are still there, somehow. They're always on at me, telling me what I should be doing, nagging about ditches and machinery and how I should keep it all in good condition. It's a hard life.'

'It wouldn't be so hard if you let me share it with you,' he said unwisely. As soon as the words were out, he closed his eyes tightly, braced for another burst of irrational anxieties.

Before it could materialise, the phone rang. They both exhaled, tension slipping away. 'Saved by the bell,' she said.

'Just so long as it isn't work,' he mumbled crossly before lifting the receiver.

'I'm terribly sorry if I'm interrupting,' came a familiar voice. 'But I wanted to thank you again for finding Clem so quickly. God, I can't tell you what it felt like to lose him.'

Den put his hand quickly over the mouthpiece and mimed 'Martha' silently to Lilah.

'That's okay,' he said. 'It's what we're here for.'

'I kept thinking about Nina and how we'd failed her by not keeping him safe. He's asleep now, poor little chap.'

'Did he say anything about why he did it?'

'Not much, but reading between the lines, I rather think it had something to do with Hugh. They were bickering at lunchtime and Hugh's looking a bit sheepish now.' She lowered her voice. 'Not that I want to blame anybody.

They're very close, compared to some brothers. I guess Clem's just extra sensitive at the moment. Anyway, all's well that ends well, as they say. I'm sure there's been no harm done.'

'I'm sure too,' he said, hoping the words sounded sufficiently confident to persuade her to curtail the call. But it seemed she had more to say.

'I was thinking, before this happened, about a conversation we had here last night. Hermione came to dinner and I asked her about Frank Gratton being Nev's godfather. She didn't give a proper explanation of how it came about, but it sounds as if she was *really* close to Charlie's mother – more so than I ever realised. This probably sounds strange to you, especially after the way I was talking on Monday, but I can't get her out of my mind. Something's been going on. And then – one of her horses damaged her shoulder, and it sounds like a really nasty animal and I was just wondering . . .' She hesitated and Den waited. 'Well, I know for a fact she didn't want Alexis to get into anything permanent with Charlie. She made no secret of that, months ago. I'm just wondering whether she got someone to ride over here on that horse and let it loose on him. Charlie, I mean. I'm sure she wouldn't have done it herself, but it does sound like the horse from hell. She calls it Boanerges.' She forced a laugh.

'Boa . . . what?'

'You know. There's a poem by Emily Dickinson? "The Railway Train". *I like to see it lap the miles and lick the valleys up.* It's one of my favourites. The last verse is *And neigh like Boanerges; then, punctual as a star, stop, docile and omnipotent, at its own stable door.* Well, I *am* an English teacher,' she concluded apologetically. 'I don't really know who the original Boanerges was, but this one's as big and strong as a train, very nearly.'

'Docile and omnipotent,' Den repeated, as if tasting the words.

'Lovely, isn't it.' There was a pause before she began again. 'Hermione says you haven't interviewed her yet. Are you planning to?'

Den sighed wearily. 'I was within a quarter of a mile of doing so when I got the call about Clem this afternoon. Every time I try, something intervenes. Can I just get this straight – what exactly are you trying to tell me?'

'That Hermione Nesbitt possesses a big strong horse and that she has a lot of history connecting her to Charlie,' she summed up impressively.

'Okay, thanks for the hint. Could anybody have taken Boanerges without her knowing about it?'

'I doubt it. She's got dogs galore and stable hands. There'd have been some sort of alarm raised if that happened. Especially as the person obviously took the horse back again afterwards. If the theory's right, that is.'

'If you don't mind my asking, what do you think of Hermione yourself?'

Martha took a long time over her reply. 'I didn't like her at all when Nina first married Nev, and she's not done much to endear herself to me since then. But she *is* fantastic with the boys. They adore her. So she can't be all bad. You know, I got the weirdest feeling last night that she wanted to *protect* them. Against Charlie, I mean. That she didn't want them to think about him or talk about him any more.'

'And yet he's the child of her closest friend and friendly with her own son.'

'That's right,' she agreed.

Lilah shifted noisily, indicating she thought the phone call had lasted long enough.

'I'll have to go,' he said. 'I'll keep you informed if anything happens.'

Martha didn't resist. 'Have a good Easter, then,' she said. 'And thanks for listening.'

Lilah, flipping through the *Radio Times* on the sofa, said nothing. Den looked at his watch. 'That took nearly twenty minutes. I'm sorry.' He went to cuddle close to her on the sofa again, but she didn't make any move to accommodate him.

'Come on, Li,' he wheedled, 'it wasn't my fault

she phoned.' Inwardly, he could feel impatience rising; sulks were a stupid waste of time in his book. But he was frightened too; he knew he would have to tread carefully.

She gave him a steady unsmiling stare.

'Shit!' He thumped a fist on the back of the couch. 'What am I supposed to do now?'

'Nothing.' She flicked her head and ran a swift hand over the short hair at the back of her neck. 'It's just . . . Martha shouldn't have phoned you here. It's starting to feel like a habit.' She stared hard at him again.

Relief flushed through him like a sweet draught of wine. He smiled broadly. 'You're jealous!' he told her happily. 'Jealous of Martha. I don't believe it.'

'And that's something to be pleased about, is it?' He could see she was having to hold on tight to the bad mood; the storm had passed once more. It felt like a game now, harmless, though potentially confusing. The rules were still unclear in his mind.

'Just for the record,' he said, 'I was praying she'd say her piece quickly and leave me alone.'

'That isn't the way it sounded to me. What was that about someone being omnipotent?'

'Docile and omnipotent,' he said again. 'Boanerges. It's Emily Dickinson.'

'*Poetry!*' she howled. 'You and Martha quote

poetry to each other and you wonder why I'm jealous.'

'Shut up, you dozy wench. I'm too tired to argue. Can we just pretend the call never happened? What she said – it can wait until morning.'

'Irresponsible sod,' she said, shifting at last so he could put his arm round her.

'You mind your language,' he mumbled, as their mouths found each other.

CHAPTER TWENTY-THREE

The phone woke them twenty minutes before the alarm would have done. Outside, birds were asking each other whether or not daylight had really arrived, and if so, was spring far enough advanced to warrant a full chorus? The sky was clear, the roads almost silent. It was 5.40 a.m.

'Cooper?' came the voice of another anonymous police message handler. 'There's been some kind of incident at the Quaker Meeting House in Chillhampton. It has been suggested you might like to get over there, seeing as how it's connected with your murder inquiry, and find out what's what.'

'Can't you give me more than that?' croaked Den blearily. 'Like what sort of incident.'

'Domestic. Neighbour reported screams. Just thought you'd want to know.' The voice was smug; somewhere along the line someone had done some unusually quick thinking and made the right connections.

'Yes. Thanks,' he said.

When he arrived at the Meeting House, there was a police car already parked outside and a small knot of villagers standing a judicious distance from the building, despite the hour. *How embarrassing for the Aspens*, thought Den, with genuine sympathy. One woman stepped forward. 'Be 'ee a policeman?' she asked.

'Detective Constable Den Cooper, madam,' said Den politely.

'Tid'n every day us gets this sort of thing,' she continued gleefully. Den recognised the type – early sixties, dumpy, with piercing brown eyes. She was clearly enjoying herself hugely.

'I'm sure it isn't,' he agreed, and pressed the doorbell, wondering how his arrival would impact on whatever might be happening in the Aspens' flat. A uniformed WPC clattered down the stairs to let him in. It was Benny Timms, one of the older, more matronly members of the local team. She smiled briefly, but seemed unsure as to how welcome his presence might be.

'What's going on?' he asked softly.

'I'm not altogether sure,' she whispered back.

'The wife's been having hysterics, but I can't get them to tell me what it's all about. The woman from the house up the road says she heard loud screams and shouting. He looks ghastly.'

'Has he been hitting her?'

'No, I don't think so. If anything, it's the other way around.'

'What?'

She rolled her eyes. 'Come and see for yourself. I suppose they might talk to you, if you already know them.'

He shook his head pessimistically. 'I wouldn't get your hopes up.'

He entered the room behind Constable Timms and scanned the scene. Clive and Mandy were both on the sofa, in their nightclothes. She was shaking and tearstained, her hands held in a tight grip by his. Clive was indeed looking ghastly. His black hair stood up in ragged spikes, his skin was grey and his short, thick beard was a sinister black slash on his cheeks and chin. 'Good morning,' said Den gently. 'I gather there's been some trouble.'

Clive shook his head heavily. 'Mandy had a bad dream. She woke up screaming and I've been trying to calm her. There's no need for you people to be involved. We're very sorry if we disturbed the neighbours. We had the window open, and the sound must have carried. This is all very embarrassing, as I expect you'll appreciate.'

'Well, sir,' Den began slowly, his mind picking up speed as he talked, 'the fact is there was a disturbance. The noise was sufficiently alarming for your neighbour to fear for your safety. With respect, it sounds as if there was something a bit more serious than a bad dream going on.'

Mandy moaned and tried to pull her hands away from Clive's grasp. Den began to wonder just why her husband was holding her so tightly. 'Let her go,' he said with a frown. 'Sir, your wife is trying to get free.'

For a moment Clive hung on, and then with a dramatic gesture he flung his hands wide apart. Mandy's fell into her lap like two dead things, revealing a scatter of torn-up paper which she had been clutching.

'What's this?' asked Den, stooping to gather a few of the scraps. They were the remains of a colour photograph. Quickly, with Mandy offering no resistance, he collected all the other fragments. There were eight in all, easy enough to reassemble. Clive made a low groan as Den laid the spoilt picture on the sofa beside Mandy.

'Is this who I think it is?' he asked.

Benny came to look over his shoulder, bemused by the sudden turn of events. 'It's somebody's little boy,' she said. 'Looks like a nice little chap.'

Den was staring from Mandy to Clive and back again. 'So this is how you recognised him yesterday,' he said to her. 'But—'

'It's not what you think,' growled Clive, shaking his head crazily from side to side. 'I never *touched* him.'

'All right, sir.' Den tried to calm him. 'Let's take this one step at a time, shall we? Would you explain why you've got a picture of Clement Nesbitt here in your flat?'

'There's no law against it, is there? It's just a simple snapshot. I work at his school. I wouldn't hurt him. I wouldn't let anyone touch a hair on his head.' His voice was rising; his eyes darted feverishly from face to face. 'It's *her*, with her nightmares and her refusal to face reality. She's the one you should be questioning, not me.'

Mandy began to cry again, loudly and without restraint. Den was at first concerned for her and then quickly suspicious that she was employing a diversionary tactic. Benny had evidently come to the same conclusion, since she put a firm hand on Mandy's arm. 'Come on, now, that's not going to help. You'll only have the neighbours telling more stories about you. You'll have to explain yourselves sooner or later, you know.'

The brisk words had some effect and Mandy

grew quieter. Den decided to leave the remaining formalities to Benny, indicating with a slight backward movement that the floor was all hers.

'Right,' she said, even more briskly, 'there doesn't seem to be any need for further questions at the moment. Detective Constable Cooper here is part of a murder inquiry, as you know, and I should imagine you will both have to be interviewed about what's happened this morning.' She looked at Den, who nodded. 'Meanwhile, I must ask you not to make any more disturbance. Can I have your assurances on that?'

Clive and Mandy murmured assent, like chastened schoolchildren.

Den cleared his throat. 'We'll need to see you separately,' he said. 'Meanwhile, I'll take this with me.' He tucked the torn-up picture into an evidence bag from his pocket. 'I don't think we should waste too much time, for everyone's sake.' He paused briefly, watching Clive carefully. 'In fact,' he decided, choosing his moment, 'I think it would be best, Mr Aspen, if you were to come with us to the police station now, and answer some questions there.'

Clive clenched his hands tightly together and pressed the double fist into his own stomach. It looked painful. 'Don't,' said Mandy. 'Clive, please don't.' She looked at Den. 'Be gentle with him,' she begged. 'He's not well.'

Den gave Clive ten minutes to get himself ready, while he and Benny went out into the village street. The Meeting House was set back from the road, with parking space in front for three or four cars. There was very little traffic; the curious neighbours had presumably all returned to their breakfasts. At least Clive wouldn't have an audience.

'What do you reckon?' Benny asked Den, as they loitered between their two cars.

'She's obviously scared of him,' Den began, before correcting himself. 'Or scared *for* him. And he's a real mess.'

'Clinging to sanity by his fingernails,' Benny agreed graphically. 'Though you can't always be sure with couples. I mean, it can be a sort of mirror image of the way it looks to an observer. Isn't there something called projection, where people dump all their own worst features onto their partner?'

Den gave her a sceptical look. 'Sounds complicated.'

'There's nowt so complicated as folk,' she quipped. 'Good luck with them, anyway. Disturbed your beauty sleep, did it? I told them not to call you.'

He grinned and rubbed his unshaven chin.

'And now you're glad they did. You looked a bit stuck when I arrived.'

She slapped him lightly on the shoulder. 'Me? Stuck! Never. But I can't pretend I was enjoying it. Something not very nice going on there. I'd bet money on it.'

'Well, while you're here, I might as well ask you—' Den leant closer, with a glance at the open window above their heads. Belatedly he wondered whether Clive and Mandy might have overheard what had been said so far. In a whisper, he said, 'Would you say he's in the running for the murder of Charlie Gratton? As a gut feeling?'

Benny pursed her lips and blew out her plump cheeks. She looked across the village street and then along its length to the junction with a small country road. She frowned. 'I wouldn't rule it out,' she said at last. 'But I would be surprised.'

Den opened his eyes wide in a parody of amazed incredulity. 'Thanks very much,' he said. 'You'll go far with insight like that.'

'You're the detective, mate,' she said, turning towards her car. 'I'd say his ten minutes are up. I'll just sit here until you've got him safely away. Have a nice day.'

But Den's day had virtually no chance of being nice after such a start. He delivered Clive to the police station only to have him whisked away to an interview room without a 'by your leave' even though it was far from clear who would do the interviewing. DI Smith and DC Bennett were both at home. Belatedly, Den realised it was Good Friday and nobody was going to thank him for bringing people in for interview. 'Either do it yourself or leave your subject to stew until a more respectable hour of the morning,' said the desk officer unsympathetically.

Den dithered, out of his depth. He knew there was no way he could question Clive without some discussion with the Inspector first. But it seemed wrong to bring the man in only to abandon him to the ministrations of the handful of reluctant Bank Holiday staff. He looked helplessly at his watch: seven forty-five.

'Call the DI at eight,' he said. 'Tell him what's happened and ask him to phone me at home. I'm going back for some breakfast.' He hoped he sounded decisive. 'And take Mr Aspen some coffee and something to eat, okay?'

The officer's jaw jutted forward mulishly, before he asked, 'Would he like butter on his hot cross buns, do you think?'

As he'd expected, Lilah had gone without leaving any sort of note. He didn't know when he could expect to see her again. This was almost the first time that his work had intruded so blatantly on their relationship and he knew it was bound to cause conflict. If he were to go for promotion – move to Exeter or even further afield, make himself available for intensive investigations – then Lilah would inevitably be required to make sacrifices. Outings would be cancelled; important events missed. Did she love him enough to make such adjustments? he wondered miserably. Were they already doomed to the stereotypical rocky police marriage, with the predictable finale in the divorce court?

He dragged his thoughts back to the job in hand. At least things did at last seem to be moving on the Gratton case. Martha's phone call couldn't be ignored; at the very least, someone should go and take a careful look at that evil-sounding horse. More immediately, the ructions at the Aspens' needed to be brought into the picture. The photograph of Clem was hard to account for with any innocent theory. Which one of the Aspens had torn it up and why? Impatiently, he waited for the DI's call. He wanted to get on with it, right now. More than anything, he wanted to speak to Mandy again, and try to coax the story out of her.

As he'd hoped, Smith summoned him back to the station and spent twenty minutes analysing the sudden acceleration of events. 'I think Clive

Aspen is seriously unstable,' Den concluded. 'One minute he's all calm and collected, the next he can't keep still and has a face like a gargoyle. Something's triggered off some sort of relapse, sir. Dorothy Mansfield – and Val Taylor – told me he had a breakdown before coming to live here. I wouldn't put anything past him at the moment.'

'Poor chap,' said the DI, to Den's surprise. 'Better go carefully with him, then.' He tapped his teeth with a biro. 'Do you think she made some sort of accusation? His wife, that is. And sent him off the deep end.'

Den blinked. 'About Clem, you mean?'

'Clem or Charlie, or both. Look, Cooper, I think *I'll* see the chap and you can go back and talk to the missus. Encourage her to open up, say it'll help Clive if she tells us the whole story. Does she trust you, do you think?'

'Can't say, sir.'

'Well, give her a couple of hours to settle down, and keep it sweet. It can't be much fun for her if her husband's gone off his rocker.'

'She did look as if she'd had enough,' Den agreed. 'Sir . . . the photo of Clem . . .'

'Intriguing, definitely. But not actually incriminating in itself. And not immediately useful in solving the Gratton case.'

'I know, sir. But—'

'I can see the way your mind's heading, Cooper. Aspen was buggering the kid, Charlie found out about it, reported it anonymously – you'd have to work on that bit, of course – so Aspen bumped him off on the horse he rides to the hunt. Got the idea from what happened to the Nesbitt woman. Thought it a fitting end. Something along those lines?'

'More or less,' Den admitted. 'And the disturbance this morning was because Mrs Aspen, having found that photo, had just come to the same conclusion.'

'Keep an open mind, son,' the DI advised. 'And go home and tidy yourself up. Ten-thirty's the right sort of time to visit Mrs A. She might even make you a lovely cup of Quaker tea.'

Den did as he was told, thankful that he lived only a few streets away from the station. It promised to be one of those days when he bounced back and forth like a yo-yo.

He had to remind himself that it was Good Friday. He had barely given Easter a thought, except to work out a complicated rota with Phil and Danny to ensure there was cover for each day. He had managed to secure the Sunday off and was supposed to be going to Redstone for a roast lunch with Lilah and her family. Otherwise it wasn't going to be noticeably different from other Bank Holiday weekends. As Lilah so often said, to a cow every day is the same; they still have to be milked every morning and afternoon.

He went back to his musings about Clive and Mandy. Did Good Friday mean anything special to them? What did Quakers do at Easter?

By some connecting process, he found himself thinking about Nina Nesbitt's grave in the High Copse garden, from which she was never going to rise again, and from there he remembered once more the details of how she died. Martyred to her cause. He had said very little to Lilah about it, but the image of Nina dropping to the ground with a small gasp would never completely go away. He heard again the sound she made – a little *Oh!* of surprise. Surprise, yes, but also resignation, acceptance, perhaps even understanding. Or had she died with absolutely no awareness of what was happening to her? One sharp blow to the face and her brain had immediately started to die. It no longer instructed her legs to hold her weight, her heart to pump blood, her lungs to draw air. But surely, Den insisted to himself, there had been time for *thought*? Plenty of time for final thoughts of where she was going and what she was leaving behind.

And Charlie Gratton? Had *he* been given time to register the transition? Had he had time to see and recognise the horse and the rider who had mown him down? Unbidden, on this day when the slow crucifixion of Jesus Christ was marked worldwide, he felt the utter loneliness of death for the first time in his life. And he shook his head in shame at the light way he had regarded it until now. The handful of murder inquiries he'd been involved in had all seemed like puzzles to be solved rather than terribly human tragedy. He'd used the idea of justice carelessly, viewed it merely as something that made life just that bit tidier. When they'd caught the person who killed Lilah's father, nearly a year ago, there had been a satisfaction in knowing the case was closed, the murderer put out of action – but he didn't remember feeling much more than that. He didn't remember giving a single serious thought to the suffering victim, dying in horror and disbelief.

He was not religious; he had scarcely ever been to church other than for school events and a few weddings. But now he allowed himself to wonder whether he'd been missing something. Now he wondered whether there'd be a place for him at the Quaker Meeting, where he might sit quietly and ponder these unwelcome new insights. With a sense of an invisible hand propelling him from behind, he went to find his notepad. There was only one person who could help him.

* * *

The voice on the phone was thick with sleep and Den remembered too late that it was still only nine in the morning. But there was no going back now. 'Mrs Map . . . I mean, Mrs Mansfield? I'm terribly sorry to wake you. I didn't notice how early it was.'

'Is that the piano-playing policeman? Cooper?' She wasn't so sleepy after all, then.

'That's right.'

'And?'

'Er . . . well, this is more of a personal call than part of the investigation,' he prevaricated. 'I was wondering, do the Quakers have a meeting today? For Good Friday, I mean?'

There was a trace of surprise in her voice. 'No, Den. We make very little of the big Christian festivals. We try to act as if every day was the same – equally special. Do you see?'

'I think so,' he said, feeling like a fool, wishing he could drop the phone back on its cradle and forget the whole thing. 'So you just have the usual meeting on Sunday, then?'

'That's right,' she confirmed. 'Unless we hold a special one for some reason, like we did last Friday.'

He forced himself to continue. 'What time is it? On Sunday, I mean?'

'Ten-thirty. We'd be very happy to see you there. Don't try to think too much about it,' she counselled him. 'Just do what feels right. You know where to find us, that's the main thing.'

'Thanks,' he managed, appalled to find his voice thickening with emotion. 'Thanks very much.'

CHAPTER TWENTY-FOUR

The phone rang again at nine-thirty, interrupting Den's light doze. The duty officer informed him he was needed. They'd had a call from a distraught woman claiming that a man intent on murder was trying to break into her house. The woman was Hannah Gratton.

Two police cars were sent speeding along the narrow lanes, one of them containing DC Cooper.

A cloud of bewildered thoughts filled his mind, as he urged the car on from the passenger seat. Was Charlie's killer stupid enough to attempt another murder? If so, he'd failed miserably, from the sound of it. Was this to be the climax of the inquiry, the *deus ex machina* that would render superfluous all their interviews and patient attempts at unravelling the mystery? Where did this new development leave the Aspens – yet another dangling loose end in Den's untidy and interrupted schedule? The familiar mixture of curiosity, apprehension and fatalism churned its way through his guts. 'It's left here,' he said unnecessarily to the driver.

The cottage was strangely calm as they arrived. There was no sign of a would-be murderer battering the door down, no stirred-up ground or pools of blood. Two uniformed police officers were walking up to the door before Den's car had been parked. Den watched as Bill Gratton slowly pulled the door open, and stood back to let the men in.

'Doesn't look as if we're needed,' said Den's companion. 'Rather a crowd in that little place, if we barge in too.'

'But I know them. They'll be glad to see a familiar face,' Den protested. 'They're part of the Gratton murder inquiry. I've got to see what's been going on.'

'Go on then,' shrugged his comrade, not really caring. 'I'll just sit here until you need me.'

Den trotted up the path and entered the house, ducking his head from long habit to clear the low doorway. The small front room did indeed feel very crowded – but with more than just people. There was an atmosphere of such strong emotion that he could almost taste it. Hannah Gratton sat curled in an armchair, her face crumpled and sodden with tears. Her brother stood beside the fireplace, away from the room, his head lowered like a wounded bull. 'What happened?' asked Den weakly.

'He's gone now,' Hannah said, looking at the limp hanky in her hand. 'He didn't hurt us – not physically. I should have known he wouldn't hurt us.'

'He ought never to have come here,' Bill's voice was rumbling and slow. 'I said to him, years ago, he was never to come here again. I said I wouldn't be able to bear the shame of it, if he did.'

Hannah reached out a hand towards him, but couldn't quite bridge the distance between them. Bill made no move towards her. 'It's all right. He's gone now,' she said. Then she looked quickly around at the men filling her living room, as if only just noticing them. 'I'm sorry I called you. I was afraid. I let myself down,' she added softly. 'It's all my fault.'

Den crossed the room to her, and squatted down beside her chair, bringing his face close to hers. 'Who?' he breathed.

She met his eyes, and smiled damply. 'I remember you,' she said. 'I'm glad it's you.'

'Who was here?' he repeated.

She heaved a shuddering breath, and more tears ran down her cheeks. 'Frank,' she said. Den realised he'd known the answer anyway.

'Charlie's brother,' Den confirmed. 'And can you tell me what he did – what caused so much trouble?'

'He's not his brother,' came Bill's gruff voice. 'He's—'

'*Wait*, Bill,' Hannah gasped. 'There's no need to say any more. It has nothing to do with the police.'

The old man shook his head hopelessly, and Den could see him shaking, one knee jittering so much it seemed in danger of collapse. But he remained silent.

One of the uniformed officers spoke. 'There's no sign of any misdemeanour having been committed here,' he judged. 'If you've got no formal complaint, madam, then we'll be on our way. It seems to be one of those days.' He smiled ruefully at his partner. 'Everybody's dialling 999. I always think there's something about Bank Holidays that makes people do strange things.'

Nobody responded. Den tried to think. 'We can't leave these people in this state,' he said. 'They've been very badly shaken.'

'We can call a doctor, or a social worker,' came the dubious reply. 'But there's no sign of any injury. And if they don't want to tell us the whole story, there's no way we can force them.'

A choking sound came from Hannah. Den peered at her, and decided she was laughing. *Hysterics,* he thought, with some alarm. What did you do with someone with hysterics?

But she rapidly controlled herself. 'Not a social worker,' she said weakly. 'There's really no need for that. We'll be all right. It's a very bad time for us – with Charlie—'

'Of course it is,' soothed Den. 'Now, is there anything you want to report? We're going to have to pay your nephew a visit, in any case. He oughtn't to have left you in this state.'

'It's not his fault,' Hannah protested vehemently. 'Don't be hard on him. He's in enough trouble as it is.'

'When you phoned us, you said you were being attacked by a murderer. We can't just forget that you used that word. You understand that, don't you?'

Hannah said nothing, but she glanced at Bill, who was now clinging to the mantelpiece like a drowning man, his face grey and twitching. Den jumped up, and took hold of him. 'Sit down, Mr Gratton. You're going to fall, otherwise.' He steered him to the sofa, where he flopped heavily and awkwardly.

'I'm calling a doctor,' said a uniformed officer nervously. 'He doesn't look too good to me.'

'Bill?' Hannah's voice was suddenly sharp. 'What's the matter with you?' She heaved herself out of her chair, and rushed to her brother. She looked up at Den – for reassurance or perhaps explanation. 'He had a minor stroke last year. It slowed his speech down, but didn't do any lasting damage. Do you think this is another one?'

Den pulled his lips back in a grimace of uncertainty. 'It could be,' he said. 'We'll get an ambulance for him.' He nodded at the other men. 'They'll be able to assess what's going on.'

It was all happening at a nightmarish pace. Bill Gratton had slumped sideways on the sofa, his eyes rolling grotesquely and short, huffing breaths coming from his mouth. Putting a restraining hand on him, trying to keep him upright, Den was aware of an unnatural heat. The man was very obviously seriously ill, and Den wondered frantically how many early signs they'd missed, and whether they could have made a difference by calling for help ten minutes sooner.

'Oh, Bill,' Hannah wept. 'Not you as well. Don't leave me, Bill. I can't manage without you. Please, Bill!' Den gently held her back, watching the old man sink into unconsciousness like a small child whooshing down a well-polished playground slide. There was even a little smile on his lips, as if the letting go had relieved him of a great burden.

When the ambulance men arrived, it was too late to save him. They could do no more than sigh and remind Den of the need for a police doctor before summoning the undertakers to convey the body to the Exeter mortuary for the necessary post-mortem.

Numb with shock, Den found himself with an arm curled tightly around Hannah's shoulders. He had never seen anyone die until a fortnight ago, and now here he was witnessing a second sudden death. He couldn't make it true inside his own head. He glanced at the ceiling, into corners of the room, out of the window, dimly aware that he was looking for the vanished Bill. He reran over and over those few minutes between moving the old man from the fireplace and hearing the ambulance men pronounce him dead. He understood the mechanics, more or less. Bill's brain had haemorrhaged, somewhere deep inside. The pressure of the blood in the wrong place, or the lack of blood to a vital area, had closed down his body's normal workings. His heart had stopped beating; his lungs had stopped taking in oxygen. Whatever the precise detail, the maintenance of life had ceased. He wondered what that meant. In the minutes following the death of Nina Nesbitt, he'd been busy with managing the crowd, calling for assistance, distracting himself from the reality.

This time, he had nothing to do but watch. He tried to imagine how it would be to die himself, and found the idea impossible. He clutched Hannah even tighter, trying to prevent his own arm from shaking.

'We need a cup of tea,' she said to him, gently removing the constricting arm. Her natural composure was rapidly returning, greatly to Den's admiration. 'There's nothing more we can do now. And really, you know, it's probably the best thing. Bill never could take too much truth. He never allowed Frank's name to be mentioned. Never for a second allowed himself to remember what happened.' She paused, watching the ambulance drive away, with the car containing the police officers following it. 'I was right, though,' she said distantly. 'There was a murderer at the door, all along.'

It was half past eleven when Den walked into the police station. He had stayed with Hannah for a while after the undertaker's men had removed Bill's body. She had told him the long-buried secret, concerning Bill and Frank and Charlie and Eloise. She had wept, not for herself, but for the things people did, and the consequences they reaped, even thirty years later. Den's own eyes had filled, as he recognised the truth in what she was saying. He had assumed that his murder inquiry was complete, and Hannah had quiveringly agreed with him. All he had to do now was unburden himself to Detective Inspector Smith.

The Inspector could see that Den was shaken, and he showed more of the unusual tact that had already come to the surface earlier that morning. He called for a cup of strong coffee and no interruptions. 'I gather there was a fatality?' he began. 'Must have been difficult – having the chap pass away before your very eyes.'

Pass away jarred on Den. Why speak in euphemisms? But he nodded anyway, and took a large gulp of the coffee.

'He seemed a harmless old chap,' he said. 'Not so old, come to that. But it's Miss Gratton I feel sorry for.' He shook his head helplessly. 'I need to tell you what she told me, sir, even though it's in confidence. I think it's important – I think it's the key to Charlie's death.' He looked up, urgency in his eyes. 'Are they bringing Frank Gratton in? They should be. We can't let him slip through our fingers now.'

Smith made a soothing motion. 'Nobody's going to slip through anything. But you'll need to persuade me before I send in the troops.'

Den closed his eyes, and took a run at it.

'Frank Gratton is Charlie's father, sir. Not his brother. At least—' he frowned '—I suppose he's his brother as well. *Jesus.*'

Smith caught on so quickly that Den suspected him of having been a step ahead all along. 'Frank was having sex with his mother? Eloise Gratton? The woman who killed herself in the pond?' His face was grim.

'That's what Hannah told me, sir,' Den confirmed unhappily. 'She's kept it a secret all these years. Of course, she wasn't in the country at the time. She came home—'

'Yes, yes, I remember. So who told her, I wonder?'

'Bill, I assume. He certainly knew about it – which is why he banned Frank from ever coming near him. They hadn't seen each other for twenty years until today.'

'Did Miss Gratton give you any clues as to how such a thing ever came to happen?'

'A few, sir. Eloise was very young – young for her age, I mean. Like a girl. She was in awe of Bill, who made it clear he thought she was a bit empty-headed and silly. Came over the old-fashioned Quaker, I imagine. Frank matured early and took it upon himself to protect her.'

'But that's a long way from having it away with her,' Smith objected. 'What on earth possessed them? Was it a one-off or did it go on for years? How old was the boy?'

'He was almost sixteen when the baby was born. I would guess it happened a few times. She was a bit of a mess, I gather. Depressed, neurotic. Silas Daggs remembers it well. It's even possible he guessed at the truth, but buried it.'

'How in the hell does he *live* with himself?' Smith burst out. 'It's sick. Disgusting . . .'

Den shook his head helplessly. 'I know, sir. But the way Hannah tells it, you have to feel sorry for him. He was only a boy. And it takes two. He loved the baby, by all accounts.'

'And did *Charlie* know who his real father was?'

'No he didn't. Hannah thinks Hermione Nesbitt might have guessed. She behaved oddly with Charlie after Eloise died. But nobody's going to voice a thing like that, are they? Not unless they're forced to.'

Smith snorted his agreement. 'So give me your theory of what happened to Charlie.'

'Okay,' Den said slowly. 'I think it was because Charlie was getting serious about Alexis, and might end up marrying her. Having kids. Someone might have told Frank about it – Hannah, probably – and he was scared that the product of incest would make a bad prospect as a father. I don't really understand how the biology of it might work. I assume Frank being a horse breeder, he would have some idea about that. He paid a visit to Nina earlier this year. My guess is he wanted to find out how big a risk there was of Charlie marrying Alexis. So, hearing what she had to say, he decided to prevent it from happening. He might have seen it as his duty. He selects his biggest, fiercest horse, rides over early one morning, and loiters about waiting for Charlie to show up. He could follow him around until he got his chance. Horse riders all look rather anonymous with hard hats on. There are riders all over the place – nobody would look twice.'

'Not bad, on the face of it,' Smith mused, a large hand cupping his craggy chin. 'Though why wouldn't Hannah herself feel a duty to stop Charlie making babies with Alexis?'

'Maybe she got Frank to do it on her behalf?'

Smith was icy calm, arms folded loosely. 'We'll have to tread carefully,' he judged. 'It'll be a shame to cause that poor woman any more suffering.'

'I know, sir,' said Den miserably. 'She's dreading the people at the Meeting hearing about this. I suppose there's no way we can keep it hushed up, is there, sir?'

Smith pushed out his lips, considering. 'Might be,' he said. 'Depends on what we decide to pin on Brother Frank. If we bring him in on a murder charge, we have to give reasons for our suspicions, and as far as I can see, there's only one road to go down on that front. And if it comes to court, they'll dig out every unsavoury little detail. The newspapers are going to think they've died and gone to heaven. Off the top of my head, I can't remember a murder trial based on mother-son incest – not a single one.'

Den shuddered, and rubbed the scarred side of his face. 'Jesus,' he said again.

'Fortunately, I don't think there's too much to worry about,' Smith continued, unperturbed. 'Because I'm not altogether inclined to accept your scenario.'

'Sir? Why not, sir?'

'Full of holes, lad. But I'm not going to blow it out of the water just yet. Now – before all this came up, you had an appointment with Mrs Mandy Aspen, didn't you? At ten-thirty?'

Tiredly, Den nodded and looked at his watch. 'I never told her an exact time,' he said, getting to his feet. 'I'd better go and do it now. Although . . .'

'No need to rush. I've spoken to Friend Clive, and you're right. He's losing it. Barely safe to be released into the community, in my view. But we'll have to let him go this afternoon, when we've had a doctor to him.'

'What did he tell you, sir?'

'That he never touched a child inappropriately in his life. That his marriage is absolutely sound in every respect, but that his wife is given to violent nightmares, which is what was going on this morning. He enjoys a nice energetic ride and follows the hounds now and then purely because it's a good country sprint and a physical challenge. He's never seen a fox killed and doesn't think he's contributing in any way to cruel practices. He thought Charlie was misguided but harmless. He told me all this with a glazed expression and his arms hugged to his chest. I think if I'd touched him he'd have turned into a gibbering wreck.'

'And did you believe any of it, sir?'

'Did I hell.'

Smith put both arms on the table, and lined his thumbs up, side by side, peering through them as if sighting down a rifle barrel. Den had seen him do this before, at moments of crisis. 'On the face of it,' the DI said slowly, 'Aspen's off the hook, now we know about Frank Gratton. But you'll find as you go on that when someone is deliberately killed, all kinds of other things get shaken out of the rafters. It's as if there's been a great storm and a lot of dead wood comes rattling down. Somebody once said that there's never a single motive for a murder. It happens because a whole lot of things come together, set off a chain reaction, and they do that because there's been a pivotal event. A spark. I'm just wondering if this spark hasn't got something to do with the Aspens. Think a minute,' he invited Den. 'You find a computer record of an unconfirmed suspicion that the younger Nesbitt kid's being abused. Clive Aspen helps out at that kid's school. Clive Aspen rides to hunt, even though he's a Quaker, and might be expected to disapprove of such a practice. Charlie must have seen him. What would that have done to relations between them? What would the other Quakers think? Clive knows the Grattons – Hannah and Bill – pretty well, after living here for three years. Does he know Frank? Has he heard whispers about Charlie's parentage? What about Alexis Cattermole?' He parted his thumbs, letting his hands fall palm upwards on the desk, as if liberating all his thoughts to fly where they might. 'Do you see what I mean?' he demanded, fixing Den with a penetrating look.

Den's head felt fuzzy. 'I think so, sir. I think you mean I – or someone – will have to go and speak to Mandy Aspen sooner rather than later.'

'Exactly,' affirmed the Inspector.

CHAPTER TWENTY-FIVE

The Good Friday switchback hadn't finished with Den yet. Quickly draining a second mug of coffee, before embarking on a return visit to the Quaker Meeting House, he was called to the phone. He was only mildly surprised to hear Mandy Aspen's Birmingham accent. 'Are you still planning to interview me?' she said, her voice sounding even more nasal than usual. 'I've been waiting in for you. And what's happening to Clive? Have you arrested him?' There was reproach in her voice.

'I'm very sorry,' Den said. 'I got called away. I was just coming over now. Your husband will be released this afternoon. We're just waiting for a doctor to check him over.'

'Oh,' she said unemotionally. 'Well, would

it be all the same to you if we had our talk somewhere other than here? I need to get out – the place is giving me the creeps.'

'Do you mean you'd like to come here?'

'Oh no. That would be even worse.' She forced an apologetic laugh. 'Somewhere in town? Would that be allowed?'

'Anything's allowed. I only want you to fill in some background.'

'I thought that little coffee place, in Market Street,' she suggested tentatively. 'It's not very far from the police station.'

Den smiled to himself. The first real conversation he'd ever had with Lilah had been in that coffee bar. He remembered her face, worried and upset at the mysterious death of her father, but she'd been nonetheless disgracefully tanned and healthy in a skimpy T-shirt. Mandy Aspen would be a poor substitute, but the place was a reasonably good choice for a rendezvous. 'What time?' he asked.

'About twelve-fifteen?'

'Okay, then. I'll be waiting for you inside.' He resolved to be early. She was probably too shy to walk into such a place alone, unless she was sure there would be someone waiting for her.

Mandy Aspen peered through the plate glass of the café window at ten past twelve, and jumped when she saw Den's face only inches away. He had deliberately positioned himself for maximum visibility, while knowing that she would want to sit in a shadowy corner. He got up to greet her, and then led the way to a much less conspicuous table. The place was half full, but the sound level was low. The hiss of the cappuccino machine was the noisiest thing in the place.

He bought coffees, and sat opposite her. 'You must be worried about your husband,' he began tentatively. 'He doesn't seem very well at the moment.'

'I'm used to it,' she said, matter-of-factly. 'Although this morning was different. When I found that photo, I knew there was trouble.' Her accent seemed to lend itself naturally to gloom and pessimism.

'What sort of trouble exactly?'

She glanced around at the neighbouring tables, but nobody seemed interested in what she was saying. 'You probably don't know, but he's had a lot of problems in the past. Even before the baby died, he was getting really stressed at work.'

'Your baby died?' Den interrupted, with rather too much eagerness. 'I'm so sorry,' he added, trying to hit the right note.

She nodded. 'I'll explain that in a minute. Let me tell you about Clive first. When it happened he collapsed with a complete breakdown. It took three years for him to get back to anything like normal. We thought we'd found new hope when we came here. This job seemed ideal at first – we thought it was heaven-sent. Hardly any pressures, surrounded by wonderful, kind people. We genuinely believed we were doing the Lord's work, that we'd been called to it on a very personal level. But it went wrong.' She sighed deeply, and wiped a hand across her brow distractedly.

'Because of Charlie?' offered Den recklessly. She blinked, frowned and shook her head.

'Charlie? No – of course not. It had nothing to do with Charlie. At least—' She shook her head again. 'If it did, that came much later.'

'Sorry. Carry on.' Inwardly cursing himself, he resolved to let her have her say uninterrupted from then on.

'Clive had therapy, you see. This woman saw him about three times a week. Clive's father paid for it. They went back into his childhood, and all the traumatic things that'd happened to him. It seemed to work fairly well. Clive likes to think everything has its own logic, that everything can be explained by cause and effect. He went on to cognitive therapy after a while, and now he doesn't see anyone. Or only once in a blue moon. The trouble is' – she sighed again – 'now he thinks *I* need therapy as well.'

'Ah,' said Den.

'Yes. Because I have bad dreams, and get a bit agoraphobic sometimes, and can't remember very much about my early childhood, he's convinced himself that I was sexually abused when I was little. And I *wasn't*. I *know* I wasn't. The idea's crazy. But he's read all these books. His therapist put the idea into his head. Whenever I can't sleep, or thrash about a bit when I'm dreaming, he tries to force me to . . . remember.'

'Sounds rather as though *he's* abusing you,' remarked Den.

'In a way he is,' she nodded, with an air of relief. 'It's getting worse all the time. He talks about denial and repressed memories and how I should have the courage to face the truth. It's like being brainwashed. And I daren't tell anybody, because they might think he's right.' She gave Den a wild look. 'And even if it *was* true, I wouldn't want to remember it now. Why should I? It would be too late to do anything about it. My dad is a very sweet man, wouldn't hurt a fly. The merest whisper of such a thing would probably kill him.'

'But you've mentioned it to me,' Den pointed out.

Mandy bit her lip. 'I know. I'm trusting you not to take it any further. I know enough about law to be sure you can't begin any sort of inquiry unless I bring charges. My problem is with Clive.

There's been something going on that I don't understand, and with these deaths, I'm getting scared.' She stopped, a hand to her mouth.

'Scared?' Den prompted.

'That he'll go right over the edge,' she said. There was a silence as Den waited for more.

'I'll tell you about the baby now,' she went on. 'It was a cot death, although Clive never accepted that as an explanation. He's become more and more convinced over the years that the babysitter was responsible. More abuse, you see.'

'Sorry?' Den was lost.

'Daniel – that was his name – was ten months old. A boy from across the road – Seamus – was looking after him. When we came home Danny was naked and Clive asked Seamus what was going on. He said the baby seemed very hot and he was trying to cool him down. Well, he *was* a bit warm, but it was nothing alarming. I never doubted Seamus's honesty. He wasn't flustered or guilty or anything.'

'And he was fully clothed himself?'

'What? Oh yes, of course he was. Good God – he was just a perfectly nice, normal boy.'

'And then—?'

She paused, swallowing painfully. 'Danny died the following night. They never found anything wrong with him. Now, of course, I blame myself, because I laid him on his face. He seemed to prefer it like that and there hadn't been any research then to say it was harmful. He'd never been ill. He was a sweet baby.'

'I'm terribly sorry,' said Den. 'What a dreadful thing.'

'Yes, well as I say, it was the final straw for Clive. He tried to persuade the police that Seamus had abused our baby, but they could see he wasn't in his right mind, thank goodness. Otherwise it would have been terrible for poor Seamus. Clive's obsessed with child abuse, encouraged by the media, of course. There are all these books, you know – I think they should be banned. They tell you how to spot the signs. Practically everything counts as suspicious, once you start looking for it.' She sighed.

In the ensuing silence, Den fitted a few more pieces of the jigsaw together. 'Clement Nesbitt?' he said. 'The photograph?'

She nodded. 'Clive thinks Clem looks exactly as Daniel would if he'd lived. Actually, there is a resemblance. He took the photo himself, at school. He's had it by the bed for weeks now.'

'Which is how you came to recognise Clem yesterday.'

She nodded again. 'Last night Clive started shouting about Charlie. He thinks I was rather too fond of him, you see. It's true I did like him. He was so appealing, such a funny mixture of

365

little-boy-lost and clever activist. And Clive was jealous of Charlie seeing so much of Clem.'

Den drew a hissing breath. 'Bad news!' he said without thinking.

'What? You mean a grown man ought not to allow himself to get attached to little boys. What a world! Anyway, that's the truth of it.'

'We have a record of an anonymous suggestion that Clement Nesbitt was being abused, about six months ago.'

'I expect that was Clive,' she said flatly. 'He tried to bring it up with the head teacher, but she dismissed it.'

'Did he suspect Charlie?'

She nodded. 'Charlie started going out with Alexis at about that time. The little boy's behaviour changed, and Clive was sure he knew why.'

'But the authorities couldn't find anything suspicious.'

'Of course they couldn't,' she said. 'It was all in Clive's own mind.'

'False accusations are dangerous, you know.' His words came slowly, because another idea was nudging at him. Something Benny had said only that morning, about projection. If he'd got the theory right, there may well be very good cause to pay very particular attention to Clive Aspen, who had managed to wheedle his way into a primary school, and whose every waking thought appeared to involve sexual abuse of children.

Nervously, Mandy pushed away her cup and reached down for her handbag. 'You don't have to tell me that,' she said. 'I've betrayed him, haven't I? But somebody has to stop him, before something awful happens.'

Den stared at her for a moment, only now grasping the depths of her own self-absorption. 'Wouldn't you say that something awful has already happened?' he demanded, with some force. She looked blank for a few seconds.

'Oh – you mean Charlie. I was forgetting. But that had nothing to do with *Clive*. Obviously it didn't. Clive would never *kill* anybody. He's far too much of a coward for that.' And she pushed back her chair, took a deep breath and left.

Once again at the police station, Den sought out his superior. 'Is the DI still here?' he asked Larry on the front desk.

'Think so,' was the laconic reply. 'Last I saw him, he looked busy with a stack of paperwork.'

Den found him on the telephone, standing at his desk. The file on Charlie Gratton was closed, as if finished with for the day. He nodded at Den, but carried on listening to the voice coming out of the receiver.

'Right, sir. That's what I think. Sorry to

trouble you. Have a good Easter.' He put the phone down, and lifted the jacket from the back of his chair. 'Okay, Cooper. That was the Superintendent. I wanted to pick his brains about what to do with Frank Gratton. He agrees with me that we haven't got enough evidence to bring him in and hold him. But he might like to answer a few questions about his poor old dad keeling over the way he did. Even though Hannah isn't pressing charges, she did make that emergency call. And we are dealing with a family at the centre of a murder investigation. So – how d'you feel about going over to Ashburton for a few words with him?'

'Now, sir?' Den's lack of enthusiasm was palpable.

'Not if you're otherwise engaged. Tomorrow would probably do. I doubt if he's going anywhere.'

Den felt torn. It wouldn't look very good if he let weariness and a sense of overload get in the way of his professional obligations. 'No, sir, I can do it this afternoon,' he said.

'Actually,' smiled Smith, 'I'd rather you went tomorrow. If he's guilty, he'll be expecting us to go rushing over as soon as maybe. Leave him twenty-four hours, and you might find him in an interesting emotional state.'

'And if he's innocent?'

'If he's innocent, it doesn't matter either way. Does it?'

Den blinked away some of the complexities, and remembered his assignation at the coffee shop. 'I've just seen Mandy Aspen,' he said. 'And to put it briefly, she told me it was Clive who sounded the alarm about young Clem Nesbitt being abused. She explained what this morning's disturbance was about. I'm not happy about him, but I can't see him killing Charlie.' He yawned uncontrollably. 'Sorry, sir. It's been quite a day.'

Smith was obviously impatient to get away, but not sufficiently so to render him inattentive. 'Another loose end tidied away,' he nodded. 'Good. I've a feeling we'll have cracked this little puzzle by Monday. Would it be a good idea to phone the Cattermoles and see if they've had any inkling about Charlie's origins?'

Den considered. 'Not easy, sir. And I really don't think they have. I'd have picked it up if so. If anyone knew, it would have been Nina. How can I ask them without giving the secret away? That would feel like betraying Hannah, and I can't see what good it could do.'

The DI shrugged. 'I thought, if Alexis already knew and was happy to stick with him regardless, she might have been unknowingly forcing the killer to take stronger measures.'

Den shook his head. 'I absolutely don't think we should say anything.'

'You might be right. Well, I'm off. You know where you can find me, if I'm needed. Meanwhile, go home and have a hot cross bun, why don't you?'

As he went to collect his jacket, Den's thoughts were whirling. Every time he identified another twist in the story – another piece of evidence or a new hypothesis – Inspector Smith seemed to have got there first. So he could either give up and let his superior get on with it in his own mysterious way – or he could strain every nerve to overtake him, to come up with something mind-blowingly conclusive, and have it complete and incontrovertible on the DI's desk by Monday.

CHAPTER TWENTY-SIX

'We all want you to stay – you know that, don't you?'

Richmond had intercepted Nev as he strolled aimlessly away from Nina's grave, apparently headed for the orchard up the hill from the house. Now he walked alongside him. 'You shouldn't feel in the way or anything.'

Nev ran a long-fingered hand through his limp hair, which was no longer tied back in its ponytail. From the back he looked sexless, hermaphrodite, a figure designed to confuse. 'I don't know,' he said feebly. 'I'm no good at all this. I thought with you and Martha and Alexis, they'd barely notice if I was here or not.'

'You're their father,' said Richmond irritably. 'What did you expect?'

'I expected to stay for a bit, make sure they'd got all they needed, make my peace with Nina – and be off again.' He looked out at the dips and rises of the crumpled Devon landscape and shook his head. 'I can't stay here – it's too enclosed, too insular. I remember my father calling it *pusillanimous*. I must be more like him that I thought, because I can see exactly what he meant. Small-minded, stuck in the past – oh, hell, I'm sorry Richmond. I don't expect you to see it like that. I'm the one with the problem.'

'You and your sons,' Richmond reminded him sternly. 'If you leave them now, I doubt if they'll ever forgive you. Or Nina.'

'What's it got to do with Nina?'

Richmond scratched his head. 'I don't suppose anybody told you what Hugh said at the funeral?' Nev shook his head. 'He said she was a pretty useless mother, and he made a list of the things she did that annoyed him. One of them was neglecting you so you went off abroad all the time. What I'm saying, I suppose, is that they've idolised you to the point where nothing you do is really your fault. Martha tells me it's quite common. They daren't even *think* bad things about you in case it makes you disappear again.'

'Thanks very much,' said Nev gloomily. 'You're

telling me I've got to stay here then, are you? Until Clem's eighteen?'

'That would be the idea, yes. But I imagine they'd settle for a guaranteed six months to start with. You know,' he continued, leading their footsteps to an even more remote corner of the orchard and glancing down at the house as if to check they weren't being overheard, 'Martha and I would have been happy to raise them as our own. And so would Charlie and Alexis. I heard Charlie say to them, the day after Nina died, that they could always rely on him; that he'd be honoured to stand in for you, whenever you were away.'

'*Honoured?* Pompous bastard,' Nev laughed bitterly. 'And what did the boys say to that?'

'Clem seemed rather pleased, I thought. But Hugh took a step back, very stiff, and said he already had a perfectly adequate father, thank you very much. I was surprised, to be honest. They both seemed fond enough of Charlie when he was around, though Martha tells me I'm blind and deaf to how anyone's feeling, most of the time. Anyway, I suppose it was bad timing on Charlie's part, talking like that when they'd just lost their mother.'

'Kids are lousy judges of character,' Nev said ruefully. 'Charlie would have made a far better dad to them than I'm ever going to.'

Richmond snorted in wordless agreement.

'They've got my ma of course,' Nev continued, after a pause. 'She adores them. Clem looks a lot like my dad, which helps. She'd never admit it, but she did love the silly old sod. Pity he pegged out when he did.'

'You would never guess,' Richmond remarked. 'She seems entirely self-sufficient to me.'

'She knew it would happen; I guess she'd prepared herself. He was sixty when I was born. I only knew him as an old man.'

Richmond had never known Sir Reginald Nesbitt. He seemed to have been forgotten by everyone except his much younger widow, in the years since his death. His knighthood was a reward for being involved in some vague capacity with the Queen's horses. Richmond seldom remembered that Hermione was officially Lady Nesbitt.

'Anyway,' said Nev, 'thanks for the reassurance that my being here isn't a problem. To be honest, I never thought it was. But I appreciate the hospitality – if that's the right word.'

Richmond's smile was sour. 'This is your home,' he said. 'When it comes right down to it, I've got no bigger claim to live here than you have. We're both appendages to the real owners.'

'Except that in my case I'm the appendage of a dead owner. That might make a difference.'

Nev's words echoed the same sourness and the men exchanged a look that acknowledged their shared status.

'I don't expect it does,' said Richmond.

Nobody at High Copse had bothered about it being Good Friday. Martha doubted whether the boys had much idea of what it signified, or even knew that it was the appropriate day on which to eat hot cross buns, since they were now available in the shops all the year round. The wholesale abandonment of Christian teaching in both the comprehensive and the primary school seemed to have happened more by inertia than from any American-style disconnection between Church and State. Morning assembly had grown too unwieldy to conduct properly any more, the timetable too crowded to permit a lengthy gathering with a hymn and a reading and a short homily from the Head. Martha found this obscurely offensive, but Nina had been dismissive when she expressed her misgivings. She saw no problem in the fact that her sons barely knew a single hymn and had virtually no knowledge of the contents of the Bible.

'A good thing too,' she had laughed. 'They can pick it up for themselves later if they're interested. I can't see that all that indoctrination ever did us any good.'

Martha had struggled to explain. 'It's not just indoctrination,' she'd argued. 'It's culturally impoverishing if they don't know about Balaam's ass and the miraculous draught of fishes, the burning bush and the fall of the walls of Jericho. They won't get the allusions to all sorts of things. It's like losing a great area of common knowledge. Like being brain damaged.' Her passion had surprised them both.

But Nina had merely shrugged. 'There's not much we can do about it. Personally, I'd be happy for them to grow up as pagans, knowing all they can about the natural environment. That's where kids these days are dysfunctional. Most of them barely know that milk comes from cows or whether a thrush is a bird or a piece of a car engine.'

The boys did, at any rate, have a sound awareness of Easter eggs. They were confident of receiving one large contribution each from Martha, Alexis and Nev and an even larger one from Hermione. Martha had caught snatches of their discussion as to where they should keep the chocolate safe from marauding dogs, ruefully recollecting the year when one of the collies had consumed four whole eggs one Easter morning, and been lavishly sick as a result.

Martha was in an odd mood on this particular Good Friday, a day when you had to work hard not to entertain thoughts of death and cruelty, regardless of your Christian credentials. If two of the best-loved people in your life had just died prematurely, you stood no chance of remaining positive. The police hunt for Charlie's killer seemed to be happening invisibly, if it was happening at all. Alexis had become silent and withdrawn. Richmond was being maddeningly hearty and the boys were inscrutable. Martha felt lonely and frustrated and aware of a growing sense of foreboding.

When Lilah Beardon phoned in the late afternoon and told her that Bill Gratton had died, Martha's first reaction was one of sardonic amusement. 'He chose a great day for it,' she said.

Lilah's inarticulate gasp of shocked surprise partially restored Martha to her senses. 'I'll tell Alexis,' she said weakly. 'She knew Hannah and Bill much better than I did.'

People were slowly assembling at High Copse, in the expectation of a meal of some kind, at about half past five. Without pausing to assess who was within earshot, Martha blurted out: 'Lilah phoned. She says Bill Gratton's dead.'

'Bill?' said Alexis with a frown. 'You mean Charlie's dad?'

Richmond muttered, 'That's the third one, then,' with something like relief.

Nev, walking into the room hand in hand with

Clem, looked round at the faces. 'What's up?' he demanded.

Nobody answered him at first. Then Martha remembered how close he had been to Charlie, how Hermione had been best friend to Charlie's mother, Bill's wife. Nev might have more feelings for Bill than any of them. She spoke haltingly. 'Bill Gratton died today. He had another stroke, they think. I don't know any details.'

'Another Quaker bites the dust,' said Alexis harshly. 'They must be wondering what they did to deserve all this.' Then her face softened. 'Poor Hannah. She must be totally flattened. Somebody should be looking after her.' She paused. 'But who, I wonder?'

Nev still hadn't said anything. When Martha looked at him again she saw bewilderment and pain on his face, and a more intense pain on Clem's small features. 'Nev!' she said sharply. 'You're crushing his hand.'

Quickly the man dropped his son's fingers. 'Why didn't you say?' he asked. The little boy shook his head and forced a smile.

'It's okay,' he said stoically.

'It's a holocaust,' said Nev. 'Or a madhouse. I can't cope with it. I don't belong here.' He looked wildly round at the faces watching him. As his eyes circled the room, he caught sight of his elder son in the doorway, watching him from the shadows. 'Hugh!' he gasped, as if guilty – or afraid.

'What's he talking about?' Hugh asked Martha calmly. 'Why's everyone looking so peculiar?'

'Charlie's father died,' Martha told him. 'Nev used to know him, when he was little. He was quite old and had a stroke. It's very sad for poor Hannah, everything happening at once like this.'

'Oh. Right,' said Hugh carelessly. 'Is supper ready yet?'

Nev laughed harshly. 'That's right, son, keep things in proportion. Little monster.'

Simultaneously, Martha and Alexis protested and moved towards the boy, as if to prevent him from hearing the words. But Hugh showed no sign of distress at the comment. He simply gazed dispassionately at his father for a moment and then went to the sink to wash his hands. Martha, still preoccupied with echoes of Good Friday and the New Testament stories, couldn't suppress a snort at the gesture. Hugh made rather a good Pontius Pilate, she thought.

Val's voice was shaking as she passed on the news of Bill's death to Polly that evening. Alexis had called, wondering whether the Quaker grapevine might have got there first. Evidently, it had not. 'Will somebody from the Meeting look after Hannah?' she wanted to know. Val had made some vague assurance and curtailed the call.

Her nervousness now was as much to do with the rift between herself and Polly as with the import of the news. In some ways she was glad to have an unimpeachable excuse to make the call.

'It's like a Shakespearean tragedy,' Polly responded. 'I know these things are meant to go in threes, but who's to say it'll stop at Bill?' Val could hear from the tone that Polly too was glad the phone call had been made.

'Steady on!' she protested. 'Don't go all superstitious on me. All that's happened is that there's been one accident, one violent death and one old man with a stroke. If I've got it right, that tall detective chap was actually *there* when Bill died . . . And he was there when Nina died, as well. Heavens!' She was suddenly almost hysterical. 'You don't think *he's* behind them all, do you?'

'Don't be silly. Calm down and tell me the whole thing from the beginning.'

'I don't know the whole story. It's been passed down a long line like Chinese whispers. There's a girl called Lilah, who knows Martha Cattermole – Nina's sister . . . '

'Yes, yes, I know who Lilah is.'

'Good. Well Lilah phoned Alexis, thinking she'd want to know, because of Charlie, and because she was fond of Hannah and Bill. Apparently Charlie's brother Frank was involved. Although that part's the most confused of all. There was some trouble centred on Frank and the police were called.'

Polly's voice rose. 'But what should we *do* about it?'

'Poll, just listen a minute. There's more going on here than either of us fully understands. Lilah warned Alexis and Martha that we should all tread very carefully. There's something behind the scenes that isn't for public consumption. There are veiled hints and long silences. I suppose there's some nasty truth yet to come out – there has to be, seeing that Charlie was murdered. Meanwhile, we have to think about Bill and Hannah. I don't know how many people from Meeting will have heard about it. It only happened this morning.'

'We can't do very much today, surely?'

'I s'pose not.'

'Tomorrow, then?' There was a breathy pause, then, 'Val? Can I come round?' The little-girl voice was both irritating and seductive. Val felt a familiar twitch in her groin. She knew that in the end Polly would overcome her hesitancy and there would be an explosive union. It had been inevitable all along, despite Val's energetic denials to Den. The game had begun two long years ago, and there was no longer much choice about seeing it through to the final whistle.

'All right, come round,' she said, as the twitch turned into a steady throb.

Den had not told Lilah the precise nature of Hannah's revelation when he phoned her just before the afternoon milking. 'You might want to give them a call at High Copse,' he suggested. 'I don't want them to hear it from me.'

She hadn't asked for an explanation, but he had added something vague about treading on sensitivities. He was being as diplomatic as he knew how, where Lilah was concerned. She had reproached him, more than once, with being unnecessarily reticent about police matters, arguing that it couldn't all be confidential. 'Anyway, I won't tell anybody,' she insisted. 'Couples shouldn't have secrets.'

'It's not "having secrets" – not the way you mean. It's being professional. You've got to be mature enough to live with that.'

She hadn't liked that, and ever since he'd done his best to make up for it. The subject recurred almost every week. 'I can cope with the dark stuff, you know,' she said. 'I know more about life and death than you do. I've seen as much of them both as you have.'

'I didn't know we were in a competition.' The

resulting sulk had lasted at least an hour.

So he gave her the task of passing on the sad news, hoping it would make her feel connected and important. He phoned later in the evening to ask how the High Copse family had taken it, and to check that she was as tired as he was and wouldn't be coming over.

'Martha said a really cynical thing. "He chose the right day for it." I suppose she means Good Friday.'

'She's probably had all she can take, without worrying about Charlie's family.'

'I had rather a rotten day myself,' Lilah changed the subject lightly.

'Me too. That phone call this morning was just the beginning. It's been one thing after another ever since.'

'You can't think of anything but this stupid murder, can you?' she snapped. 'Aren't you allowed to have a life apart from your job?'

He grunted as if she'd hit him. 'Lilah, I saw a man die today. That's what happened to me. It doesn't make any difference that I was working at the time. It happened to *me*, Den Cooper. And tonight I can't think of anything else, even if I want to. If you can't bear with me until this is sorted, that's up to you. And if I can't share my bad times with you, then that's a great pity. It isn't my problem if you can't accept what I do for a living.'

'Okay,' she said, her voice deceptively soft. 'Point taken. I'll go now. It sounds as if I'm more of a nuisance than anything else.'

He had a natural proclivity for the truth; anything else always seemed to result in trouble, sooner or later. 'Not a nuisance,' he corrected. 'But a bit more than I can deal with just now. Good night – and I'll see you on Sunday.'

'Night night,' she said with a catch in her voice.

Now I've made her cry, he thought despairingly as he put the phone down.

CHAPTER TWENTY-SEVEN

It was dark when Barty White heard the knock on his door. He was already halfway down the hall, thanks to the alarmed barking of his dogs. Nobody visited Barty unannounced. He threw the door wide and allowed the three terriers to surge out without restraint, to assess the acceptability of the visitor. The barking quickly diminished, to be replaced by rumbling growls. A man then, Barty concluded, trying to focus on the silhouetted figure in front of him.

'I'm sorry to come round so late,' came a strained voice. 'It's been a bad day and I haven't been able to get on top of things.'

'But—' Barty was bewildered. He lived in a quiet valley some miles from Chillhampton;

spontaneous visits after dark were unheard of. 'On top of things?' he queried, picking the least comprehensible part of the remark.

Clive laughed, sending shards of alarm through Barty. 'Well, can I come in?'

There was no choice. Barty stood aside and gently moved the dogs away with his foot, clearing a path for the Meeting House Warden.

Having been shown into Barty's living room, Clive took a seat gingerly. The bungalow was generously proportioned, built on a plot of Barty's own land, across the lane from the original farmhouse where he'd lived all his adult life. His son was there now, while Barty enjoyed retirement with his Jack Russells.

He switched on the overhead light, making Clive blink and cringe. *He's off his head*, Barty thought with detachment. He could imagine no conceivable reason for the visit; he had no business with Clive Aspen apart from the running of the Meeting House and the shared Sunday morning meetings. And Hotspur. Surely the fool hadn't come about a horse at this time of night?

'I want to talk to you.' He frowned fiercely at Barty. 'Something has happened to me and there's no one else who'll listen.'

'Well . . .' Barty began, bemused.

'Things are getting so complicated,' Clive said earnestly. 'You know – what Charlie Gratton said to me about following the hounds. *You* understand, don't you? You let me borrow your horse, after all.'

Barty shook his head despairingly. 'What brought this on?' he asked, unable to keep a certain briskness out of his tone.

'Charlie,' Clive said in a whisper. 'He saw me at the hunt. I never thought there'd be protesters there that day. I thought they'd go after the mid Devon lot. I thought it would be safe just to follow, anonymously. It's such a good ride, you know. Well, of course you know – I borrowed your horse. And he behaved like a lamb. After that stupid girl got herself knocked out—'

'Killed,' said Barty. 'She was *killed*.'

'Well, yes, she was. And Charlie was wailing and carrying on like a banshee. But he'd seen me, before it happened. He gave me such a filthy look . . .' Clive shuddered and put his hands over his face. 'I didn't know how I'd face him after that. So I went on a long ride. A gallop. Couldn't disappoint poor Hotspur, could I? We had a great time. And you know you said I could use him whenever I liked. So I borrowed him again, on Sunday afternoon . . . and something happened.' He stopped speaking, glancing sideways with a horrible glint of excitement in his eyes.

'I still don't see—' Barty began, wishing he'd had the sense to keep the chap on the doorstep.

The dogs were arranged comically in the doorway of the living room, watching Clive with great attention. Barty was glad of their presence. 'I don't see . . .' he tried again, before realising that he *did* see. Or he thought he did. And if he did, it was a vision he'd much rather not have been burdened with.

Warily he moved towards Clive, one hand outstretched. 'That's enough, Friend,' he said soothingly. 'Don't say anything more. It was good of you to come and see me, I don't get many visitors these days. Everybody's always so busy. One thing about Friends, they look after their own. This trouble with Charlie – it should bring us all together. Nobody's going to worry now about you being at the hunt. I've known Friends do much worse than that.' The nonsensical words were flowing with little conscious thought: just so long as they calmed and reassured the man enough for him to decide he'd done what he came to do, and leave without any trouble.

Barty felt at a real disadvantage; the younger man was so much bigger and stronger than him. If he said the wrong thing, he had no confidence that Clive would remain harmless. However loud he shouted, however much his dogs barked, still nobody would come. His son, Paul, was accustomed to a lot of noise from the dogs and would ignore it, even if he heard anything.

He tried not to think about what Clive had just told him. It had sounded horribly like a confession to murder and Barty felt deeply ill-equipped to deal with such a situation. The man was unhinged, barely responsible for his words and actions. And then there was the wretched Mandy to worry about. Could Barty allow himself simply to pack the man off, knowing the state he was in? Slowly the implications crowded in on him, and he knew he must make a series of painful decisions. The first had already formed, without his realising it; he could not let Clive depart to wreak whatever damage he might.

'There, there,' he said fatuously, reaching a tentative hand out and patting Clive's shoulder. 'Let's have a cup of tea and talk this thing over, shall we? You make yourself comfortable and I'll go and put the kettle on.'

The phone was in the hall. He closed the door firmly behind him and stretched the instrument as far away from the living room as he could. Then he dialled 999, his heart thumping like a sledgehammer.

Unable to sleep, despite the early start and the avalanche of events which had kept him frantically busy that day, Den found himself – much to his own surprise – obsessively reconstructing the death of Nina Nesbitt, of all people. It was now just over two weeks since it had happened; he hadn't yet given himself time to relive it in full and precise detail. Other things had forced themselves in front of it, overshadowing it, but never wiping it from his mind.

He had been too closely involved in trying to breathe life into the dead woman to observe very much of what took place in the crowd. The hunt itself had been cancelled, with reasonably good grace. The appalled and appalling wails of grief coming from Charlie Gratton had merged with the general background noise as people shouted instructions and attempted to dismantle the complex assembly of horses, hounds, followers and protesters. One or two isolated images stood out: Clive Aspen on a dark-coloured horse with a red ribbon tied around its tail; the arrival of a Land Rover containing Richmond, Clem and Hugh from High Copse – summoned, as he subsequently learnt, by Val Taylor on her mobile phone. But above all, Nina's limp body, her face unbruised – evidence in itself that the blow had killed her instantly, before the flesh could react in the normal way to violence. She had looked like a sleeping princess in a fairytale, albeit in jeans and donkey jacket, and there seemed to be no reason to prevent her children from coming near. Clem had frowned, puzzled, not yet anywhere near an understanding of what had taken place; Hugh, more knowing, had pushed a fist into his mouth, his face contorted. There had been a long wait for a police doctor to arrive, the ambulance men withdrawing, shaking their heads and explaining that this was no longer a job for them.

And Den remembered Hermione Nesbitt striding forward, the crowd parting automatically to let her through. She had seized both boys, gripping them tight, one under each arm, and pulled them away from their mother. 'You've seen enough now,' she'd said, in a voice startling in its gentleness. 'You can come home with me.' Gradually the scene had emptied. Undertaker's men took Nina to the hospital mortuary for a post-mortem which seemed to Den like a desecration of that perfect, unmarked body. More damage would be done in the interests of law and science than had occurred when she died. He knew it was foolish to care so much.

Charlie Gratton had been almost the last person to leave. He had not approached Nina's body close enough to touch, but hovered nearby, gasping and quivering with grief or shock or possibly even guilt. Nobody had gone to his aid, which in retrospect struck Den as strange. He stood in an island of distress, arms wrapped around himself tightly. A few children stared at him openly, but the adults averted their gaze. So much pain, so nakedly displayed, was more than they could take.

Pressing his face into the pillow, fighting to banish the disturbing images from his mind and fall into the oblivion of sleep, Den felt dampness around his eyes. Such a waste of vibrant life! No wonder it had been followed by a sequence of events hardly less shocking and senseless. He felt himself caught in a web of old secrets and new grudges, perpetuating misunderstandings and a profound shame. Lilah's self-absorbed complaints made little impression. Things would settle down again between them, he assumed – and if they didn't, then he'd manage as best he could without her.

News of Bill Gratton's death was slow to circulate. When the ambulance had come and gone outside the cottage on Friday morning, not a soul in the village had noticed. The Grattons' cottage was out on a limb, more than a hundred yards from its closest neighbour. One or two might have dimly heard Frank's angry hammering on the door, but could never have imagined that it presaged anything so dramatic as death.

Hannah had asked the police to tell Silas, and Lilah had made the call to the Cattermoles as Den had asked her to. Silas had no desire to pass the news to anyone else. Val and Polly assumed that if *they* had heard about it, then everybody had.

And so it was, on Saturday morning, when Dorothy Mansfield went to call on Hannah, on a routine visit with no real purpose, she was completely unprepared for what she would find.

Usually, she would open the front door, and call out if there was nobody visible. This morning, the door was locked. Dorothy rang the bell, which made a throaty croak, betraying how little it was used. When nothing happened, she moved to the front window and peered in. Bill was almost always to be seen in his chair by the fireplace. The sight of it empty was disconcerting. More curious than worried, Dorothy followed the brick path round to the back of the house. Surely the kitchen door would be standing open, and Hannah would be found hanging out washing or putting in some early potatoes.

The back door wasn't open, but neither was it locked, so Dorothy was able to gain entry. 'Hannah?' she called. 'Where are you? Is everything all right?'

A wordless reply came from above her head. Dorothy hurried to the foot of the stairs. 'Hannah?' she called again, her voice more urgent now.

The faint sound was repeated, more firmly, and the visitor mounted the stairs.

Hannah was in bed, her face a caricature of

her usual soft features. Dark patches, like bruises, marked her cheeks, beneath each eye; harsh grooves outlined her chin, like a ventriloquist's dummy. There were scratches along one jawline. 'My God!' Dorothy gasped, holding onto the door frame. 'What in the world's happened to you? Have you been mugged? Where's Bill?'

Hannah's blue eyes looked hot and sore. She stared at Dorothy with a deep frown. 'He's dead,' she said.

Dorothy looked around foolishly for the body. 'Dead?' she echoed.

'Yesterday. The police were here when it happened. He had another stroke.'

'But – what about *you*? Have you been here all night on your own?'

'Obviously. Why not? There's nothing to hurt me now.' The words came dull and dead.

Dorothy kept one hand on the door frame, and formed a fist with the other. She sucked air through a narrow gap between her front teeth. Then she spoke. 'I won't ask all the obvious questions,' she said. 'You can tell me whatever you think I should know. But you're going to get out of bed, now, and pack a bag with enough things for two or three days. Then you're coming home with me. No arguments.'

'You won't want me in your house when you know the whole story,' said Hannah, making no move. 'Nobody will want to speak to me again.'

'I'm absolutely certain that that isn't true,' said Dorothy. 'There isn't anything you could have done that would make it true. Even if you did something truly terrible – killed Charlie, for instance – and I can't really see how you might have done that – but even if you did, then I'd still be happy to speak to you. I'm a Friend, Hannah. I hope that counts for something. Wash your face and get dressed.'

Hannah managed a weak smile. 'I didn't kill Charlie,' she said softly. 'In fact, I suppose you could say I kept him alive. I'm just so terribly sorry that I couldn't go on protecting him.' Tears filled the new grooves in her face, as if they'd previously carved them out, like canyons. As Dorothy watched, the gentle Quaker formed claws from her own hands and deliberately drew them down her cheeks, digging with all her strength. Blood welled slowly as pale ridges formed around the wounds. Dorothy was horrified.

'Stop it!' she screamed. 'Hannah, you mustn't do that.' She knew now that something more dreadful than Bill's death must have taken place. She gripped her friend's hands and pulled them away from her face. Both women were shaking.

'Come on,' Dorothy crooned, as if to a suffering animal. 'Come with me, my dear. It's all over now.'

Hannah relaxed; her hands dropped out of Dorothy's grasp. 'What shall I bring?' she said helplessly.

Dorothy maintained a trickle of comforting chatter as she found a few essentials and put them into a bag. Already she was feeling less afraid; a warm feeling of righteousness washed through her. Curious she might be, but curiosity was unworthy, and its suppression was virtuous. It might be difficult to accept whatever grim truth eventually emerged, but she knew she would be able to forgive the weak souls who'd committed whatever evil acts had led to Charlie and Bill's deaths. Indeed, Dorothy silently concluded, this was the kind of challenge she'd always longed for. A real test of her Quaker faith. Something robust stirred within her; something exhilarating. 'I'm going to keep you in my sight until you feel better,' she said firmly.

'Feel better,' Hannah echoed dully. 'I can't imagine that day will ever come.'

Dorothy shook her head, pursing her lips in a pout of disapproval. 'We'll see about that,' she said.

CHAPTER TWENTY-EIGHT

The uniformed police made a clumsy job of handling Clive Aspen. Barty's phone call had admittedly been difficult to decipher, made as it was in a breathy whisper and containing implausible phrases such as *scared for my life* and *confessing to a murder.*

So they only sent one car, which took half an hour or more to make the convoluted journey through the lanes. When it arrived, its two occupants found an elderly farmer standing at his own front door, beckoning them urgently. Three yapping Jack Russells added to the confusion.

The old man led them into his front room, where a younger man sat with his hands clasped around a cold mug of tea, his gaze fixed with horror on something invisible. 'He's gone into some sort of trance,' said Barty in a low voice, as if he didn't want to wake his guest. 'Been like it for twenty minutes or more.'

One of the policemen had heard in some detail about the events at the Grattons' cottage the previous day, and had a working knowledge of the individuals involved. 'Here we go again,' he remarked. 'Going down like ninepins, you Quakers. And what might the trouble be, sir?' he asked Clive loudly.

Clive ignored him. Barty intervened, more confident now he had reinforcements. 'He's had mental trouble before,' he told them. 'He turned up here over an hour ago, talking about Charlie Gratton. God knows why he chose me to speak to. But I think he was trying to tell me that it was him who killed Charlie. He got himself into a state because Charlie saw him at the Meet – where the Nesbitt woman was killed. He borrowed my horse – Hotspur. He's sixteen hands or so and high-spirited. It helps me to have someone to take him out. You'll have to take him with you,' he finished, with a look part sorrowful and part triumphant. 'He's not right in the head. Not responsible for what he's done.'

'Hold on a minute, sir,' said the second policeman. 'Are you telling us that this chap has confessed to killing Charlie Gratton?'

Barty nodded impatiently. 'His name's Clive Aspen and he's Warden of the Meeting House in Chillhampton. He never did like Charlie.'

The first officer bent over and tried to take the mug of long-cold tea out of Clive's rigid hands. 'Mr Aspen,' he said firmly, 'you'll have to come with us, sir. We'll take you somewhere safe where they'll look after you.'

'Catatonic,' said his partner smugly. 'That's catatonic, that is.'

The word woke Clive up with startling suddenness. He quivered and looked directly into the bending man's face. 'Who are you?' he said angrily. 'What have you been saying about me?' He stood up, tall and intimidating in his long black coat.

'We're police officers, sir. We were called because you didn't seem very well. Mr White was worried about you. We think you might need some medical attention. If you'd just come with us—'

'No!' Clive spoke with controlled emphasis. 'No, thank you,' he amended. 'I'm perfectly all right. I've already spent a large part of the day on your premises and I can't say I enjoyed the experience. I've got my car outside. I'll go home. My wife will be worried about me if I stay out any longer.'

The policemen exchanged quizzical glances, and then looked anxiously at Barty. 'Mr White tells us you've been saying some strange things to him. About Charlie Gratton.'

Clive smiled again, urbane now, and self-possessed. To Barty the transformation made him seem more insane than ever. 'I'll be pleased to speak to you in the morning, if you think it's necessary,' Clive offered. 'But for tonight, I really think I should go home.'

The situation was sticky – even Barty could see that. He wouldn't have known what to do in the policemen's position, either. They'd merely seen Clive frozen, almost, as one officer had already observed, catatonic. They hadn't seen the repressed violence; the staring eyes; the turmoil of rage and shame and self-disgust. They couldn't have any idea what he was capable of.

'He isn't *right*,' he said urgently. 'These things – they come and go. You never know from one minute to the next how he's going to be. His wife might not thank you—' He stopped. Clive was directing a gaze of astonished reproach at him. 'Er . . .' Barty dithered. 'Well, at least call somebody for advice,' he ended weakly.

Apparently this was a good idea. 'I'll go and call Control,' said one of the officers, heading gratefully for the car outside, as Clive spread his arms in a Christlike gesture of innocence and accommodation. The three men waited for the much-needed advice.

It took over ten minutes and the tension in the room rose steadily. Barty fidgeted with a collection of objects on a table near the window; Clive walked slowly across the room and back again, over and over again. The second policeman stood stiffly, arms folded.

At last the officer returned, looking distinctly uncomfortable. 'Well,' he began, 'it seems there was some disturbance at your home early this morning, Mr Aspen. No harm done, but your wife was apparently very upset. Now, sir, I'm sure you'll understand that we can't risk a repetition of that sort of thing. We're trying to contact your doctor and get him to meet us at the police station. It'll be down to him what happens next, in all probability.' He paused and scratched his head. Then he looked at Barty. 'We'll leave you in peace, then, sir,' he concluded.

Barty tried to feel relieved. It was out of his hands now. Except it wasn't. 'It isn't as simple as that,' he said unhappily, as Clive gave him another look of injured bewilderment.

'Maybe not,' agreed the policeman. 'But let's take it a step at a time. Mr Aspen, please come with us now.'

The three of them waited for Clive's next move. He glanced at a row of china figures on

401

Barty's mantelpiece; their owner clearly saw them flying off and smashing, as the policemen struggled to subdue a suddenly violent captive. But it didn't happen. Clive merely smiled again, something forlorn and childlike on his face, and walked towards the door.

Barty didn't follow. He waited for the sound of the car engine to fade and then he locked the door. His dogs followed him from room to room, reduced to chastened silence by his obvious distress.

He felt very little better on Saturday morning. He owed it to the Meeting to give an account of what had happened – and he felt particularly bad about poor Mandy. He assumed that Clive had been permitted to phone her and explain what was happening, but this latest crisis was only going to increase her woes. She hadn't seemed to Barty to be a woman of much inner strength, in the years she'd been at the Meeting House. Now he wondered if he ought to revise his opinion; anyone who could stick with such an unpredictable husband and still stay sane must have more guts than most. In any case, the Quaker way was to ensure that she was cared for and Barty couldn't assume that someone else would do it. The Meeting had always been small; it had never been easy to evade the many tasks and responsibilities that went with membership. He couldn't even assume that anyone else knew that Clive was in trouble. There had been a complete lack of communication for a few days now – no calls from Hannah or Dorothy, and even the importunate Miriam had left him alone for longer than usual.

From long habit, he performed the outdoor tasks before having his breakfast. The dogs were let out and then fed. Although no longer farming, he had a small barn in which he kept rabbits and poultry and they had to be attended to. He often thought that without his residual collection of livestock he would have died long ago – not so much from boredom as a lack of purpose. Without animals or birds depending on him, needing the routines of feeding and maintenance, there would have been nothing worthwhile in his life. As it was, he chatted and whistled as he did his rounds, and pretended to himself that he was still an active farmer living off the land.

When he finally went back indoors it was nine-thirty and he steeled himself to phone Hannah and Bill and describe what had taken place the previous evening. He rehearsed the words, avoiding any overt criticism of Clive, and resisting the obvious inference that he had killed Charlie. Let people form their own conclusions on that subject.

But the phone rang and rang in a house he somehow knew was empty. What day was it? Saturday – they could have gone into town on the weekly bus, he supposed, although it would be unusual; Bill seldom went anywhere these days. He'd have to try Dorothy, as the only remaining sensible Quaker he felt comfortable talking to.

But before he could do that, he heard a female voice outside. 'Coo-ee?' it called. And there was only one person he knew who could still unselfconsciously speak as if she'd stepped out of a *Bunty* cartoon strip.

Miriam Snow had heard the news about Bill Gratton from the postman at eight that morning. It was her custom to waylay him if she saw him approaching her front door and engage him in a brief chat. She wasn't the only one, and he had picked up the news from the occupants of one of the other houses, whose son was a local policeman. It seemed extraordinary to Miriam that she had not been informed directly by Hannah or one of the other Friends. She was rather annoyed at being the last to know, as she assumed she must be.

Everything seemed to be falling apart, what with the police asking questions about Charlie and everyone apparently retreating into their own little worlds. Where there had once been a solid, supportive Quaker Meeting, there was now a fragmentary collection of disasters, with nobody to hold things together. Val and Polly were always busy, and Miriam knew they regarded her as feather-brained; Dorothy Mansfield was even more dismissive. Silas Daggs was little more than an appendage to the Grattons. Which left only Barty.

She had gone through the list twice, a little smile deepening as she did so. She was right – Barty was the only one she could approach for comfort and advice. More than that, they seemed to be the only two who had been personally unaffected by all the calamities. It made obvious sense to seek him out, and discuss with him what should be done.

Although accustomed to walking long distances, this time the urgency was too great. She would have to use her bicycle and go round by the lanes. This was hazardous, and exhausting, but there was no avoiding it. The bike was in good working order, and she wasted no more time.

Thanks to undimmed hearing, she was able to dismount and cower in the flower-decked banks every time a vehicle came past, in the narrower stretches of lane. Primroses, dog violets and rich yellow celandines were squashed as she pressed into them to avoid one large lorry. *Soon*, she thought crossly, *it will be completely impossible to use these roads except in a motor vehicle.*

There didn't seem much point in even teaching children to ride bikes any more – and what was the pleasure if you had to dress in so much protective armour first? She of course refused to wear any sort of cycle helmet herself.

But she reached Barty's farmyard unscathed, and was greeted enthusiastically by his dogs. When she called out, the man himself came to the door within moments, and ushered her in with fair grace. She hadn't permitted herself to anticipate his response in advance. She knew well enough that he was embarrassed by her ill-concealed feelings for him.

'I suppose you've heard about Bill?' she began, almost accusingly.

He stared at her blankly. 'What about him?'

'Oh, Barty.' Miriam was penitent. 'I thought everyone knew but me. It seems he died yesterday morning.'

Barty swayed, blinked, frowned. He glanced back into the hallway, at his phone. 'I was just trying to call them,' he said. 'Where's Hannah?'

'I have no idea.'

She met his eyes and her heart did its usual girlish dance. He was such a *sweet* man! Never loud or hasty, but imbued with the Quaker habit of slow consideration of every angle, a refusal to make unfounded judgements. Barty had been an example to her when she first attended Meeting, and his brief but welcoming words had felt like a blessing.

Now he did an unprecedented thing: he reached out and took her hand. 'Come and sit down,' he invited. 'You must be tired.' He smiled at the bike behind her. 'Cycling isn't as easy as it used to be. And I've got something to tell you,' he added, with a worried look.

'Oh dear,' she squealed. 'Not more bad news I hope?'

He sat her down in the same chair that Clive had occupied the evening before and went to make more coffee. His kitchen was untidy, the washing-up still waiting from the previous day; he had to use his only two remaining mugs, one of which had a crack in it. Things like that no longer seemed to matter.

Miriam waited quietly for him, for which he was thankful. He had to admit she had a nice face; the blue eyes today were slightly less vacuous than usual. She had more spirit than he'd credited her with, riding her bike down those lanes, with milk tankers and horse boxes trying to force her off the road. And he supposed he should be grateful, in a way, for her abiding affection. There was something steady and appealing in it; many men his age would have envied him.

He gave her the drink and told her briefly about Clive. 'They were going to call a doctor to

407

him. The poor chap's had mental trouble before, of course.'

She said nothing at first, which struck him as unusual. Then she spoke, her voice broken, as if a new vein of thought or emotion had just been breached. 'I know I seem silly sometimes,' she said with dignity. 'Always throwing myself headlong into new things. I never seem to strike the right note with people. It's been the same all my life. But I do care, very much, about all this. It's terrible to think of Charlie being deliberately killed, and poor Bill dying like that. I suppose it was the shock about Charlie that did it. And now Clive.' She looked at him, and he was struck by the transparency, the sincerity of her gaze. 'I didn't like Clive,' she admitted. 'I didn't even *try* to like him. So gloomy and self-righteous. But perhaps he was just fighting inner demons. Do you think that's it?'

Barty sighed. Something seemed to fall away; some outer shell of armour. He took her hand again, shyly. 'I didn't like him either,' he said. 'And last night I was fearful of him. I thought he'd do me harm. When I phoned the police it was with my own welfare at heart, not his. We're all imperfect creatures, it seems. We muddle on, doing what we do, and making all kinds of messes as we go.' He smiled at her, eliciting a tremulous response. They both felt something kindling between them; Miriam with a delight so intense she felt faint, Barty with more resignation than excitement. Sometimes you couldn't fight these things and it would, he supposed, be good to have human company in his declining years.

They stood side by side as Barty telephoned Dorothy and gleaned some limited details about Hannah's state of mind. 'She has only been here a little while,' said Dorothy. 'She hasn't told me much yet.'

With some reluctance Barty gave a brief account of Clive's breakdown, again making no reference to Charlie's death. 'Someone will have to go and visit Mandy,' he said. 'And it sounds as if you've got your hands full.'

Dorothy gave a tight laugh. 'You could say that,' she said. 'You might try Val and Polly. Or Miriam.'

'Leave it with me,' said Barty, squaring his shoulders.

Miriam had obviously been thinking. 'That young detective – the one who's investigating Charlie's death – he asked me if I rode – horses, not bikes. I presume he asked everybody that.' Barty nodded. 'Well, Clive rides, doesn't he? He spoke about it once at Meeting. How it clears his head and makes him feel at one with nature.'

'He borrows my Hotspur when he wants a really good gallop. We never made too much of it at Meeting – with all you animal rights people making every sort of fuss. He rode to hounds the day Nina Nesbitt died. He didn't expect anyone to see him. Never thought there'd be a protest that day.'

Miriam pouted thoughtfully. 'So *Charlie* saw him,' she said. 'Which must have been awkward for Clive. What a silly thing to do.'

'Worse than silly in Charlie's eyes. Though he wasn't Mr Sensible himself when it came to the hunt.'

Miriam withdrew slightly. 'Hunting is indefensible,' she said primly. 'Barbaric in this day and age.'

He shook his head. 'If you take hunting away, there's precious little left to us,' he said obscurely. 'I mean – mankind is already living too much inside its own head. People have moved too far away from the land, from muck and pain and a sense of how it all fits together. The hunt is primitive, I grant you. Maybe even barbaric. But it isn't wicked or evil. Those arguments of Charlie's were beside the point. And it isn't about jobs or culture or any of that. It's about . . .' He shook his head again helplessly. 'It's about denying our place. Human beings are hunters, just as tigers and wolves are hunters. If we forget that, we don't deserve to be here in the world at all.'

Miriam's mouth opened and closed twice more. Then she went back to her chair and sat down slowly. 'I don't really understand,' she admitted hesitantly. 'But I can tell it's something you believe deeply. I never heard you talk like that before – with such passion. I just thought, of course you were a farmer, you're bound to have the sort of opinions a farmer would have. But Barty, you sound more like a philosopher than a farmer to me.'

He laughed. 'Maybe a man can be both,' he said, almost flirtatiously.

She wagged a finger at him. 'You got us off the subject,' she chastised. 'We have to think about Charlie and how he died. Did the policemen last night say anything about him?'

'Quite a lot,' he said heavily. 'They're sure to be thinking it was Clive that did it.' The words brought relief and sadness. 'He more or less told me he did,' he added, reaching again for Miriam's hand.

CHAPTER TWENTY-NINE

Den was one of the last to hear when Frank Gratton was apprehended and taken in for questioning. He didn't know about Clive Aspen's evening adventure, either, until nine o'clock on Saturday morning. Detective Sergeant Danny Hemsley, back from his course and anxious to catch up with developments, phoned him and told him to cancel all plans for the day, thanks to unfolding events. 'We've got two contenders for the hot seat now,' he said. 'And they're both in a right old state. The Aspen chap only just escaped being sectioned last night – the doctor was within a whisker of signing the doings, when something made him think twice about it. Said we should wait till morning. And of course Mr A. is all sweetness and co-operation today. His wife's sitting in reception making a nuisance of herself. You should be here, Den. This is your bag more than anyone else's.'

'I was coming in anyway,' said Den. 'I'm down for the rota today.'

Frank Gratton was first in line for questioning. DI Smith was doing the honours when Den arrived. The interview lasted thirty minutes, with Den waiting impatiently for the outcome.

The Inspector emerged, rubbing his hands thoughtfully. 'Morning, Cooper,' he said. 'How's things?'

'I don't know, sir,' said Den, a little disgruntled. 'I need to do a bit of catching up. Any luck with Brother Frank?'

'Yes and no, as they say. Yes, he freely admitted he was Charlie's biological father. Seemed quite glad to get it off his chest. He said he'd tried to tell the Cattermoles, when Charlie took up with Alexis, but they wouldn't listen. And no, he did not kill the lad – and *lad* was the word he used. He seemed almost amused at the suggestion, actually. His manner's odd, but then I've never interviewed a chap who's slept with his mother before. I wasn't sure what to expect.'

Den did not smile; the jokes were too obvious, the idea too uncomfortable; the implications too unhappy. Smith grew serious, as if remembering the circumstances, but Den felt wary. It was not a good idea to present yourself as morally superior to the man above you on the ladder.

'Did you ask him to explain? I mean, the stuff with his mother?'

'He was only too keen to tell me,' said Smith. 'Not that he made a lot of sense.' Den waited as the Inspector gathered his thoughts. 'You were right that it was at least as much her as him. He never really thought of her as his mother, in the usual way. She flirted with him, played with him – you know, with his winkle when he was little. He thought it was the same for everybody until he got a bit older and had a few rude awakenings at school. He learnt then to keep it all secret, pretending it wasn't happening, even to himself. But he loved her. Being around her got him all excited. When he was fourteen it got deadly serious. She'd come into his room at night.' Smith sighed sadly. 'It's not so different from the usual story with fathers and daughters, when all's said and done. She was the adult and he was the child. You have to see it that way – she abused him.'

'But she got pregnant and she drowned herself,' said Den. 'Makes you wonder just who the victim is.'

'They're *all* victims,' growled the DI. 'Which

414

tends to be true in most of these family tangles.'

'And how is he now he's unburdened himself?' asked Den.

'Like a man waiting for execution. As if nothing matters any more.'

'But you think he's guilty, in spite of what he says?'

'I'm not sure he is, damn it. It all fits too neatly and life isn't neat, in my experience. The man's grief-stricken about old Bill. Maybe about Charlie as well. He's too bloody *decent*,' he burst out, greatly to Den's surprise. Smith clenched his fists and shook them in mock rage. 'I don't mind telling you I'd love to be able to pin this on him and go home for a nice relaxing Easter, but I've just spent ninety minutes with a man I wouldn't object to spending a week in a small tent with; a man I'd be happy to call *friend*. Sorry, Cooper, but there it is.'

Den followed a stray lateral thread. 'Exactly where was he when you went to find him? It must have been pretty early.'

'Oh – haven't you heard? He was in church at 7 a.m. The vicar found him weeping and when he approached him, Frank said he wasn't fit to be in such a place.'

'And the vicar called us?'

'No, no. They don't do that sort of thing. But the church had a burglary recently, and some

415

woman across the village green saw him going in and raised the alarm.'

'Poor Frank.'

'Yes,' said Smith.

Den rallied first, after a few moments of gloom. 'Then it's Clive Aspen,' he said. 'It fits him just as neatly.'

Smith shook his head, the thick neck creasing as he did so. 'Watch your logic, son,' he advised. 'It's not an either/or situation. Frank's not off the hook, Aspen's a basket case, and there are others to be borne in mind. First priority is to have a thorough look at the Ashburton place. Forensics are on their way, and I want you and Phil to join them.'

'Yes, sir,' said Den heavily.

'But first you can come with me to talk again to Aspen. His wife's getting on everybody's nerves, sitting there like some sort of plaster saint.'

'What happened exactly? More ructions at the Meeting House? Danny says he came close to being sectioned.'

'Much better than that. He went to the home of a Mr Bartholomew White and more or less confessed to killing Charlie Gratton. All hearsay, obviously, and he was in a highly disturbed frame of mind, according to the chaps who brought him in. Probably not responsible for his words or actions. The interesting question is – what set him off? Why did he go there and say what he did?'

'Has he got a solicitor with him?'

'Insists he doesn't want one. Says he can handle it all himself. The doctor's seen him again this morning, and he's calmness personified. Come on then, see if you can help open him up. He knows you.'

'Which may or may not be helpful,' said Den ruefully. 'He and I haven't formed much of a relationship. I think I'd rather spend a week in a deep, dark cave than in a tent with Clive Aspen.'

'Keep an open mind,' said Smith. 'You might discover his better side.'

Clive sat upright at the small table, chin resting on folded hands, arms propped on his elbows, the picture of a patient man. There was something clerical about him, or martyred. He looked up trustfully at Inspector Smith, ignoring Den completely.

'Mr Aspen, I'm sure you know we're investigating the death of Mr Charlie Gratton. I understand you've already been questioned by Detective Constable Cooper here and that he was called to your home again yesterday after a domestic disturbance. We are also aware of a question mark over the alleged abuse of a young boy called Clement Nesbitt, who is part of a family with which Charlie Gratton was very closely connected. Now these are matters on which we would like you to cast some light. Last night you are reported as making some admissions to Mr White of Hill Farm Bungalow, which if true will perhaps make you reconsider your decision not to have a legal representative.'

'What exactly are you asking me?' said Clive with a faint frown.

Inspector Smith smiled gently and lifted his chin in a display of confidence. 'We know Mr Gratton was deliberately killed, and we know that you've been very disturbed by this occurrence, in recent days. We'd like you to fill us in and explain the connection, if you can, sir.'

Clive blinked twice. He took his chin away from his hands and brought his fingertips together, the picture of a university professor – or a psychiatrist. The sense of a game being played out between the two men was acute. Den remembered how Smith had been with Gerald Fairfield, Master of Foxhounds, and began to understand the Inspector's style of working. And how enjoyable it must be: there was a twinkle of relish in Smith's eyes.

Clive spoke calmly, if reluctantly. 'I knew Charlie Gratton for three years, since coming here to take up the post of Warden to the Meeting House. I became aware subsequently that he had argued against the selection of myself and Mandy on grounds I have never properly understood. He was a birthright Quaker, from a family of Quakers going back generations. Mandy and I are Quakers by convincement. We've been in membership for six years. We have been surprised at the level of involvement with animal rights organisations within the Meeting. At times it has seemed to us that it has been deleterious to the spiritual welfare of the Meeting and we have done our best to counterbalance it. You might deduce from this that I had a personal dislike of Charlie Gratton.'

'Indeed we might,' Smith agreed. 'Perhaps you could be a little more specific. Is Mr White correct in stating that you made a confession to him last night? That you told him you rode his horse to High Copse and deliberately trampled Charlie Gratton to death with it?'

Clive Aspen smiled tolerantly. 'I don't believe I said any such thing.'

'But is it true? Is that what you did, two Sundays ago?'

'I rode Mr White's horse in the general direction of High Copse, along a bridle path that I think borders their land and then goes off towards Cornwall. But I took a detour, avoiding High Copse altogether.'

'Why?'

'Because I didn't want to meet any of them, not after Nina's death. Not after Charlie abused me. I went as far as Bradstone Church. Do you know it, Inspector?'

Smith shook his head. 'Is this what you tried to tell Mr White?'

Clive waved the question aside as irrelevant and continued his tale. 'Bradstone Church is extremely beautiful,' he said earnestly. 'Inside, it's as plain as any Meeting House. You can see the workmanship, you can feel the presence of the men who built it seven hundred years ago or more. St Nonna's, they call it.'

Smith and Den itched to stop his ramblings, but were unable to interrupt effectively. Clive went on speaking regardless. 'Anyway,' he said, 'I had a conversion.'

'I beg your pardon?' Smith spluttered. 'A *what*?'

'I was converted, there in the graveyard. I'm not a Quaker any more. That's what I went to explain to Barty White. But it didn't come out properly. It all connects, you see. Little Clem, Charlie Gratton, the horses, the church – it's all part of one great picture, full of meaning. I went to him because I thought he would understand. But I was overcome with unhappiness for Charlie, who was so wrong-headed. He made me very unhappy, you know. I hated him.'

'But did you kill him?'

'No, I did not. Of course.'

In the pause that followed, Den stirred impatiently and looked anxiously at the DI. 'Cooper,' Smith invited, 'is there anything you'd like to ask Mr Aspen?'

'There is, actually, sir. Just a small point, although I think it's relevant.' He faced Clive squarely. 'What does a red ribbon on a horse's tail signify?'

Clive was plainly thrown off course by the question. Then he shrugged. 'It's a courtesy thing, where horses are gathered together. It means the animal is liable to kick out without warning.'

Smith glanced quizzically at Den, who continued, 'And I understand that on the day that Mrs Nesbitt died, you were mounted on a horse wearing just such a ribbon?'

Clive nodded impatiently. 'Hotspur, yes. Barty White and I have an agreement that I can use him any time. It's good for the horse. Without me, he'd probably have been sold by now. He's very high-spirited, but he has always behaved perfectly with me. He's an excellent mount. But to be on the safe side, I put the ribbon on him. I don't really think it was necessary.' His gaze returned to Smith. 'But I was telling you what happened to me,' he persisted, as if Den had been a briefly irritating distraction.

'Just bear with us a little longer,' begged Smith. 'How did Charlie Gratton react to your presence at the hunt on March the twenty-fifth?'

'I didn't see. I kept away from him.'

'Might he have felt betrayed?'

Clive inhaled deeply. 'It's possible.'

'And might you not therefore have felt embarrassed, even ashamed?'

Clive smiled scornfully. 'Not enough to make me want to murder him. The very idea is ridiculous.'

'We have reason to think that you believed Clement Nesbitt was being sexually abused,' Smith said, with no change of expression. 'And that you anonymously alerted the authorities to it, last September.'

Clive tensed and his face turned a shade paler. 'How—?' he began, before stopping himself. 'That has nothing to do with anything, now. It's all in the past.'

'But you did make that phone call?'

Clive nodded.

'I understand you have no children of your own?'

Another deep inhalation. 'No, but I'm quite sure you're aware that we had a little boy. He died in his cot when he was ten months old. He'd be just nine now. Neither of us dealt effectively with the loss at the time, and that contributed to my illness.'

'But you're confident that you've dealt with it now? I note that you work on a voluntary basis at the local primary school?'

'I love children,' said Clive. Den shuddered at the mismatch between the words and their delivery: a strong statement of emotion expressed robotically. 'I have a genuine commitment to their welfare.'

'To the extent of watching for signs of abuse everywhere you go? Wanting to keep them safe from all the ills and dangers of the world?' Smith oozed sympathy and understanding.

'It's every citizen's moral duty,' said Clive.

'I suggest, Mr Aspen, that you believed Charlie Gratton to be the abuser of young Clement, and you took it upon yourself to punish him.'

'By riding over him on Hotspur?' Clive's eyes flickered as if reading an autocue. 'I assure you I did not do that, Inspector.'

Den indicated the need to ask another question, which Smith graciously permitted. 'Why did you have a picture of Clem Nesbitt in your flat?'

Clive hesitated. 'You wouldn't understand,' he said, with some sign of agitation. 'I can't explain it to you.'

'Please try, sir.'

'Our baby – Daniel, he was called – had the same fair hair. The same pointed little chin. The likeness struck me. I took the photo at school one day. There's absolutely nothing sinister about it.' His explanation was identical to Mandy's, Den realised.

'Mr Aspen, would you please tell us honestly, did you believe that Clem Nesbitt was being sexually abused?' Den hoped he wasn't spoiling any delicate strategy of the Inspector's, by being so direct; he was encouraged by Smith's passive acceptance of the question.

Clive's mouth worked oddly. He kept his eyes fixed on the desk. 'I think he was frightened and unhappy. His whole demeanour changed last autumn, a few weeks into the term. It was at the same time as Charlie Gratton started spending a lot of time at High Copse.'

'And you leapt to a wholly unjustified conclusion, didn't you, sir?'

Clive raised his eyes to meet Den's for the first time. 'I don't think so,' he said stubbornly.

Raising a forefinger to interrupt Den, Smith returned to the fray.

'This . . . um . . . *experience* you had at Bradstone. Was anyone else there at the time?'

'No, of course not. Except—'

'Yes?'

'There were other riders on the road outside. It's a very quiet road. There's a large farm close by and two or three houses. One of the houses has a stable block, not far from the church. There was a commotion from the horses. I'd tied Hotspur up near the church gate and he joined in. Someone was riding a big horse quite fast along the path. It rises steeply up from the river valley and I heard the hooves.'

'But you didn't see it?'

'Only a brief glimpse through the trees. It was definitely big – I'd say a hand bigger than Hotspur. But I wasn't very interested. You see—'

Smith held up his hand. 'Yes, I know. You were otherwise engaged,' he said. 'Have you ever been to High Copse Farmhouse?' he added suddenly.

Clive shook his head minimally. 'Never,' he said.

'And you deny killing Charlie Gratton?'

'Absolutely.'

'All right, sir. Interview terminated at . . . 12.45 p.m. on Saturday 10th April. You're free to go, Mr Aspen, but I strongly suggest that you stay in close touch with your doctor, in the light of last night's episode. It strikes me that you are in need of help, although I'm not officially qualified to judge, of course. We can provide you with an emergency number, if the situation flares up again over the next two days. Your wife is waiting for you at the front desk and she undertakes responsibility for your wellbeing. Do you understand, sir?'

'Of course,' said Clive, standing up slowly, leaning his weight on the table momentarily, as if about to fall. Den realised he probably hadn't slept at all the previous night. 'Thank you, Inspector.'

Den waited for the post-mortem on the interview, trying to guess Smith's conclusion from the bizarre encounter he had just witnessed. The two men went to the canteen for a much-needed lunch. 'Gut feelings?' the Inspector prompted.

'A clever nutcase,' Den began. 'All over the place as far as normal emotions go. Definitely ought not to be let loose in a primary school.'

'But did he kill Charlie?'

Den hesitated, rerunning Clive's flat denial, rummaging inside himself for the elusive gut feeling. 'Maybe not,' he managed indecisively. 'I mean, the motivation isn't very strong, is it? And how would he have known where to find Charlie that day?'

'Spur of the moment? Riding over there on the offchance? Red mist sort of thing?'

Den scratched an earlobe. 'I don't know, sir. There doesn't seem to be the slightest scrap of evidence, other than the fact that Hotspur was known to kick out. And what about that other horse he says he saw?'

Smith shrugged. 'The place is crawling with horses. And he might be trying to throw us off the scent. So we're a little way off a conclusion yet. But let's not despair, eh?'

'I'm still going to Ashburton, then?'

'Oh yes. And when you get back from there, you are finally, *definitely*, going to talk to Lady Hermione Nesbitt. It might be five o'clock, or even later, but you're not going home until it's done. And then, once you've written up all the reports, and assured me there are no more unturned stones out there, you can have tomorrow in peace – probably.'

'Right, sir.'

Smith rapped a finger on the table. 'I'm not unhappy with your work on this, Cooper, but I'm not blinded with admiration, either. However it ends up, you'll have learnt something. Whatever mistakes you've made on this one, I won't want to see them made another time. Understand?'

Mistakes? The choice of word didn't bode too well for his chances of promotion. 'I'm sorry, sir,' he said meekly.

'I'm not telling you off, lad. I just want you to stay on your toes. Now, I've warned Phil you two are in for a heavy afternoon. He's coming in at two, so you've got half an hour or so to gather your thoughts. The Moor's going to be thick with grockles, and it's a fair old way to Ashburton. Off you go, now.'

'Right, sir,' said Den.

CHAPTER THIRTY

Den decided to go for a short walk while he waited for Phil Bennett. Walking often helped to settle his thoughts, and the Gratton murder had got under his skin in unexpected ways. It had been peculiar from the outset, linked as it was in his mind with the bizarre death of Nina Nesbitt. If Frank Gratton – who stubbornly remained as Den's favourite suspect – had killed Charlie, then the death of Nina would turn out to have no connection, unless something momentous had taken place during Frank's meeting with her not long before she died, which Den doubted. The Cattermoles presumably had done no more than inadvertently provide the venue for the deed. *Full of holes, lad*, DI Smith's comment reverberated, and Den could see what he meant. Motive, yes; means, definitely. Opportunity, however, was very much less obvious. How did you hang about inconspicuously on a large horse in someone else's field, waiting for your victim to happen by? At the very least, you'd need information on where he was likely to be at a given moment. And for that, Frank would have needed to be in communication with someone at High Copse. In which case, it seemed, after all, that the Cattermoles may have had a part to play in the killing of Charlie.

He turned his thoughts to the events of the previous morning, and the revelations from Mandy Aspen. Whichever way you looked at it, Clive Aspen was going to need watching. The Social Services would probably have to be brought in, and the old sledgehammer and nut routine would be set in motion. Teachers interviewed, references checked, children observed; unlikely scenarios put forward as obvious fact.

Den was as confused and uneasy about child abuse as anyone. He was, however, convinced that it was much too easy to cause real harm in the pursuit of faint suspicions; that it was even possible to introduce a climate of damage where all was harmless innocence before. His natural common sense cried *Witch-hunt* and *Hysteria* when listening to some of the more excessive briefings from so-called experts on the subject.

With his mind still focused on Clem and the complexities inherent in extracting objective truth from a child, he decided he'd been enough of a wimp for one day. If he walked briskly, he could get as far as the edge of Dartmoor and back before he had to meet Phil. Up Station Road, straight on and like magic you were on the Moor before you knew it.

From the hill above the town he could look back over a grid of new houses where once there had been fields. He remembered roaming free with the family dog, getting out of the house where his parents were too bound up with each other to take much notice of him.

Outside the last row of houses before the edge of town, he noticed a little boy crouched on the pavement, intently examining something at his feet. About six or seven, with a halo of curly blond hair, he was a child of eye-catching beauty. Den's instant reaction was to regard him as a potential victim. Any predator could come along in a car, and scoop up the child in seconds. The whole thing was so vivid in his mind, he could actually feel the small, wriggling body against his own chest, as if he himself were the abductor. He almost approached the child, to tell him to get home, where it was safe.

And then he stopped himself. There was in

reality nothing dangerous in what the lad was doing. His home was a few feet away, his mother probably keeping an eye on him from one of the windows. He was old enough not to run in front of any cars – which was by far the worst hazard. With a deep frown, Den carried on walking, accelerating his pace slightly, in case the sight of him alarmed either the boy or an observing parent.

Something new had occurred to him, something that was slowly taking shape in his mind. Something about the whole logic of society's attitude to the abuse of children. Hadn't he just demonstrated this to himself – and become aware of the most uncomfortable implications? Because the general assumption now was that no child was safe out in the streets alone, didn't that actively *encourage* the idea of damaging any child thus encountered? Didn't it give the message – this child is fair game? It's breaking the rules, behaving irresponsibly, giving itself up as a sacrificial victim? No wonder Clive Aspen had become so obsessed.

And there was something of a catch-22 about all this. Society made loud, hysterical noises about the evil wickedness of child abuse, and kept all its children under lock and key to protect them. But by so doing, it conveyed a general expectation that any child not adequately protected was fair game, there for the taking.

Den knew it was all very well to theorise. He knew what had happened inside himself for a fleeting second. He had seen the little boy as an object of beauty, something it might be gratifying to *touch inappropriately*, as the social workers would say. He had felt the tingle in his own balls, like a tiny current of electricity. It wasn't enough to know that he would never – *ever* – act on it. That didn't matter. He had glimpsed the possibility, understood what the great mass of ordinary self-deceiving people said they would never be able to understand. He didn't think he was uniquely perverted or disgusting. Den believed that if it had happened to him, it could happen to virtually any man alive. And if that was true, then wasn't his work as a police officer utterly futile, if not impossible?

Or was it in fact even more important than he thought? If everyone was naturally tempted to misbehave, then society required discipline and law enforcement for its very survival. It hung together like a carefully constructed archway, with the police force as the keystone, keeping it all in place. It felt like a precarious role to be playing.

Forcing himself back to the murder of Charlie Gratton for the hundredth time, he applied the new revelation to the people he'd met over the past ten days. Many of them might qualify as abused children. Frank, seduced by his own mother during the bewildering years of adolescence; Hugh and Clement, shared around the family while their father effectively forgot their existence; Mandy Aspen, bizarrely abused in retrospect by her obsessive husband. And then, he thought ruefully of his own Lilah, who had not enjoyed the most healthy of relationships with her volatile father. He wondered what the emotionally inadequate Nev Nesbitt's early years had been like, and those of the three fatherless Cattermole girls. The more you delved, the less 'normal' anyone's life appeared to be. The surprise, really, was that there weren't more murders and abuses perpetrated by these damaged individuals.

He walked as far as the fringe of Dartmoor, where gorse flourished. He could see brilliant yellow flowers glowing luminous in the afternoon light. He remembered his mother saying, *When gorse isn't flowering, love's out of season*, every time they visited the Moor. It had seemed to him just another foolish country saying that gained currency only by being regarded as quaint by people who scarcely knew gorse from blackthorn. But now it provided a welcome counterbalance to his grim musings on the human condition. And it made him think of Lilah. He had parted from her on a sour note and he ought not to leave it that way.

He turned round, thinking that if he hurried he might have time to phone his fiancée before going to Ashburton. He had not taken a phone with him when he went out. Much of the purpose of the walk had been to escape human entanglements for a while.

But Phil was early and impatient to be off. Den could see that the afternoon was disappearing fast and they needed to reach Frank Gratton's stables.

Easter Saturday afternoon saw Alexis galvanised into action, as if possessed.

'We're going to get this house clean,' she announced. 'Wash away all the gloom and doom and focus on the future. Boys, don't even think of going anywhere. I need your help.'

Hugh made a hissing noise, interpreted by them all as annoyance. 'I'm going over to Granny's,' he said.

'You can go later. Clem – what about you?'

The younger boy glanced tentatively at Hugh and shrugged. 'I'm going to Granny's as well,' he said, without looking at her.

'Then we'd better get started right away.' She assembled an impressive collection of buckets, brushes, sponges, dusters. She vacuumed the living room carpet and rolled up the rugs. She fetched a ladder and climbed up it to tackle the picture rail, coated as it was with a sooty black deposit. The skirting boards were hardly any better, and she set Clem to scrubbing them clean.

Martha, swept along by the energy and by something oddly appropriate in the timing, did her share. 'Let me have the ladder,' she said. 'We'd better take down the curtains and get them cleaned.' Alexis made her wait until the picture rails were finished and then turned her attentions to the windows themselves.

'Where's Nev?' asked Hugh as he reluctantly swept cobwebs from walls and furniture with a long-handled feather duster. 'He should be helping.'

'He's around somewhere,' said Martha. 'We don't need any more people in here. We'd just get in each other's way.'

'Nina would laugh at us,' Alexis said, glancing down at Clem, still diligently cleaning the skirting board. 'But we can't go on as we did when she was here. It was her fault we never did any cleaning. She despised such housewifely activities. But it's different now. We're going to be *normal*. For the kids' sake, if nothing else.'

Martha shook her head, eyebrows raised in bewilderment. 'I don't know about that. But this room's looking better already.' She returned to her struggle with the curtain hooks, stretching perilously from the top of the stepladder.

'Careful!' Alexis warned. 'You'll have to get down and move it before you can reach the last ones.' She hovered beneath her sister.

'Phew,' panted Martha. 'What a smell up here! Old dust and cobwebs and smoke from the fire, all mixed together. We should be ashamed of ourselves.'

'Rubbish! It's not a sin to let your curtains get dirty. You know what'll happen, don't you? If we put them in the machine, they'll disintegrate. It's only the cobwebs holding them together.'

'Then we'll get new ones,' said Martha.

'And we'll paint every room. Smarten the whole place up. Who knows – when things settle down a bit, we might even think of moving.'

'We can't move,' came Clem's thin voice. 'Not ever.' He stared at his aunt with huge eyes. 'What about Mum?'

'That's right,' said Martha, descending from the ladder and putting her arm round him. 'We can't leave Nina. Who'd buy a house with a grave in the garden, anyway?'

'Well, that's that, then,' said Alexis nastily. 'Meanwhile we're going to keep on at this dirt and filth. I won't live like a tramp any longer. I've had enough.'

Martha was placatory. 'Fine by me. I've no

objection to doing some cleaning. Just don't talk about moving. Whatever you decide to do is your own business, but Richmond and the boys and me are all staying here.'

'And Nev,' said Hugh from the corner.

'Yeah,' echoed Clem, pulling away from Martha. 'It's his *duty*.'

Martha and Alexis looked at each other and then at the child. Nobody spoke. Martha swept dust and dog hair from her black leggings. Clem kept rubbing at the same short stretch of skirting board.

'You're right about one thing,' Martha said with artificial brightness. 'This place certainly is filthy. First thing on Monday I'm going to Plymouth to buy one of those fancy new vacuum cleaners with a transparent stomach. Richmond can pay for it. I can't wait to see what it picks up – probably enough hair to make a whole new dog, for a start.'

Nobody even tried to laugh.

On the same afternoon, Silas Daggs was also doing a bit of overdue cleaning. The corgi was sixteen years old and had forgotten everything it had ever been taught about lavatory arrangements. Silas knew he should confine it to the kitchen, where the lino was easier to clean, but he hadn't the heart, so there were frequent lapses on the living room carpet. Even he could smell it on this mild afternoon. He threw open the window and tried to assess the extent of the task.

The carpet was a good one. He remembered when it had arrived, in a large van with a lot of other items. He hadn't expected to be lumbered with so many of his grandfather's possessions, but he hadn't objected, either. He and the old man had got along very well, back in the days when Silas was in his thirties and increasingly unlikely to find himself a wife or follow any conventional way of life. His grandfather had understood; they'd gone walking together, birdwatching and speaking little. 'You're my favourite,' he'd confided. 'The others would make poor use of my good things.'

Hannah had been in Africa and Bill was courting the doe-eyed Eloise, who anyone could see was never going to set the Tamar on fire. She'd been raised on the Moor with four or five older siblings, miles from anywhere. She'd been like a child from a fairytale, who had never quite adjusted to living in the twentieth century.

Silas was uncomfortable with his inheritance, obscurely guilty. He tried to make up for the imbalance in small ways. He watched helplessly as Eloise imprisoned herself in the little house, scared of the big world outside, scared of just about everything except her firstborn, the silent and inscrutable Frank.

Silas had visited regularly, bringing her a basket of eggs or fruit from the garden. He would sit and talk to Bill for a little while and then go off to find Eloise and little Frank, doing his best to make them laugh, showing them tricks with lengths of string, pointing out different birdcalls in the garden. He even took them a puppy he'd come across on one of the farms; a little collie which they kept for a few months and then passed to someone else when it demanded too much exercise and attention. Eloise had a couple of cats, but Silas noticed she never let them onto her lap or showed them any affection.

He wondered now whether he'd done more harm than good by somehow encouraging her to stay as she was, voluntarily shut away from civilisation in the little cottage, welcoming Bill home from his work with the dairy, waving Frank off to school and then drifting through the day in silent isolation. Silas wondered if he could somehow have got her out, if he could have found her a little job, helped her to make friends, join in with village life. She went to Quaker Meeting, of course, and took her share in the smaller tasks, but she never seemed to belong. He assumed that nobody now remembered her at all. Even Barty White, who had known her for a few years, was unable to conjure an image of her now, thirty years later.

And so Silas knelt stiffly on the good Persian carpet and rubbed a damp rag over it, hoping to remove the stains and smells left by the dog. *What a life*, he thought grimly as he worked. *It all goes for nothing in the end*. Bill and Charlie both dead and Hannah losing her wits in Dorothy's upstairs room. It was all due to Frank, of course. Everything had always been due to Frank, right from the very start. Old Sarah Beamish had called him a changeling child, a reject from the fairies, and even stolid Silas could see what she meant. Frank Gratton was from a place of darkness, and Silas had come to fear him in the same confused and awestruck way Hannah and Bill had feared him. For Silas had guessed the secret, long, long ago.

CHAPTER THIRTY-ONE

Dorothy Mansfield watched the disintegration of the Quaker Meeting membership with horrified disbelief. Throughout Saturday afternoon her telephone kept ringing as messages of disaster mounted up. Mandy Aspen told her she couldn't take any more responsibility for the Meeting House because Clive had been questioned by the police and had just announced he was no longer a Quaker.

'What is he then?' asked Dorothy in exasperation.

'He's an Anglican,' said Mandy, in such a hollow tone that Dorothy couldn't help but laugh.

Silas Daggs had rambled incoherently about

Hannah's nephew Frank. One or two of the things he said caused Dorothy's spine to prickle. She cut him short, afraid of the revelation she was already coming close to guessing.

Miriam Snow rang, so full of burbling good cheer that the contrast with everyone else's gloom was grotesque. When Dorothy told her there would probably not be anybody at Meeting next day, Miriam refused to listen. 'Barty and I will be there,' she said happily. 'We want to share our joy with everyone.' Dorothy gave up.

Which left only Val and Polly. Dorothy decided to pre-empt the inevitable by phoning Val. 'I'm just warning you that Meeting tomorrow will be very sparse,' she said. 'I'm not sure how much you know of what's been happening?'

Val's voice was strained. 'I know Bill died,' she said. 'And . . . has Clive been arrested?'

'No! Why ever would he be?'

'I thought perhaps . . .' Dorothy could hear the long, shaky intake of breath. 'I think he's been abusing little boys,' Val said in a rush. 'I've turned a blind eye for a long time. I know what it does to a person's reputation to be under that sort of suspicion, but it's bound to come out now.'

Dorothy did not want to hear any more. 'Don't

tell me about it,' she said crossly. 'You of all people know where your duty lies. Just do it, and leave me out of it.'

And with that she unplugged the phone from its socket and returned to the task of consoling the heartbroken Hannah Gratton.

Val mustered all her courage and phoned the Meeting House. Mandy answered and listened in silence as Val poured out all her suspicions, breaking all guidelines about inappropriate disclosures. When she petered to a halt, Mandy spoke. 'Rubbish! It was Clive himself who made the report about the Nesbitt boy. He knows now he was wrong. *Wrong*, do you hear? Leave me alone, Val. The whole truth will come out soon enough. I can't take any more for now.'

Clive was standing in the doorway between their bedroom and the living room. She turned away from him, gritting her teeth against further tears. A vision of her marriage as a heavy object, suspended over an abyss by the slenderest of threads, came to her mind's eye. One more episode like last night and this morning, one more unkind word like those he had just spoken, and she would go. She could already see herself, carrying a single suitcase, catching the bus to Exeter, the train to London, or – even better – Birmingham, where she would start a new life without him. The feeling of freedom and lightness that went with this fantasy was in itself a sure sign that it was the right thing to do. Clive wasn't going to get any better. She'd never be able to convince him that the only source of disturbance in her life was Clive himself.

Well, she wasn't going to play the game any longer. It would destroy her if she didn't get out. She looked at him, where he had started noisily tidying up a small pile of newspapers and letters, as he did every day; he could never go to bed until everything was completely clear. All the surfaces empty and clean; the cushions straight; the curtains tightly closed. Mandy often felt as if she lived in a sort of limbo, where every personal possession was removed from her at nightfall. In the morning, she had to begin over again, searching through drawers and cupboards for the book or needlework of the day before. Part of her rapidly-strengthening vision of the future was a blessedly cluttered home, where she could put a thing down one day and find it undisturbed the next.

'I mean what I say,' she told him. 'I'm not staying here any longer. I'm going to pack a bag and take the car and go to my mother's.'

'You'd desert me, would you?' She could see fear in his eyes, although his voice gave no hint of it. 'So much for wifely duty. "In sickness and in health" you promised. But there's nothing the matter with me now. I keep telling you – what happened before was a result of trying to force myself to live a dishonest life. I was keeping the lid on so much that it had to fly off in the end. You know that.'

'And now you're living truthfully?' The sarcasm was like a blow in the face. She saw him wince.

'Now I've seen my mistake, of course I am. Can you doubt it?'

'Your truth is not the same as mine,' she said, more gently. 'From here it looks as if you've built up a whole mountain of nonsense with not a *grain* of truth in it. I wonder whether you're even capable of recognising truth any more.'

It felt wonderful, as if her feet were no longer in contact with the ground. The heady exhilaration of finally saying what she really felt, telling him her own true thoughts, was immensely liberating. It didn't matter now if he hit her, if he ran screaming down the street, if he called her the most terrible names he could find. She was free.

He narrowed his eyes and rested two white-knuckled hands on the edge of the table he'd been clearing. Mandy almost giggled; he looked so much like a pantomime villain. She stared at him in fascination. Clive was *exactly* the sort of figure people must imagine when they wanted to scare themselves. Tall, dressed in black, bearded, unsmiling. The giggle died away. She took a step back, fearing for her own battered mental stability.

'Goodbye, Clive. I'll be gone in ten minutes.'

Den sat beside Phil as they drove over the Moor to Ashburton, the sun sinking in the sky already. He leant his head on the rest behind him and closed his eyes. Thinking of Clem Nesbitt, he remembered a dream from the night before, about his own biological father and his mother's second husband and young Gary. The dream had been painful. Den and Gary had been playing football in a park when their two fathers appeared and started shouting. At first Den had thought they were merely shouting instructions on how to tackle, and he had been intent on earning their approval as Gary dodged and grinned and sneaked the ball from between Den's long legs, but gradually he understood that his own father was fighting with Gary's. They were wrestling, arms locked together, trying to throw each other to the ground. Den forgot the football and ran to the men. His mother appeared, screaming at Den to stop the fight.

The two faces were red with exertion and anger. They were fighting over *him* and he was supposed to choose one over the other. 'Dad!' he shouted. 'I choose Dad!' knowing the name applied to both contenders. His mother sank to the ground in tears.

Children are lousy judges of character, Den reminded himself now.

Phil broke a long silence with a comment about the heavy workload the day had brought them. 'What time are we meant to get home this evening?' he grumbled.

'It's all right for you – I've got to see the Nesbitt woman after this. It'll be dark before I even reach her at this rate.'

A forensics team met them at Frank Gratton's stables, with little of importance to report thus far. Den and Phil were expecting to don the protective clothing and help with a search of the house. Den was not eager; rummaging through the contents of a suspect's home always felt like a gross invasion of privacy. The exertion of legal force over the wishes of the individual was a violence that bothered him. In at least half the occasions on which he had searched a private home, the suspect turned out to be innocent, or at least not proven guilty. Twice he had been part of a team that literally ripped a place apart. They cut the seats from dining chairs, pulled up fitted carpets, took every book down from the shelves, shaking each one in turn. In both cases, not a thing had been found. The guilt he felt at the destruction still remained with him.

In Frank Gratton's case, there was mercifully little need for such brutality. Bloodstains on clothes; horseshoes fitting Charlie's scars: these were the only kinds of evidence they could feasibly hope to discover.

The stables had a deserted air. No dogs came running to challenge them. Nothing stirred in the house. Frank, forewarned of the invasion, had opted to make himself scarce, it seemed. Den could hardly blame him, despite the theoretical requirement that the homeowner be present during a police search.

And then a vehicle came up the lane leading to the farm, driven by a young woman. She braked hard beside a woodpile and jumped out of the pickup. She was tall with broad shoulders and a long ponytail, and looked about twenty-five. She wore a sleeveless singlet under an unbuttoned man's check shirt. Phil made the wordless sound of approval that men everywhere made at such a sight.

'Frank's stable hand,' muttered Den.

'This is more like it,' said Phil laddishly.

'Hello!' called the girl. 'Frank asked me to

be here, instead of him. I hope that's all right? Is there some trouble?'

'You probably know that his brother died nearly two weeks ago,' said Phil, trotting towards her. 'Charlie Gratton? Kicked to death by a horse.'

The girl frowned. 'But he lives *miles* away. What's it got to do with Frank? He never goes to see any of his family.'

'Could we all go into the house now? We have to conduct a search.'

'Well, I have to feed the horses. I thought you just wanted—'

Two white-clad forensics men emerged from a far building, beyond the stable block. They strolled towards Den, looking like aliens. 'We need to examine the horses,' said one. 'Are they all out in the fields?'

The girl hesitated. 'All but two. You might already have seen them? A Shetland mare and her new foal. I think you can safely assume they didn't trample anybody.'

'Making how many in total?'

'Eight, including the foal.'

'Could you fetch the other six in, please? We have to look at their feet.'

Den discreetly detached himself. One of the forensic men was experienced with horses and knew what he was doing. They would have to take plaster casts of each hoof in turn – a task that was not going to be simple.

'Give me five minutes,' said the girl, with a resigned sigh. 'I'll get them into that stable there, look. After that, it's up to you. They're all perfectly quiet, so you should be okay.'

'We need to ask you some questions,' said Den.

She paused. 'Which comes first? Horses or questions?' She looked from one pair of men to the other.

'If we walk down to the paddock together, maybe we can combine the two,' Den suggested, still reluctant to embark on the search of the house.

'Okay,' she shrugged. 'You're the boss.'

'Are you here every day?' he began.

'Yes. I'm here every afternoon, to exercise the hunters and get them ready for the classes. Frank teaches adults to ride. I do some feeding and grooming, but Frank does most of it. He drives himself too hard.'

'Can you remember whether you were here on Sunday and Monday, 28th and 29th of March?'

'I would have been, yes.'

'Was Mr Gratton here as well?'

'I don't remember for sure, but there's a diary that'll have the lessons in. If he needs an alibi, I can check the exact times for you.'

'Did he never have any visitors from the Okehampton or Tavistock area, to your knowledge?'

'Only Mrs Nesbitt,' she said carelessly.

'What? Nina, you mean?'

'No. Her name's Hermione. Quite a grand lady.'

'How often did she come?'

'Not that often. Once a month, at most. Usually on a Monday or a Tuesday. I think she goes to Buckfastleigh afterwards. She's keen on bees and goes there to talk to the monks. I went with her once. She's very well-informed.'

'Sounds as if you like her.' Sadly, it occurred to him that the visits might well cease from then on. Routines assumed to be permanent were another casualty of violent events. Everything for Frank Gratton was about to change.

Phil was struggling to keep up. 'The old girl from the Tamar Valley? Mother of Charlie's best mate? Am I getting this right?' He looked to Den for confirmation.

Den nodded curtly. This was no way to conduct an interview with a possible witness. Before he could form another question, there was a sudden shout, followed by the clip-clop of a cantering horse.

'Bloody hell! What do they think they're

doing?' the girl cried. 'They've let Jasper escape.' The forensics men had gone ahead of the threesome, and opened the paddock gate. Six horses had crowded eagerly towards them, looking for their beloved master. They had jostled the men in good-natured impatience, and before order could be restored, one large black individual had got himself through the gate. Sensing a change of routine and an intoxicating chance of freedom, he began to head determinedly up the lane towards the road.

The girl ran for her truck, in great distress. 'He'll get killed!' she gasped. 'If he gets onto the road, something'll hit him.'

And he will get onto the road, thought Den coolly. *He'll be there already, at that speed.* He remembered seeing a dead horse in a road, years before. The huge body, with the elegant neck twisted and the lips drawn back in agony, was something he never wanted to see again.

With amazing speed and dexterity, the girl turned her vehicle and sped after the horse. Den wondered how she thought she could save it, and realised she was relying on him and the others to help. 'Come on!' he ordered the three others. 'We'll have to go up there and stop the traffic.'

It turned out to be much easier than he

feared. The horse had not chosen to run along the road, but had charged straight across it and into the grounds of a large house opposite. The girl jumped out of her truck and ran after the absconder. Den and Phil, emerging from the end of the lane, were unsure of what to do. 'Hope she doesn't want us to round it up,' said Phil. 'I'm not very good with horses.'

'Nor me,' Den admitted. 'But we'd better be ready to head it off if it tries to get back onto the road.'

On foot they followed the girl's route, through the open gates leading to the house. Feeling important, Den dragged the big iron gates closed after them. 'That should do it,' he boasted.

The house at the end of a long, curving drive was ivy-covered, gabled, lead-mullioned. It appeared to boast two or three acres of well-tended lawns and gardens. 'That horse could do some damage if it starts playing up,' said Phil.

Simultaneously they saw the animal half-hidden in a shrubbery, and the stable girl walking calmly towards it, hand extended.

'She's brave,' said Den. 'That's a big horse.' Abruptly, the words triggered a vivid flashback to the death of Nina Nesbitt. This horse was very nearly as big as Fairfield's hunter and probably every bit as agitated. 'Christ!' he exclaimed. 'What if—'

'Steady!' Phil soothed. 'She's got it, look.'

Den began to shake. Two people had died already because of horses. He couldn't be sure it wouldn't happen again, especially if this horse, belonging to Frank Gratton, was the very one that had killed Charlie. He tried to run, but his legs had become boneless. 'Be careful!' he called.

His voice didn't carry very well, but either his shout or the presence of three strange people and a large animal in the garden, alerted someone in the house. A woman in her thirties emerged from the front door and started shrieking. 'What's going on? What are you people doing?' At her heels a Jack Russell dog ran round in lunatic circles.

Den, to his shame, screwed his eyes tight shut as the girl held onto the halter on the horse's head. On the insides of his eyelids he saw it pull back, rear up, strike down on her with murderously sharp hooves. A hissing intake of breath from Phil confirmed his fears and he forced himself to look.

She had grasped the halter, but the horse was indeed yanking backwards, dancing nervously as the dog skittered up to it and yapped even louder. The girl kicked out unambiguously.

'Shut up, you stupid little beast!' she shouted, loud enough to make the creature pause for a moment.

'Jacky!' called the woman. 'Come back here!' The pause extended. The horse jerked its head once more, pulling the girl's arm up to its full extent, but she didn't let go.

'Come on,' said Phil. 'Let's do something useful.'

Order was quickly restored. The woman from the house cornered the dog and tucked it firmly under her arm, where it continued to yap, though with less urgency. The horse gave itself up with a good grace, Phil bravely holding onto the halter alongside the girl. 'That took guts,' Den said to her, a little embarrassed. 'I thought it was going to . . . hurt you.'

She laughed. 'No way. This is Jasper. He's as gentle as a kitten. Gentler – he hasn't even got claws. You could lie on the ground with nothing to protect you and he'd just step carefully over you. These are riding school horses, for heaven's sake! They have to be a thousand per cent trustworthy.'

'They're all like that, are they?' Den was watching his theories about Frank scatter to the four winds. 'Wouldn't he have kicked that dog if it had run at him from behind?'

'Definitely not. It was *me* that kicked the little

bastard, not Jasper.' She glanced apologetically at the woman holding the dog. 'Oops! Sorry, but he was being an awful pain.'

The woman did not seem very forgiving. 'This is the second time one of your horses has churned up my lawn. It's not going to be a regular occurrence, is it?'

Den felt called upon to make a gesture. 'I'm really sorry,' he said ruefully. 'It was our fault. We're here on a Ministry inspection. One of our men let the horse out – very stupidly. He's a novice around horses, I'm afraid.'

The girl and Phil both stared at him for a few seconds, before deciding to let the story stand. Then with a sense of anticlimax they trooped back to the stables, where the forensic men had shyly retreated some time earlier.

'Have you chaps got those hoof prints yet?' Den asked them briskly.

'Not quite,' one of them admitted, in stark exaggeration. It was obvious they had not even begun the task.

'Well, we'll leave you to it. Miss . . . um . . . will help you. We've got to be somewhere.' The fact that he had neglected to ask the stable girl her name struck him as both deeply unprofessional and rather fitting. He was confident there would be no need to officially report her testimony. The forensic examination of all the riding school mounts and their hooves was a waste of time, too, but he didn't say so.

'Have we?' Phil blinked.

Den watched as horses and people milled about the paddock, and then shook himself. 'Yes, we have. I don't know about you, but I'm going to pay a call on Lady Hermione Nesbitt.'

CHAPTER THIRTY-TWO

There was an increasing sense of urgency as Den and Phil sped back to Okehampton, exacerbated by Phil's implacable insistence on stopping at a garage and buying two large sandwiches and two bottles of sugary fizzy drinks. It was almost six-thirty when they finally pulled up at the police station again. 'You can make the report – what there is of it. I'm going straight off again,' said Den, practically pushing his colleague out of the car.

Phil tried to speak, to ascertain for certain whether they really were abandoning the notion that Frank Gratton was their killer. 'What's the DI going to say?' he worried. 'We never did what we were meant to.'

'Just leave some notes on his desk,' Den snapped. 'Nobody's going to read them today, anyway. If there are any matching hoof prints, it'll be taken out of our hands.' But he knew that wouldn't happen. He knew for sure now that Frank did not possess a murderous horse. He was shouting the final words out of the window as he revved the engine and drove away.

He knew it had been a huge mistake not to interview Lady Nesbitt sooner. He remembered her at Nina's death, how authoritative she had been, how genuinely concerned for her grandsons. He also remembered the contemptuous glance she had thrown at the weeping Charlie. Like a gradually developing photograph, the picture was coming into focus. Lilah had commented on how many strong women there were in this story – Hannah, Martha, the matriarchal Eliza and the daunting Hermione herself. And how weak the men appeared by comparison . . .

The drive to Hermione's was once again indirect and time-consuming. A few Easter holidaymakers were still exploring the area along the Tamar, enjoying the fine evening and the westering sun. Their cars were either parked obstructively or dawdling down the narrow lanes. Den forced himself to avoid reckless overtaking and aggressive tailgating; his car was not identifiably that of a police officer and he had no real justification for undue haste, other than desperately wanting to reach his destination before darkness fell. And to get his questions answered once and for all.

His map showed Hermione's home as yet another imposing mansion, set on a hillside a few miles north of Gunnislake. It turned out to have a short approach drive and a view far superior to that from High Copse. The Tamar was an impressive river for much of its length, and at this point, sliding loopily between steep wooded hills, at its best. There was scarcely any sign of human habitation for miles. Villages straddled the two A roads – the 388 and the 384 – but the triangle between them was sparsely inhabited.

The land levelled out behind the house and a large paddock was bordered by a sturdy post-and-rail fence. Den shook his head at the plethora of equestrian facilities laid out before him. No wonder Hermione was friendly with Frank – his place must have been a home from home, despite the inferior quality of his buildings. Lady Nesbitt's house and grounds, on the other hand, had been spared no expense in a comparatively recent refurbishment. The area in front of the house was immaculately tarmacked, the surrounding lawns well tended. But the

Range Rover was parked crookedly beside a wall – doubtless concealing a lavishly-stocked garden or tennis court – covered in mud and with one headlight broken.

Although obviously not a working farm, it appeared that there was a substantial area of land attached to the house. Den scanned the acres in the fading light in vain, for evidence of a horse, before leaving his car and rapping the heavy iron knocker on the solid oak front door.

He half expected a maidservant in a frilly apron to greet him, but it was Hermione herself who flung the door wide in an oddly appealing gesture. As with Gerald Fairfield, Master of Foxhounds, Den's instant intuition was that here was an innocent person with nothing to hide.

She narrowed her eyes and cocked her head to one side like a big, heavy bird. 'I know you,' she said.

'Detective Constable Den Cooper, ma'am,' he confirmed. 'I was present at the death of your daughter-in-law. I expect that's where you saw me.'

'Terrible business,' she said, in a gruff voice. If he hadn't been face to face with her, he would have taken her for a man. 'It should never have happened.'

'It must be very difficult for you,' he offered.

'Especially as she was trying to prevent the hunt—'

'No,' she corrected him, the deep voice now suggestive of something painful, something carefully buried. 'No, it wasn't unduly difficult. We'd got used to each other, but there was no love lost. I'd say it was far worse for the boys. Those children have known some very divided loyalties, one way and another. Anyway – do you want to come in?' She opened the door wider, invitingly, but he felt her holding her breath; felt the tension – or was it apprehension? – in the air. 'I admit I'm surprised by your timing,' she remarked.

Den took a deep breath, and struggled to order his thoughts. 'I'm sorry,' he said. 'It's been a very full day. And thank you, I will come in for a few minutes.'

She ushered him into a small room, furnished like a study. The window looked out onto the front garden and the paddock beyond. The gathering darkness made it hard to see much.

One by one, his suspects were turning into uncomfortably likeable characters. For a full fifteen minutes earlier that day, he had been quite certain that Hermione had killed Charlie Gratton, just as he had been sure about Frank and Clive Aspen, in their turn. Now the ideas all seemed ridiculous.

'I came to talk to you about Frank and Charlie Gratton,' he said. 'We were told today that you're on friendly terms with Frank, and you visit him regularly?' Like someone sacrificing his queen in a final desperate move, he added, 'You probably don't know that he has been an object of our interest as a possible perpetrator of Charlie's killing.'

Her weathered cheeks turned a darker shade and her eyes widened in disbelief. 'That's utterly stupid,' she said angrily. 'By what dim-witted thought processes did you reach that conclusion?'

Whatever Hermione's background, she had a disarming way with words.

'I can't go into that,' said Den politely. 'But I do need to ask you certain questions. I understand you have a large horse here, which was responsible for hurting your arm a week or so ago?'

'Boanerges, yes,' she said shortly. 'He's out at the moment.'

He looked at her closely. 'Out? In the dark?'

She moved to the window. 'It's not really dark yet,' she said, as if trying to convince herself.

'Is he with someone?'

'Of course he is.' He knew something was coming then; her face was hardening in some sort of inner struggle. She turned back to him and looked up into his face, eyes hungry for something. Understanding? Forgiveness? 'Boanerges is out with the boys,' she said. He felt her admit defeat. A decision had been made.

'Boys? Do you mean your grandsons?'

'Clem and Hugh,' she nodded. 'They've gone off for a ride. Hugh takes Boanerges and Clem has a smaller mare. They're both excellent riders. Well they would be, with their background.'

Den's heart was in an icy grip. 'But it's *dark*,' he repeated. 'And are they due back soon?'

'I promised them flapjack,' she said distractedly, a hand to her throat.

'Flapjack?' he echoed.

She shook herself and blinked rapidly. 'This is too much for me,' she said abruptly and sat down on a leather chair in front of an oak desk. 'I knew I wouldn't be able to hide it if you people ever decided to come here. I knew I shouldn't even try.'

'Frank Gratton?' he prompted, knowing he was being a coward, merely delaying the inevitable, knowing the question was completely beside the point; knowing too that he was no more ready than Hermione to confront the heartbreaking truth. 'What makes you think we've made a mistake about Frank?'

'One simple thing,' she said, playing along

gallantly. 'Frank didn't care enough about Charlie to kill him.'

Den put a hand on her arm, slow and heavy with sadness. 'Are you certain about that?' he said. 'I'm not sure I can believe it.'

'Frank isn't the person you're looking for,' she insisted, her eyes meeting his.

'I think you're trying to protect him,' said Den, as if reading from a script.

'It would be very unfair if he were to be blamed for Charlie's death.'

'I'd like to ask you about Charlie's origins,' he pursued with an effort. 'I gather you were close to his mother.'

He could see the struggle going on inside her. 'Who have you been talking to?' she asked sharply. Then she shook her head. 'Yes, I was the only friend she had when Charlie was born. The district nurse asked me if I would keep an eye on her. She had terrible postnatal depression, you see.'

'But your own son was only a year old, and Frank Gratton is his godfather. So you knew her well before Charlie was born.'

'It was a long time ago,' she whispered.

'Lady Nesbitt – we know who Charlie's father was. I don't want you to try and hide it from us.'

She looked at him again, the aristocratic matriarch, the indomitable countrywoman, and her eyes filled with tears. 'You mustn't blame Frank,' she said. 'It wasn't his fault. She was so *dependent* on him, and Bill was useless.' A flash of anger crossed her face. 'I've never been able to bear Bill since then. So righteous and punitive, and so cruel to the wretched boy.'

The noise outside was faint at first. A boyish shouting, the neigh of a horse. Hermione got up slowly and Den followed her to the front door. They stepped outside and stood on the lawn. The figures in the paddock were shadowy, mere patches of darker grey in the twilight.

'The boys don't seem to have been very fond of Charlie,' Den commented, unnaturally casual, trying to defer the moment when he would have to fully understand, and live for the rest of his life with the understanding. 'They only have eyes for their father.'

'They don't know what's good for them,' she said. 'Children never do. They always seem to make the wrong choices. Has anyone told you how much Charlie loved them? If their father had come to grief on one of his outlandish jaunts, Charlie would probably have tried to adopt them. But they'd never have been won over by him. They were unshakeably loyal to Nevil, the little fools.'

Den was watching the two silhouetted riders. One was on a medium-sized pony, trotting steadily towards the house. Clem's face looked pale, his expression unreadable at such a distance. Behind him came a much larger animal.

'Hugh's a wonderful horseman,' said Hermione again. 'It runs in his blood. Not many boys of his age could handle Boanerges.'

Den didn't ask. The answer was only too obvious. The animal was a rich chestnut, at least as big as the one that had killed Nina at the hunt. As he watched, the boy cantered it alongside the top rail of the paddock and then forced it to a violently sudden stop. The horse reared up, the boy clinging effortlessly to its back, laughing loud enough to carry across the intervening distance. 'He's always making him do that,' Hermione remarked, almost idly. 'It looks worse than it is. I don't think he's ever fallen off.'

Den wasn't seeing the reality before his eyes. He was seeing a curled-up figure on the ground beneath the great hooves. He was seeing the boy deliberately charging at Charlie. Compelling the horse to rear and then stamp down on the unprotected man. Charlie, who had caused the death of his mother; Charlie, who would take on the role of father if anything happened to Nev; Charlie, who was probably going to marry Alexis and be there all the time, forcing his unwanted love onto Hugh and Clem his brother.

Den's heart inflated, impeding the operation of his lungs. This was the realisation he had never wanted to dawn.

'You don't have to protect him any more,' he said tightly to Hermione.

CHAPTER THIRTY-THREE

Forensics were called out in the dark Easter Saturday evening. Den rode in the back of a police car with Hugh and Nevil Nesbitt. Nev babbled wildly, unable to get to grips with what was happening.

'Hugh would never *do* such a thing,' he insisted frantically. 'Tell them, son, it's all a stupid mistake.'

Hugh said nothing. He sat in the back of the car watching the dark lanes outside.

'You didn't do it on purpose, of course you didn't. Granny should never have let you go out on that horse. You couldn't control him properly, a massive beast like that. It was a horrible accident.'

'Dad—' began Hugh, before lapsing into another silence.

'Yes? What? Tell me, Hugh.'

'I didn't lose control of him. He does everything I want him to.'

'Shush!' Nevil cast a worried look at Den. 'Don't say any more.'

'It wasn't an accident, Dad,' Hugh repeated. 'I did it so you'd stay with us. We didn't want Charlie for our father.'

The choking sob that came from Nev was agony to hear. Den tried to close his ears to it. He was in no mood to offer sympathy to Nevil Nesbitt.

They all assembled at the police station: Nev, Hermione, Martha and a social worker. Martha and Hermione were not present at the questioning, but sat with Den in another room. Martha wept. 'I had no idea,' she repeated, over and over. 'It never occurred to me.'

Den believed her, aware of how much it mattered that he should. 'What about Alexis?' he asked, when she was calmer.

She frowned in anger and suspicion. 'I don't know. I couldn't swear to it either way. She might have guessed, I suppose.'

'And if she had?'

Martha moaned softly. 'It wouldn't make any

difference now. She and I have been pushed apart by all this. I haven't been able to understand her lately – she's been like a person with a secret. I can see that now.'

'And Clem?' he almost whispered, confronting a question he knew to be acutely painful.

Hermione spoke up, with shocking ferocity. 'Clem was in thrall to his brother. I saw it all, but couldn't do anything. Can you remember how it is for children – how there is no way any adult can hope to ensure justice? All I could do was look on and wait for Hugh to grow up and leave Clem alone. I would even have paid for boarding school, but his mother wouldn't hear of it. By protecting Hugh, I think I did protect Clem as well, at least a little. He was frightened and sad, but he'd learnt how to avoid arousing his brother's worst side. When it was obvious that nobody had even considered Hugh as Charlie's killer, everything relaxed a little. But we all three of us knew, deep down, that it would come to this in the end.'

Martha wept afresh. Den had an image of the pale child showing him round the orchard, seeming glad to be away from his brother. Dark thoughts crossed his mind. 'Hugh forced him to keep quiet. To lie and pretend. Clem was there that Sunday, with his bike. He went home alone, while Hugh stayed with you. He must have been terrorised, scared rigid.'

'Hugh's not a monster,' Hermione broke in. 'It's the way he's been brought up. Too many crosscurrents, too much freedom. He's never been properly disciplined.'

Martha nodded miserably. 'Nina didn't believe in it. And if one of us told him off, he just went over to your place to be indulged and spoilt.' She looked up at Hermione. 'I think you're partly responsible for this.'

Hermione closed her eyes and said nothing.

Den felt immensely weary. He rubbed the tender side of his face, which was tingling, as it did when he was tired or upset. 'Families,' he said, and Martha just nodded. It seemed to sum the whole thing up rather neatly.

He left them, almost dead on his feet from weariness. It was half past nine. There were still things he had to do.

First he called Lilah. It felt like several days since he'd seen her, instead of barely twenty-four hours. 'Happy Easter,' he said cautiously when she answered the phone.

'Same to you,' she returned. 'How's the murder coming along?'

'It's finished,' he said flatly. 'With the usual whimper.'

'No rejoicing then? No sense of a job well done, a source of satisfaction?'

'Hardly any of that,' he agreed. 'This job's a bugger – which you probably knew already.'

'And mine's the job from hell. Join the club.'

'We're still friends then, are we?'

'Oh Den, I'm really sorry. I'm infantile. I should have been helping you, not nagging for attention. Am I allowed to know who did it? Who did kill Charlie?'

'Hugh,' he said. 'Young Hugh Nesbitt. On his grandma's horse.'

'An accident then? Surely not deliberate?'

'Absolutely deliberate, I'm afraid. He didn't want Charlie usurping his father's rightful place.'

'Oh shit,' she choked.

'That's about it,' he agreed.

Next morning, feeling foolish and nervous and unsure, Den Cooper walked into the Quaker Meeting at twenty-five past ten. Dorothy Mansfield and Silas Daggs were in their places; Val Taylor and Polly Spence were on a bench near the back, shoulder to shoulder; and behind Den sat Miriam Snow and Barty White.

Slowly the silence deepened, as the tiny group began their Meeting for Worship. It was Easter Day, but there were no outward manifestations of this: none of the exuberance shown by other Christian churches on this day of the Resurrection and hope. Den's thoughts whirled as he covertly glanced from one person to another, wondering what was going on inside their heads. Wondering, too, what in the world he thought he was doing there. He had received brief smiles of acknowledgement from Miriam and Barty, and a more obvious welcome from Dorothy, that betrayed no hint of surprise.

He assumed that none of them knew the outcome of the murder inquiry; they were still very much preoccupied by the death of Bill Gratton and the collapse of his sister Hannah. He assumed, too, that every person present had been shaken and disturbed by recent events. And yet the atmosphere was profoundly calm. There was something sweet in the air, partly the scent of the spring flowers in a simple vase on the central table, but also something less tangible. As if all unpleasant thoughts and deeds had been left at the door, and those present had brought nothing but their better side.

The seat was hard and Den felt the muscles tighten in his back as he fought to keep still. He let his eyes close and tried to empty his mind. Images of Hugh Nesbitt on the massive, murderous horse; of Frank Gratton cowering in shame in a village church; of Mandy Aspen being shaken into making false accusations by a deeply disturbed husband – all came into his head and then drifted away again. He was learning simply to observe them, without rushing to interpret or deny.

Then there was a sound at the door. Footsteps and a single brief whisper. He let the next breath finish before opening his eyes. Passing in front of him were two figures – a man and a woman – on their way to the far end of the bench on which he sat. Without warning, Den's eyes filled with tears, rushing from nowhere. He closed them again, rubbing swift fingers beneath each lower lid, trying to sweep the droplets away. He felt intensely conspicuous and impossibly foolish. But somehow it didn't matter. He could feel Dorothy watching him, accepting, understanding.

After all, he reminded himself, he had reason to cry. The world was a profoundly sad place at times. He glanced sideways, quickly, apologetically, to where Hannah Gratton sat beside her nephew Frank, holding tightly to his hand.